"JOHN MACGILLIVRAY AND I HAVE KNOWN EACH OTHER ALL OUR LIVES."

"Yes," he said, tracing his fingers along the soft skin of her forearm. "And I have envied him that privilege before."

Anne felt the heat of his breath against her wrist. "You have?"

"I have envied every man who has known you longer than I have."

His lips were on her wrist again, and now they were following the tingling path already conquered by his fingertips. The cuff of her sleeve had fallen below her elbow, and when he reached the chenille barrier, he turned and pressed his lips into the curve of her neck.

His mouth was warm, his tongue hot and moist where it swirled up to flirt with her earlobe, then scrolled a provocative path down to the collar of her robe. Anne could barely hold her head steady. The seduction would end before it had even begun.

"Jealousy," he murmured, "can be a terrible thing. Almost as terrible as pride."

She might have had the wit to think of a response but for the thrill of his lips on her.

"Stop," she gasped. "You must stop. I cannot bear it."

"You can. And you will, for I have not even begun."

PRAISE FOR MARSHA CANHAM
AND HER PREVIOUS NOVELS

Swept Away

"EXCITING, SEXY AND FUN...filled with spies, intrigue, danger, swordplay and a grand passion...a writer whose talents know no bounds." —*Romantic Times*

Pale Moon Rider

"CAPTIVATING...Lush and sensually explicit... Canham has written a grand adventure full of heroic men and dastardly villains, and with a beautiful heroine who has spirit and determination, and even saves the hero on more than one occasion." —*Booklist*

"This gripping tale kept me up well into the morning. Tyrone will steal hearts and haunt dreams. Renee is enchanting and full of fire. Don't miss this new arrival by Marsha Canham."
—*Affaire de Coeur*

The Blood of Roses

"Completely enthralling!...A powerful love story... Written like a well-played chess game, the reader is everywhere and becomes one with the scenes."
—*Heartland Critiques*

"Marsha Canham sweeps you into Catherine's love story with characters that leap from the pages.... She completely captures the essence of this era with an emotional intensity that will stun and thrill readers."
—*Romantic Times*

Marsha Canham

Midnight Honor

A Dell Book

Published by
Dell Publishing
a division of
Random House, Inc.
1540 Broadway
New York, New York 10036

This is a work of fiction. Names, characters, places, and incidents
either are the product of the author's imagination or are used
fictitiously. Any resemblance to actual persons, living or dead,
events, or locales is entirely coincidental.

Copyright © 2001 by Marsha Canham
Cover illustration by Alan Ayers
Cover design by GTC Design

ISBN-13: 978-0-440-23522-4

ISBN-10: 0-440-23522-7

Manufactured in the United States of America

Published simultaneously in Canada

April 2001

10   9   8   7   6   5   4   3   2   1
OPM

This is for my husband, Peter, who, after twenty-eight years of marriage, has learned to tread lightly and duck fast during those heady days and nights known as Deadline Hell. For my son, Jeffrey, my daughter-in-law, Michelle, and my Munchkin, Austin: Even though there are no palm trees in town, the days are warmer when you are around. To the Intrepids, the Loopies, and the readers/cyber-friends at A2R and RBL, my thanks for keeping me company at two and three in the morning when my characters keep me awake and pounding at the keys. Special thanks to Ruth Mounts for giving me a title that inspired so much more angst than just "Book Three." And to Adrienne Ball, friend and publicist, who threatened to pout for another year if I did not mention her somewhere in this book.

Author's Note

The phrase "labor of love" has been used so often, I think it sometimes loses its meaning, but in this case, with *Midnight Honor*, there is no other way to describe it. I actually started writing the story ten years ago, right after I had finished *The Pride of Lions* and *The Blood of Roses*. I had met Colonel Anne while doing research on the Jacobite Rebellion and knew she was a strong enough character to carry a story of her own. No, she *deserved* a story of her own. I started it, but put it aside after a hundred pages or so because I knew I had been in Scotland too long and needed to distance myself from Culloden for a while in order to do Anne justice. Nearly every year after that, I took out the folder and leafed through the pages I had written, but each time I put them back again knowing I wasn't ready, that I still retained too much from the first two books to enable me to look at Anne's story with a fresh eye. Okay, I'll admit it: I was more than a little afraid I had used up all the emotion and impact of the rebellion in the pages of *The Blood of Roses*.

Three years ago, Marjorie Braman offered me the chance to revise and update both *The Pride of Lions* and *The Blood of Roses* for reissued editions. I had just finished writing one Regency, *Pale Moon Rider*, and was contracted for a second, *Swept Away*, but retyping the two Scottish books in the computer made all the little hairs on the back of my neck stand on end. The story was there in my mind, the characters kept nudging their way into my thoughts even as I was chasing coaches through the streets of London. The only question remained: How do I write a story about a woman in love with two vastly different but inherently similar men? How do I make the challenges and sacrifices of all three characters as believable and as heart-rending for the reader as they are for the characters themselves? And how do I make the gentle readers who lambasted me at the end of *The Blood of Roses* understand that the real tragedy isn't in the loss, it is in the forgetting?

Anne and Angus Moy, John MacGillivray, Gillies MacBean, even Fearchar Farquharson, were real, living, breathing people; heroic figures out of the past who, I hope, will allow me my poetic license in weaving my story around them. I have been warmly rewarded by correspondence from the descendants of Lochiel and Alexander Cameron; I can only hope the MacKintoshes will be as kind.

"*These deeds, these plots, this ill-conceived folly born of midnight honor . . .*"

— *UNKNOWN*

Prologue

*T*he fear was like a blanket, smothering her. Having witnessed and survived the obscene terror of Culloden, Anne Farquharson Moy thought she could never be truly frightened again, yet there were times her heart pounded so violently in her chest, she thought it might explode. Her mouth was dry; her hands shook like those of a palsied old woman. The slimy stone walls of her cell seemed to be shrinking around her, closer each day, and the air was so thin and sour she had to pant to ease the pressure in her lungs.

And then there were the sounds. . . .

They were as bone-chilling and piercing as the screams that haunted her dreams day and night. She had watched the prince's army die on the blood-soaked moor at Culloden, had seen the rounds of grapeshot fired by the English ranks spray into the charging Highlanders and cut them down like the pins in a child's game of bowls. She had heard the dreadful, unimaginable agony of fathers cradling fallen sons, brothers dragging themselves on mangled limbs to die beside brothers. And she had heard their cries for mercy as the English completed the slaughter by stabbing and mutilating those wounded souls they found alive on the erstwhile field of honor.

The sounds she heard in her gaol cell were the soft, barely audible groans of a dying faith, of crushed pride, and of the utter, complete hopelessness that permeated the walls of the old stone courthouse in Inverness.

She was alone in her cell. Cumberland had called it a luxury, for there were easily a hundred half-starved men crowded into an area that normally held no more than twenty, some with festering wounds who were too weak or feverish to roll out of their own waste. An oatcake and small tin cup of water were the daily ration. Pleas and prayers went unheeded. The weak eventually grew too frail to squander their strength on such futile measures and simply died in silence. The stronger ones clung to their rage and sat huddled in dank corners, showing their defiance the only way they could: by continuing to live.

How, indeed, could they show any less courage than the tall and straight-backed Lady Anne Moy, who had spat her contempt in the porcine face of Butcher Cumberland with such magnificent defiance? He had come to the prison three times over the past six weeks offering to free her in exchange for giving king's evidence against the Jacobite leaders. All three times she had sent him away spluttering German oaths under his breath.

It was a heavy burden to carry on such slender shoulders, and Anne had come closer to accepting his offer on that third visit than she cared to admit. But he had made it in the open courtyard, below windows filled with the strained, haunted faces of the brave men who had already lost so much in a cause that had been doomed from the outset. If all she could do was give them this last shred of pride and honor to cling to, then it was little enough. It was also a sacrifice that grew pitifully smaller in importance with each day that passed, each hour that saw another rack of Jacobites hung for treason, each minute that brought the inevitability of her own death closer and closer.

Her once lustrous red hair was dull and matted with filth. Her skin was gray and the flesh had shrunk from her bones, leaving her body gaunt and always cold in spite of the spare blanket one of the kinder guards had smuggled through the bars. Deep purple smudges ringed her eyes, and her hands were stained black, her nails cracked and torn from repeatedly pulling herself up to the narrow window cut high in the cell wall.

She held one almost transparent hand up to the murky light and could not entirely stifle the sob that rose in her throat. She was so thin she could no longer wear the ring Angus had given her on their wedding day. It had fallen off one night, and she had become nearly frantic groping through the straw and filth that littered the floor until she had found it.

That was the closest she had come to weeping since her arrest. The closest she had come to screaming out an oath to the devil himself if he would take her away from this place.

She did not even know if Angus was alive or not. Cumberland assured her that he was, miraculously clinging to a thread to be sure, yet Anne had no reason to believe him, certainly none to trust him. The royal toady had said himself that belly wounds were the quickest to mortify despite all the skills a surgeon could bring to bear.

Anne curled her fingers into a tight ball and pressed them against her lips.

A gleaming, fat tear squeezed between her lashes and streaked slowly down the length of her cheek to her chin. It hung there a moment, glistening like a liquefied diamond before a tremor shook it free and it dropped unnoticed among the other stains that darkened the bodice of her dress. The once lovely gown was filthy, the silk rendered colorless and torn in a dozen places. The layers of ruffled linen petticoats she had discarded after the first week of confinement now served as her bedding. Her cloak had gone to ease the fevered chills of another prisoner. Over the weeks, she had bartered her shoes, her gloves, even the tiny rosette buttons that had adorned her bodice for a taste of cheese or an extra crust of black bread.

When she had nothing left to trade, one of the *Sassenach* guards had suggested other ways of earning favors, but the first time he came into her cell at night, he left doubled over, his ballocks damn near kicked into his pockets.

She had expected him to come back, with friends, but she never saw his ugly face again, and one of the men in a nearby cell whispered a reassurance that she would not. No one would ever see him again for the insult he had paid to their valiant Colonel Anne.

They did not know that the cruelest insult had already been delivered by Cumberland himself. Nor did they know it had been Anne's own blade that had pierced her husband's belly.

Chapter One

The track was narrow and deeply rutted, slushed with puddles of melted snow. The two riders kept their horses on the frozen deer grass wherever possible, and several times abandoned the road entirely to cut across a field, or shave the corner off a moor in order to shorten the journey from Moy Hall to Dunmaglass. Anne Farquharson Moy was dressed for the hard ride and wore plaid trews, a warm woolen shirt, and a leather doublet. A long length of tartan was wrapped around her waist and draped over her shoulders to further blunt the icy effects of the wind. Her bonnet was pulled low over her forehead, stuffed full of her long red hair. In her belt she wore a brace of Highland dags, the heavy steel pistols loaded and primed, and she was comfortable with the knowledge that she would use them without hesitation should the need arise.

Riding beside her was her cousin, Robert Farquharson of Monaltrie, also dressed for the bitter cold, swaddled in plaid. When the wind snapped at his kilt, his legs were bare beneath, the skin red, but he was accustomed to withstanding the raw weather.

Robert had been waiting in a grove of trees close by Moy Hall at the appointed time. When Anne had joined him, they had exchanged but a few frosty whispers before setting out across the frozen landscape.

Great care had to be taken when traveling from home these days. There were three battalions of government troops stationed in nearby Inverness, Highland regiments formed up under the command of John Campbell, earl of Loudoun. Patrols were regularly sent out from Fort George to scour the countryside day and night, and anyone could be arrested or taken away to prison without benefit of either a warrant or a trial. Several local clansmen had been dragged from their homes just this past week, their only crime being the sprig of thistle worn in their bonnets to show support for Prince Charles Edward Stuart.

Anne glanced up as a thick blanket of cloud crawled across the moon. She could smell more snow on the way and was grimly thankful for it. Snow—the driving icy crystals that were indigenous to the clear Highland air—would make the night safer for her, safer for everyone.

Her grandfather had sent an urgent message to her earlier in the day. Despite the terrible risks involved to both parties, he had requested a meeting at the home of John Alexander MacGillivray, a laird of some considerable influence who possessed a reputation fearsome enough to keep Lord Loudoun's patrols at a wary distance. Anne strongly doubted that even the news of Fearchar Farquharson's presence at Dunmaglass would inspire the lobsterbacks to venture too close, though she had heard recently the reward had been doubled for the old gray fox's capture.

At one hundred and thirteen years of age, Fearchar Farquharson was a spry walking history of Scotland. He had seen six kings take the English throne since the Restoration and had endured each one's particular remedy for the "Scottish problem." He had fought his first battle nearly a century before when James Graham, the Duke of Montrose, had raised an army of Highlanders in an attempt to save the doomed Catholic monarchy. He had fought for the Stuart cause again in 1689, when England had first dared to invite a German Hanover to wear the crown, and he had played a major role in the failed uprising of 1715. Some reverently referred to him as the "wee de'il in plaid," but to Anne, he was simply Granda', a stubborn old warrior who had reached his venerable age on the assumption that he was destined to survive as long as it took to see the Stuarts restored to their rightful place on the throne of Scotland.

His best hope for victory had landed in the Hebrides in mid-July. Charles Edward Stuart had embarked from France equally determined to reclaim the throne of England and Scotland in his father's name. In August, he had raised the Stuart standard at Glenfinnan and proclaimed himself Regent. To the astonishment of nearly every arrogant-minded Englishman who thought their army invulnerable, he had led his Highlanders to Edinburgh and recaptured the royal city, then dealt the government troops a resounding defeat at Prestonpans. Capitalizing on his victories, the prince had secured the Scottish borders and marched his army deep into the very heart of England.

Derby was one hundred and fifty miles from London; upon hearing that the Stuart prince had ventured unchallenged to within striking distance of the throne, the English king had ordered his household packed and loaded into waiting boats, prepared to flee at a moment's notice.

Fearchar—indeed, all of the Highland clans loyal to the Jacobite cause—had raised such a resounding cheer at the news that it was said to have echoed the length and breadth of the Great Glen. He had been all for setting out, on foot if need be, to join the brave and courageous army, even at the unthinkable cost of breaking the oath of fealty that bound the entire Farquharson clan to the will of their laird Angus Moy, The MacKintosh of Clan MacKintosh, Chief of Clan Chattan.

To Fearchar and others like him, the shame was nearly untenable that Angus Moy had not called out the clan and marched to Glenfinnan in support of their valiant prince. Instead, Angus had been one of a dozen influential lairds who had taken commissions in the government army and thereby bound their clansmen to remain at home—some even to take up the Hanover colors—while their prince marched bravely forth to meet his destiny. Fearchar had been one of the most outspoken dissenters; as a result, there was an outstanding warrant for his arrest, as well as for the arrests of Anne's three cousins.

Raised without benefit of a mother, Anne had spent most of her youth in the brash company of Robert, Eneas, and James Farquharson of Monaltrie. Out of ten children, eighty-six grandchildren, and too many great-grandchildren to count, these four progeny were the stars in Fearchar's sky. They were his hope, and he considered them to be Scotland's promise, for they were as fearless and proud as the mountains and glens that bred the fiercest, boldest hearts of courage. They were Highlanders and Jacobites who proclaimed their loyalty as openly as they wore the white Stuart cockade in their bonnets.

At the outset of the rebellion, Anne's cousins had joined Fearchar in the mountains, tirelessly tramping the miles between Inverness and Aberdeen, between Aberdeen and Arisaig, to keep the clans informed of events happening south of the border. They had been the first to report the stunning victory of the Highland army over General Sir John Cope's troops at Prestonpans, first to report the prince's march south into England and the subsequent fall of Carlisle, then Manchester, and finally Derby.

But for the small inconvenience of being a woman and married to the clan chief, Anne likely would have joined them. She was closer to them than to her own siblings—three silly sisters who were content with their stitchery and nursery chores. She had relied on her cousins to teach her the important skills—how to ride like the wind, how to hunt, to shoot a musket and bow—and to that end, she could toss a dirk into a plover's eye at twenty paces or, if the mood came upon her, down a pint of fiery *uisque baugh* without batting a long auburn eyelash. She had been as distraught as they when Angus had forbidden any of the clan to ride to Glenfinnan, as disillusioned, hurt, and angered when he had subsequently donned the uniform of the Black Watch and raised a battalion of four hundred clansmen to join the Hanover regiments under the command of Lord Loudoun.

Anne shivered and hunched lower in her saddle, not wanting to think about how enraged her husband would be if he knew she was riding to Dunmaglass to meet her grandfather. He had expressly forbidden her to have any further contact with her outlawed kinsmen lest word of her affiliation with rebels reach the ears of Duncan Forbes, Lord President of the Court of Session. But forbidding Anne to see her family was like forbidding fruit to ripen on the vine. Outwardly she may have striven to look and act the part of a gentleman's wife, shunning her trews and doublets for the silk underpinnings and stiff whalebone corsets of a proper married lady. Inwardly, however, she was still "Wild Ruadh Annie," and if her family needed her, she would go to them. Blood was thicker than any bonds made by marriage vows.

Ruadh Annie, truth be told, had never given much weight to the state of holy matrimony. Growing up, she had known it would eventually be a necessary evil, as would the vow of obedience she would be required to pledge to her husband. There had not been any shortage of suitors eager to tame the red-haired wildcat, but had someone predicted that she would one day become the mistress of Moy Hall, the Lady Anne MacKintosh, she would have laughed until tears ran down her face.

She imagined Angus's reaction would have been much the same. Born in the Highlands, but educated in England and widely traveled, he had not had the faintest inkling he would one day inherit the mantle of chief, let alone be obligated to honor an agreement forged when he was still riding ponies and wearing knee breeks.

Anne had been a waddling sprite of two when Fearchar had secured her future by betrothing her to a MacKintosh. It did not matter that Angus was twelve years older than she and a fourth son, not destined to inherit more than a comfortable livelihood. It was a union that would bring together two of the largest clans amongst the dozen that had amalgamated to form the powerful Clan of the Cats. It was also probable that Angus's father had agreed to the arrangement only because he assumed—or hoped—the pug-faced, barefooted toddler would succumb, long before she came of an age to marry, to one of the many childhood diseases that ravaged the Highlands.

No one could have anticipated Lachlan MacKintosh's own death a few brief years later, or that those same indiscriminate childhood diseases would remove, one after another, his three eldest heirs in line of succession. With the swiftness only fate can deliver, the title and estates were conferred upon Angus, who, having had no thought of inheritances or weighty mantles of responsibility, had been living on the Continent. He had been absent for so long, in fact, and was so far out of touch, it took nearly four months for word to reach him that he was the new Chief of Clan Chattan.

The tall, elegant gentleman who arrived at Moy Hall was not like any of the rawboned, braw lads who had been flirting shamelessly with Anne and stealing kisses behind the haystack. He was reserved and articulate, a scholar and a brilliant mathematician who was so thorough and businesslike, he startled the dust out of countless ledgers and tally books throughout Invernesshire. The MacKintosh estates, which had been run haphazardly for a decade or more, came under a stern and caustic pair of pewter gray eyes—the same shrewd eyes that uncovered the articles of betrothal negotiated by Fearchar Farquharson and Lachlan MacKintosh nearly two decades before.

He was not shy in his attempts to have the agreement voided, since it was hardly a suitable alliance for a powerful clan chief. In an effort to arrive at an agreeable compromise, he arranged for a meeting with Fearchar and they had remained closeted in the library at Moy Hall for eight long hours. Fearchar proved to be a worthy opponent. Not even the demand to honor the original dowry of twelve thousand merks—an astronomical sum to a man whose greatest asset was his word—bowed the gnarled old warrior and within the prescribed time he returned to Moy Hall bearing a pouch of coins in the full amount.

Anne had entered the church in Aberdeen with a sinking heart and leaden feet, aware that the vows she was about to take would not only bind her to a man who did not love her and did not want her, but also condemn her to a life of whalebone stays and frilly petticoats.

She had been fully halfway to the altar before she saw her husband for the first time. The sunlight, streaming through a stained glass window, had lit the chestnut waves of his hair like a gleaming crown. Wearing a blue grogram coat over a satin waistcoat richly ornamented with embroidery and gold lace, he had been dressed in the formal *breacan an fheile*. A tartan of green-on-black plaid had been draped over his shoulder, pinned with the silver-and-cairngorm brooch bearing the clan crest and motto. The light had flared blue along the shaft of the dress sword he wore at his side, and the air had sparkled with a million floating dust motes, all of which seemed to pour around his shoulders like a silver stream.

Angus Moy was, quite simply, the most beautiful human being she had ever set eyes upon, his face so perfectly sculpted that no one feature overawed another. His mouth, his nose, the metallic gray of his eyes had surely been fashioned by the faeries to stop a woman's heart, and Anne's was no exception. How long she had stared through the crystalline silence, tongue-tied and wooden-limbed, she had no way of knowing.

The groom had not moved either, but it was to be suspected it was more because of horrified surprise, for Anne was no petite, fine-boned flower trembling at the thought of being plucked. She was tall and amply proportioned, with a tautness in her legs and arms that had been honed by years of riding and swaggering about with her cousins. Her face was freckled from the sun, and although her hair had been tempered by pins and combs into a semblance of respectability, the wind had played havoc with a few fiery strands that dangled down her back and over her shoulders.

Eneas actually had to prod him into moving forward to take her hand, and when they had faced the minister, they both seemed paler for the experience.

"I am thinking about him," she said aloud, startled out of her reverie by a cold slap of night wind. "And if I think about him I will turn around and ride home. Or I will never be able to go home again."

"Did ye say somethin', Annie?"

She looked up sharply. "No. No, I was just cursing the wind."

"Aye, well, it'll ease off once we get through the pass."

Instead of answering she tucked her chin back into her plaid and prayed her huge gray gelding would keep a steady foot as they crossed the saddle of land between the two hills known as Garbhal Beg and Garbhal Mor. Here, the icy gusts were strong enough to tear the breath from her lungs, the howling as loud as a dozen banshees screaming into the night.

Not until they were through the pass and beginning their descent did the dreadful wailing cease and the wind die off enough to allow Anne to wipe her eyes and look out across the sprawling expanse of the valley below.

The clouds had thickened, reducing the moon to a clotted glow high above. Snow lay in a thin crust on the slopes and gave shape to the tumble of rocks that littered either side of the track. It was there, from one of the deep, black crags, that she caught a hint of movement.

Taking her cue from Robbie, she released one gloved hand from the reins and slid it beneath the folds of her tartan. Her fingers closing around the scrolled butt of her pistol, she withdrew the gun from her belt, her thumb cocking the hammer in the same smooth motion.

"Easy on, the pair o' ye." The muffled voice came out of the shadows, low as a heartbeat. "Ye were that late, we almost sent riders out tae search."

"I had to be sure the household had gone to bed," Anne said with a sigh.

The dark shape of Eneas Farquharson, oldest of the Monaltrie brothers, detached itself from the jumble of rocks and, without waiting for assent, swung himself up pillion-style behind Robbie.

"Yer husband is still in Inverness, is he no'?"

Her pride stung a bit at the knowledge that her kinsmen thought Angus dangerous enough to watch his every move. "Aye. He's away visiting his mam until tomorrow."

"She serves up a rare joint o' beef, does the Lady Drummuir. We supped wi' her just last night an' the taste is still on ma tongue."

Unlike her son, the Dowager Lady MacKintosh was a staunch and extremely vocal Jacobite who proclaimed herself too old to worry about repercussions.

"You took a terrible risk riding into Inverness."

Eneas shrugged. "Ye ken Granda' when he has a thought in his heid. Or the scent o' real meat up his nose."

Anne shook her head and resheathed her pistol. "How is Mairi? And the children?"

"She sends her love. So dae the bairns."

Anne felt another tug on her heartstrings. She had not seen Eneas's wife or children since the families had been forced into hiding. "I brought some things for you to take to them—warm clothes, shoes, food." She patted the bulging sacks draped behind her. "And some books so Mairi can keep them up with their schoolwork."

She could not see it through the wiry froth of beard that covered the lower half of his face, but she could sense his big grin. "Aye, they'll be thankin' ye for that."

"I'll not be thanking *you*"—she scowled halfheartedly—"if I waken in the morning coughing my lungs into my hands."

"Bah. Ye're made o' sterner stuff than that, an' ye know it. Granda' was out just a wee while ago takin' his bath in the stream. Had tae crack through the ice first tae dae it."

Anne shuddered and hunched deeper into her tartan. "How is he?"

"Och, healthy as ever. Skittish, but, with seein' ye again, as ye ken he must be if he took a proper wash."

Eneas chatted happily about his family all the way down the slope. There were thick stands of pine trees skirting the glen, serving to buffer the wind and allow a stillness of sorts to settle over the bowl of the valley. At the far end, a large two-story stone house sat tucked against the edge of the forest; behind that she knew there was a hundred-foot sheer drop to the loch below. There was only one approach to Dunmaglass, and someone must have been watching between the slats of a shuttered window, for no sooner had the horses drawn up in front of the house than the door swung open, throwing a garish slash of yellow light across the snow.

Anne blinked into a lantern as it was swung up into her face. It was held by James, the third Farquharson of Monaltrie and twin to Robbie, younger by six minutes. All three of Anne's cousins were of middling height with short, stalky legs and barrel-shaped torsos hewn out of solid muscle. They shared the familial blue eyes and red hair, though in the twins

the latter was thick and straight and stuck out above their ears
in a way that made them always look slightly demoniacal.

Anne dismounted and Jamie swore a streak in Gaelic,
hugging her with enough force to spin her around off her feet.
He barely waited until she had caught her breath again before
he snatched the bonnet off her head the way he used to do
when they were children.

Her hair tumbled down in a wealth of unruly curls and she
would have boxed his ears for the impertinence if she was not
so happy to be reunited with all three of her cousins. She was
even more eager to see her grandfather again, and, linking
arms with the twins, she urged them toward the open door.

Dunmaglass, albeit larger and better appointed than most
stone houses scattered through the glens, was typical of one
belonging to a Highland laird who gave more weight to what
was practical than to what was pretty. The ground floor consisted of two main rooms, one the kitchen and pantry, the
other a parlor for taking meals and entertaining guests before
the comfort of an enormous open hearth. Solid wood planks
covered the floor where once, to judge by the faintly redolent
scent that no amount of beeswax could quite disguise, sheep
and goats had been penned inside as a pragmatic measure to
save them from the worst of the winter freezes. In the absence
of livestock, there were chairs and a long pine table, an over-
stuffed sofa of indeterminate color and age, and a large
braided rug made of many twists of old rags. A staircase
against a side wall gave access to the sleeping quarters on the
second floor.

Fearchar Farquharson sat at the end of the table closest to
the heat of the fire, with his bony knees spread wide apart, his
ancient walking stick planted between them to support his
hands. His skin was the texture of wrinkled parchment,
draped in folds from the sparse white wisps of his hair to the
ragged collar of his coat. His fingers were dried brown twigs;
the bared shins that poked out from beneath the hem of his
kilt were not much more than bone and grizzle with a transparent layer of weathered skin overtop.

Only the eyes were still sharp and vibrant, the blue as
piercing as the steel edge of a dirk.

"Och!" He thumped the floor loudly with his stick and

cackled. "Wee Ruadh Annie! So ye've come, have ye? Gillies here didna think ye would, but I ken'd ye would. Weel! Why are ye just standin' there like a blin' lump? Come here an' gi' an auld mon a kiss."

Anne dropped to her knees before him, laughing as he welcomed her into his arms with a hug of amazing strength.

"It is so good to see you, Granda'," she cried. "And good to see you looking so well."

"Och, weel, it takes a mout longer f'ae these auld bones tae stir of a morn, but they dae. Miles get longer, clachans farther apart, but aye, I'm hale n'braw, thank the Laird above. Here, let me look at ye, lass. God strike me deid, but ye're a fine sight f'ae these tired eyes. An' what's this?" He reached boldly forward and laid a hand on her belly. "Wed four years an' still nae bairn on ye? Christ in a crib, had I ken'd yer husban' wouldna be up tae the task, I'd ha' wed ye tae wee Gillies here. He'd've known how tae fill ye wi' babbies. He'd've had three sprouted an' anither well planted by now, an' ye'd've both had a mout o' pleasure puttin' them there."

Anne sighed, accustomed to her grandfather's coarseness, but she could tell by the look on "wee" Gillies's face that he still suffered for it.

MacBean was a stout, rawboned Highlander who stood barely above five feet, but what he lacked in height he more than made up for in the width of his massive shoulders. His face was as craggy as the mountain range he called home, yet he could blush as swift as a lass at the wrong turn of a phrase—especially any phrase involving those mysterious creatures of the opposite sex. He was painfully tongue-tied around women of any age, a vulnerability that amused the old gray fox no end.

"Ye look like ye've a bone stuck in yer gullet," Fearchar snorted. "Speak up, mon. Can ye nae work up enough spittle tae say hallo tae wee Annie?"

Already as red as raw meat, Gillies burned an even hotter shade as he nodded and murmured, " 'Tis bonnie tae see ye again."

"And you, Gillies. I'm glad to know you've been taking care of Granda' for me."

The stick rapped on the floor again. "I take care o' masel', lassie. I only keep these belties wi' me tae see *they* stay out o' trouble. Ye've seen The MacGillivray, have ye not?"

Once again Annie followed the authoritative end of the walking stick and noted the shadowy figure seated well back in the corner of the room. A pair of long, muscular legs were stretched out and crossed at the ankles; arms the thickness of small tree trunks were folded over an equally impressive expanse of chest. Dunmaglass was his home, and it was his neck that would be stretched on a gibbet if any of them were caught holding a clandestine meeting.

John Alexander MacGillivray was a rare oddity in the Highlands. Not only did he stand a full head taller than most men, but his hair was the burnished gold of ripe wheat. He was not particularly handsome in the usual sense; his mouth was a touch too bold, his eyes were frighteningly black, and his jaw was fashioned from a square, immovable ridge of solid granite. But his smile could turn a woman's thighs to jelly, and rumors of what lay beneath his kilt could send her wits flying out the nearest window.

Anne had known The MacGillivray most of her life. His smile could still raise a flush of gooseflesh on her arms, and while her wits and thighs were safe enough, it had not always been so. Indeed, there had been a time when Wild Ruadh Annie and Big John MacGillivray were veering toward becoming much more than just friends.

"Lady Anne," he said quietly, nodding.

"MacGillivray."

It felt awkward addressing each other with such formality. Then again, it had been many a year since she had shadowed her cousins around to all the fairgrounds in the hopes of wagering a penny or two on MacGillivray's wrestling skills. In fact, it had been after one arousingly successful day when he won all five bouts he had entered that he had taken Anne out behind one of the booths and kissed her for the first time. It had been a hot day and he had been stripped to the waist, his muscles oiled and gleaming in the sunlight. . . .

"Come," Fearchar said, startling Anne as he dragged an empty chair closer to the fire. "Set yersel' doon, lassie. Ye must be chilled frae the long ride. Ye'll take a dram tae warm yer bones?"

Anne smiled. "Aye, Granda'. A bit of warmth would not go amiss."

The old warrior chuckled and waved a hand by way of a signal to James, who produced a stoneware jug of *uisque baugh*. Fearchar removed the bung and tipped the crock to his lips, taking two deep swallows before he passed it to Anne.

She accepted it warily, hesitating when she saw the bright and entirely involuntary film of water sparkle in his eyes. "Your own, then, is it?" she asked in a wry murmur.

"Aye." He sucked at a large mouthful of air to cool his throat. "An' I'll thank ye tae notice I've no' lost ma touch."

Anne braced herself and raised the jug. She matched the two hearty swallows her grandfather had taken, determined not to choke as the fiery Highland spirits slid over her tongue and scorched a path through her chest into her stomach. Once there, though, a fireball exploded, searing through her veins, boiling into her extremities, where it scalded the nerve endings and left the flesh numb with shock.

When she could, she followed Fearchar's example and took an enormous mouthful of ale from the tankard that had appeared magically at her elbow, swallowing in broken gulps that set her cousins, Gillies, and even the stone-faced MacGillivray laughing.

"Mary Mother of Christ," she gasped. " 'Tis a wonder you've not burned a hole clear through your bellies!"

Fearchar smacked his lap and gave a gleeful cackle. "Blew up three stillmen, but, when they thought tae take a pipe afterward."

"I'm not surprised." She took another cooling mouthful of ale and wiped the foam on the back of her hand. "Though I'm sure you've not brought me all the way out here tonight just to prove you can still brew up the barley with the best. What has happened? Why are you here in Inverness when you know full well every soldier in Fort George would trade their firstborn sons to collect the reward the *Sassenachs* have put on your head?"

Fearchar's happy expression faded and he glanced quickly at the other men in the room before gathering a rattled breath to speak.

"Ye've no' heard, then."

It was not a question so much as a painful wrench of emotion, and Anne's first thought was that someone must have died. Someone close to her. Someone whose death her grandfather did not want her hearing from a stranger.

"Has something happened to Angus?" she asked in a whisper.

Fearchar scowled and cursed under his breath. "Yer husband is as fine an' fit as he were when he left yer bed two days ago. Fitter than he has a right tae be, ye ask me."

"Then what—?"

"The prince has turned his army around. They're in retreat."

"Retreat!" Her mouth dropped open in surprise. "But . . . but that's not possible! They were only a few days' march out of London—you sent me word of it yourself."

"Aye, an' now we're here tae tell ye the army is turned away," Robbie said quietly. "We're tellin' ye that General Wade is closin' in on their right flank wi' five thousan' men; General Ligonier is on their left wi' another seven thousan'; an' comin' straight up their backsides is the Duke o' Christ-less Cumberland wi' a few thousan' troops he's brought wi' him off the battlefield in Flanders. That puts about twenty thousan' in all between the prince an' London, an' the chiefs decided it were just askin' too much f'ae our brave lads tae try tae fight their way through. Not when they've had no support frae either end—none frae here, none in England. Two hundred men, we were told, is all that joined up since they crossed the River Esk, where they were promised bluidy thousands."

"They should have known better than to trust promises," MacGillivray said from the shadows. "The king of France promised thousands o' troops, an' how many did he send? None. He promised guns an' ammunition an' money as well to pay the men for the crops we'll not be able to plant come the spring. What did we get? More o' nothin'."

"Crops?" Fearchar glared angrily over his shoulder. "How can a man think o' crops when his king an' country need him?"

"When his family is starvin' an' his children are dyin'

from the cold, that is all he thinks about," MacGillivray answered flatly. "He worries if they have a roof over their heads an' if they have enough meat to tide them over the winter. Why do ye suppose so many men on both sides slip away in the night? It's no' because they're afraid to fight or to die in battle. It's because they want to take a coin or a bit o' bread back to their wives. That's all a simple man cares about."

"An' you?" Eneas asked. "What dae *you* care about, MacGillivray?"

"Me?" Someone moved and an errant shaft of lamplight cut across the Highlander's face, revealing a disdainful curve at the corner of his mouth. "I care about what ma chief orders me to care about. Just like the rest o' ye. That's why we're here debatin' the whys an' wherefores o' battles fought an' not fought instead o' bein' out in the fields fightin' them." His eyes glittered like two chips of black ice as he looked in Anne's direction. "Because we've all been forbidden to do much else, have we not?"

Anne endured the derision in his eyes as long as she could before faltering and turning away. She was reminded, every single hour of every single day, that men like MacGillivray and Gillies and her cousins would be in Derby now with the prince's army if Angus had not bound them to their oaths. She also knew that if not for so many other lairds like Angus who had chosen caution over passion, the Jacobite army would have been equal to anything the English could muster against them. The five thousand brave men who had followed the Stuart prince to Derby would be ten, fifteen thousand strong and would not now be enduring the humiliation of a retreat.

"They've not been defeated yet, have they?" Anne whispered. "Just because they are being prudent and returning home to Scotland, that does not mean they do so in defeat."

Fearchar rallied somewhat. "No one has said aught about a defeat! As it happens, the prince has sent word tae all the clans that he only plans tae wait out the winter before he strikes south again, an' he's already proved he has the heart an' courage tae dae it. All he needs tae dae is come home an' build up the strength o' his army. He needs tae hold the throne o' Scotland f'ae his father an' drive these *Sassenach* basthards out o' Inverness an' Perth. He needs"——Fearchar leaned forward for emphasis——"*all* o' his lairds an' chiefs tae believe in him enough tae *want* tae make Scotland their own again."

"Angus wants an independent Scotland as much as the next man," she insisted calmly.

"Then why is he no' in Derby wi' his prince? Why is he wearin' a captain's uniform f'ae a company o' the king's Black Watch, an' why is he in Inverness this very night suppin' at the bluidy table of Duncan bluidy Forbes?"

"He is only trying to keep the peace—"

"Peace?" Fearchar straightened. "Aye, I've nae doubt they all want a piece o' the spoils! Him an' MacLeod an' Argyle. Och! Argyle wants a piece o' Lochaber so badly there's no need f'ae Forbes tae pay him wi' Judas gold."

Gillies MacBean arched an eyebrow and ventured gingerly into the fray. "Argyle never needed a bribe tae fight the Camerons, especially after he heard the *Camshroinaich Dubh* was back in Lochaber."

"Ewen Cameron?" Fearchar's eyes rounded out of their creases. "He's risen up out o' his grave?"

"No' the auld Dark Cameron," Eneas said gently. "The young one. Lochiel's brither, Alexander."

"Oh. Och, aye. I ken'd that," Fearchar grumbled, and waved his hand to dismiss his own lapse of memory. "I ken'd wee Alasdair were who ye meant all the while."

With almost the next breath, his shoulders slumped forward and his head bowed over the support of his walking stick. Like a bladder losing air he seemed to collapse in on himself until he was just a rounded bundle of rags and wispy gray hair.

"Granda'!" Anne started to reach out, but Robbie waylaid her hand.

"He does that now an' then. Just drops off, has a wee nap, then sits up like as nothin' has happened. He'll be right as rain in a few minutes, mark my words."

"I dinna have to mark your words, Robbie. I can mark how thin and tired he is. He is far too old to be hiding in the hills and living out of caves!"

Jamie came to his brother's defense. "Aye, well, ye can be the one tae tell him so, then, cousin. I'm certain he'll listen tae you, where he just clouts the rest o' us wi' his stick an' ignores aught we say. He were determined tae come here tonight an' here he came, a pox on the snow, a pox on the wind, a pox on the thousand militia swarmin' around Inverness."

"Two," Annie said softly, stroking a fold of her grandfather's tartan. "It will be two thousand by week's end. The MacLeod and The MacKenzie of Seaforth have pledged to send more men to reinforce Loudoun's defenses around Fort George."

"How do ye know this?" MacGillivray asked sharply.

"I hear things. I see things." She shrugged and looked over. "Sometimes Forbes will send a message to Angus and . . . and sometimes he might be careless and leave his desk unlocked."

"I didna think Angus Moy was a careless man."

"He is not," she admitted. "It sometimes requires a hairpin to make it seem so."

Jamie and Robbie grinned. Eneas only frowned. "If he catches ye tamperin' wi' his locks, he'll no' look on it too kindly, lass."

"He would hardly be overjoyed to know I was here, either. He is sick to death of all this, Eneas. He is sick to death at the thought of more bloodshed, of Highlanders killing Highlanders."

"Aye. That's why he's raised a regiment of MacKintoshes to fight f'ae Hanover. That's why he spends a treat o' time at Culloden House drinking claret wi' Duncan Forbes."

"Moy Hall is less than ten miles from Culloden House! How could he possibly avoid contact with Duncan Forbes?"

"I do," MacGillivray said easily. "An' Dunmaglass is closer."

"Own up to it, Annie," Eneas said. "He's been away too long an' he's simply no' willin' tae risk his lands an' fortune on anither war. It's in his bluid anyway tae lay back an' see which way the wind blows. His grandfather was one o' the first lairds tae disarm the clans after The Fifteen. His father was one o' the first tae swear the oath of allegiance tae the Hanover king so his lands an' titles wouldna be forfeit. There were many a clansman who cursed him f'ae that; many who have long memories an' will never fight under the Hanover flag regardless if yer husband drives them barefoot out intae the snow an' burns the roof down o'er their heads."

"He would not do that," Anne countered angrily.

"Nor would a true Scot question his rightful king," Robbie said heatedly. "When The Stuart called f'ae his sword, he would give it. Simple as that."

"Are you saying Angus is not a true Scot?"

"Wheesht, Annie. Calm yerself." Eneas glared ominously at Robbie before continuing. "No one is sayin' any such thing about The MacKintosh. He's a good man, a fair man; he must be, or ye would have run a dirk across his throat long ago."

The demand to hear the unspoken reservation came through clenched teeth. "But?"

"But . . . he hasna proved he's the leader this clan needs him tae be. Oh, aye, he can tally sheep an' count rents, an' he can hold a pretty audience when two crofters are fightin' over the boundaries o' their land. But he disna listen tae the hearts o' the men. They want tae fight, Annie. They would fight the devil himself if they had a leader willin' tae take them intae battle. And if he's no' the one tae do it, they'll look elsewhere f'ae a sword tae follow."

She looked slowly from one cousin to the next, then from Gillies MacBean—who studiously avoided making eye contact—to The MacGillivray. By then, all the fine hairs across her nape had prickled to attention and the skin along her spine felt as if spiders were skittering up and down it.

"That's why you've called this meeting, isn't it? You're planning to break from the clan," she whispered. "You're planning to break your oath to Angus and you're going to join the prince."

"I'll no' lie by sayin' we havna been thinkin' about it," Eneas admitted. "Trouble is, three or four men willna make a lick o' difference. On the other hand, if we had three or four thousand—"

"You'll not get three *hundred* clansmen to follow you, Eneas Farquharson! You may be able to frighten and bully them into holding secret meetings and sticking a sprig of thistle in their bonnets, but asking them to break clan laws is another matter altogether. They would lose their homes. They would be men without a badge, without honor."

"They would be fightin' f'ae their king, f'ae their faith, f'ae their pride."

"Their pride would be fleeting. The glory would pass and they would be looked on as men who could not be trusted to uphold their word. Oh, not right away perhaps, for in victory there is always benevolence. But there would come a time when it would be remembered that they broke their oaths when so many stayed firm, and it would be held against them."

"There are some willin' tae take that chance."

"Are you one of them? Are you willing to forfeit your home? To lose everything your family has fought so hard to build? Are you willing to have your names struck from the kirk registry, and your children denied their birthrights?"

"Better ye should ask me could I bear tae look in ma wife's eyes if I kept ma sword buried under the thatch instead o' raisin' it by the prince's side," Eneas said quietly. "Some things are worth fightin' an' dyin' f'ae, Annie. Mayhap ye would understand that better if ye were a man."

She shot to her feet with enough vehemence to nearly tip the chair into the fire. "My not being a man has nothing to do with what I feel in my heart. I would walk onto the battlefield beside the lot of you if that was what my laird commanded. I would fight as hard and kill as many *Sassenachs* as the rest of you, and I would spill their blood just as proudly, never dare say that I would not!"

"We dinna doubt yer loyalty f'ae a moment, Annie," Fearchar said, having been startled awake by the crash of the chair against the iron grate. "In fact, it's the fire in yer eyes an' the courage in yer heart that we want."

"You have always had my heart, Granda'. You have never needed to ask for it."

"This time we do. Too many o' the lairds willna break their oath f'ae the very reasons ye said, but they might if they had a leader. Nay, nay"—he scrubbed his hand in the air as if erasing words from a slate—"that's no' right either. They blessed *all* want tae be leaders, an' tae that end, they'll fight themselves bluidy before they're ever out o' the glen. What they need is someone who is as cunning as Forbes, as shameless as Loudoun when he offers rewards o' land an' gold to any man who signs the roster, someone they can trust who has the power tae bring them back intae the clan again regardless who wins an' who loses."

Anne could think of no one who could fill such an overwhelming charter, but then she frowned and looked at MacGillivray, the tall golden lion of the Highlands, and once again her breath left her lungs on a gust. "You, John? They've asked you to do this?"

Before he answered he drew his legs in and sat straight in the chair. He rose slowly, the top of his head seeming to stretch forever into the shadows near the ceiling before he walked into the brighter circle of firelight. The creamy wool of his shirt took on a luminous glow, the radiance spreading upward to touch the strands of his hair. The blackness of his eyes reflected a sudden wily glint that could very well have come from Lucifer himself.

"Ye give me too much credit, lass. It's not me they're after askin'," he said quietly. "It's you."

Chapter Two

$\mathscr{A}$t that same moment, at almost the exact spot in the narrow pass between Garbhal Beg and Garbhal Mor where Anne had stopped to take in the beauty of the glen below, one of MacGillivray's sentries cocked the hammer on his flintlock and aimed at a shadowy figure walking up the hill. The other man must have heard the faint click of the ratchet, for he stopped and held up his hand while he whistled a low trill to identify himself. He was warm, his tunic and kilt dry, his senses keen after a hot meal and couple of hours in front of a crackling fire. The sentry was happy enough to welcome the relief. His beard and eyebrows were caked with crystals of frost and his toes were numb despite the nest he had made for himself in the bracken.

Releasing the hammer again, he shrugged the snow off his plaid and stretched his legs with exaggerated motions to ease the stiffness that had locked them with cramps after several hours in the cold. There would be broth and ale waiting for him in the sheltered heat of the stables—him and the others who stood watch over the snowy silence of the glen.

None of them actually expected any trouble, for it was an ugly night and the English were not known for their eagerness to leave the protected garrison at Inverness after dark. Truth be told, most of the sentries had pulled their plaids over their heads to seek what comfort they could until it was their turn to be relieved.

The two men said a few words, cursed the thickening snow in hearty Gaelic, then parted company with a wave. Neither one of them was aware of the two other shadowy figures who had crept stealthily to the edge of the fir trees and watched the exchange with narrow-eyed surprise.

Unlike MacGillivray's sentries, they had anticipated no relief whatsoever and were dressed for the cold, each in his own manner. The Highlander wore his breacan belted into pleats around his waist with the ends of the wool wound warmly around his shoulders. His bonnet was pulled low over his forehead; his beard shielded everything below the beaklike nose, leaving only a narrow strip free for his eyes.

The English officer's scarlet tunic was concealed beneath a voluminous black greatcoat. He was temporarily hatless, but the fresh white flakes of snow barely survived a moment or two on the dark cap of hair before they dissolved into tiny beads of water. He was clean shaven, his face a hard mask of concentration softened only by the shallow puffs of steam that gave substance to each breath.

"How many more do you suppose are up there?"

"Could be two," said the Scot. "Could be twenny. MacGillivray is a cautious bastard; I'm surprised we managed tae get as close as we have."

The major cursed under his breath, for he had not even been aware they were on MacGillivray's land until a few moments ago and he was just thankful *he* had been cautious enough to order a circuitous approach through the woods.

"Have we any idea who those two riders were?"

"Could ha' been any one of a barrel full o' rebels come tae meet with the auld bastard."

"You are absolutely certain Fearchar Farquharson is in that cottage?"

"As certain as I am o' the nose on ma face. Lomach saw the youngest Monaltrie in Inverness today an' followed him here, an' if he's inside yon house, so are his brithers, an' so is their granda'. Like apples in a barrel."

"Yes. And that barrel belongs to Dunmaglass."

"Ye're leakin' a bit o' piss worryin' about The MacGillivray? He stops a lead ball just as easily as any ither man."

The English officer turned his head to stare at the Highlander. "I am sure he does. But how many of his men will be spitting lead at us before we even have a chance to get to him? There could be a dozen more burrowed into those blasted rocks, the same again inside the house and barn—none of them chosen for either their poor aim or their reluctance to demonstrate it. We have fifteen good men I would as soon not squander on an attack that holds little promise of success." He turned his gaze back to the house. "Besides, the old fox is worth much more to me alive than dead, for he attracts these rebels like flies to dung and we merely have to watch him to see who comes to pay homage."

The Highlander expelled a hoary breath. He knew there was no use arguing with the *Sassenach*, though it galled him to have to let such a plum opportunity slip through his fingers. He owed the arrogant MacGillivray a scar or two for past insults.

Hugh MacDugal of Argyle was not paid to eat gall, but he was paid—and paid well—as a tracker. His nose was as keen as that of any bloodhound and it was no idle boast to say he could follow an ant through a forest in a rainstorm. Just as the MacCrimmon clansmen were known for piping the sweetest music in all of Caledonia, the MacDugals had bred generations of hunters. Hugh's services, along with those of his brother Lomach, had been contracted by the English within hours of the Stuart prince raising his standard at Glenfinnan.

Major Roger Worsham, on the other hand, had only arrived in the Highlands a fortnight ago. Unlike most English officers who treated the posting at Inverness like an exile, and who familiarized themselves first with the local whisky, second with the local whores, Worsham had remained aloof and apart, preferring his own company when he was not otherwise engaged in army matters. He reported directly to Lord Loudoun, yet he was not yet attached to any specific regiment. Rumor was he had been sent to Inverness by the Duke of Cumberland himself.

Worsham started to edge back into the denser cover of the trees, and with a vigilant glance around the rocks, MacDugal followed, keeping low until the shadows and increasing snowfall were likely to mask any hint of movement. Despite the thickness of the fir trees, the rest of the men were clearly visible, the scarlet of their tunics glowing a dull blood red against the bluish gloom of their surroundings.

"If we're no' gonny attack, we'd best move further back," he advised. "Otherwise *we'll* be the apples in the barrel."

Worsham detected the derision in the tracker's voice and thrust a thumb down between each finger to adjust the fit of his leather gloves. "I have seen enough anyway. It's too bloody cold to stand about watching the smoke rise from the chimney. Keep half of the men here with you, MacDugal, and put them where you will. I'll take the rest back with me to Inverness. When MacGillivray's guests leave—or if any others arrive—I want them followed."

"By this flock o' bloody lobsterbacks? In this snow they'll stick out like licks o' flame."

"You have a better idea?"

"Aye. Take the lot o' them back tae Inverness wi' ye. Lomach an' I will manage on our own."

Worsham searched for the dark blot of the other tartan-clad Highlander, but having no success, settled his gaze on MacDugal. "I don't want to lose Farquharson in these hills."

"Ye won't. Old as he is, he's nae daft enough tae leave Dunmaglass tonight. No' with The MacGillivray guaranteeing his safety. An' mark my words"—he paused and screwed his eyes upward to look at the sky—"it'll get a fair sight worse out here afore it gets any better."

Within the hour, Eneas had arrived at the same conclusion. "Snow's gettin' heavier," he murmured, glancing through a slat in the window shutters. "If ye're determined tae go back tonight, Annie, ye'd best be leavin' soon."

Since staying away from home all night was not an option she could even briefly consider, Anne looked reluctantly away from the fire and nodded. She had not said much in the past ten minutes or so. Fearchar had dropped off again and the twins had carried him away to his bed. Gillies had volunteered to fetch more wood, though she suspected he only wanted an excuse to remove himself from the tension that had filled the room since The MacGillivray's startling announcement.

"Me? They want *me* to lead the clan away?" Anne had gasped.

MacGillivray had only shrugged his big shoulders and she had not been sure if the smile playing across his lips was intended to express his amusement or his derision.

She had turned then, to stare at her cousins and grandfather. "You cannot be serious."

"We're deadly serious, lass," Fearchar declared. "Ye're the only one can dae it."

"Surely not the only one."

"Onliest one the men will listen tae. Ye're the wife o' the chief. Ye're a Farquharson. Ye're ma granddaughter, an' by God's grace ye've more courage in yer wee finger than Angus Moy can lay claim tae in his entire body."

"He is not a coward, Granda'," she insisted quietly.

"He just disna want tae fight. Well an' good then, we can fight wi'out him. I've gone through all the laws, lassie, an' there's naught says a woman canna lead the clan. I grant ye, it's never been done afore, but then we've never had an army marched all the way tae London afore either! We've never had a prince willin' tae risk everythin' he has tae walk in the mud alongside his troops! We've never had a general like Lord George Murray, nor have we ever had brave men the likes o' Lochiel an' Keppoch an' Lord John Drummond willin' tae risk everythin', tae lose everythin' tae fight f'ae Scotland's freedom. All ye need, lass, is the signatures of a hundred lairds willin' tae acknowledge ye as their leader an' the law says ye can send out the *crosh tarie* an' call the men tae arms."

For generations, the burning cross had been sent out across the Highlands as both a demand for clansmen to answer a summons by their chief, and a threat of punishment by fire if they failed to show up at the appointed time and place.

"The signatures of a hundred lairds?" She offered up a sound that fell somewhere between a scoff and a curse. "Is that all? No armor, no mighty Excalibur, no steel helmet with horns growing out of the sides?"

"Ye'd not actually be expected tae ride intae battle," Robbie said, taking exception to her mockery. "Ye'd have tae appoint a captain wi' hard fightin' experience behind him tae lead the men onto the battlefield."

"One of you stalwart fellows, I suppose?"

"No' me," Jamie said, raising his hands in self-defense.

"Damned right, no' you," Robert agreed. "Ye have enough trouble leadin' the way across a moor."

Jamie glared. "If ye're referrin' tae last week at Killie-crankie, how was I tae know the ground were thawed?"

"Thawed? Ye were up tae yer armpits in bog an' squealin' like a stuck pig when we caught up tae ye. Took us two hours tae haul ye out an' two days afore the stink washed off."

"Enough." Eneas's voice cut sharply between the two before addressing Anne. "We didna mean tae spring this on ye so sudden, nor have we come wi' a half-cocked idea. We've asked some o' the lairds what their answer might be if they were given a petition bearin' yer name, an' if it interests ye tae know, we have twenty-seven willin' tae sign already—an' that's no' includin' any man here."

Anne did not know what to say. Twenty-seven lairds were ready to break their oath of fealty to their chief, and they were willing to do it on her say-so. Part of her was appalled, certainly. Respect and unquestioning loyalty to the authority of the clan chief was ingrained from birth; what they were suggesting was tantamount to treason within the clan. Another part of her—the part that had reveled in riding the moors with her cousins—was admittedly excited, too, for it meant there were at least twenty-seven lairds who had not laughed her grandfather out of the room and slammed the door behind him.

"Ye dinna have tae give us yer answer tonight, lass," Fearchar said. "Sleep on it. Think on it. Watch yer husband dress in his fine scarlet tunic a time or two afore ye make up yer mind."

"I don't have to think about it," Anne said quietly. "The answer is no. What you are asking is . . . is just not possible. It's utter madness, in fact."

"Annie," Robbie began, "it's f'ae the honor o' the clan."

Her gaze cut to her cousin. "Don't you dare try to justify this by telling me it's for the honor of the clan. It may have worked four years ago, but it will not work now."

"But Annie—"

"And do not *but Annie* me." Her anger flashed in Eneas's direction. "Four years ago you all insisted I marry a man I had never even seen before, a man who had to be threatened and badgered to honor an agreement *he* had neither sought nor wanted. But marry we did, and you justified the threats and badgering by claiming I had an obligation, that the union was for the good of the clan. Well . . . you may not take your vows and oaths seriously—or perhaps you only take them seriously when they suit your moods and motives—but I do. Angus is my husband. He is also my laird, and I'll not break the vows I made just because it is no longer of any benefit to the Farquharson clan that I keep them. If you want another Joan of Arc, you will have to look elsewhere for someone to ride the white charger."

Jamie and Robbie started to retort with arguments in their own defense, but Anne turned her back to the room and no longer listened. In truth, it *had* taken the combined efforts of all three cousins and her grandfather to coax her into going through with the wedding to Angus Moy. The fact it had not turned out to be the hated, dreaded, feared ordeal she had envisioned had nothing to do with her resentment now. They had used her like a pawn once to get what they wanted; she was not about to let them use her again, especially since it was only her name they wanted, and not even her.

"Dinna let it eat at ye, lass," MacGillivray murmured, coming up and handing her a newly refilled tankard of ale. "Ye were right to tell them to go to hell. 'Tis a foolish thing they're askin' an' ye're better off stayin' out of it."

Anne was tall for a woman, and accustomed to meeting

most men on eye level, but to look into MacGillivray's eyes, she had to physically tilt her head upward.

She smiled and was about to thank him for the ale when she remembered Eneas had said none of the men in this room had signed the petition. That would include MacGillivray, who had sat like a big cat in the shadows throughout the discussion, undoubtedly harboring his own opinions on the foolishness of what they proposed. On the other hand, there was no lack of respect for him among his peers, and his clansmen were bonny fighters; not a one would remain behind if he gave orders to take up arms. He would have been Anne's first choice to lead anyone into battle, and she could well understand if his pride had been left a little stung that it was not his name on the petition.

The faint grin that had been pulling at his mouth widened, giving Anne the distinct impression he knew exactly what she was thinking.

The proof of it came on a soft laugh. "I aspire to be nothin' more than what I am, Annie. Had they asked me, I would have throfted them out the door on the toe o' ma boot."

"Yet you did nothing to *stop* them from asking me."

"Mayhap I was curious to hear yer answer."

His eyes were like deep black pools and, try as she might, she could not look away. Nor could she stop herself from asking, "Had I said yes, what would you have done?"

His head tipped to one side and his gaze made a slow, leisurely study of her face, taking in the smooth curve of her cheek, the slight upturn at the end of her nose, the lush fullness of her lower lip. When he was finished, his smile had been lost somewhere in the stillness and Anne had forgotten what she had asked.

"We'll never know what might have happened, will we?"

Somehow she knew he was not talking about petitions or signatures or rebellions. He was back with her behind the booth at the fairground and his hands were deep in her hair; his hard, oiled body was hotter than the sunlight, and his mouth was introducing her to sensations she'd had no idea she was capable of feeling.

"Ye'd best be on yer way, Annie," Eneas said from the window. "I'll have Gillies bring the horses round."

"Yes," she said, glancing over at him. "Thank you."

When she looked back, MacGillivray had moved away from the hearth and returned to the shadows, taking whatever memories had been disturbed with him.

Chapter Three

Anne hurried up the darkened staircase to the second floor of Moy Hall. She had removed her boots after squelching two or three steps inside the rear door, and her stockinged feet made no sound on the waxed wooden floors. The ride from Dunmaglass had been without incident, though Eneas, who had elected to act as her escort on the way back, had periodically called a halt to look over his shoulder and study the gusts of swirling snow.

Shivering and red-nosed, Anne arrived at her bedchamber and released an audible sigh of gratitude when she saw a fire blazing high in the grate. She had half unwound her plaid, shedding clumps of ice and melting snow onto the floor all the while, before she stiffened and turned slowly to stare at the fireplace again.

"It is a cold night. I thought you might appreciate the heat. I even had your maid draw a bath, although I expect the water has cooled by now."

Anne's hands clutched the woolen folds as she followed the voice. Angus was seated in the armchair in the far corner of the room. His coat and waistcoat had been discarded, his fine lawn shirt was loosened in a deep V down his chest, his booted feet were propped on a tapestry stool. Seeing her husband lounging in much the same position MacGillivray had assumed for most of the evening brought the tiny hairs along her forearms standing up on end.

"Angus?"

"You were expecting someone else?"

"No. No, of course not, but—"

He held a crystal glass in his hand and began to swirl the contents round and round. To judge by the near-empty decanter of claret on the table beside him, he had been there for quite some time.

"I . . . I thought you would have stayed the night on Church Street," she said lamely.

"My dear mother would not have thanked me for imposing myself on her hospitality."

"I am sure she does not think upon it as an imposition."

"It is if she is stockpiling guns in the wine cellar for Prince Charles or hatching plots to storm the citadel at Fort George." He took a slow sip of wine and let his gaze wander speculatively over her wet and bedraggled appearance. "Besides which, I thought my wife might appreciate my company on such a cold and blustery night. Imagine my surprise and disappointment when I found an empty house."

Anne's cheeks warmed as she draped the heavy tartan over the back of a nearby chair.

"Granda' is in Inverness," she said, having no wish to play any more games of cat and mouse this night. "I went to see him."

The pewter gray eyes narrowed sharply. "Fearchar? He's here? What the good Christ is he doing anywhere near Inverness?"

Anne forced another measured breath between her lips. It was a rare occasion when her husband used profanity in front of her, even more rare than the times he presented himself with the ends of his cravat trailing unwound down his chest and his shirtfront opened haphazardly over the dark swirls of hair beneath. His manners were normally as polished as his appearance, and in four years of marriage she had yet to witness any major disruption in either. This—the gaping shirt, the mud showing on the soles of his boots, the disheveled lock of chestnut hair fallen over the brow, and the near-empty decanter of claret—evoked a sensation not unlike holding a lit fuse in front of a keg of gunpowder.

Nor did his eyes do anything to ease her apprehension. They were fastened on her like gun barrels, following her every move as she took off her bonnet and set it alongside her plaid.

"He came to tell me about the prince's army retreating from Derby. He was surprised I had not already heard the news from you."

"Your grandfather's sources are better than the Lord President's. The army dispatch only reached Inverness late this afternoon."

"And you rushed right home to tell me?"

She saw his mouth tighten at her sarcasm and she could have bitten her tongue off at the root, for it occurred to her—too late to save the slow burn in her cheeks—that he might have done exactly that.

He held her in a fixed stare for a moment longer, then resumed swirling the contents of his glass. "You are aware, are you not, of the dangers involved with being caught in your grandfather's company?"

"He was careful, I was careful. No one saw me leave the house and I met no one on the road."

His gaze flickered downward again and settled on the twin steel-butted dags tucked into her belt. "Please do not tell me you went out on a night like this . . . *alone*?"

"Robbie met me at the bridge. Eneas brought me home."

That almost brought forth a groan. "Sweet Jesus. Your cousins are here, too?"

"All three of them." She paused and some reckless inner demon could not resist adding, "Eneas sends his fondest regards."

Angus's mouth tightened further, for he and Eneas Farquharson of Monaltrie were not exactly the best of friends. Eneas had waited for Angus outside the church the day of their wedding and pinned him against the wall by a fistful of his fine grogram jacket. He had pressed his lips to the blade of his dirk and sworn a solemn oath to personally carve out The

MacKintosh's heart should there ever be a whisper of mistreatment against their Annie. Angus had heard him out, had suffered the double threat of brute strength and glittering steel without a word, then had coolly straightened his clothes and walked away. To Anne's knowledge, they had not spoken since.

"Does Fearchar know the countryside is swarming with militia?"

"It is not the first time Granda' has been named on an English warrant," Anne said. "He knows who his friends are . . . and who would sell him out for a few copper pennies."

"A thousand pounds is hardly a few coppers."

"Nor is it thirty pieces of Judas silver."

The barb struck home, for Angus had been apportioned somewhat more than thirty pieces of silver to form up a regiment of MacKintosh men to serve under Lord Loudoun's command. According to Duncan Forbes, the compensation was intended to provide the men with uniforms and weaponry as well as the half shilling a day they earned in pay, but few Highlanders saw it as such. Not when wealthy lairds insisted on several thousand pounds sterling over and above any expectations of costs.

Anne did not wait for a rebuttal—not that one appeared to be forthcoming. She walked toward the dressing room instead, dragging the sodden ribbon out of her hair as she went.

"I am cold and tired. Can we not talk about this in the morning?"

"Actually, no. Since I have been sitting here for the past three hours with all manner of imagined and creative explanations for your late-night absence running through my mind, I would rather talk about it now."

She paused at the door and cast a small frown in his direction. Although his voice was as smooth as satin, there were fine white lines of tension bracketing his mouth, and while the hand that held the wineglass was no longer swirling it, the contents continued to shiver.

Her gaze flicked involuntarily to the neatly turned sheets on the bed. The bedchamber itself was half of a four-room suite, the largest in Moy Hall, with two suitably well-appointed dressing rooms that divided Anne's bedroom from his. In the first three and a half years of their marriage, they had slept apart only a handful of nights; most of the time they had shared—and enjoyed—the massive canopied bed in Angus's room.

In the last six months, however, the opposite had held true, and the strain between them had become so obvious, even to the household servants, that the maids had begun to turn down both beds.

"Surely you could not have been thinking I was with another man," she said softly.

His hand curled around the stem of the glass and his mouth formed a small pucker before he met her gaze. "Frankly, no, that was not my first thought, but I admit it was one of them. And in truth, it might have been preferable over some of the alternatives. The mind . . . conjures all manner of things on a dark, windy night."

"I am sorry if you were worried. But I truly thought you would stay the night in Inverness."

"And that makes it all right to gallop around the countryside with loaded guns in your belt?"

"I was hardly galloping about the countryside. I was at Dunmaglass."

"Ah."

There was enough innuendo in that one little sound to make her search his face a second time. The exercise proved to be futile, as it always was when his guard was up—which seemed to be most of the time these days. When he chose to retreat behind his well-groomed mask of indifference, regardless of what he was thinking, regardless of whether he was in a rage or the height of despair, his eyes, his expression gave away nothing. There were occasions Anne envied his ability to detach himself so completely, and others—such as now—when she resented it with all the passion of her Highland blood.

The notion that he might have thought . . .

But that was foolish. The very idea that he would even suspect she had gone to see John MacGillivray . . .

"I went to Dunmaglass to see Granda'," she said evenly. "He was the one who set the place for the meeting, not I."

She watched him empty the dregs of his wineglass, then

reach for the decanter to refill it. "If you were so sure I was not coming home tonight, you could have invited him here. You've done it before, have you not?"

Anne chewed on the edge of her lip. Indifference might be the mask he wore, but ignorance was never a question, and not knowing how to answer the charge, she merely evaded it. "He is my grandfather. He wanted to see me; I obliged."

"I am your *husband*. I *expect* to see you when I come home."

"Perhaps if you were at home more often," she retorted, "those expectations would be more happily realized."

She went into her dressing room, and when she was out of sight, she leaned against the wall and closed her eyes. She heard a sharp sound as the base of the glass hit the table, but when he did not appear in the doorway as she half expected him to, she covered her face with her hands and slowly shook her head, cursing her tongue for its impetuousness.

But Angus had indeed pushed himself out of the chair and was halfway to the dressing room before he thought better of it and stopped. He could see her through the lighted crack between the door and the frame, and his jaw clenched hard enough to set the muscles in his cheek shivering.

"I . . . have never forbidden you to see your grandfather—or any member of your family, for that matter," he said after a long moment. "I only hoped you would see the need for discretion."

"I saw a greater need to take some food and warm clothing for the children. Do you know they all fear for their lives and must live in a cave now? Eneas says the little ones are brave and they do not complain, but it's bitter cold most of the time and they both have heavy chests and . . . and Mairi suffered a miscarriage last month. She slipped on some rocks . . ."

Her voice trailed away and Angus watched her lower her hands. She folded them over her belly as if she were feeling the tearing loss herself and her face crumpled to expose a terrifying vulnerability. He took a halting step forward, then another, but by the time he had convinced himself she would not slam the door on him, the opportunity was lost.

"I am . . . genuinely sorry to hear about Mairi," he said

gently. "But at the moment, it is your health I am more concerned with. The water in the bath should still be warm. Hardy has been adding fresh buckets every half hour or so. I . . . can have him bring more, if you require it."

"No. Thank you. It is fine."

He looked up as she passed before the narrow slice of light again, her hair streaming down her back like a red silk curtain. As he watched, she gathered fistfuls of the curls and twisted them into a haphazard pile on top of her head, catching all but a few straggled wisps between a pair of mother-of-pearl combs. That left her neck and shoulders exposed, and, when she turned slightly, the pale white swell of her breast.

Anne emerged a short time later, her body rendered shapeless in a thick chenille robe. Risking a glance into the corner, she saw that her husband was still there. His head was leaning back against the upholstery and he was staring up at the ceiling, seemingly engrossed with the patterns the firelight made on the ornate plaster moldings.

She unfastened the combs from her hair and started working out the tangles. It was still damp from the melted snow, and the first few strokes of the hairbrush proved stubborn as always, but she was grateful to be doing something that did not require conscious thought. The long ride to Dunmaglass and the meeting with her grandfather had left her more exhausted than she cared to admit, and she was down to her last reserves of strength. She had half hoped Angus would have retired to his own chamber by now, for she was as confused as she was tired, and did not think she could withstand any more confrontations.

More important, she had never deliberately lied to Angus and did not particularly want to start now, so she prayed he would not ask her for any more specific reasons why Fearchar had called her out on such a cold, bleak night. She could scarcely believe the irony of it herself, being asked to lead a rebellion within the clan when she had worked so hard to dampen the rebellious streak within herself.

Anne's hand faltered in the middle of a brushstroke.

She had tried, she really tried hard to be a good wife, to learn the manners and demure behavior that would not embarrass her husband in the company of his peers. She struggled daily to erase the harsh edge from her brogue, to learn to walk and talk with the proper decorum; she fought a constant battle to curb her emotions, to be more like the frosty, aloof women whose faces were in danger of cracking if they laughed out loud.

She used to laugh a great deal, the sound hearty enough that it often won a reluctant smile from her more reserved spouse—and not just the smile he gave out so freely and falsely in company, but the slow, lethally sensuous smile he usually reserved for the privacy of their bedroom.

Sighing, she rested the brush in her lap for a moment.

Despite the circumstances surrounding their wedding, he had never given her any reason to question her ability to please him as a woman, nor had she ever given him any basis to suspect she went to his bed each night merely to fulfill her wifely obligations. There were times she could have wept from the sheer pleasure of feeling his hands, his mouth on her body. And there were times, when the lights were low and he was deep inside her, she imagined she could sense a longing for intimacy that went beyond the physical act of their union. Times when the urgency of his whisperings and the hungry rovings of his hands and mouth were as contradictory as they were confounding. He was a skilled, generous lover, and his body betrayed his pleasure in ways no amount of mental discipline could control. In turn, he awakened needs within her that made her more than willing, and often shamelessly eager, to go to his bed at night.

The very notion that he had sat in the dark and suspected her of having a lover was ironic enough to almost make her smile. There were countless times over these past six months when she had sat in that same chair and wondered the same thing about him.

Angus had never given her any reason to believe he had been unfaithful, but men were inherently sly creatures when it came to such indiscretions. Married men, especially handsome, worldly men accustomed to the courts of Europe, were expected to keep mistresses; it was as commonplace as keeping two sets of plate in a household, one for special occasions, one for everyday use. Few of his peers would have understood any reluctance on his part to sample the less inhibited beauties who seemed to arrive by the shipload each time the English garrison was reinforced. Wild Rhuad Annie was the kind of woman a man took behind the stable to toss her skirts above her head for a sweaty romp. She was not the kind men married or to whom they remained faithful.

Yet Angus had not touched her, sweatily or otherwise, in over a month, and she suffered a genuine melancholy for the lack. The tingling in her body now had less to do with her quick scrub and proximity to the fire than with the heat in his eyes as they watched her every move. His shirt being carelessly unfastened did not help her powers of concentration either, nor did the movement of his fingers as he absently stroked the stem of the wineglass.

Her own fingers fought the urge to press down into the junction of her thighs, to stop if she could the ache that seemed to be growing there by the second. But having discovered there was more to marriage than arranging dinner parties and keeping track of seventy household servants, Anne could not simply command her body to go cold. Nor could she act as if the patterns thrown by the firelight were more intriguing than the remembered feel of his breath on her neck or the sensation of his fingers skimming across her breasts.

No, she did not want to argue with him. She wanted to throw off her robe and sprawl naked on the hearthrug like a harlot if that was what it took to bring him out of that wretched corner.

Anne looked down at where the brush rested in her lap. According to the rules of polite society, it was considered *très gauche* to actually be in love with one's own husband. Was it also wrong to want to feel his arms around her, or to enjoy the physical pleasure of his flesh moving inside her?

"Here, let me help."

Startled, Anne turned and found Angus standing beside her, his hand outstretched. She had not heard him get up or walk across the room. And because, for the moment it took him to lean over and gently prise the hairbrush out of her hand, she had no idea what he was offering to do, she remained warily still, only following him with her eyes.

"You look as if your arms are ready to fall off."

"I can manage," she whispered.

"I'm sure you can."

Without further ado he took up the brush and moved behind her. It was the first time he had ever done such a thing, and in her indelicately aroused state she was not all that certain she could bear him doing it now.

He began by dealing quickly with the fiery disorder, using a man's brusque, no-nonsense efficiency. But when the brush began to run smoothly from her scalp to the ends of the curls, his movements slowed as well, and the strokes became noticeably more deliberate. Before too long the tangles and the dampness had been banished and on each silky pass of the brush, the gleaming strands began to crackle with static. The surface of Anne's skin tingled with the same needle-prick sensations. She sat breathlessly still, her heart pounding like a blacksmith's hammer, wondering if he could possibly be aware of the unbelievably erotic sensations that were rippling down her neck, down her spine, and pooling in her belly.

The edges of her bathrobe started to quiver where the chenille gaped slightly over her breasts. A particularly long, sensual sweep of the brush set off a corresponding wave of pinpoint implosions between her thighs, and her lips parted around an audible gasp.

The brush stopped.

She could not move, she could scarcely even breathe, and when he reached forward to run his fingertips along the curve of her neck, she almost could not stop herself from climaxing then and there. He used the excuse of gathering up the errant ribbons of hair that had escaped his attention, but when she parted her lips and released a second nearly soundless whimper, he abandoned the pretense and the caress lingered. His fingers went back and trailed across the warm, smooth curve, though there were no more errant wisps to catch.

The next challenge came as he split the one thick tail into three sections, and she realized he was attempting to plait her hair.

"I can do the rest," she offered.

"No, no. I have started it, I'll finish it. Besides, I have probably watched you do this a thousand times, how difficult can it be?"

He made a few ineffectual twists before Anne smiled and reached around to relieve him of the task. Their hands met and brushed together, but he did not move away; he caught her wrist instead and held it a moment before raising it and pressing it against his lips.

"I lied to you earlier when I said that your being with another man was not my first thought. Reinforced by two bottles of claret, I thought I had arrived at a fairly obvious conclusion. Nor was the beast soothed overmuch when you said you had gone to Dunmaglass."

"John MacGillivray and I have known each other all our lives."

"Yes," he said, tracing his fingers along the soft skin of her forearm. "And I have envied him that privilege before."

Anne felt the heat of his breath against her wrist, his fingers skimming into the crease of her elbow, and it took her two attempts to form the words "You have?"

"I have envied every man who has known you longer than I have," he confessed.

It was likely the claret speaking, Anne thought, but if that was what it took, she would arrange to have a gallon by his chair every night.

His lips were on her wrist again, and now they were following the tingling path already conquered by his fingertips. The cuff of her sleeve had fallen well below her elbow and when he reached the chenille barrier it was a simple matter just to turn and press his lips into the curve of her neck.

Anne could barely hold her head steady. His mouth was warm, his tongue hot and moist where it swirled up to flirt with her earlobe, then scrolled a provocative path down to the collar of her robe. His hand was gently peeling aside the chenille, causing rivers of new sensations to flow downward, and Anne feared she was so near the brink of an orgasm already, the seduction would end before it had even begun. Moreover, he would know at a glance how aroused she was, for the skin across her breasts had shrunk so tight, the buds of her nipples were like small, ripe berries.

Without removing his mouth from her body he came slowly down on one knee before her. He pushed the robe off her arms and his hands smoothed over her breasts, cupping them in his palms. He wet each nipple with his tongue then watched, fascinated, as the firelight glistened off the blushed tips.

"Jealousy," he murmured, "can be a terrible thing. Almost as terrible as pride."

Anne might have had the wit to think of a response but for the thrill of feeling his lips part wider and slowly take her breast into his mouth. She melted forward, her fingers twisting into his hair, and he obliged by sucking harder, chafing her flesh with his tongue until she started making small smothered sounds in her throat.

But when she would have slipped off the edge of the chair and joined him eagerly on the hearthrug, he stopped her. His lips released her flesh with a soft, wet suckling sound and his hands went down to her thighs, coaxing them apart. A disbelieving heartbeat later, he was pushing that same warm and teasing mouth into the V of feathery copper curls, and Anne had to grip the edges of the chair to keep from lurching right off.

Her warning cry brought his hands around her hips to brace her through the first ungovernable rush of pleasure. His tongue prowled and probed. It thrust deep between the slippery folds and traced swirling patterns on flesh that shivered and tightened with each wave of gratification.

"Stop," she gasped. "You must stop. I cannot bear it."

"You can," he murmured. "And you will, for I have not even begun."

He ignored her moaned protest and his tongue pushed deeper, joined now by the wicked skill of long, tapered fingers—skill that had her clutching at his shoulders, and had her writhing so dangerously close to the edge of the chair that eventually he had no choice but to lift her and set her down on the rug beneath him. Once there, with nothing to hamper her pleasure or his, he hooked his arms under her knees and raised them until she was as open and exposed as the harlot she had craved to be only moments ago. This time, when her climax came, she had nowhere to go but up, up, straining into each shattering wave of ecstasy until she was in real danger of fainting.

Angus relented, but he abandoned her only as long as it

took to kick off his boots and peel away his breeches. Anne watched through heavy-lidded eyes as he pulled his shirt up over his head and flung it away in the shadows. She sighed as he removed his smallclothes, for he stood thick and proud before her, his arousal bucking up against his belly. When he saw where her gaze lingered, he lowered himself between her thighs, but stopped just short of touching her. Instead, he brought her hand forward and bade her wrap her fingers around him.

Anne let her hand glide over the hard shaft of flesh. The veins were prominent, the head smooth and sleek with the proof of his own intemperate arousal. She watched the response in the pewter gray eyes as she continued to pull and push, and she knew, when he was about as full and hard as he would ever be, there was no more time for teasing.

He came into her arms again and there was no hesitation, only hunger. She dug her fingers into the hard muscles across his back and welcomed the first powerful thrust with a cry of joy. As big as he was, she stretched eagerly to accommodate him, aware of every heated, surging inch of him. The pleasure shattered her again. And again. She could feel his flesh growing impossibly harder, thrusting into her with the full power and strength of his possession.

He whispered a ragged command and she raised her knees, locking her ankles together at his waist. He reared up, his face taut, the muscles across his chest and shoulders bulging, gleaming with his exertions, and she saw him give an apologetic little shake of his head, as if he could delay the inevitable no longer. He arched his torso and plunged his hips forward one last time, erupting hotly within her. She shared every shudder, every shiver, every liquid throb of his release before the sheer force of their expended energies brought them melting together in utter collapse.

Even then he continued to rock gently inside her, his flesh as unwilling as hers to relinquish even the smallest quiver of pleasure. From somewhere she found the strength to open her eyes; when she did, she saw the mirror image of their bodies twined together in the pattern of shadows on the wall, a sight that was more intoxicating than any ten bottles of fine French claret.

She ran her hands up from where they had been so urgently grasped around his buttocks and smiled faintly at the dampness she could feel on his shoulders and across his back. Angus Moy did not sweat, as a rule, nor did he pant or grin like a cocky adolescent who has just discovered the real reason why ministers spent so much time in the pulpit lecturing against sins of the flesh.

"Forgive me," he murmured, capturing her lips beneath his. "You said you were tired. I did not mean to keep you from your bed."

"A bed would be nice," she agreed. "Eventually."

"Eventually?" He said it as if the word held a wealth of possibilities and Anne parted her lips around another sigh, feeling him stir inside her.

"I'm still there," he whispered. "God knows how, but I am still there."

"Yes," she gasped, curling her hips up to savor the delicious thickening. "And right there is where you will remain, my lord, until neither one of us has the strength to say nay."

Chapter Four

When Anne opened her eyes again, the room was completely dark. There was not even a ruddy glow from the fire with which to orient herself, and it took a moment to realize she was no longer in her own chamber; she was in Angus's big bed with the heavy draperies closed to keep out the drafts. Outside the velvet cocoon, she could hear the wind moaning against the window, rattling the panes of glass with frequent wintry gusts. Inside, there was only the sound of her own breathing and a depression beside her that was still faintly warm, suggesting she had not been alone very long.

Her husband's nocturnal habits had always baffled her. While she could remain in bed as long as the covers were warm and the pillow soft, Angus rarely stayed an entire night abed regardless of how long a day he'd had, or how late an evening. A light, restless sleeper, he would often be up well before the first servant rubbed the crust out of his eyes. Many a time Anne would waken to find him reading or sitting at his desk catching up on his correspondence. He claimed it was a habit he had acquired in his travels through Europe. In order to see and do all there was to see and do, he had learned how to get by on a meager two or three hours of sleep each night.

Anne did not think there was a castle anywhere in the world that would inspire her to rise before dawn and travel twenty miles by horse cart just to glimpse an illusion of battlements floating above a cloud of mist. She was even less likely to cram her feet into shoes with three-inch glass heels just so she could dance the night away in some Russian princeling's court. She preferred the beauty of the glens and ancient keeps right here in Scotland, and there was no greater pleasure on earth than running barefoot through a field fragrant with heather.

With one possible exception, of course.

Her smile was decidedly complacent, as was her whole body. It had been so long . . . too long, since she'd wakened with her nose buried in pillows that smelled of the sandalwood oil Angus used to dress his hair. The scent was distinct and uniquely his, another luxury acquired abroad, for he disliked the chalky feel of powder and rarely tolerated the itch of a wig.

Mewling through a delicious stretch, she savored the feel of soft linen sheets against her naked body. She felt woolly and drugged, as if someone had given her laudanum and the effects were slow to wear away. Her lips were tender, her cheeks lightly chafed by stubble, and when her hand brushed over her breasts, she found they were still responsive enough for the nipples to gather instantly into tight, crinkled peaks. A languorous shifting of her hips brought attention to a welter of other sensations, most notably the throbbing sleekness between her thighs.

A faint sound from the other side of the curtain made her lift her head off the pillow. She listened a moment, then rolled quietly to the edge of the bed and ran her hand along the velvet until she found the break where the curtains joined. Careful to guard against the rustling of the mattress, she leaned over and used the tip of her finger to open a sliver between the panels.

At first she saw nothing for the lack of light. The night lamp glowed in its sconce beside the dressing room, but the wick was turned low, the flame too miserly to give off more than a pinpoint glow and a smudge of smoke. Something in the texture of the shadows drew her gaze to the desk, however, and after a few moments of concentration, she saw Angus seated in the leather chair where he usually scratched out his letters. He was not writing anything now, however; he sat with his elbows propped on his knees, and his head bowed forward, his chin cradled in his hands.

Anne nudged the velvet wider. "Angus?"

When he did not move, or acknowledge her whisper, she moistened her lips and tried again. "Angus . . . are you all right?"

He expelled a long breath. "I'm fine. Go back to sleep."

"Why are you sitting in the dark?"

"It isn't dark," he said, raising his head. "It's just . . . quiet."

Anne drew her legs up and swung them over the side of the bed. She had been carried into the room naked and it was measurably cooler outside the curtains. He was wearing the robe he normally kept beside the bed, and with nothing else at hand, she pulled the top cover off the bed and wrapped it around her shoulders before she emerged.

"I trust that is not your subtle way of telling me I snore, milord?"

His face was just a pale blot against the shadows, so she could not see if her remark won a smile as she approached. The robe was dark blue, the quilted brocade cool to the touch when she ran her hand across his shoulder.

"Anne, honestly I am fine. You should go back to bed before you catch a chill."

"Will you at least let me stoke the fire for you? See, there are still some embers—"

"If *you* want a fire, I will build one for you, otherwise . . . please. I just want some time to *think*."

Anne recoiled slightly from the sudden sharpness in his voice—a voice that only a short while ago had been reduced to low and silky groans against her flesh.

"I'm sorry. I . . . certainly did not mean to intrude." She pulled the blanket higher around her shoulders. "Perhaps you would rather I just returned to my own room?"

He caught her hand before she could turn away. "No. No . . . Anne, I'm the one who is sorry. I . . . I don't want you to go. Not at all. Please. Here, come and sit with me for a minute. My head is pounding like thunder and my belly feels full of lead ballast."

"So much for feeding you a gallon of claret each night," she murmured.

"What?"

"Never mind. 'Twas a silly thought anyway."

Angus pulled her into his lap, and she curled warmly into the curve of his shoulder. "I truly am sorry." He ran a hand down her back to smooth her straggling waves of hair into place. "I did not mean to bark at you."

"And I did not mean to interrupt you. I will go back to bed if you want me to."

He debated the offer for a moment before pressing a kiss into a crush of her hair. "No. I like you right where you are."

Anne sighed and snuggled closer. A few seconds later, the soft edge of regret she had heard in his voice made her tilt her head surreptitiously upward to study his face in the gloom.

With the effects of the claret worn away, was he now embarrassed by their behavior during the night? As much as she imagined lust would be regarded as a decided weakness by a man who always kept such a tight rein over his emotions, he had seemed determined to make up for his lack of attentiveness over the past weeks. Was he now wondering how to face her across a plate of breakfast sausage, knowing where she had had her mouth only hours before?

An uncomfortable flush spread through her body and the lush, rich sense of contentment so recently acquired threatened to vanish between one heartbeat and the next.

"Is it something I have said . . . or . . . or something I have done that is troubling you?"

Angus took a moment to ponder his answer before he shook his head, dismissing the question. "No, it is nothing to do with you. Nothing you need concern yourself with, at any rate."

His tone could not have been more patronizing had he patted her on the head and offered her a sweet.

" 'Twere a fine romp, lass. Ye've done a bonny job distractin' me," she said with gentle mockery, "now off ye go an' peel the tatties. Aye, milord, I'll just do that, I will. An' should I muck out the stables whilst I'm at it?"

He stared at her through the gloom, one dark wing of

brow curling upward. "A distraction? Is that what you think you are?"

"It's not what I want to think, but you leave me little choice when you as much as shout: 'Go back to bed and don't bother me.'"

Angus opened his mouth, then snapped it shut again, the warning implicit if he tried to discount the charge with more platitudes.

"I did not shout."

"You said it yourself: You barked. At any rate, you sounded angry."

"Not with you, Anne. With myself, maybe, but not with you. Well, yes, all right, I will confess I was angry earlier tonight, but that was only because I was worried. I had a lot of time to think about a good many things, including what your presence in my life means to me."

She frowned. "What does it mean? A warm body in your bed when you need one, a hostess at your table, someone to count linens and occasionally scold a servant for not applying enough wax to your tables?"

"*My* tables?"

"If you will recall, I came here with nothing but the clothes on my back, so aye, they are your tables, your chairs, your curtains, your plates, and I have never been encouraged to think of them any other way."

His hand shifted restlessly on her shoulder, and she knew he was remembering the flower arrangement she had made the first week she had come to live at Moy Hall. She had been out for a long walk and collected some sprigs of heather and bluebells—truly a scrawny offering, in hindsight, but at the time, she had thought it pretty enough to put in an odd little china vase she had seen in the drawing room. Within the hour, the flowers were gone and the maids were tittering about the "weeds" the valet, Robert Hardy, had found in the master's valuable antique vase. Angus had never mentioned the incident, but it had taught her a painful lesson in making presumptions.

"I was not aware you still felt like a guest in your own home," he said quietly.

"Sometimes I do, yes. And other times . . ."

He tilted his head forward as she bowed hers down. "Other times?"

"I am quite aware I am an inconvenience," she said softly. "Even an embarrassment."

Angus straightened his head again. "I will grant you that some of the time you can be extremely headstrong and opinionated. You also have a disconcerting habit of saying exactly what is on your mind without pausing to think of the repercussions—and not just within the privacy of these four walls. I will even go so far as to say that you are probably not what every man has in mind when they think of a quiet, sedate country life. On the other hand, if that was what I had wanted—"

"You could have married Margaret MacNeil or her lovely French cousin, Adrienne de Boule. Indeed, I was told they were both sorely distressed when they heard you were obligated to take a sow's ear to wife."

"I cannot imagine anyone comparing you to a sow's ear."

"Then you should listen more carefully to the gossips. Regardless, I doubt the likes of Mlle. de Boule would ever cause you a moment's worry by riding out in the middle of the night with guns in her belt, nor would she disgrace you by using the wrong fork or spoon. She would likely feel at home seated next to Duncan Forbes at a dinner party, and would never dare ask why in God's name you wear the uniform of the Black Watch when it shames nearly every one of your clansmen who see you in it."

The instant the words left her tongue she regretted them, for they struck him like a cold slap in the face. His body stiffened and the hand that had begun to wander beneath the folds of the quilt withdrew as if it were on a spring.

"So. We come back to that again. As always."

"It is not something we can just ignore when the mood does not suit us."

"No, we certainly cannot. And I would say the mood here has been pretty well shattered."

The leather creaked as he shifted forward, inviting her to leave his lap. When she did, he stood and crossed over to the fire, bending down to light a taper, which he then used to bring a pair of candles on the mantel to life. In the bright yellow flare, Anne could see his face was set in harsh lines, his jaw was squared, his mouth compressed into a flat line. His hair was still boyishly disheveled, the dark waves falling forward on his cheeks and brow, but where it should have softened the impact of his anger, it only emphasized the swiftness with which he could turn from considerate lover to dispassionate overlord.

"I suppose I should have asked you earlier, but I thought . . . well, never mind what I thought," he said. "I expect Fearchar called the meeting because he wanted to know if I had any intentions of changing my mind; if I intend to release the lairds of Clan Chattan to join the prince's army if that is what they wish to do?"

"He was hoping it would be what you wished to do."

"Join the ranks of an army in retreat? I may not have the military expertise of the Farquharson clan, but I am inclined to believe this is not the best time to declare one's support."

"Had you declared it earlier," she said evenly, "perhaps they would not be in retreat."

"Do you honestly think a few hundred men would have made a difference?"

"Not alone, no. But if the few hundred MacKintoshes had joined with the MacLeods and the MacDonalds and the dozens of other clans who chose to stay at home and safe-guard their family assets, there would have been thousands and yes, that might have made a difference."

The taper had burned down to his fingers and he tossed the charred scrap into the fire before walking over to the window. He lifted the curtain aside to look out, but it was still black as sin and there was little to see. When he turned back, he shoved his hands into the pockets of his robe and glared at her, his eyes eerily reflecting two hard points of candlelight.

"Perhaps you are right," he said. "Perhaps I should have included you in some of the discussions I have been having with my conscience. Not that I haven't heard all the arguments already, of course."

Anne said nothing; she stood on ice cold feet, her toes curling nervously into the carpet.

"Do you honestly think I want to force good men like Fearchar and Gillies MacBean and John MacGillivray to keep an oath that galls them to the very bone? Do you think I enjoy the sullen stares, or the sound of men spitting at me behind my back? Do you think, for one blessed moment, that a day does not go by without my agonizing over the decisions I have had to make?"

"You did not have to make them on your own," she reminded him.

"Ahh, well, yes, you would think it would be easy just to gather all the lairds of Clan Chattan together and arrive at a consensus of opinion. But I have discovered it is easier to mix oil and water than it is to get two Highlanders to agree on any given point of an argument. Twenty of them in a room together could well result in a hundred opinions, ninety-nine of them ending in bloodshed and swordplay. No." He shook his head sadly. "Part of the joy that comes with the mantle of chief is that such burdens are mine and mine alone to bear. How easy it would be if it weren't." He paused and held up a hand to forestall her interruption.

"Unfortunately, there are more than two thousand families who depend on my leading with my head, not my heart. For each man I order to take up arms in a reckless and ill-conceived plan, there are easily twice as many women and children and babes in arms who would be the first to suffer the consequences for such blind arrogance. You despair for your nephews and nieces having to live in caves now? Imagine a thousand others who could find themselves without a roof over their heads, their homes burned to the ground, their fields scorched, their livestock slaughtered. Imagine their fathers, sons, and husbands arrested and put on transport ships bound for an indentured life in a foreign land."

"The English cannot arrest every man in Scotland," she argued. "And those they did might prefer such a fate to being forced to wear the Hanover colors and fight for a *Sassenach* king they despise."

"You believe they would prefer to fight for a king who has done nothing to even acknowledge the sacrifices they are willing to make in the name of loyalty? James Stuart has been in exile for sixty years. He has grown fat and indolent living off the sympathy of other fat, indolent monarchs who spout words of indignation and outrage even as they mock the very notion of his ever reclaiming the throne. Did he even have enough confidence in his own cause to come to Scotland himself? Good gracious, no. He sent his inexperienced, vainglorious pup of a son instead—a man who had yet to see a battlefield, much less possess the wherewithal to overthrow a country. And not just any country, mind you. *England*, for God's sake. The most powerful military force in the world."

"He defeated them at Prestonpans," she argued valiantly. "His army took Edinburgh and Perth and Stirling, and he has raised the Stuart standard in English towns all the way to Derby."

"Lord George Murray led the army at Prestonpans. If not for him and men like Donald Cameron of Lochiel, I doubt Charles Stuart would have had a thousand men follow him away from Glenfinnan. As for raising his standard in English towns, I warrant they were torn down the instant the dust settled behind his retreat."

Her fingers clenched around the folds of the quilt but Angus held up a hand for her to keep her silence a moment longer.

"But even if . . . *even if* the improbable had happened and the Jacobite army had marched all the way to London, how long do you suppose he could have remained there? The English managed to rally thirty thousand within a week of the prince crossing the border, and they would have had five times that many had a real threat been made against the capital city. They also have the means and resources to feed and clothe and *pay* an army, and to keep them well supplied with guns, cannon, and ammunition. Our men have to beg for food and wrap their feet in scraps of cloth when their shoes wear out. We also rely entirely on outside sources to supply us with guns and ammunition, whereas the English have a fleet of five hundred ships in a navy that could blockade the coastlines so tight the fish would turn away."

"We have strong allies," she countered fiercely.

"Indeed we have. Two of England's most powerful enemies: France and Spain. If ever there was a chance of gaining support or sympathy within the ranks of the English military, it died then and there. After fighting hundred-year wars to keep France on the other side of the Channel and repelling an invincible armada with fishing boats and bonfire beacons, it is not likely they would invite either nation to encamp on their shores now. As for their being such fierce allies—where are they? King Louis promised forty thousand men and shiploads of guns and gold. To date, he has sent two worm-eaten hulks with a cargo of mismatched cannonballs—which, as it happens, are useless without the cannon to fire them."

Anne turned her head. "You have done a fine job of convincing yourself our cause was lost before it even began."

"I am only being realistic, Anne. As soon as the prince set foot on English soil, he was lost. Had he stopped at the border, had he consolidated his victories, reinforced his garrisons, called for recruits to guard our homes and our freedom against another English invasion . . ." His voice fell off suddenly. "Well, we will never know what might have happened, will we?"

"It isn't too late. We could still help to defend our borders."

"Against thirty thousand vindictive Englishmen in a winter campaign? You know full well, when the prince crosses the River Esk back into Scotland, half the men he has will melt away and go home to their farms and families. He'll be lucky to keep the other half intact long enough to reach Edinburgh. Then again, if the reports are true . . ." He returned to his desk and opened the top drawer, hesitating but a moment before he withdrew a sheet of paper. Anne had seen enough official documents to recognize military seals and government stamps, just as she knew the grandiose flourish that identified the signature of John Campbell, fourth earl of Loudoun, commander of the English troops garrisoned in Inverness.

"Cumberland's army is less than two days march behind the prince. If that is the case, he may not even make it as far as the border, and then the subject of whether or not he could defend Scotland against an invasion would be moot."

"Two days!"

"And this report is forty-eight hours old."

Anne's breath stopped again as she looked into her husband's face. "What are you going to do?"

"Truthfully? I am going to pray that whatever happens

happens several hundred miles from here. That it happens quickly and with the fewest possible repercussions for the rest of the country. What is more, as unpleasant and unpopular as it may seem to your grandfather and your cousins, I am going to do everything in my power to protect my home, my family, my clan."

"Even if it means taking up arms and fighting *against* the prince?"

"The men of Clan Chattan will not be fighting anyone," Angus stated flatly. "They will be deployed as guards and sentries only; I made that quite clear to Lord Loudoun at the outset."

"And if it happens they are on duty guarding the glens and bens around Inverness, acting as sentries when they see the prince riding up the road . . . will they lay their muskets aside or will they be ordered to fire upon him?"

Angus bowed his head and exhaled through pursed lips. "I pray each night it will never come to that, just as I have prayed each night both sides would come to their senses and find a way to resolve this thing peacefully."

"This thing," she murmured. "Can you not even bring yourself to put a name to it? It is war, Angus. War. And in war there must be a side that wins and a side that loses. What you have done, what you continue to do by supporting the English, is only helping the wrong side win."

"*Your* wrong side," he said with quiet emphasis. "I am trying very hard not to have one."

"Yes, I can see how hard you try. The dinners at Culloden House, the soirees at Fort George, the government favors and promises of land and estates in exchange for your cooperation. It must be very difficult pretending not to enjoy all the flattery and attention."

"I try to take it in stride," he retorted dryly. "Should I assume, by the charming look of derision on your face when you mentioned Culloden House just now, that you have forgotten the dinner party we are *both* expected to attend there tomorrow night?"

"Dinner party?"

"To celebrate Lady Regina Forbes's eightieth birthday?"

"Oh good God, I had completely forgotten!" Her eyes

widened with disbelief. "Surely you do not expect me to attend! Not to spend an entire evening in the same room as Duncan Forbes and that bilious Earl of Loudoun!"

"Culloden is a large estate, I have no doubt you can find enough walls to act as buffers. And yes, I do expect you to attend. Whatever your feelings may be toward her son, the Dowager Lady Forbes has done nothing to deserve your enmity or your contempt. Even my mother has consented to leave her lair for the occasion, and if the Dragon Lady can manage to keep her tongue between her teeth for the evening, I see no reason why you cannot make a similar effort. That will, of course, include refraining from insulting the other guests or drawing your knives over every imagined slight."

"I have never worn knives to a formal dinner," she snapped.

"Then you have obviously never been looking in a mirror when your temper is roused." He paused a moment, forcing himself to regain control. "Well?"

"Well, what?"

"I plan to leave here around six P.M.; may I anticipate the pleasure of your company in the carriage, Lady MacKintosh?"

Anne turned and walked toward her dressing room. At the doors that led through to her own bedchamber, she stopped and looked back over her shoulder. "I expect you will know the answer to that at six P.M. tomorrow, my lord. As will I."

Chapter Five

*A*ngus was in the library when the clock on the mantel struck six. He was dressed in an elegant long jacket of rich hunting green velvet over a skirted waistcoat made of a paler shade of green silk. The latter was embroidered with bands of clustered ivy leaves, while the front facings of the doublet were stiff with ornate scrolls of gold thread, the cuffs folded back to allow a rich display of ruffles about the wrists. The short breacan kilt was red-and-green tartan; his calves were sheathed in hose of dark red wool with green fretting. His shoes were buckled in silver, and a scabbard of soft kid leather chased in gold was draped from shoulder to hip and held his dress sword. As was his favor, he wore no wig, but his hair had been plied with hot tongs at the temples, the length gathered into a neatly bound tail.

He had not seen Anne all day, had not received any messages to indicate whether she would be accompanying him to the party or preferred him to attend on his own and remain there until hell froze over. Despite his excesses of the previous night, he'd had two large glasses of claret in the past fifteen minutes while he paced and watched the hand on the timepiece crawl inexorably toward the twelve. Normally, she strived to be punctual and was more often than not early. Angus had caught a glimpse of her personal maid, Drena, scurrying down the hallway earlier, but he had deemed it unworthy of him to stop a servant to inquire if his wife was dressed for an evening out, or an evening at home.

He adjusted his sporran for the tenth time in as many minutes and ran a finger between his neck and cravat to ease some of the tightness. His valet, Robert Hardy, had assisted him in dressing, as usual, and while the tall, thin manservant rarely expressed his opinions in words, his mood could generally be gauged by the amount of tension he applied to the neckcloth or the brusqueness in his hand as he brushed specks of lint off the velvet coat.

Tonight he had all but battered Angus's shoulders with the vigor of his brushstrokes, and if the starched linen had been wound any tighter his master's face would have turned blue.

Hardy, a staunch and proper manservant for many years, had initially been affronted to the verge of seeking employment elsewhere when he heard of his master's impending marriage to a red-haired hellion. He had been as disdainful as the rest of the servants, until the day he had found Anne up to her elbows in blood, trying frantically to help one of the scullery maids who had cut herself on a fireplace grating. Not only had quick thinking saved the girl's life, but Anne's knowledge of wounds and stitchery had likely saved the arm. Since most highborn ladies would have been more inclined to scream and faint rather than ruin a silk gown with bloodstains—a servant's blood, no less—Hardy began to view the erstwhile hellion with a grudging measure of respect. He began to communicate, by barely perceptible nods and shakes of the head at first, which forks or spoons were to be used with each course during a long formal meal. Eventually, he laid out an entire, elaborate setting for a formal banquet, explaining each piece and its purpose. This progressed to teaching her how to plan menus, and when he discovered that her education had stopped at a rustic, poorly spelled scrawl, he discreetly arranged for a tutor to visit each day until she was able to copy out full pages of poetry and prose in an elegant script. At her further shy request, he added lessons in elocution, carriage, and deportment. She balked at learning how to embroider or play the pianoforte, but she enjoyed sketching and showed a genuine flair for painting with watercolors.

Hardy, governed by ingrained and unbreakable rules of conduct, had kept Angus apprised of each new accomplishment. The laird, in turn, had discussed other interests she mentioned in passing, so that when the suggestion came from Hardy, she would not feel obligated or guided by her husband's hand in any way.

It was reward enough for Angus just to see the pride shining in her eyes after each new achievement. He had no burning desire to see her transformed into a preened and perfumed chatelaine; on the contrary, he still smiled when he remembered the looks on the faces of several starched visitors when she had come running into the room, flushed and out of breath, her hair scattered around her shoulders, her feet bare and her skirts rucked up to avoid the nipping teeth of the puppy in hot pursuit.

Anne had entered his life like a small storm. The sound of her laughter across the dinner table had left him staring on more occasions than he cared to admit, not because he disapproved of the sound, but because he wondered why it had never been there before. The thought of his mother joking with his father, whether alone or in company, was as foreign to him as the notion that they must have been intimate on at least four occasions through their marriage.

Last night he had gently chided Anne for speaking her mind, but how he envied her the freedom to do so. How he wished he were free to admit how desperately he wanted to be as open and honest with his emotions as she. But the MacKintoshes could trace their lineage back to King Malcolm IV, who reigned in 1153, and there had not been one day in his youth that he had not been reminded of it. Nor had he been allowed to forget that it was the misguided zeal of his grandfather, who had righteously declared for the Jacobites in the ill-fated Fifteen, that had cost the clan dearly in forfeited fines and estates. It had taken nearly two decades and a sworn vow of allegiance to the English king to restore the family titles and position.

Angus had not asked for the burden of becoming clan chief. In fact, there had been some debate among the other lairds that the title should fall to Cluny MacPherson, for they were unsure of a man whose leadership had never been tested, a man who had spent ten years on the Continent attending operas and studying the ancient languages of dead poets.

Angus Moy would be the first to admit he was a scholar, not a fighter. He appreciated fine art, music, literature. He had been taught to fence by a Spanish master, but had never fought a duel, never wielded a broadsword or fired a pistol in anger. To his secret mortification, he had once vomited at the sight of a beggar's hand crushed to bloody pulp beneath the wheels of a wagon.

He had been appalled the first time the lairds of Clan Chattan had gathered to acknowledge his title and confer upon him the traditional oaths of fealty. Many of them had arrived in velvet and lace, but an equal number had stalked into the hall, their faces bearded and sullen, their *clai' mórs* slung across their backs. He was quick to discover that very little had changed in the decade he had been away, which was to say that nothing much had changed in the past six hundred years of feudal law. While the Lowlands had more or less come to accept the progressive realities of English rule, and were even learning how to prosper by exporting wool and coal and raw iron, the Highlanders still clung to the clan system that had always dominated the mountainous regions. Lowlanders embraced the fair practices of the courts and knew that just because they had been born on a farm did not mean they had to die on a farm. In the Highlands, the crofters could not even marry without the permission of the chief, let alone sell a bale of wheat without giving nine tenths of any profit to the overlord.

Angus had needed no one's permission to marry; he could have nullified the agreement between his father and Fearchar Farquharson with a slash of a pen. Yet he had humored the old gray warrior. He had invited him to Moy Hall and listened to his arguments, knowing all the while exactly what he was going to do.

As it happened, Angus had seen Anne Farquharson before he had even set eyes upon the elegant ivy-covered walls of his home. She had been riding across the moor, her waist-long hair whipping out in a fiery red wake behind her. He had first thought she was on a runaway, for the stallion was huge and powerful, his hooves thundering through the waves of deer grass like a rampant charger. But then he had seen two men in hot pursuit—her cousins, he would later learn—and he had seen her halt on the crest of a hill to mock, with a crudely upthrust finger, their paltry efforts at catching her.

The image of her face, as breathtakingly beautiful as the Highlands that rose in untamed splendor around her, had stayed branded on Angus's mind for days afterward, and had kept intruding on his thoughts each time he opened his mouth to argue with Fearchar over the terms of the betrothal. It should not have intruded. It should not have affected the way he thought or acted or even breathed at times—and yet it did.

Even now, after four years of marriage, Wild Rhuad Annie could still leave him stripped breathless. She could render his palms damp and his groin aching with memories of her body sliding hard over his. She could set him pacing in a library, adjusting collars and cuffs, posing in front of a window with an assumed nonchalance every time he heard a footstep out in the hallway.

Angus finished the last warm mouthful of claret and checked the clock again. It was ten minutes past six. The invitation had said seven, though dinner could not be fashionably served until ten. It would take at least an hour to travel the frozen miles to Culloden House by carriage, and while it was the height of bad taste for a guest to arrive on or near the actual stipulated hour, Angus could not reasonably delay his departure much past six-thirty. Seven at the very latest.

He could, of course, not go at all. He had even less desire than Anne to see the smug, pretentious faces of Duncan Forbes and his phalanx of strutting English bloodhounds. But he was trapped as surely as if there were a boot planted solidly at the back of his neck.

He was not aware he had closed his eyes until the faint whisper of silk on wool prompted him to open them. He turned, just his head at first, and by such slow fractions of inches it took several seconds to complete the motion.

More than long enough for the flush to rise in Anne's throat and darken her cheeks.

She was definitely not dressed to remain sitting at home

by the hearth. She shimmered against the darker hallway like the luminous wing of a dragonfly, the bell-shaped expanse of her skirt spreading wide enough to fill the doorway. The bodice of embroidered pale gold silk was cut square, the stomacher molding her waist and descending in a flattering, deep V. Her breasts were pressured upward, rising softly over the upper edge of silk, and although an admiring eye might linger there in appreciation of the creamy half-moons, it was eventually drawn upward to the slender column of her throat, then higher still to the carefully piled extravagance of gleaming red curls.

Angus tried to blindly set his glass on the mantel, missed, and had to take his eyes away from Anne for a moment in order to steady the crystal base on the stone. When he looked back, she had swept inside the room, the slitted panels at the front of her skirt flaring stylishly over the rich layers of petticoat beneath.

"I am sorry I am late. Drena had a deal of trouble with my hair."

"The delay was well worth it," he murmured. "You look lovely."

Compliments, as always, left Anne flustered and she gave her hands a nervous twist in the direction of the side table. "Are we in a dreadful hurry, or might I have a sip of wine before we leave?"

"Of course you may." He glanced past her shoulder to where Hardy hovered just out of earshot. The elderly valet came forward at once, signaling another servant, who was burdened under an armload of capes, to wait off to one side.

After Angus nodded to indicate he would take another, two glasses of wine were poured and set on a silver tray. The first was presented to Anne, who exchanged a furtive glance with Hardy before taking it. His eyes gave away nothing, no hint that he could detect the harsh bite of Highland spirits on her breath, but her hand was visibly unsteady and her mouth dry as tinder.

Throughout the morning and most of the afternoon, she had been determined to send down a message that she was too ill to venture out tonight. She felt hurt and betrayed, resentful and not a little confused by the conflicting actions of her husband and the emotions they had aroused. She had sent for Hardy, then waved him away again, sent for him and dismissed him without delivering any messages to anyone but the Almighty, who had heard her cursing fluently once the doors were closed.

Having hardly slept a wink in the last twenty-four hours, her nerves felt frayed, raw. It normally required enormous preparation in her mind and body before she could tolerate her husband's *associates* with any measure of reasonably civil demeanor. Because she interpreted "reasonable" as meaning not spitting in their faces or calling them cowards and traitors, Angus had not often pressed her into accompanying him to formal affairs held at Culloden House or Fort George. By the same token, it was because he *had* spared her the discomfort of enduring all the political bombast and conceits that she had ultimately decided to join him tonight.

Moreover, it was true what he had said about his mother. If the Dowager Lady MacKintosh could sit through an evening without fisting either Duncan Forbes or Lord Loudoun in the nose, then Anne Farquharson Moy, Lady MacKintosh, could do the same. Conversely, if the Dowager did let swing, as she had one memorable afternoon a month ago in the marketplace, Anne did not want to miss it by being ten miles away in a blue sulk.

Somewhat bolstered by the thought, she took the wine and drank it down in one tilt. It was strong and sweet and she might have asked for another had Hardy not swept past and peremptorily relieved her of the empty glass.

"Well then," Angus said, setting his own untouched dram aside. "If you are ready—?"

She turned and preceded him out into the hallway. A moment later Hardy was assisting her with her cloak, a voluminous wool garment with a fur lining and a hood spacious enough to accommodate the most elaborate hairstyle. While a maid fussed with clasps and gloves and muffs, Angus donned his own outer garment, which, on this formal occasion, was a long, broad length of tartan wrapped around his shoulders and draped over one arm.

The carriage was already waiting at the front entrance of Moy Hall, the door held open by a footman as Anne and Angus emerged from the house. It was a clear, dark sky, the air laden with contrasting smells of ice and woodsmoke, and as she paused to draw a crisp breath into her lungs, Angus slipped his hand under her elbow to guide her across the rug that had been thrown down to protect their shoes. Small swirls of wind-driven snow danced along the ground beside them, sliding under Anne's skirts and twirling up her legs. She did not object as Angus sat beside her and covered them both with a lap robe of unsheared sheepskin, but neither did she invite any inane conversations as she settled into the corner and kept her face turned to the window, the flare of the hood preventing any unnecessary or unwanted eye contact.

Culloden House was situated in the midst of a beautifully landscaped park. It had a commanding view of the Moray Firth to the north and the impressive battlements of the Grampian mountain range to the south. The house itself stood three stories tall and boasted eighteen bedrooms, all with marble fireplaces, fountainous crystal chandeliers, and brocaded silk wall coverings. One of the grander country estates in the area, it had once belonged the MacKintoshes, but had been sold in the early part of the previous century to pay off bad debts.

The stone pillars that sat on either side of the gates, as well as the wide circular drive, were dotted with torches and lamps. Every window in the house was ablaze with light, so many that a glow had been visible in the sky long before the carriage carrying Anne and Angus had rolled over the last hill.

Anne's mood had not improved much through the miles of silent travel. Her expression was plainly glum and her fingers had worried a seam of her gloves into a tangle of loose threads. Once or twice she had stolen a peek at Angus, but the interior light was muted by a shade of pressed horn and she had not been able to see much more than his profile. She knew he was tense, however, by the way the muscle in his jaw flexed. She suspected he was holding entire conversations inside his head, anticipating ways he might ward off potentially inflammatory subjects with his Jacobite mother and wife together in a room full of the Elector's representatives.

He was well aware he was playing with fire bringing her here tonight and it puzzled her somewhat that he would even do it, much less be so adamant about her attending—especially when word of the prince's retreat would likely be a heated topic of every conversation. In spite of his insistence that her absence would be misconstrued as an insult to the Dowager Lady Forbes, there would be few who would regard her presence as anything other than an affront.

Unfortunately, it was too late to balk now. They were through the gates and in the drive, pulling to a halt near the sweeping front staircase. When Angus helped her out of the coach, he held her hand a moment longer than necessary.

"What is it? Is something wrong?"

The hood of her cloak had slipped back, revealing her cloud of red curls. The blue of her eyes seemed to glow brightly in the torchlight, and her cheeks, kissed pink by the cool air, were fairly luminous against the darkness behind them.

"No," he murmured. "Nothing is wrong. I . . . I just wanted to say again how lovely you look tonight."

Anne's breath stopped as she returned the favor by looking into her husband's face. He was heartbreakingly handsome in daylight, doubly so by candlelight, as regal and aristocratic as one would imagine royalty should be. His gray eyes were deep set and surrounded by long, dark lashes. His nose was fine and straight, his mouth so near sensual perfection she doubted that any woman could stop herself from staring at him. Last night, that mouth had been everywhere on her body, bringing her incredible pleasure. Tonight what would it bring?

"Shall we?"

Anne's cloak was removed inside the foyer. The day rooms, parlors, and family dining hall were on the ground floor, all lit by multitiered chandeliers, with the south-facing rooms giving access to the rear terraces and manicured gardens. The second story boasted an arched hallway with eighteen-foot ceilings supported by solid oak columns; it housed the grand ballroom, which, for the next few hours, would be converted into a banquet hall. Following the meal, the tables would be cleared away and dancing would commence, the musicians playing tirelessly through until dawn.

The upper floor with its multitude of bedrooms was reserved for important guests or those who had traveled too far to consider returning home the same night. In happier times, ten miles would have been deemed much too great a distance after a long evening, but Anne doubted the invitation to remain over had been extended once the reply acknowledging her attendance was received.

Duncan Forbes and his wife, Mary, stood at the top of the stairs, greeting their guests. Beside them was their only son, John, and his vapid bride of less than a year. Neither father nor son was striking enough to have drawn attention in a crowded room. Both had sallow complexions that were not flattered by the heavily powdered periwigs curled as tight and precise as their personalities. They had long, sharp noses and protruding brown eyes, mouths that were thin and stern, chins whose characters could have benefitted from beards.

Another relative, the Reverend Robert Forbes, stood alongside a nephew, Douglas. The latter was modestly more invigorated in appearance than the rest of his family, for he possessed a youthful, almost handsome face. If the reputation he was developing with the ladies was accurate among the gossips, he was also a throwback to his grandfather, the late and greatly lamented "Bumper John" Forbes, who had begun the tradition that was still in evidence—that of opening a large anker of whisky and setting it alongside the host and hostess, the contents to be ladled generously into cups to welcome each guest.

It was Bumper John's widow who was celebrating her eightieth birthday, not a moment too soon. A tiny, wrinkled gnome with the familial brown eyes bulging from beneath a ridiculously oversized wig, Lady Regina Forbes perched on a thronelike chaise between her son and grandson. In one hand, she clutched an ear trumpet that she was barely able to lift; on the other, she wore so many rings it drooped like a deadweight over the arm of the chair.

While Anne waited with her husband to be officially

welcomed to the celebrations, her gaze strayed along the crowded hallway. Splashes of red from bright scarlet uniform jackets were predominant among the male guests, their various companies denoted by facings of blue and yellow, buff, and green. Women wore every shade of silk imaginable, their throats glittering with jewels, their laughter tinkling in the air like crystal prisms. Fully three quarters of the visitors were military officers, and at least half that number wore the kilt identifying them as belonging to a Highland regiment. Anne readily recognized members of the MacLeod and Campbell clans, The MacKenzie of Seaforth, The Munro of Culcairn— a thoroughly disagreeable fellow who had lost an eye in the Fifteen and wore the hideous scarring like a badge. One by one she saw them turn and stare as she and Angus mounted the final step to the second floor, their conversations fading to an obviously tense hush.

Had it been just Angus arriving at the party, she suspected they would have met him with gregarious shouts and much shoulder-clapping. In her eyes, however, they were all traitors trying desperately to justify their treachery, and if Angus's jibe about unsheathing visual knives was to be believed, she would have liked to meet each cold stare in turn and hold it until they bled away into lifeless heaps.

Sensing as much, Angus hastened her forward, presenting her first to the Reverend Robert Forbes. He was an innocuously pompous man given to making sermons out of common sentences, and he did not disappoint now. He offered the usual droll observations on the weather, then bemoaned the fact that his parish was so far away in Leith as to make more frequent visits to Inverness an impossibility. His wife, too dull to realize she was expected to offer nothing more than a stiff nod to Anne Farquharson Moy, exhausted her repertoire of compliments. By the time she had praised Anne's gown, and said how lovely it was to see her again, the silence behind them was almost deafening.

Angus was received with the utmost cordiality by both Duncan Forbes and his son, who greeted him with the traditional *cend mile failte*—a hundred thousand welcomes—and a glass of ladled whisky. But when he, in turn, bent over to shout birthday wishes in the dowager's trumpet, both men deliberately tipped their chins a notch higher so they could look down along their noses at Anne. Their wives were less subtle. They allowed their gazes to travel slowly from Anne's unpowdered hair to her shoulders to her waist to the hem of her skirts, leaving her with the distinct impression she had not bathed in hot enough water. Their delicate little nostrils flared and their pinched little lips formed puckers that suggested no amount of silks or perfumes could disguise the odor of countless stable floors and sweaty sex that clung to her.

"Be that de'il o' a gran'faither o' yourn still alive?"

Startled, Anne felt the dowager's bony hand clamp around her wrist. Somewhere in the back of her mind she recalled hearing whispers of a torrid affair years ago between Fearchar and Lady Forbes, and she guessed by the sudden twinkle in the rheumy eyes that the older woman was remembering it too.

"Yes. He is still very much alive."

"Eh? What's that ye say?"

Instead of bending to speak into the ear trumpet, Anne merely raised her voice. "I said yes, my lady. My grandfather Fearchar Farquharson of Invercauld is very much alive and healthy. I am sure he will be pleased to hear you asked about him."

The dowager cackled. "Fleas, has he? Aye, well, he alus were a hairy mon, but a guid scrub wi' lye soap will burn the wee bastards out o' their roosts. Mind, I wouldna kick him oot ma bed just f'ae the sake o' a few hornie-gollachs. Alus gave a lass a right guid tickle, he did. A pintle ye could ride the whole blesset night long an' still have some left f'ae the morn. Eh?" She batted the side of her wig to straighten it and glared at her son for dislodging it in his haste to whisper in her ear. "What are ye on aboot now? Flush what? Speak up, mon, I canna hear ye over all this blather."

The fact there had been no blather whatsoever to conceal the exchange darkened the Lord President's complexion and caused him to signal a quartet of footmen standing nearby. They lifted the chaise and carried the dowager into an adjoining room, with the current Lady Forbes and her pallid daughter-in-law scurrying after them.

"You must excuse my mother," said Duncan Forbes once the confusion had cleared. "Not only does her memory wander, but it seems she grows less concerned each day with what she says and to whom she says it."

"If I live to be eighty, I would like to think I could claim the same privilege," Angus said, smiling.

The two men exchanged curt bows and Angus led Anne away, noting as he did that her glass of whisky was already half empty. Most of the conversations resumed upon a telling look from Duncan Forbes, but like the blade of a plow cutting a new furrow, there was a clear path of silence where Lord and Lady MacKintosh walked.

"I do not suppose this would constitute a duty served," she murmured.

"You are doing just fine, my dear," Angus said, his voice equally low. "And no, it would not."

"MacKintosh!" The booming voice of John Campbell, earl of Loudoun, parted the cluster of guests. He was a big man, not overly tall but wide enough around the girth and across the shoulders to test the skill of a tailor. His cheeks wore a constant blush from the cobweb of fine red veins, and he had what was most likely the largest nose in all of Scotland, thick and bulbous at the end, pitted like a sea sponge. "Pleased to see you here tonight, Captain. And your lovely wife, of course. Lady Anne. A pleasure."

He came forward with a flock of scarlet-clad officers in his wake, most of whom looked rigid enough to crack if they bent over.

"You know my wife, of course?"

The two women traded forced smiles. Of all the men present this evening, Anne harbored the least tolerance for Lord Loudoun. As commander of the government troops in Scotland, he had been the first to approach Angus with the "offer" not to arrest him, not to have his lands and titles attained, not to billet troops at Moy Hall or confiscate his possessions, rents, and livestock, in exchange for forming up a regiment of MacKintosh men to wear the white horse of Hanover on their caps. Together with Duncan Forbes, he had made every laird of any importance similar offers, and those who had stubbornly refused were either locked away in the Tolbooth or hiding in caves.

When the earl bowed politely over Anne's hand, his eyes went no lower than the brimming edge of her bodice. "It has been an inordinately long time since we have had the pleasure of your company, Lady Anne. Angus, I know you have already met my new adjutants, but permit me the honor of presenting them to your wife: Lady Anne MacKintosh, Major Roger Worsham and Captain Fergus Blite, both arrived within the past fortnight from London."

Anne was happy not to have to stare into Loudoun's face a moment longer than necessary, but neither of the two new officers was any blistering prize as an alternative. Captain Blite was spectacularly ugly, his face marred by a milky white coating over one eye. The major was a slight improvement in that his features were almost pristinely handsome, but his back was stiff, his knee bent slightly forward to show the tightness and fit of his breeches to best advantage, and the sly smile he wore clearly indicated he had already heard a great deal about the red-haired Jacobite mistress of Moy Hall.

Standing by his side, a slender white hand hooked possessively through his elbow, was yet another reason to bring Anne's jaws grinding together.

Adrienne de Boule was petite and fine-boned, her hair dark as coal under the severe dusting of rice powder. She was French, and spoke in a delicate accented whisper calculated, no doubt, to require men to always lean forward to hear what she was saying. Her skin did not need mercury washes to bleach it white; her eyes were large and dark and expressive, with a thick fringe of black lashes that could be batted to good effect.

They were stirring up a veritable breeze at the moment as her gaze fastened on Angus, and when he bowed over her hand, she took a deep enough breath to seriously deplete the supply of air in the room and to make her breasts—which were prominent enough without assistance—come perilously close to popping over the top of her bodice.

"Lady MacKintosh." Worsham was still smiling, oblivious to the fact that his companion was on the verge of lifting her skirts if Angus gave the smallest indication of interest. "It is both an honor and a privilege to finally make your acquaintance. I apologize for being somewhat lax in bringing myself out to Moy Hall before now, but can assure you the oversight will be corrected forthwith."

Anne dragged her attention away from Mademoiselle de Boule and responded to the major's pledge with a brittle smile. "There is no need to trouble yourself, Major. I am rarely at home these days myself."

"You have business that takes you away at all hours?"

"No. But I am rarely at home to uninvited visitors."

The major arched an eyebrow. His eyes were so pale a blue as to be almost colorless, but they darkened now as the centers flared with intrigue.

Loudoun, meanwhile, cleared his throat with a gruff *harrumph*. "You heard about the trouble last night, I trust?"

Angus was slow to pull his gaze away from Worsham. "Trouble?"

"Mmm. A skirmish on the Inverness road last night between Major Worsham's patrol and some rebels."

"Three of my men dead," Worsham offered. "Several more injured. The leader of the rebels was hit and went down, but his men carried the body away before we could ascertain an identity."

"I had not heard about it," Angus said with a frown.

"No? I had men following the tracks, but they lost them in the snow. Near Loch Moy, as it happens."

"A good choice," Angus acknowledged. "The woods are thick and the ground rocky enough in places to conceal the tracks of an army."

"I will have to remember that," Worsham said, and the pale eyes flicked back to Anne again. "I trust you would report it upon the instant were you to see anything untoward in the vicinity? Any . . . wounded men, for instance. Or a large party of armed rebels."

"Oh, upon the instant," Anne agreed.

Worsham smiled again and Anne felt a chill run up her spine.

"You know," he said, "I have the most extraordinary feeling we have met before."

"I am sure we have not, Major."

"You were not out riding across the moors late last night by any chance, were you?"

The boldness of the question took Anne by surprise, as it was undoubtedly intended to do, and it was Angus who answered with a wry laugh. "Last night? Last night my dear wife was giving me a sharp piece of her tongue for having had too much to drink through the afternoon and squandering the venison roast she had ordered up for our evening meal."

Worsham's pale eyes glittered. "And yet my instincts, especially where a beautiful woman is concerned, are rarely mistaken. Perhaps you have been to London, my lady? To the theater or opera?"

"No, sir," Anne said carefully. "I have never been to London, nor have I had the smallest desire to visit, for I have been told it is a dark, dreary place. They say that it always rains, and the smell of offal is so thick in the streets that it clings to all who hail from there."

It took a moment for the veil to come off the insult, but when it did, the major's throat turned a mottled shade of scarlet. As stiff as his back was already, he managed to square his shoulders into blocks, and if not for the sudden skirling of a chanter from the far end of the hall, the tightly pressed lips might actually have pulled back into a snarl.

As it was, Anne felt Angus's hand grasp her arm and steer her over to one of the oak columns, ostensibly to clear the way for the pipers to call the guests into the banquet room. Over the strains of the Forbes's *piob rach'd,* Angus leaned down to whisper in her ear, "Just for your own information, Major Worsham is rumored to be one of the Duke of Cumberland's favored protégés. He sharpened his teeth serving under General Henry Hawley and has

spent the last six months in Flanders slitting throats by moonlight."

"He's a bloody *Sassenach*," Anne whispered back. "And
he does not frighten me."

"Well, he should. I strongly doubt the last *man* who told
him he smelled like shit is able to smell anything at all."

Chapter Six

*A*nne's esteemed mother-in-law laughed with the gusto of a man. "Ye told him he smelled like what?"

Nearing seventy, Lady Drummuir had the robust girth and forthright manner of a woman who had lived too long and seen too much strife to worry about petty gossips and social-conscious peers—several of whom snapped open their fans at the sound of her gaiety.

"Like shite?" She wiped her eyes, the laughter jiggling the prodigious expanse of her bosoms. "That'll be the second time in the spate of a week, then, he's been told he needs to bathe wi' more care, damned *Sassenach*."

The dinner had progressed smoothly enough. The avid appetites of more than sixty guests had been tempted with courses that included collops of beef, smoked salmon, saddles of venison, and huge bowls of poached sea scallops swimming in butter. Most of the focus, therefore, had been on the extravagant quantities of good food and wine—both of which had been in short supply in recent months. To be sure, there were the occasional bursts of laughter and rousing cheers from the sea of redcoats surrounding Lord Loudoun as they offered periodic huzzahs to celebrate the retreat of the Jacobite army. Angus, because of his rank and privilege, was situated somewhere in their midst, but Anne and Lady Drummuir had chosen of their own accord to sit much farther along the table, where the company consisted mostly of older crones and homely spinsters.

And a few surprises.

Anne was already in her seat when she glanced along the table and saw a familiar mane of tarnished blond hair. Granted, it was combed smooth and bound at the nape, but there was no mistaking the massive shoulders and dark brooding eyes of John Alexander MacGillivray.

Anne would be the last one to express surprise at seeing a known Jacobite sympathizer seated at the Lord President's banquet table. Apart from the fact he was a wealthy and powerful laird in his own right, it was most likely MacGillivray's black-market burgundy that the guests were drinking, for his clansmen were as renowned for their smuggling ventures as they were for their warlike independence. He would have been invited, as Anne had, out of a sense of courtesy, and like Anne, he had probably come out of respect for the Dowager Lady Forbes.

She managed to pass him a fleeting smile before being drawn back into the conversation with Lady Drummuir.

"He had the nerve to bring a troop of men to my house an' search the cellars," she declared with an impressively indignant flaring of nostrils. "He claimed he'd heard a rumor the Jacobites were hoardin' a supply of lead shot in my wine tuns. I told him no' to be such a daft bastard; the tuns were used to store the powder, the prince had all the balls."

Douglas Forbes, the Lord President's nephew, actually chewed twice on his mouthful of black pudding before he caught the pun, at which time he nearly choked. Etiquette and civility had dictated that a member of the immediate family must be seated near the ladies MacKintosh, and he had actually volunteered for the privilege. He was between Anne and Lady Drummuir, and through the course of the meal there had been several occasions when he required a sharp clap between the shoulders from one or the other.

It was the dowager's turn this time and she obliged with a hearty cuff that nearly sent him across the table. "There now, laddie, take a wee sip of wine. Yer torment is almost over. See there? The ladies are heavin' off their fine fannies to go take a winkle, an' the men are takin' their brandy an' cigars in the drawing room so the lads can clear away the tables."

"I assure you it has not been a torment, Lady Drummuir," he said with a grin. "Far from it." He noticed Anne moving, and stood quickly to hold her chair as she rose. When she thanked him for the courtesy, he flushed and stammered out an emboldened invitation. "If you would not regard it as being too presumptuous, Lady Anne, I would be spectacularly honored if you would grant me the pleasure of a dance later this evening. If your time is not already spoken for, that is. And of course, if you would care to dance. With me, I mean."

Anne took a moment to admire the throbbing shade of red his ears achieved.

"Spectacularly honored? I do not believe anyone has attributed such merits to a mere dance. In this case, although I thank you for asking, Mr. Forbes, I suspect your uncle would prefer if you did not."

"So long as the preference is not yours, Lady Anne, my uncle can go shoot himself in the foot."

She laughed and tipped her head. "You offer too much temptation, sir. The honor would be mine, and I should like very much to dance with you."

The lad was so thrilled he started to escort her out into the hallway, but The MacGillivray was suddenly beside them, the glint in his eye advising Douglas Forbes to melt onto the floor with the other gnats instead.

"I need a word with ye," he murmured, barely moving his lips as he walked Anne to the end of the dining hall. "Slip down the stairs an' meet me in the library soon as ye're able."

He did not wait for her answer, nor could she think of one on the instant, startled as she was by the request. At the door, she watched him bow and stride off down the hall, gallantly excusing his way through several dozen chattering females.

"A prime piece of lusty manhood is that MacGillivray," Lady Drummuir mused, slipping her arm through Anne's as they followed at a more sedate pace. "If I were forty years younger, I'd no' have to rely on gossips to tell me what was under that kilt of his. Aye, a hundred pairs of thighs will weep when they hear the news he's finally decided to wed."

"He has?"

"Ye've no' heard? He's thinkin' of asking after Elizabeth Campbell of Clunas—or so the faeries tell me."

The dowager's faeries comprised a network of spies as extensive as anything the British military had in the field. If they said John MacGillivray was taking a bride, it was just a matter of picking out a frock to wear to the church, and Anne wondered if that was what he wanted to speak to her about. If so, she was happy for him. Truly, she was. John was a fine man, loyal and honorable, with none of the airs or arrogance borne by many who turned heads wherever they walked.

Try as she might, however, she could not call forth a clear image of Elizabeth of Clunas. Nothing came to mind beyond plain brown hair and a great many freckles.

"I said—" The dowager's voice cut sharply into Anne's reflections. "Odd he did not mention it to you."

"Why should he?" Anne said.

"No reason. No reason at all, though I would have thought he might have said something last night when ye visited Dunmaglass."

Anne just turned and stared.

"Och, lass, ye'd be surprised the things I know. For instance, I ken what your gran' wanted to speak to ye about, too, an' ye were wise to turn him down. No good could ever come of splitting the clan. Too many are split already, an' wounds like that will never heal. Never."

"Does it not tear at your heart," Anne whispered back, "to see our clansmen wearing the uniform of the Black Watch? To see Angus in uniform leading them?"

"Child, ma poor heart has been torn so many times over the years, it should have lost the ability to beat long ago. God knows it is in shreds over some of the choices Angus has made, but he's my son an' I love him. Though I may rail an' rant an' stomp about like a blathering fool, an' have no doubt one day Duncan Forbes will have me dragged off to prison in the hopes the rats will bite off ma tongue, I'll not put a knife in Angus's back. I ken he is only doing what he thinks is best for the clan."

"Whether the lairds agree or not?"

"Neither you nor I will live long enough to see the day all the lairds of Clan Chattan agree on a single point. Ye must have noticed: He's called only on those who have no qualms wearin' the black cockade."

It was true enough, Anne thought. Angus had been careful selecting the men to fill Loudoun's requirements; he had known better than to order men like The MacGillivray or The MacBean to take up arms for the Elector's army. They likely would have shot him out of hand and tossed his body down a well, never to be seen again.

"Angus has promised me . . . he gave me his word our men will not be involved in any fighting," Anne said with quiet intensity. "He insists they are to be engaged as guards and sentries only."

"That would be bonnie," Lady Drummuir agreed. "Though I dinna see how he can keep to such a promise. Not when Forbes and Horse-Nose Loudoun will make a point of placing the Highland regiments in prominent positions."

"He will keep it," Anne insisted. "He has never lied to me or broken his word, despite all that has happened, and I do not believe he will do so now."

"Aye, well then, we'll both keep the faith, shall we? He's a good lad when he's no' being so bloody pigheaded. Naturally, if ye tell him I said as much, I'll deny it, for it does no harm to keep yer sons a wee bit afraid of ye." The dowager's gaze strayed to where Lady Regina Forbes and her chair were being carried into an adjacent room. "Poor soul. Not only is she frail as a leaf, but have ye ever seen skin that color on aught but a corpse? I suppose I must go an' pay ma respects, though if that slack-witted daughter-in-law of hers says the smallest word to me, I'll be windin' up ma fist again."

Anne kept company with one of the spinsters for a few moments, then excused herself to casually follow some of the other guests as they drifted downstairs. She would have done so even if The MacGillivray had not requested a moment alone. The interminable hours spent at the dinner table had been a strain on her nerves and the thought of the upcoming dancing was more than enough to make her want to seek out a quiet, shadowy corner somewhere to wait for Angus to say they could leave. He had caught her eye several times during the various courses, his expression anxious each time, as if he were wondering who he could approach to act as his second should either his wife or his mother offer an insult that could not be retracted. He had not followed her out of the dining room, and the last glimpse she'd had, he was standing in a corner conversing with Duncan Forbes.

When she was fairly certain no one was paying her any notice, Anne made her way down the stairs and along the huge vaulted hallway to a rear corridor leading off to the left.

When she rounded the corner, she stopped and looked back again, feeling more like a thief than a guest, for while it was one thing to caper about the countryside in the dead of night, it was quite another to be caught skulking around in the Lord President's library.

The tall double doors were standing slightly ajar when she approached. The hallway was well lit and there were no guards cordoning off any areas of the house, yet she still felt like an interloper and walked with her skirts raised to lessen the sound of her petticoats brushing over the floor. She peered between the opened doors but could see very little of the interior. The room was barely lit, and she suspected that if MacGillivray was already inside, he had perhaps extinguished some of the candles and lamps to make it less hospitable to any guests who might be ambling by.

She drew a deep breath and casually pushed the doors wider. Staying within the bounds of the light that came from the hallway, she walked almost to the center of the room before halting again.

"Hello?" she called softly. "Is anyone here?"

It was a large, scholarly room, darkened by wood paneling, muted further by rows of crowded bookshelves that rose twenty feet to the ceiling. Two shell-shaped alcoves were framed in crimson draperies that hung above the arch and fell in deep swags on either side, tied back with thick ropes to match the braided gold fringing. One of the alcoves contained an upholstered chair for reading in the natural light; the other housed French doors that opened out to the terrace. A huge cherrywood desk occupied the space between the two windowed bays, set beneath a large tapestry depicting a medieval battlefield with archers and knights in heavy armor.

The air was musky, redolent of leather and paper, as silent as an ancient scriptorium, and Anne made one full, slow revolution, awed by the sheer number of books, curious as to who might actually have read them all. She found her answer in the gilt-framed portraits that were hung between the sections of shelves; they were men with the stern faces and long chins of academics, nary a soldier or warrior in the lot.

"As grim an' dull as they come," MacGillivray agreed, stepping out of one of the alcoves. "Nae wonder Forbes is such a heroic fellow. That one"—he hooked his thumb derisively in the direction of one pinch-lipped ancestor— "looks as though he just took a mouthful o' sheep dung but disnae have the guts to spit it out."

"This is very dangerous," Anne said. "If someone should walk by and see us here we would have the devil of a time explaining ourselves."

"Two old friends, taking a breath o' fresh air. Where's the harm?"

Aside from the obvious trespass, she thought, the harm was in the lack of light, the heavy shadows, and the crooked, challenging smile on his face. It was in the not-so-casual gleam in the unfathomable black eyes, and in the memories of a hot afternoon behind a booth at the fairground.

"Come," he said, indicating the French doors. "We can talk out on the terrace."

It was cooler outside, but because the bulk of the house gave them shelter against the wind it was a fresh change from the candle smoke and cloying perfumes.

She walked to the far end of the promenade and stood a moment looking out over the crystalline stillness of the gardens before she turned and met the dark eyes.

"I hope you've not brought me out here to talk about

Fearchar's proposal from last night. Since you were relieved to hear me turn him down, I cannot imagine what else there is to be said."

"I was relieved, aye. But no' for the reasons ye may have thought."

"You would have signed a petition supporting me as clan chief?"

"Are ye sayin' ye dinna think ye would make an able leader?"

"I would make as good a leader as any man, and a better one than most," she said evenly. "I simply did not think you, of all people, would approve a woman in that position."

"Well, if ye're pressin' for a confession, I can think of better positions for a lass, aye," MacGillivray murmured through an enigmatic smile. "But I've seen ye prick the rumps o' yer cousins with a sword, an' I've watched ye bring down a stag with a single shot. I've seen ye lead the three o' them into a mêlée against twice yer number, an' I've heard the crowds cheerin' for 'wild rhuad Annie' when ye came away bruised, but not too bloodied to keep ye from throwin' yerself back into the fray. Mind, that was before ye traded yer powder horn an' firelock for fancy silk skirts an' fine lace ruffles. An' before ye started talkin' like a lady and sippin' yer soup from a spoon, instead o' the side o' the bowl."

"I could say the same for you," she countered, launching an eyebrow upward as she inspected him boldly up and down. His enormous shoulders were clad in the full formal dress of a gentleman, with doublet, waistcoat, and ruffled sleeves complementing the red-and-blue plaid of his kilt. "Clean shaven, your hair curled and tucked into a ribbon while you sup at the Lord President's table. Your buckles are polished and"—she leaned forward, sniffing the air delicately—"is that French water I smell? With your fiancée not even here to enjoy it?"

His eyes narrowed. "Who told ye I had a fiancée?"

"Lady Drummuir, if it matters . . . which it should not."

"No," he mused. "It should not. No more so than the cause o' the burn on yer cheeks that was not there yesterday." He reached up through the darkness and ran the tip of his finger along her chin and throat. "Ye should tell yer husband to use a sharper blade when he shaves. 'Tis a shame to chafe such fine, smooth skin."

Anne backed away, her heart giving one loud slam against her rib cage. "I hardly think Angus's shaving habits are a matter we should be discussing."

"Nor are ma intentions toward Elizabeth of Clunas."

She started to say, "I fail to see—" but snapped her mouth shut again and hugged her upper arms against a sudden chill. "You said you had to speak to me about something. We will be missed in a few minutes."

"You, mayhap. I've already made ma excuses."

"You're leaving already? But—?"

"Savin' a dance for me, were ye? Sorry to disappoint, but I've paid ma respects an' not a drop o' blood shed but ma own." He reached inside the front of his coat and, for a split second, his face was turned to the light, revealing a new twist to his smile—that of pain.

When he withdrew his hand again, the fingers were wet and shiny, slick with blood.

"My God! What happened to you?"

"It's naught but a wee hole," he said, waving away her concern. "The shot went in an' out clean enough."

"*Shot?* You were *shot!*"

"A wee bit louder, lass." He scowled and looked up at the second-story windows. "I dinna think they all heard."

"Shot," she hissed. "What do you mean you were shot? When? Where? And what the devil are you doing here playing the gentleman fool?"

"Aye, playin' is the word for it. For if I'd not come tonight, actin' as if nothin' was amiss, I'd likely be swingin' from a gibbet by morn's mornin'."

Anne shook her head even as she reached down and struggled to tear a strip of linen from the bottom layer of petticoat. "I don't understand."

"After ye left last night, one o' the lads said as how he thought he heard horses in the woods. We went out after them, an' sure enough, found where a troop o' bloody redcoats had been hiding in the trees near the edge o' the glen. They were easy enough to follow in the snow, but—"

She looked up sharply. "It was *you*. You were the 'rene-
gades' the major mentioned earlier."

MacGillivray only shrugged. "He's no' as stupid as most
Sassenachs. He left men to watch their backs while they rode
away. One o' them saw us an' gave off a warning shot. Before
we knew it, the soldiers came in at the gallop an' we were in
the middle of a fight."

She straightened and folded the linen into a thick wad.
Batting away his hand with his objection, she eased his jacket
open, fitting the makeshift bandage snugly beneath his waistcoat. His shirt was already dark with blood; some of it had
started to seep through the brocade vest.

"You have to leave and get this tended to before you bleed
to death."

"Aye, I will do. But I thought I should warn ye first."

"Warn me? About what?"

"There were another set o' tracks leavin' the glen. Two
men. They followed you an' yer cousin Eneas most o' the way
to Moy Hall."

"*Most* of the way?" she parroted.

"Ma lads lost all the tracks after ye crossed Moy Burn.
Did Eneas keep to the water for a bit?"

She nodded. "I thought he was being overly cautious,
but—"

"There will be no such thing as over-cautious from here
on out, lass, not unless the thought of a gibbet appeals to ye."

"It does not." Anne shivered and glanced back at the
house. "He asked me if I had been out riding on the moor last
night."

"Who did, the fancy major with the ghostie eyes?"

She nodded. "Angus laughed it off. He said I was with
him all night. Whether or not the major believed him—" She
shrugged. "There are not too many places our tracks could
have been going, other than Moy Hall."

"Aye, but his men dinna know who they were followin',
do they?" he asked quietly. "Ye were not exactly wearing yer
silks an' laces."

"Yes, but . . ."

"But nocht. If they truly suspected it were you, ye'd have

irons clapped around yer wrists by now. An' if ye say Angus covered for ye..." He paused, as if her husband's actions surprised him as much as they had her. "Was he no' in Inverness last night?"

"He came home early. He was waiting for me, in fact, when I returned. Needless to say, he was not happy to discover I had been out."

"He didna raise a hand to ye, did he?"

Anne looked up, startled to hear a sudden change in John's voice. "No. No, of course not. Angus has never even raised his hand to swat a fly in anger, not in the four years I have known him."

He said nothing, but after a long moment, she heard his teeth chatter through an involuntary shiver.

"You have to leave here at once," she said. "Come, I'll see you safely to the door."

"Now that truly would be a foolish idea. Stay here. Count to fifty or so before ye go back inside, an' have a care no one sees ye leave the library. Go back up the stairs an' find Angus. Stay fast by his side an' he'll see ye through the rest o' the night until ye're home safe."

"What about you? Will you be all right?"

He looked down to where her hand rested on his forearm. "It would take more than a pea-sized ball o' English lead to bring me down, lass. Ye mind what I said, though, an' stay close by yer husband."

"Be careful."

He held her gaze a moment, then crossed the terrace and vaulted over the low stone balustrade. She heard the crunch of his shoes on the frozen ground for a minute more, then it was lost to the sounds of the party on the floor above.

MacGillivray had been shot, and she had been followed. There had been English troops in the woods at Dunmaglass, and if they had been watching The MacGillivray's home, they must have known Fearchar and her cousins were inside.

But had they followed Fearchar to Dunmaglass, or had they been watching Dunmaglass all along? If it was the former, it would mean her grandfather wasn't as wily an old fox as he fancied himself to be, and he could be arrested at any time.

If it was MacGillivray who had fallen under government scrutiny, it might be because the English were anticipating the very thing that had brought Anne out in the middle of the night: plans to split the great Clan of the Cats into two factions. They would be justifiably alarmed; Inverness was in the heart of MacKintosh territory, and the prospect of a thousand sword-wielding clansmen taking to the hills, men renowned for their ability to stage bloody raids and vanish into the night, would surely cause the latrines within the garrison walls to overflow. Loudoun and Forbes would do anything within their power to prevent such a division, even if it meant arresting the clan chief without proof of any wrongdoing.

The silent progression of logic brought Anne's fingers pressing against her temples, and it took every last scrap of willpower to keep from following MacGillivray over the stone wall.

But of course she could not. John was right: She had to go back upstairs, find Angus, and act as if nothing had happened.

Her head was throbbing like an over-swelled bladder, and the novelty of fresh air no longer held any appeal. Guessing she could easily have counted to several times more than fifty by now, she retraced her steps to the library. The latch on the French doors proved to be stubborn, and she had just cursed it into place, had barely stepped clear of the alcove, when she was stopped cold by the sound of voices in the outer hallway. The footsteps were brusque and purposeful, making their way toward the library door.

Anne glanced quickly around, but there was nowhere to hide. There was nothing but a bank of windows behind her, with a two-foot section of wall on either side forming the arch.

Without stopping to think about it, she reached quickly for the gold ropes that held the curtains swagged to either side. The heavy crimson folds fell across the opening of the alcove, closing it off from the main room. Desperately, Anne caught the fabric and steadied it, then retreated against the French doors, feeling open and exposed to anyone who might glance out an upper window. Beyond the flimsy wall of velvet, the voices and footsteps marked the introduction of several men into the library. The outer doors were closed, followed by the sound of more serious, forthright steps bringing someone over to the desk.

"I will feel a damned sight better when these are locked away," came the gratingly familiar voice of Duncan Forbes. "I suppose one must admire the resolve of a courier who has been given specific orders to deliver a dispatch directly into the recipient's hand, but a damned inconvenience nonetheless."

"You were inconvenienced?" Lord Loudoun's laughter was coarse. "The very delightful Miss Chastity Morris's teats were practically in my hands, and I suspect she would have willingly placed them there in another moment had Worsham not come to fetch me away."

"Your pardon, my lord. I have no doubt you can regroup and reacquire."

"Only if you agree to lead a diversion to keep my wife distracted elsewhere."

Polite laughter indicated there were at least two or three more men present who had accompanied Duncan Forbes into his study. Anne glanced around the shadowy alcove again, distressed to see how the smallest slivers of light sparkled off the gold threads in her frock. Worse still, her farthingale consisted of a series of descending hoops that held her skirts out in a graceful bell shape. Crushed as she was against the glass panes of the door, the hem was thrust out in front, the outermost edge almost teasing the length of velvet curtain.

As carefully as she could, she gathered the folds of silk and inched them back out of harm's way.

"Any word from Hawley?" asked a sober voice in the group. "Is he sending reinforcements from Edinburgh?"

"General Hawley has but two thousand men and orders to hold Falkirk, Perth, and Stirling. I doubt he could spare a stableboy at the moment."

"If there is any truth in the report we received yesterday, there are only five thousand men in the whole of the prince's army. Ill-equipped, demoralized . . ."

"We have underestimated their resolve before," Worsham interrupted in his quietly insidious voice. "And it would not behoove us to do so again. Major Garner, I understand your dragoons were amongst the first to engage the rebels at Colt's Bridge, and again at Prestonpans?"

Anne put a face to the English officer's name. Hamilton Garner was tall, blond, and arrogant, with the cold green eyes of a cobra. His dragoons had run away from the Highland army at Colt's Bridge without exchanging a single shot. At the battle of Prestonpans, slightly more than three thousand Jacobites had defeated General Sir John Cope's army of twice that number in a morning ambush. Major Garner had been among the shamefully few to stand and fight, but he had been captured. Eventually, because the prisoners vastly outnumbered the victors, he and the others had been released on their own parole, promising not to take up arms against Prince Charles again. Garner had broken that parole the instant he was free. He had ordered the cowards under his command to be flogged within an inch of their lives, and testified against five officers hanged in the public square.

There were rumors suggesting the major's fight was not just with the prince, that he bore a personal vendetta against one of the prince's most daring and successful captains, Alexander Cameron—the *Camshroinaich Dubh* whose name had conjured ghosts out of Fearchar Farquharson's past. Lady Drummuir, with her reliable legion of spies, had heard that Cameron had won Hamilton Garner's betrothed in a duel, that he had married the woman himself—a *Sassenach*—and taken her home to Lochaber. He had also been at Colt's Bridge and Prestonpans, and Garner's rage, having seen him there, knew no bounds. He had sworn to track his enemy to the ends of the earth if it meant killing every Jacobite single-handedly in the pursuit.

"These rebels do not fight in accordance to any known military order," Garner protested now. "I cannot begin to recount the number of times I have attempted to enlighten General Hawley to this unpleasant fact. They creep about in the darkness, wading through bogs, emerging covered in mud and stink. Any lines they form are ragged at best and break at the first screech of encouragement from their infernal pipers. They discharge but one round from their muskets and toss them aside, reaching our lines with their claymores in hand, while our men are still bent over their weapons, priming them for a second shot. They will even fling off their plaids and skirts if the bulk of their clothing hampers them. Imagine that, if you will. Scores of screaming, half-naked devils descending upon you, wielding swords as tall as any normal man."

There was a pause, then an indignant *harrumph* from Lord Loudoun. "They fight like barbarians, sirs. They eat cold oatmeal and animal blood, for God's sake. They are a clamorous, disorganized rabble, and the major showed exemplary fortitude flaying the skin off the back of any man who did not instantly set aside the terms of his parole."

"Indeed," Worsham murmured, nonplussed by the earl's rant, "for where is the merit in upholding a soldier's oath when one is dealing with cattle thieves and sheep-fuckers?"

Anne, listening from behind the curtain, felt the blood boil up into her cheeks. Her lips parted in an attempt to gather more air into her lungs but the effort was hampered by the tightness of her stomacher. The urge was growing to fling the draperies aside and confront the lot of them, and indeed, her temper was such that she might well have thrown caution to the wind and done exactly that had the next voice not stopped her cold.

"Come now. You are too harsh on my neighbors. We are not all enamored of our farm animals. Some of us prefer all those lovely English lassies you have had transported up from London."

Another round of lusty laughter acknowledged Angus Moy's remark.

"Indeed, the whores are cleaner than most," said another man. "And decidedly more eager than their Highland counterparts."

Worsham's voice rose above the second round of ribald laughter. "But your wife, sir," he said to Angus. "She seems a fiery little vixen with energy to spare. Surely you are not tossing her into the stew pot as well?"

Anne held her breath, her fingers clenching tight around the folds of her skirt. She fully hoped to hear the lethal hiss of steel as her husband drew his sword to cut the envisioned smirk off the Englishman's face, but she was shocked to hear him respond with an exaggerated sigh.

"Alas, I grew weary long ago of my wife's . . . various energies. And of trying to curb either her tongue or her penchant for supporting lost causes."

"Women," said Duncan Forbes, "can be bellicose creatures at the best of times. Pretty to look at, intriguing to bed, but if they are not taken firmly in hand on the walk back from the altar, they can be the cause of one blasted migraine after another. Even my son used to despair at times of his Arabella's simpering, but a few sound beatings put her quickly to rights. Perhaps you've just been too lax on her, m'boy. A good throuncing once in a while never hurts; shows who's master and who is just there by the grace of our benevolence."

"I will keep that in mind," Angus said with a low chuckle.

"She is a Farquharson, is she not?" Major Garner posed the question over the sound of Forbes closing and locking a cupboard in his desk. "Related to the old man and his trio of foot soldiers?"

"He is her grandfather," Angus provided.

"And you see no need to rein her in?" His surprise was as apparent as Angus's nonchalance.

"Frankly, we've told him not to," Loudoun answered. "She is the old bastard's pride and joy, and so long as he thinks she has the freedom to come and go as she pleases, he will stay in contact with her. Especially now. I warrant Fearchar Farquharson knows within a mile where the rebel army is and where they will be going after they cross the border."

"My money is on Glasgow," Forbes said. "The Pretender will be desperately short on supplies and will not want to risk a march to Edinburgh without regrouping."

"Neither will he want to delay recapturing the royal city," Garner suggested. "He must know the reserves he left behind were forced to abandon their positions when Hawley came north. Yet he will believe, like every Stuart king and queen before him, that the key to holding Scotland lies with holding Edinburgh."

"I agree," Loudoun said heartily. "Which is why Hawley has asked *us* to send reinforcements to *him*. Three thousand men, to be precise, which will strip us to the bone, but well worth the risk if we can end this thing sooner rather than later. I had thought to hold off until morning discussing your reassignment, Angus, but I see no point waiting. The general has specifically requested Royal Scots brigades—what better way to shatter an army in retreat than to have them face their own kind across the field of battle, eh?—and since your men are more than ready for active duty, I'll be sending your MacKintosh brigade back with Major Garner. I believe, Major, you intend to depart at week's end?"

"Sooner, if possible," Garner said. "I am just awaiting the arrival of a supply ship."

Her eyes closed, Anne felt every scrap of energy drain out of her body. Her knees grew weak and her hands trembled; her fingers lost their grip on the silk panels of her skirt and the hem slid forward, brushing the bottom edge of the velvet curtain.

"There you have it, then, Angus. Angus? Are you with us, man?"

"What? Oh. Yes. Yes, of course, I was just lost in thought there for a moment."

"You'll be in the thick of it soon enough, my man, no time for losing yourself anywhere. We will be relying on you to help hold Edinburgh and keep the rebels trapped until Cumberland can bring his army north. In the meantime, make it a priority to find out what your wife knows. It can only benefit us to be aware of the prince's intentions ahead of time, and a wife who knows her husband is going away for an extended period of time is often inclined to reveal more than she might otherwise do."

"I doubt the threat of my absence would cause anything but relief these days."

"Whisper in her ear," Forbes said. "Tickle her on the chin, promise her you will keep your powder wet and your wick dry, whatever it takes to placate her. We are running out of time, here, and your efforts will not go unrewarded. Lochaber was once MacKintosh territory; it could well be again."

"I will do my best, sir."

"I have no doubt you will."

Chapter Seven

*A*nne did not know how long she stood in the darkness of the alcove after the men had departed. She was too stunned to think. Too angry. Too disillusioned. Too hurt. Her husband's betrayal went so far beyond her grasp she felt as though it must have been someone else's voice she had heard, not Angus's.

She thought she should cry, but somehow that was not appropriate either. A small, insidiously cruel part of her felt more like laughing—that was what you did when you stumbled across the village fool, was it not? But just who had been played for the bigger fool she was not yet certain. She had wanted so desperately to believe the man she married was inherently good and honorable, she had never even considered the possibility he was a consummate liar, a manipulator, a traitor. Lochaber was indeed a ripe, lush plum, and if that was what Forbes and Loudoun had offered for his cooperation, then it was far more than thirty pieces of silver; well worth deceiving a wife and betraying a prince.

Had he thought a night of passion would make her malleable and docile? Had he thought a night of sweet lovemaking would make her betray her grandfather and cousins' whereabouts to him? She had, of course, but that was after the fact, for the dragoons had already been sent to watch Dunmaglass. And if he was just "humoring her" as Loudoun had ordered, why had he lied to Worsham about her whereabouts last night?

She pressed her hands to her temples and squeezed. It was just too confusing. There were too many contradictions to try to sort through, when she could barely think her way clear to what to do in the next five minutes.

Anne looked down. Her skirt was crumpled where her hands had crushed the fabric. While she absently tried to smooth the creases, she turned her head and glanced out the window at the panorama of stars smeared across the sky, wondering how everything could look so lovely and tranquil when her entire world had just been turned upside down.

Something . . . a noise, a rustle, a soft squeak of a floorboard . . . intruded on Anne's thoughts and she frowned. She stared at the curtain for a long moment, then edged forward on silent toes to peer cautiously through the fringed edges, wondering if, unbeknownst to her, one of the officers had remained behind. Forbes had locked something in his desk, nervous that it was in his possession. Perhaps he had left someone behind to guard it.

She heard the sound again and bit off a scream as something small and furry darted under the hem of her skirt and scampered out the other side.

"Jesus God in heaven!" she gasped, clapping a hand to her breast. It was a mouse. A damned mouse!

She lashed out with her foot, accomplishing little more than stubbing her toe and tangling a heel in the bottom hoop of her farthingale. Extricating it brought forth another muttered curse, after which she pushed one panel of the curtains aside and ducked back into the main room, happy to leave the rodent with sole possession of the alcove.

The library appeared as it had before, though darker now that the outer doors were closed. A very faint undercurrent of sound filtered through the silence, indicating the ball was getting under way overhead. Musicians would be tuning their instruments. Footmen would be weaving their way through the guests, balancing silver trays laden with wine and punch. The chairs set around the perimeter would already be occupied by the crones and matrons, their fans cooling their faces, their heads tilting together over a choice remark about the fabric of someone's gown, or another's shocking display of cleavage. The soldiers would be inspecting the women, trying to decide who would most likely accompany them into a shadowy corner and relieve a few lusty needs.

Anne's gaze wandered down to the Lord President's desk. It was a massive, solid affair built with deep drawers on each side of the wide kneehole. The top two drawers on either side had small brass lockplates, as did the long flat one in the center; almost without thinking, she reached up and withdrew a thin steel pin from her hair.

Running her fingertips along the smooth, polished wood, she glanced at the door again, then bent over and, with a steady hand, fed the end of the pin into the center lock. It was a simple, single ratchet mechanism not unlike the one in Angus's study, and it gave on the second turn.

The drawer slid open soundlessly and Anne peered inside. There were papers—half-written letters, mostly; none of them seeming important enough to come from a late-night courier—several sticks of sealing wax, and two large gold stamps, one embossed with the Forbes coat of arms, the other with his seal of office. The drawer on the left opened as easily, and it contained a second locked box which took all of two seconds to work open. The sight of a sizeable cache of gold coins barely caused a twitch in the set of her jaw, nor did the contents of the third and final locked drawer.

Frowning, Anne glanced over the top of the desk at the door before sinking down in a crush of silk skirts. She had distinctly heard Forbes turning a key in a lock, but the other drawers opened without effort.

It was when she was pushing the last one back into place that she noticed the oddity. The drawers on the left pedestal were much shorter than those on the right; they were barely as deep as the length between her palm and elbow, whereas those in the other bank could accommodate her arm from fingertip to shoulder. She ducked down and searched again, finding nothing on the first pass of her hand. On the second, with the help of a candle hastily lit with flint and tinder, she felt the scar of a small keyhole embedded in the wood and, beside it, the faint line of a seam that, if one did not know where to look, would appear to be part of the grain.

"Clever bastard," she muttered, confirming her suspicion by peering at the outer side of the desk, where the ornate carvings and curlicues concealed two thin hinges discolored with a dark patina to blend into the carved patterns on the wood.

Wasting no more time on admiring the carpentry, Anne applied the hairpin, cursing softly when the lock proved to be more complicated. It succumbed eventually, and when she swung the false drawers aside, the first thing she saw was a packet of dispatches bound and wrapped in a leather pouch. There were other bundles, other papers, all of which earned a cursory inspection before she discarded some and added others to a pile on the floor beside her.

When she reached the limit of what she thought she could safely conceal on her person, she pushed the false front of drawers back in place. Since she had never quite mastered the art of *locking* anything with a hairpin, she had to hope no one would come looking for any of the missing papers until morning.

She stood, lifting the layers of her overskirt, underskirt, and petticoat to bare the frame of her farthingale. Between the fourth and fifth rib of whalebone, a pocket had been sewn onto the strips of linen. Her protest to Angus the previous night about not wearing knives to a formal affair was forgotten as she reached inside the pocket and removed the wickedly sharp dirk. The bundles of papers made for a snug fit, and with nowhere else to conceal the dirk, she rearranged several books on a nearby shelf and shoved the weapon well back behind them.

With her hand pressed flat over the constricting tightness of her bodice, she took a moment to catch her breath before ensuring her skirts were straight and orderly again, her hair was not missing a curl, and she had not left anything behind. Everything seemed to be the way she had found it apart from the curtains on the alcoves, and they had obviously gone unnoticed earlier. As a final precaution, she ventured into mouse country one last time to open the French doors, leaving them ajar enough to suggest an alternate means of entry and exit.

Back at the main door, she paused and pressed her ear to the wood. She cracked it open a sliver of an inch, then two, then boldly threw her shoulders back and walked out into the hallway, a rueful expression on her face as if she had just taken a wrong turn.

The pretense was not needed. Apart from one red-faced couple who emerged from another darkened niche farther along the hall and refused to even meet her eye, she saw no one until she reached the vicinity of the entrance hallway. The weight of the bundle hanging from her farthingale made it feel as if her skirt were dragging at a tilt, and as she passed before an ornately gilded mirror, she fully expected to see the evidence of her guilt reflected back. Surprisingly enough, she saw only a tall, pale woman in gold silk whose eyes were possibly a bit too rounded and dark, and who had to force herself to stop and lean toward the polished surface as if to adjust a displaced curl.

If luck was in any way on her side, Anne reasoned, the theft would not be discovered until she was long gone, and even then she, a mere woman, would hardly be considered the prime suspect. Once she was safely back at Moy Hall and able to think clearly again, she would decide what to do with the stolen papers, but for now, she had to get out of here. She had to regain her composure and act as if nothing were amiss, as if the horrendous pain twisting inside her chest were not there at all.

"My dear, are ye all right?"

"What?" Anne started as Lady Drummuir reached out and touched her arm.

"Ye look as if ye've seen the ghost of William Wallace."

Anne swallowed. "I'm fine, just tired. Have you seen Angus?"

"Since the last time ye asked not two minutes gone? Nay. Nay, I've not."

Anne searched the crowded room, but although she saw Lords Forbes and Loudoun laughing at some unheard triviality, there was no sign of her husband. A servant walked by and she signaled for a glass of wine, which she emptied in three swallows and replaced with another.

Meanwhile, couples were lining up in two swirling columns of color that formed the opening lines of the contredanse. She located Adrienne de Boule, the sapphire blue silk of her gown shining like a jewel under the thousand candles in the chandelier overhead. Her partner was the green-eyed Major Garner—a suitable match, Anne thought belligerently, though she almost wished it were Angus, if for no other reason than she would know where he was.

Farther along, the young Mr. Forbes was dancing with one of the MacLaren sisters—who could keep track of their names when there were seven who all looked frighteningly alike? He craned his neck at every turn to try to catch Anne's attention, but she ignored him.

With her foot tapping impatiently to the music, she started her search at the far end of the cavernous room again, skimming past the clusters of uniformed officers, the tables of refreshments, the curtained recesses where twenty-foot-high arched doors opened onto stone balconies . . .

Her gaze faltered and flicked back to the doors.

When she had first entered the library, the curtains in the two alcoves had been swagged and tied with gold cords. But when she had paused at the door before leaving and glanced back . . . they had both been lowered!

She fought the instant surge of panic and forced herself to remain calm, to think as hard as she could and remember *exactly* what she had seen when she looked back from the doorway. Both curtains had been tied back when she entered, she knew that much without a doubt, but regardless of how she tried to change the image in her mind, both sets of drapes were also hanging free when she departed. Someone must have been in the library with her! Someone who had stayed behind? Or someone who had crept back after the others departed?

Just before she'd had her wits startled by the mouse, she had heard a noise she had thought sounded like a stealthy footstep. Whoever owned that footstep must have heard her kick the bejesus out of the mouse and ducked into the second alcove, lowering the panels as she had done to conceal himself.

But if that was what had happened . . . it meant that someone had seen her searching the Lord President's desk! Someone had seen her pick the lock, steal the papers, then stash them away under her petticoat!

Lady Drummuir jumped at the sound of breaking glass,

gasping when she turned and saw blood welling through Anne's fingers. "Good God, child, what have ye done?"

Anne had not been aware of squeezing the wine goblet or of its shattering in her hand. She was only vaguely conscious now of the dowager holding her hand away from her dress and shouting at one of the servants for a clean cloth.

All she could think of was that someone had been in the library with her, watching her steal important papers from the locked desk of the Lord President of the Court of Session.

"Och, ye've gone an' cut yerself, dearie. Here, let me wrap it so ye dinna drip all over yer fine gown. Cheap bloody glass, that's what it is," the dowager snorted. "He's had all his crystal and silver plate packed into boxes an' sent to London for safekeeping. It's nae wonder the plates didna crack under the weight of the bread, an' the cutlery not bend each time ye touched it to yer lip."

Anne allowed herself to be led out of the ballroom, her hand bundled in a napkin. A few of the ladies near the exit gasped and swooned for the benefit of the men in their company but for the most part the accident hardly drew notice. She was taken into a small parlor, where water and more cloths were fetched, along with Doctor Faustus MacMillan, a short strut of a man with bloodshot eyes and rolled sausages for fingers. Under Lady Drummuir's caustic eye, he bathed the latticework of small cuts and bound the hand in clean strips of linen. He was just finishing when Angus and Lord Forbes came through the door, the former looking genuinely concerned as he went down on one knee beside Anne's chair.

"What happened? I was told there had been a mishap, that you were bleeding."

The doctor glanced over the top of his pince-nez. "Nothing too serious, m'lord. Cut herself on a glass, she did. More blood than bother."

"It was a silly accident," Anne said in a whisper. "The glass broke when I lifted it off the tray."

"Your hand—?" Angus started to reach for the bandaged hand, but Anne flinched away from his touch.

"My hand is fine. There are a few small cuts, nothing that will not heal in a day or two. It was foolish to even bring the doctor away from the party. I could have tended it myself."

She tried to keep the words from sounding as though they were spat from between her teeth, but because they were, it was difficult to measure any success.

"Are you certain . . . ?"

"I am absolutely certain. Please, do not worry yourself any further."

"Worry?" Forbes exhaled a breath and clasped his hands behind his back. "He was damned near beside himself, dear lady. Blanched like a lovesick swain, I vow, and with good reason, for I confess my own heart skipped a beat or two. Point out the clumsy lout who gave you a broken glass and I'll thrash him myself."

"It was no one's fault but my own," Anne said coldly.

"An' ma son's," Lady Drummuir added, casting a narrowed accusation in Angus's direction. "If she hadn't been so distracted wonderin' where ye'd taken yerself off to, she might have seen the glass was cracked."

"You were looking for me?" Angus glanced at Anne.

"No. I mean yes. I . . . I wanted to tell you I was leaving. I have a dreadful headache and I wanted to tell you I was going home."

"Home?" Forbes frowned like an indulgent father. "Nonsense. You will stay here the night. I'll have a chamber prepared at once, and—"

"No!" Anne shot to her feet. "I mean . . . no, thank you. I would prefer just to go home. There is no need for Angus to leave," she added. "I will be perfectly fine on my own."

"Don't be absurd," Angus said. "Of course I will take you home."

In desperation, Anne turned to appeal to her mother-in-law. "Please—?"

Lady Drummuir frowned, but bustled forward at once to take charge of the situation. "All this blather over a few wee cuts. There's surely no need for anyone to work themselves into a turn: It's not as if the lass is in peril of bleedin' to death. I was of a mind to find ma bed anyroad, so Annie will simply come home with me. Angus, ye can come fetch her from Church Street in the mornin' if ye're of a mind. Or ye can come away now if ye dinna trust me to see her safe, but I'll warn ye I've been in a fair mood all night to clout someone over the head, so ye'd be takin' yer chances if ye do."

Aside from a small tic that shivered in Angus's cheek, he had no recourse but to offer his mother a small bow of compliance. Anne had no choice either; she had to take his arm when he insisted on escorting them to the front door, but there was not one step taken when she did not fear the next would bring shouts and a demand for her arrest. By the time the servants had fetched their cloaks and brought Lady Drummuir's coach to the door, she could feel the dampness between her shoulder blades, and her head was so light she was not even aware of Angus kissing her on the cheek or murmuring his promise to see her first thing in the morning.

And then she was in the coach. The door was closing, being latched. They were pulling away from Culloden House and she could see Angus silhouetted against the torchlights, his arm raised in farewell. The purloined dispatches were a lump against her thigh—almost as obtrusive as the one in her throat.

Obviously whoever had been in the library with her had decided to play a cat-and-mouse game of his own.

Chapter Eight

"I canna believe ye took such a risk," Lady Drummuir said, shocked almost beyond speech. Once they were through the gates she had demanded explanations, and because Anne desperately needed to confide in someone, she spilled out everything that had happened since her meeting with John MacGillivray in the library. "I canna believe ye had the ballocks to break open the Lord President's desk. With a hairpin, ye say?"

"It was a rather simple lock."

"Still an' all, Miss, 'tis not exactly the kind of talent one expects in a laird's wife."

"I was the granddaughter of a reiver first," Anne reminded her.

"Aye, an' that alone would have justified clappin' ye in irons on the spot. The real surprise if, as ye say, ye think someone saw ye, is that no one has released the hellhounds on ye yet."

The "yet" hung between them a moment, twisting this way and that in the silence to impart all manner of unpleasant consequences in the minds of both women.

"Why do ye suppose that is? Why do ye suppose ye're not riding in the company of a dozen redcoats right the now?"

Anne bit her lip in genuine confusion. "I don't know. When I saw Forbes in the parlor with Angus just then . . ."

She had lost a year of her life in that single moment, and still could not believe she had been allowed to walk away from Culloden House without an escort of lobsterbacks.

"Ye have no idea who might have been watchin' ye in the library?"

"No. I was certain everyone had gone. At one point, I thought I might have heard . . ."

"Yes? Ye thought ye might have heard what?"

Anne shook her head. "I thought I heard a footstep, or a creak on the floorboard, but I was so distracted and angry and confused . . . then I saw the mouse, and—"

"And ye cried out an' near stomped it to death, giving whoever it was plenty of time to slip into the other alcove."

Anne nodded, her face pale. "That must be what happened. But if it was Forbes or one of the other officers, why was I not stopped? Whoever it was had to have seen me take the dispatches and hide them, so why was I not confronted in the ballroom or the parlor and shown to be a thief?"

The dowager frowned, obviously asking herself the same questions.

"The one hope," she said finally, "the *only* hope is that it wisna one of the men who was there earlier, for I canna see any of them not nip-tongued with glee at the thought of strippin' ye down an' arrestin' ye with the proof of treason hangin' off yer skirts. Still an' again," she added, playing her own devil's advocate, "had they shamed ye an' arrested ye in such a public manner, might they not have worried what the other lairds would have done? Better to wait until ye were away from Culloden, where it could be done without danger of swords bein' drawn."

After staring at each other for a moment, both women reached up simultaneously and unlatched the windows beside them, lowering the sashes enough to poke their heads through and study the darkness of the road behind them. Apart from the muted pinpricks of light marking the cottages they were passing, the road was a clear, dark ribbon cutting through the tree-lined parks on either side. They were nearing the outskirts of Inverness, following the banks of the Moray Firth, and if anyone had pursued them from Culloden, this would present the perfect stretch to overtake them.

Anne remained hanging over the window sash until her cheeks were chilled and the wind had torn several curls loose. When she retreated inside again, the dowager had already affected repairs to her own coif and chose not to comment on their brief lapse of dignity.

"There is a third possibility," she said. "An' that would be that ye were not the only one curious to see what the Lord President had locked away in his desk."

"You mean someone else at the party set out to rob him?"

"We were not the only ones who would have preferred to stay at home an' tattoo our arses with sharp sticks. The MacGregor was there with his son, the brace of them standin' stiffer than iron pikes. MacPherson an' Strathbogie, MacFall an' MacKillican, were in the corners, the lot of them lookin' in as black a mood as The MacGillivray, an' likely gone just as quickly once homage was paid, though surely not with the same urgency as Big John. One of them could as easily have been in the library as another."

The women exchanged a glance, then looked away, neither one convinced, and again the silence stretched between them, broken only by the rolling of the carriage wheels over the rutted road.

"Are ye dead certain, lass, that ye heard what ye say ye heard?"

It had only been a few short hours ago that the dowager had defended her son by saying he was only doing what he thought was best for the clan, and Anne knew the strain in her voice was not caused entirely by fear for her personal well-being.

"I heard Forbes tell him to ply me with kindness in order that I might confide in him anything Fearchar told me about the prince's army. I also heard Angus say that he . . . that he was weary of my various energies and my penchant for supporting lost causes."

Lady Drummuir expelled a sigh that bespoke the full weight of her seven decades. "So now ye feel it is up to you to dash off in a mad fit o' vengeance?"

Anne had not said as much, had not even made the decision in her own mind, but she did so now without hesitation. "Granda' was right. There is no one else of equal rank the lairds will follow. Nor is there any son or brother to send by way of preserving the honor of the clan."

"I ken what ye're sayin', child, but the danger—! Will ye strap a *clai' mór* to yer back and pistols on yer hips, an' will ye ride onto a battlefield with blood in yer eye? Aye, yer heart is in the right place, I grant ye, an' aye, ye'll likely stir enough shame in the clan to get the proxies ye need, but the lairds will want a man to lead them."

"I will give them a man," Anne said quietly. "I will give them John MacGillivray."

"MacGillivray!"

"He is obviously willing to fight, and so are his men."

"Och, he's not a man to toy with, Anne," the dowager cautioned. "He's like a great blooded stallion who may appear to be broken to the saddle, but once he has the bit in his teeth, ye might not be able to rein him in again."

"I am none too certain I would *want* to rein him in," Anne declared with more confidence than she felt. "And it is Angus who should be worried, not me."

The dowager lapsed into silence again and turned to stare out the window as the coach passed St. John's Chapel and slowed to make its turn into the tree-lined avenue leading to Drummuir House. It was a large and stately William and Mary mansion built of mellow red brick and sandstone quoining, and because it sat so near the river, there was always a sheer layer of mist blanketing the encompassing parkland.

"Times like this," Lady Drummuir sighed, "I can almost feel sorry for Duncan Forbes. He was ever an annoyin' man, but everythin' he has done, he has done because he honestly believed it would make for a stronger Scotland. Not two years ago he wanted to send Highland regiments to Flanders to fight alongside the English. He said if men like Lochiel an' Lord George Murray were away in Europe fightin' the Dutch, who would be at home to stir a rebellion? An' it's true, I suppose, for they would not have been here to meet the prince at Glenfinnan, he would not have been able to raise an army, an' all this strife could have been prevented—an' mayhap that would not have been such a terrible thing."

"Is that what you would have wanted? To have slowly

bowed to all the English demands and commands until there was no longer any Scotland?"

"There will always be a Scotland, Anne Moy! But must we always drench the glens in blood to prove it?"

"English blood," Anne replied softly. "Aye, if we must."

"Faugh! Ye're as stubborn as yer granda'."

"Is that such a terrible thing as well?"

The dowager did not turn to address the remark, but her gloved hand crept across the bench and, finding Anne's, gave it a small squeeze.

"No, lass," she whispered. "'Tis just the envy of an old woman ye're hearin', for if I could, I'd be up on that magnificent stallion alongside ye."

When Angus came to Drummuir House the following morning, he was not alone. Major Roger Worsham was by his side, his scarlet tunic fastidiously clean, the brass buttons gleaming, the edges of his wide buff lapels looking as if they had been cut by a razor.

His face was equally officious, his jaw set in stone, his eyes gazing unblinking at their surroundings as they were shown into the yellow drawing room—a regal chamber with walls lined with yellow silk damask. The same fabric covered the sumptuous sofas and delicate chairs that were in turn complemented by gilt-edged paintings and pale buttercolored wood moldings. It was a room normally reserved for formal occasions—which did not escape Angus's notice—dominated by a huge white marble fireplace that was as cold as the expression on the dowager's face when she appeared nearly half an hour after their arrival to greet them.

"Angus."

He inclined his head slightly. "Mother."

"Major."

Worsham cocked an eyebrow. "Madam."

"Now that we ken who we all are, ye might want to tell me why ye've come poundin' on ma doors before the hour was decent enough to do so. Lady Anne is still abed, an' I havna had time to even strop ma corset on tight enough. I trust ye havna come here lookin' for yer balls again, Major, for we MacKintoshes seem to be in short supply ourselves at the moment."

That set the tone fairly bluntly and Worsham offered a smirk. "I pray you forgive the early hour, but when Captain MacKintosh mentioned he was coming here, I thought I would accompany him and save us both a later inconvenience."

"Well, ye're too late for breakfast an' too early for dinner."

"The thought did not occur to put you to any trouble."

"Good, for 'twould never have occurred to me, either. If ye've come to fetch Anne home, ye've wasted a trip as well," she said to Angus. "She fancies she might stay with me a few days."

"A few days? Is she ill?"

"She's healthy as a dray horse. Since when can she not visit with her mother-in-law, if she so chooses?"

"Of course she can, but—"

"Then I'll tell her ye have no objections. She keeps a small wardrobe here, so there's nae need to send for claythes or necessities. Will ye be wantin' me to take her a message?"

"Actually, since my business is with the Lady Anne, we should prefer to speak to her in person, if we may," said Worsham.

"An' what business might that be, Major?"

"A trifling matter. It should not take too much of her time."

Lady Drummuir's bosom swelled with the same threat of violence that flared her nostrils, but her intended riposte was thwarted by a quiet voice from the doorway. "It is quite all right. I am here."

Both men turned as Anne walked into the room. It was immediately apparent that she had not taken time to trouble with her corset or her hair, for the latter was loose and fell in soft red waves over her shoulders. Her modesty was preserved by a loose-fitting *contouche* of white muslin with delicate lace ruffles bordering the neckline and spilling from the cuffs. Peeping from beneath the hem as she walked were more ruffles that rustled slightly as they brushed the surface of the carpet.

She stopped in front of one of the tall, square-paned windows, and with the bright beams of sunshine behind her, the combination of glowing white muslin and fiery red hair gave both men pause. As a calculated distraction, it was effective, for the muscles in Angus's jaw flexed and, despite his best efforts to prevent it, a flush of warmth crept up his throat and darkened his complexion.

Worsham's reaction was more feral. The pale eyes narrowed and a speck of saliva glittered at the corner of his mouth.

"You wanted to speak to me, Major?"

The perfunctory address, absent of any social niceties, brought his attention swiftly back to her face. "I trust you are not suffering any ill effects from last night? I heard you cut your hand."

She lifted her hand and turned it, showing the bandages. "It was nothing. A clumsy accident."

"Nonetheless, Lady Forbes was discomfited and wished me to express her regret over the unfortunate incident."

"I am certain she did not sleep a wink. However, there was no incident, sir. A glass broke. I happened to be holding it at the time."

"Indeed. And you are right; there were other, more pressing concerns at Culloden House this morning. It seems someone took the liberty of creating some mischief."

"Mischief? How so?"

"One of the guests mentioned he saw you in the vicinity of the Lord President's library last night shortly after midnight," he said, deferring a direct answer. "Is this true?"

Anne pursed her lips as if perplexed. After a moment, her brow cleared and she nodded. "Yes, I believe I may have been, though I could not swear to the exact hour. I'm afraid I overindulged at the supper table and was feeling uncomfortable. I sought a quiet hallway, hoping a few turns might help. Unfortunately, it only left me feeling somewhat light-headed, and"— she held up her hand—"thus the accident."

"Did you happen to see anyone else in the hallways while you were . . . walking off your discomfort?"

"No, I don't recall . . . wait. Yes. Yes, I saw a young couple emerging from one of the rooms—I'm sorry, I do not know the manor well enough to tell you which one—but they seemed as startled to see me as I was them. I believe they had also been seeking a few moments of privacy away from the noise of the ballroom."

Worsham nodded slightly to acknowledge the supposition. "Major Bosworth was the one who reported seeing you in the vicinity. He did, however, neglect to mention he was not alone."

"I'm not surprised," Anne said evenly. "I doubt Lord Ian MacLeod would be any too pleased to hear his daughter had been anywhere private with an English officer. Neither would her betrothed."

The pale blue eyes narrowed again. "Whereas a married lady seeking a liaison with an individual of her own ilk would raise fewer eyebrows?"

Anne returned his gaze without so much as blinking. "I warrant that would depend on the identity of the individual as well as on the nature of their liaison."

"An interesting choice of words, Lady Anne. Forgive my temerity in asking, but what was the nature of your liaison with John MacGillivray?"

Anne's reaction was completely involuntary as she glanced at her husband's face. It was not much of a flicker, over in the flash of an instant, but it had the same effect on Worsham as the scent of fresh blood to a hawk.

"MacGillivray?"

"Yes. You were observed whispering together outside the dining hall moments before the hour in question."

"I do not recall that we were *whispering,* sir, although I expect he may well have paused to bid good-night. I hardly remember."

"You did not see him again downstairs?"

"No. I did not."

"And would you tell me if you had?"

"No," she said simply. "I would not. Now, if you are quite finished—"

"I am told your relationship with John MacGillivray goes much deeper than just a casual friendship."

"Then you were told wrong, sir. John MacGillivray is an honest, honorable man, loyal to his clan and to his country."

This time her eyes cut openly to Angus before returning to Worsham. "He was ever my friend, yes, and I'm proud to say so to anyone who would ask. But there was never anything more between us."

"Nothing that would prompt you to lie for him? Or protect him?"

"John MacGillivray hardly needs my protection, sir."

"Where is this line of questions going, Major?" Angus asked, his annoyance evident in the way he removed his gloves and slapped them down on a nearby chair. "And I should tread very carefully with your answer here."

"As you know, someone was in the Lord President's library last night and stole some rather . . . sensitive papers."

"By God," Angus murmured angrily. "And this is why you accompanied me from Culloden House? So you could accuse my wife of theft?"

"Her whereabouts at the time of the robbery were unaccounted for, as were MacGillivray's."

"Well, she has accounted for them now. She has also said she did not see MacGillivray, though if you had asked me, you might have saved yourself a trip."

"You?"

"Indeed. I saw and spoke to MacGillivray in the lower hallway just after our meeting in the library. He had already paid his respects to the dowager Lady Forbes and was begging my leave, as he had a matter of some urgency to tend to in Clunas this morning and wanted an early start. I believe he said it was to do with the health of his fiancée, Lady Elizabeth of Clunas, who was prevented from attending last night because of illness. He was quite beside himself with worry, which would explain his seeming distraction. I believe they are to be wed next month, though he has been singularly smitten with the lovely lady for some time now. At least, she was all he could speak about the previous evening—to the point I was damn near distracted myself."

"Ahh, yes." Worsham's eyes took on a predatory gleam again as he confronted Anne. "I believe we were discussing your whereabouts Thursday evening when we were interrupted last night."

Anne, remembering MacGillivray's warning that someone had followed her and Eneas away from Dunmaglass, hesitated a fraction of an instant with her answer, long enough for Angus to release another impatient huff of breath.

"And I shall interrupt you again, sir, by reiterating the fact that my wife and I were both at home Thursday evening. If you care to recall, I told Lord Loudoun that John MacGillivray was also with us, playing cards until the small hours of the morning, at which time the pair of us, having consumed several"— he glanced uncomfortably at Anne who was, in turn, staring wide-eyed back at him—"well, yes, all right, rather more than several bottles of strong spirits, both had to be carried to our beds. If you saw my wife whispering with MacGillivray last night, and if what she said to him was anything like the dressing-down she gave to me earlier in the day, I can promise you it would have scalded your ears red."

A muscle jumped in Worsham's cheek as he looked from Angus to Anne. She barely noticed, for she was still staring at her husband. He had done it again. He had lied for her *and* MacGillivray, giving them both alibis that only a man with absolute, incontrovertible proof would dare challenge. It was clear the major did not have any such proof, and Lady Drummuir wasted no time in taking advantage of his hesitation.

"Shall I have Gibb show ye out, Major, or can ye find yer own way to the door?"

Worsham looked from one face to the next, obviously not pleased with the way things had gone. His fists curled momentarily as he considered his options, but in the end, he merely offered a curt nod and strode out of the drawing room, his boots sending an angry echo back along the hall.

The dowager waited until there was silence before she spoke again. "I'm not thinkin' ye made a friend there, Angus, love."

"He's a pompous fool and lucky I did not draw my sword."

"Aye, ye're a real threat to a man who likely picks his teeth wi' his saber." Her sarcasm earned a stony glare and she moved toward the door. "I've a rare need for a morning tot of *uisque*. Shall I have Gibb fetch some coffee, or would ye prefer something stronger as well?"

"Nothing for me," Angus said. "I will not be staying long."

"As ye like."

When his mother was gone and the door was firmly shut behind her, he turned his attention to Anne, who held his gaze for all of two seconds before averting her eyes and staring out the window.

"You *should* be embarrassed," he said with ominous silkiness. "You have more nerve than—" but an adequate comparison failed him and he settled for a heavy sigh. "I am almost afraid to leave the two of you here alone, for fear of the plots you and Mother might hatch together. Please tell me, at least, that last night's stupidity was unplanned."

She looked at him in surprise. "You don't actually believe him, do you, that MacGillivray and I stole away for a secret tryst!"

"A tryst? No. But I do believe you were engaged in some sort of foolery, though whether it was before or after you picked the lock and stole the papers out of Duncan Forbes's desk, I do not know. And please, do not waste both of our time denying it; I was there, I saw you."

Someone else might have fainted dead away from the shock, or at the very least reddened with guilt, but to Anne's credit—and Angus's grudging admiration—she merely gazed at him across the beam of sunlight that was slanting brightly through the window between them.

"It was you in the alcove?"

"I thought I had seen movement behind the curtains, a shadow at the bottom that was blocking the sliver of moonlight one moment and gone the next. After we left, I watched the door for a few minutes to see if anyone came out, and when no one did, I went back inside. My hand was an inch away from the damned curtain when you squealed and started dancing about, and when I realized it was you, my first instinct was to rip the curtains down and see if you were alone; the second was to step aside and save you the embarrassment if you were not."

"Save *me* the embarrassment? After what I had just heard, I should think you would be the one who was shamed beyond measure. Or was it someone else I heard who sounded pleased to be joining General Hawley in Edinburgh, someone else who claimed he was bored with his wife's politics? Someone else who lied when he promised me *so sincerely* that our clansmen would not be involved in any real fighting?"

"Do not attempt to steer the conversation away from your own actions," he warned smoothly, not even having the grace to answer any of the charges. "Do you have any idea what could have happened to you had you been discovered skulking behind that damned curtain eavesdropping on official military business? Can you even conceive of how lucky you were that it was I who came back to the library and not Worsham or that other bastard, Garner?"

"At the time, I can honestly say I was not feeling anything but betrayed."

He looked away for a moment, not completely successful this time in stanching the flow of heat that mottled his throat and cheeks.

"Do you still have the dispatches or did you give them to MacGillivray?"

"Do you not even intend to defend yourself?"

"Against what? You have already made up your mind that I am guilty of all charges."

"You have left me with little choice. You made me a promise; you broke it. You lied to me after swearing you would never do so. And at the time you swore it with such passion and conviction, I . . . I almost thought . . ." The words broke off as she caught her lip between her teeth and bit down hard. "I almost thought you meant what you said. That was, of course, before I discovered how much my . . . *antics* . . . bore you."

"At the time I made you that promise, I honestly believed it was possible to keep it."

"It has only been two days. Has so much changed since then?"

Angus raked his hand through the dark locks of his hair, scattering whatever semblance of order remained of the stylish waves and curls. "Yes. Yes, by God, it has. It changed the instant I had to swear to Colonel Loudoun that MacGillivray was with me on Thursday night, that it could not have been he who attacked Worsham's men. You can see how well the major believed me, for it directly contradicted his report that stated MacGillivray was at Dunmaglass, under the close scrutiny of his crack troop of dragoons."

"Then why did you do it?"

"Not to sanction his actions in any way, I promise you. I did it because more than likely there were soldiers at Culloden House waiting to arrest him. Because he was once a friend as well as a clansman, and because I thought if he was implicated in any way, the charges would eventually spread farther afield and end up on the doorstep of Moy Hall. That was, of course, before I stood in the library and watched my wife take a hairpin to the Lord President's locked desk. And before I saw her remove papers and military dispatches that could earn her an extended stay in a gaol cell if, indeed, she avoided the executioner's ax long enough to enjoy prison. For that reason, my dear, you will have to forgive me if I do not feel as though I should be standing here defending *my* actions."

Anne's chin revealed the first hint of a tremor, and her eyes had grown so wide and had achieved such a piercing shade of blue, it seemed some of the color tinted the whites.

"I did not know about the attack on Worsham's men," she insisted softly. "I did not know John was involved, not until later, when he told me he had been shot."

"Shot?"

She nodded. "In the shoulder."

Angus clenched his jaw and pursed his lips, visibly drawing on all of his strength to keep a flood of invectives from exploding forth.

"Do you," he asked through his teeth, "still have the dispatches?"

"No. Your mother thought it best not to keep them in the house."

"Dear God." He closed his eyes and pressed a hand to his temple. "What did she do with them? Where did she send them?"

Although her voice was fiercely steady when she replied, "I do not know," the lie was in her eyes and Angus did not need a map to follow the course. The courier who brought the dispatches had come directly from France; the papers he carried were from one of the spies Forbes had planted high in the service of King Louis's royal court. Fearchar Farquharson would know exactly what to do with the documents once he opened them and realized what he held in his hands.

"What do you plan to do now?" she asked softly.

The question drew him away from his thoughts for a moment. "Do?"

What he wanted to do was throttle her, but he clasped his hands behind his back instead and avoided her gaze the way she had avoided his earlier. He looked out the window in time to see a falcon glide past, floating effortlessly on the wind currents, its wings outstretched and motionless. Only the head moved, the eyes searching relentlessly for prey, the wickedly hooked beak open in anticipation. It required no vast stretch of the imagination to compare the falcon to Major Roger Worsham, for the officer's eyes held the same carnivorous gleam, his expression the same calculating stillness as he studied his quarry.

If Worsham suspected Angus of lying about MacGillivray or Anne, the question that should concern them more became: What would *he* do about it?

Angus knew Anne was watching him, waiting for his answer, and he took a further moment to settle his emotions before he faced her. "What am I going to do? I am going to go home and make the necessary preparations to depart for Edinburgh."

"I see."

"Do you? Because I do not see where I have a choice, madam. I am an officer in His Majesty's Royal Scots Infantry, and if I refused to obey a direct order, I would likely find myself a fugitive skulking about in the hills alongside your grandfather and cousins."

"Or you could say the word, and a thousand good men would join you in marching to meet the prince. If you did, and if you asked me to go with you, I would proudly ride at your side every step of the way."

"Would you?" He moved forward, his body cutting through the shaft of sunlight as he reached up and took her face between his hands. "What if I asked you to leave with me now? What if I asked you to come away from here and sail with me to France?"

Her eyes grew even more impossibly wider, bluer. "France?"

"I have friends in Paris; we could stay there until things settled down again. This will all be over in a month, two at the utmost."

The brief shimmer of hope that had flared in her eyes faded again. Her sense of disbelief and confusion was as easy to read as nearly every other volatile emotion that crossed her face, and for once Angus wished she could be more like the Adrienne de Boules of the world, a blank page on which nothing was written that one did not want to see.

"This is my home," she said, reaching up to gently but firmly extricate herself from his grasp. "It is where I belong. Running away will not change anything, nor will it do anything to breach this wall you have thrown up between us."

Her rejection, her condemnation cut him to the bone, and he doubted she would listen now even if he did attempt to explain that the wall had been put there deliberately to try to save her from the very pain she was feeling now.

He stared at her mouth, remembering how willing and eager it had been to answer his whispered pleas only two brief nights ago. How in God's name was he supposed to just turn around and walk out that door knowing that if he did so, she would hate him? How would he be able to close his eyes again and not see her, not hear her, not be haunted by the image of her body moving urgently beneath his?

His arms dropped down by his sides. "I'm sorry. I should have known better than to ... well, I just should have known better. Please forgive me, and forgive this intrusion. I will not disturb you again."

"Angus——?"

"All things considered," he added curtly, "perhaps it is for the best that you stay here. There are no battlements or cannon mounted on the walls of Drummuir House, but I warrant you will be safer here with my mother blocking the doors than you would be anywhere else. And ... if you can ... I suggest you get a message to MacGillivray; convince him to remove himself from Dunmaglass for a while. He might not be too open to taking advice from me at the moment, but Worsham is as bloody-minded as they come, and it would be wise if John put himself out of reach."

"I will send a warning to him," she said, bowing her head, refusing to let him see how close she was to tears. "Thank you."

"Do not thank me, Anne. If he was standing before me right now I would be more inclined to give him to Worsham myself than expose you to any further risk."

Startled, she looked up into his face, but there was nothing there to ease the tightness in her chest. The mask was firmly in place, his eyes so cool and distant she could scarcely believe he had just asked her to run away with him to France.

The constricting pressure became too much to bear and she turned her face away, missing the action of his hand as it rose toward her shoulder. It stopped the width of a prayer away from touching her before the long, tapered fingers curled into a tight fist and withdrew.

"If you need anything while I'm gone, you know where I keep the strongbox."

"I will be fine. I bid you have a safe journey to Edinburgh. An unsuccessful one, to be sure, but safe."

He studied her profile, saw the bright jewel of a tear trembling at the corner of her eye, and he knew if he did not leave at once, that very moment, he would not be able to leave at all.

"If there is nothing more—?"

"No," she whispered. "There is nothing more we need to say to each other."

Angus nodded. Moving woodenly, he retrieved his hat and gloves from the chair, then glanced back at the window. Anne had not moved. She stood fully in the path of the sunbeam, the light turning her skin luminous, gilding the flown wisps of her hair fiery red and gold.

"Shall I write from Edinburgh?"

"If it pleases you to do so."

He expelled a breath and put his hand on the doorknob. "I'll write, then."

The door opened easily enough but his feet could not seem to make it fully across the threshold without stopping again.

"Anne . . . I know I have been somewhat of a disappointment to you lately, that I have likely not proven to be the husband of your dreams. But regardless of what happens or does not happen in the coming weeks, I do not want to leave without telling you that I have considered myself a very lucky man these past four years. Extraordinarily lucky, in fact, and I . . . I want to thank you for that. Perhaps some day, when this is over, you might even be able to find it in your heart to forgive me."

Anne said nothing—she could not; she was crying too hard—and a moment later, the door clicked softly shut behind him.

Chapter Nine

John MacGillivray woke to the sound of whispered voices. They were low and indistinct, clouded by the quantity of harsh spirits he had downed the night before. He had barely made it home to Dunmaglass from Culloden, and when he'd stripped off his blood-soaked waistcoat and shirt and seen the torn stitches, he had known there was only one way to seal the raw edges of flesh. As luck would have it, he had found Gillies MacBean curled up on the floor in front of the hearth fire, his plaid wrapped around his shoulders, the prodigious depth of his snores indicating he had not been sleeping long. Following the skirmish with the English soldiers, it had been his duty to escort Fearchar Farquharson deeper into the hills and to settle him with a strong guard of clansmen. Jamie Farquharson had returned to Dunmaglass with Gillies and was stretched out beside him on the hearth, his plaid likewise pulled over his head.

Before the whisky had taken hold of MacGillivray's senses, he had ordered Gillies to thrust the blade of a knife into the fire and heat it red hot. When the steel was glowing and the bottle of whisky was empty, John had gripped the side of the table and ordered Jamie to hold his arms. He had snarled at MacBean to do it right the first time, for he had his hand on his sword, a fine pistol on his hip, and he would not hesitate to use them on the two fools if they blundered.

The smell of burning skin and sizzling blood had set every iron-hard muscle to trembling, every nerve screaming, but the pain had been mercifully brief before he had slumped forward into a drunken stupor.

Now he was hearing the whispers. They overlapped and seemed to echo within themselves, the words becoming a muddle of shushes and wheeshts and soft feminine sighs. He remained very still, afraid to open his eyes lest he find himself suspended on white clouds with heaven above and the fires of hell below and a flock of serious-minded seraphs debating whither he be sent, up or down.

Something icy cool touched his forehead and he opened his eyes a slit, relieved to see no bright lights, no diaphanous wings hovering over him. The whispering had stopped as well, but he sensed he was not quite in the clear yet, for there was a lingering specter standing by the side of the bed. For half an eternity, he just stared. If it wasn't an angel then it was something sent by the devil: a wee spookie his mother used to call them, a vision of something you dreamed about so long or wanted so badly that the devil used it to torment your soul.

His own personal chimera was just standing there looking down at him. Her face was a pale oval in the lamplight, her hair spilled around her shoulders in a shimmer of flames. She wore a white shirt and men's trews, and he could see where her breasts pushed softly against the cambric, unhindered by any foolish whalebone garments.

If it was a vision, it was real enough to tempt his hand upward. And when his hand encountered solid flesh, he could no more control the desire to pull her down beside him than he could the need to draw her beneath him and sink his flesh into her until the vision faded and disappeared.

Anne gasped when she felt MacGillivray's hand close around her wrist. Having been assured by Gillies MacBean that he was still sleeping his way through a heavy fog of whisky, she had remained behind a moment, intending only to straighten the covers he had thrown off and perhaps take a cloth to the beads of moisture that gleamed on his brow. She had felt no signs of fever when she touched his skin, but standing this close to the bed she had seen what the shadows and disheveled covers had shielded from the view she'd had inside the doorway.

His entire left side was exposed in a magnificent display of strength and sinewed power, from his shoulder down the extraordinary length of his body to his toes. His chest might have been chiseled out of solid granite, his arms and shoulders of oak. His legs were furred with hair as blond as that on his head, with tufts of copper sprouting at his armpits, thicker and darker at his groin. Nesting there was evidence that the rumors she'd heard about his prowess had more than a little foundation in fact. And there was where her gaze stalled and her breath stopped, for even as she watched, his flesh began to stir and grow.

When his fingers curled around her wrist, she was sufficiently off balance to offer no resistance as she was pulled forward and down onto the bed beside him. The startled cry that formed in her throat was smothered when his mouth crushed over hers, and no sooner did she part her lips to attempt another cry, than his tongue launched an instant, lusty invasion. She tried to twist free, but he was already rolling on top of her, trapping her legs beneath his, and trying to push against him was like trying to push a mountain out of the way—one with determined hands, hot lips, and a shockingly huge protrusion of flesh that was already jutting thick between her thighs.

His tongue swept her mouth and probed deep on each thrust, reducing her cries to strangled gasps. When he shifted, cursing the trews that proved a stronger deterrent than her frustrated cries, she renewed her struggles and this time, the heel of her hand caught him high on the wounded shoulder, causing him to jerk back with a roar of pain.

For the moment it took his senses to clear, he glared down at her, his lips drawn back in a primal snarl. The long golden locks of his hair had fallen forward, the ends tickling her cheek, the denser mass near the scalp throwing up more shadows to mask his face from the light, but there was enough to see his expression turn from rapine lust to blinking confusion.

"Annie? Ye're real, then?"

"Of course I'm real, you great oaf. Heave off me!"

"Christ," he gasped, easing back. "Christ, Annie . . . I'm

sorry. I didna ken . . . I mean, I thought ye were . . . For the love o' God, what's that stench?"

"I am afraid the stench is of your own making," she said, glancing pointedly at the blackened flesh over his wound. Glistening under the shiny layer of unguent Gillies had applied to ward off infection, the smell was similar to that of rotted fish.

He released her at once and, seeing how further disturbed the covers had become, snatched them hastily above his waist. Anne wriggled free. With her mouth still wet and pulsing with the taste of him, she scrambled clumsily off the bed and retreated to a safe distance. There she attempted to cover her embarrassment by tugging her clothes back into order.

John rolled onto his back and gazed around the room in further bewilderment. "This is ma bedroom, is it no'?"

Anne cast an acerbic eye around the piles of clothing thrown hither and yon, the half-full slop jar at the side of the bed, the globs of congealed wax on the table where oil and a good scrubbing stone had rarely ventured. "It would appear so."

"What the devil are ye doin' here? What time is it?"

"It is past four in the afternoon, and I've come from Drummuir House to return a favor."

"A favor?"

Something glimmered briefly in his eyes and Anne quashed it with a frown. "Not that kind of favor, blast you. Sober yourself! I've come to return the favor of the warning you gave me last night."

He scratched a hand through his hair, leaving a bright plume standing straight up over his right eye. "Warning? Wait, wait. Turn yer back, lass, an' give me a chance to find ma claythes."

She saw his kilt draped over a chair and tossed it to him before she headed for the door. "When you're decent, come down the stairs and I'll bandage your shoulder proper. In the meantime, you might want to give your head—and something else as well—a soak in cold water."

A muffled Gaelic curse, graphic enough to make her smile, followed Annie as she descended the stairs. Gillies was there, bending over the fire. Two other clansmen lurked in the

corner with Donuil MacKintosh, the young man sent by the
dowager to escort Anne to Dunmaglass. Outside, the yard
bristled with more clansmen. Taking no chances this time,
there were men in the forest and up on the hillside; the outer
ring of sentries had been expanded far beyond the steep and
rocky nipples of Garbhal Beg and Garbhal Mor to provide
ample warning of anyone approaching the glen.

"Will ye take an ale, m'lady?" Gillies asked, straightening
when she came into the room.

"I will. But only if you stop calling me 'my lady.' The way
you say it, I want to look over my shoulder and see who has
come into the room."

Gillies reddened and grinned. "Aye. I'll do that."

"Annie," she prompted.

"Aye," he murmured. "Annie."

Jamie Farquharson held out his own tankard. "I'll take another
dram, if ye're tippin' the crock. Ma throat's dry as a dusty fart."

"Then you'd best have coffee, if that's what I smell boiling
over the fire. And you'd best get it while you have the chance, for
I've a mind the laird of the house will be needing the entire kettle
before he can make a proper count of his fingers."

"A pox on coffee," came MacGillivray's bellicose voice
from the bottom of the stairs. "I'll have an ale as well."

He strode into the room, his footsteps heavy and dragging,
one eye closed, the other glowing red with burst veins.

Anne took up a tin cup and ladled steaming black coffee
out of the kettle, setting it in front of him as he slouched into
a chair at the table. "I need you with a clear head, John. You
can get sotted again later, after I've left."

"Ye sound like ma old mam," he grumbled, but took a
grudging sip.

While he muttered his way through two cups of coffee and
a dozen fried eggs, Anne found a linen sheet and tore it into
strips. She carefully bathed his wound, then applied a fresh
coating of lard and crushed willow ash before wrapping the
bandages. By the time he had drained his third cup and
finished half a plate of oatcakes, his eyes were more white
than red and his skin had lost some of its greenish tinge.

"All right, lass," he said. "I've chased the demons out o'
ma blood; will ye speak at me the now?"

She wiped her hands and went to fetch her woolen short-coat from the hook. Tucked into the quilted lining was the bundled sheaf of dispatches she had taken from Duncan Forbes's desk. She had felt no qualms lying to Angus when he'd asked her if she still had them, for if she had admitted they were not two feet away, strapped to her thigh, she was not altogether sure he would not have tossed her robe over her head and taken them.

When she set the leather-bound packet on the table in front of John MacGillivray, he took a final sip of coffee and wiped his lips on his cuff.

"What's this, then?"

"Can you read French?"

He snatched the papers up with a frown. *"Bien sûr je peux lire français, Mademoiselle Haut Âne.* Latin, too, if ye have need of a few scriptures read to cleanse ye of the sin o' pride."

"I only ask," she explained, wary of his belligerent mood, "because I can barely speak enough words to say good morning and good night. The dowager read these aloud, and we were neither one of us entirely sure if we understood what they mean, but if we're right, and if you interpret them to mean the same thing, then we must get these papers to the prince as fast as ever we can."

He studied her a moment longer, his eyes probing hers with a thoroughness that left her as breathless as the kiss had earlier.

"Fetch the light closer," he said to Jamie, and reached for the leather-bound packet. A flick of his thumb and forefinger unfastened the ribbon binding the edges of hide, and only when he drew out the folded sheets of paper did he release his visual hold on Anne and look down.

Jamie slid the lamp closer and turned up the wick without waiting to be asked. Both he and Gillies had taken chairs around the table, the latter craning his neck to see the words, though to him they were nothing more than scratches on a page.

John read through the documents once, skimming over some of the phrases that were too complex for the initial pass. But when he read it a second time, then a third, he not only sounded out every syllable, he mouthed each word in soundless disbelief.

He finished and glanced over at Anne. "Where did ye get this?"

She told him, and he stared until a blink returned his thoughts to what he held in his hands. "What did ye think it meant when ye read it?"

Anne moistened her lips, warmed by the excitement she had seen gleaming in his eyes. "I think it means a treaty has been signed between the French and the Dutch, that the Dutch have pledged not to raise arms against the French for a period of no less than two years, during which time the countries will work together to negotiate amicable terms for a permanent peace."

John nodded. "Aye, that's how I read it."

Jamie lifted an eyebrow. "An' so? The French an' Dutch have made a treaty. What of it?"

Anne shuffled through the sheaf of documents she had retained—the extra documents she had taken from the Lord President's desk—until she found the one she wanted, then separated it from the rest.

"These are memoranda listing the approximate number of men in each division of the government's armies. The Duke of Cumberland, for instance, boasts a complement of eight thousand men, all veterans he brought back with him from Flanders. Among them he claims Dutch regiments numbering upward of six thousand men."

Jamie scratched his beard. "Aye, an' so?"

"So," MacGillivray said, beginning to grin. "Cumberland's forces are the only ones who have seen actual battle; the raw recruits servin' under Wade an' Ligonier an' Hawley have spent most o' their time marchin' on parade grounds an' shootin' melons off o' fence posts. That was why most o' them turned tail an' ran at Prestonpans; they'd never seen a bloody battlefield, nor stood eye to eye with a man who was chargin' at them full bore, eager to gut him on the end of his sword. I'm no' sayin' they're any less of a threat for it; sheer numbers put them at five, six times the size o' the prince's army, an' sooner or later their bullets hit their marks, but in the time it takes them to find their steel, Cumberland's Dutchmen could cut us down by half."

Jamie nodded as if he understood, then glanced surreptitiously at Gillies, who shrugged.

"It means," Anne explained, "that without the Dutch brigades, Cumberland would be gelded. And if the French and Dutch have signed a treaty, it means the Dutch can no longer engage in any act of war against any of France's allies"—she paused and spread her arms wide—"which includes us."

"Ye mean they canna fight the prince?"

"Not unless they want to break the treaty."

MacGillivray rubbed a hand across his jaw. "No wonder Forbes was anxious to lock the news away. It could take weeks for word of the treaty to cross the Channel; longer still for either Holland or France to send an official representative. By then, the battles might all have been fought. Aye, Annie, ye're right. We must get this to the prince at once. Jamie, lad, with a fast horse beneath ye, how long would it take ye to make Aberdeen?"

"Aberdeen?" Anne frowned. "But the prince's army is west, not east."

"Ye're a day behind in yer news, lass. Clunas sent word last night that Lord Lewis Gordon is in Aberdeen gatherin' another army to ride out an' join forces with the prince."

"Aberdeen," she whispered. "That must be why Colonel Loudoun is sending reinforcements to Edinburgh, and why he told them they must hold the city and keep it out of rebel hands."

"How do ye know this?"

"Angus has orders to take his Royal Scots regiments to Edinburgh before week's end."

In the bitter silence that followed, Gillies softly muttered, "Mary, Mother o' Jesus."

"Jamie! Have yer boots grown roots into the floor?"

Farquharson's head snapped around in response to MacGillivray's voice, which came out in a far more commanding bellow. "Nay. I'll leave soon as ma horse is saddled."

"Go by way of Clunas an' tell Fearchar what ye're about; he may know a quicker way to get word to the prince. Take a dozen o' ma men with ye an' stop for no one. Strap this packet to yer waist an' guard it like it was yer manhood. Ye want those to go as well?" he asked Anne, pointing to the papers spread in front of her.

"Yes. Yes, of course they would be of more value to . . . to . . ." She stopped, moistened her lips and pushed deliberately to her feet. "I also want you to take a personal message to Granda', Jamie. I want you to tell him I've changed my mind. If he still has the petition, and if he still thinks the lairds will agree to follow me, then I'll gather what MacKintosh men I can and lead them to Aberdeen to join the prince's army."

All three men froze and gaped at her.

"Ye will?" Jamie asked eagerly. "Ye'll send out the *crosh tarie* an' lead the clan to war?"

"I don't know about burning crosses, but I'll do what I can to plead, bribe, or threaten every man of honor left in Invernesshire to join us. There is just one thing, however," she added, raising her voice to ward off the anticipated burst of howling. "We all know there is no petition on earth would see them agree to follow a woman onto the battlefield, and because of this"—she stopped and held MacGillivray's black gaze locked to her own— "we will only succeed if John MacGillivray rides by my side and agrees to take full command."

Like following the play of a ball tossed back and forth, the bearded faces of Gillies and Jamie swung around to join her in staring at MacGillivray. He had thrown a shirt over his bandaged chest but had not bothered to tie the laces. His kilt had been pleated in haste, his hair was uncombed and still stuck straight out like the mane of a lion, but his jaw was set and his eyes fierce, making Anne wonder how any mere Englishman could see such a fearsome sight across a battlefield—multiplied several thousandfold—and not run away screaming in terror.

"Will you do it, John?" she asked. "Will you fight for Scotland?"

"No."

His answer so startled her that she was bereft of speech for the full minute it took him to refold the dispatches and tie them back into the leather pouch.

"No," he repeated on a quiet sigh. "But I will fight for what Scotland means to you."

It took a further heartbeat for the words to sink in, but when they did, both Gillies and Jamie gave off a hoot of joy. They roared and stomped their feet, they leaped in circles and clapped hands to each other's shoulders, dancing an impromptu reel to imaginary pipes. The two clansmen half dozing in the corner were drawn into the ruckus, as was Donuil MacKintosh, yet while the shouting and cheering swirled around them, Anne and MacGillivray were still staring at one another across the width of the table, the air seeming to hum between them.

" 'Tis the same thing, is it not?" she asked with a small frown.

He shook his head. "No' the now. But mayhap by the time we reach a battlefield, it will be."

Chapter Ten

On December 20, Charles Edward Stuart crossed the River Esk and led his army back into Scotland. Men of every rank fell on their knees after they forded the icy waters, giving thanks to their God, their king, and their prince for bringing them safely home.

With the English no more than a day's march behind them, the prince divided his ragtag troops into two divisions. He led one across the high, mountainous route to Glasgow, while his commanding general, Lord George Murray, led the second and was forced to take the longer, slower route by way of the low roads, for they also hauled munition wagons and what few cannon they had not spiked and left on the other side of the river.

Fully half the Stuart army was barefoot, their clothes reduced to rags, their bellies sunk against their spines. Still, they were the stuff of legends. Five thousand poorly provisioned, ill-equipped Highlanders had outwitted and outmaneuvered the combined forces of Generals Wade, Ligonier, and Cumberland.

Conservative estimates put the government forces at close to thirty thousand, converging from three different directions and heading north into Scotland to avenge the insult to their king and country. Some days the plumes of smoke from the advance campfires of Wade's army could be seen by the retreating vanguard of the prince's troops.

Two things slowed the progress of the Elector's troops, then halted it altogether. A hellish storm struck just after the Jacobites crossed the river, pelting the English with snow and sleet, raising the level of the already turbulent waters higher than even the most foolhardy commander would dare attempt to ford. Secondly, the Duke of Cumberland received an urgent dispatch from London, warning him of a massive fleet of French ships bound for the northeast coast. Cumberland removed himself from the chase at once and ordered Ligonier to the old fortress city of York, knowing all too well that if the French were ever allowed to gain a toehold on English soil, it could extend the war by months.

The "urgent message" had in fact come from the pen of a gray-haired old fox who had drifted off to sleep twice while composing it, and the only French ship that landed did so well north of where Cumberland anxiously watched the coastline. While the battered old frigate did carry troops, they amounted to fewer than three hundred who served in the personal guard of Lord John Drummond. Of more pressing value to the Jacobites gathering at Aberdeen were the guns and ammunition in her holds, along with the four chests of gold Drummond had managed, at long last, to prise from the French king's coffers.

Jamie Farquharson arrived in Aberdeen while the ship was still offloading its cargo. Upon reading the documents he carried and realizing the significance of the Dutch treaty, Lord Drummond immediately removed his blockade runner's garb and declared himself the official representative of King Louis in Scotland. As such, he sent formal notice to the commander of the six thousand Dutch veterans serving under the Duke of Cumberland, advising him to return home at once lest he violate the terms of the new treaty.

Cumberland was understandably furious as he watched nearly three quarters of his veteran troops march out of camp. Moreover, at the end of a futile three-week vigil, with nary a French sail in sight, he was forced to acknowledge that he had been duped. This time, when the enraged duke turned his eyes and army north to Scotland, he did so with a vow to carry his royal cousin's head to London and leave it spiked on the gates of his father's palace until the flesh rotted and fell off the bone.

Colin Mor heard sounds in the glen long before he ventured out of doors to identify them. Hearing what started as a low, distant rumble, he had initially closed the shutters against an approaching storm. But when the disturbance grew louder and closer, it started breaking into patterns that were distinctly man-made; the rolling of wheels on the rutted earth, the shuffle of many footsteps, the creak of saddle leather and the muted jingle of harness traces.

Colin stood outside his clachan, the door open and tilted on its rope hinges. Dusk had come early on this January evening, and there was just enough ambient light to turn the heavy mist into a gray, soupy miasma. Cold and wet, the fog had settled into the bowl of the glen earlier and rendered anything beyond the reach of a child's throw opaque. It was certainly not the kind of night that would inspire travel, nor was Colin's tiny glen anywhere near a main thoroughfare. His small sheep farm was, as his wife often lamented, in the middle of nowhere, with high craggy peaks to the north, dense tracts of fir trees to the east and west, and a swampy elbow of the River Dee at their backs. The closest kirk was Kildrummy, with the city of Aberdeen another thirty miles down the river.

His wife, Rose, was standing behind him now, a bairn on her hip, two more clinging to her skirts.

"What is it, Colla?" she asked in a terrified whisper.

He shook his head, tilting it to one side as if that would help him hear more clearly. The fog was distorting the sound and the direction, making it nearly impossible to tell if there were ten men or a hundred, if they were a hundred paces away or ten. He did not have to work half so hard to hear Rose's fearful breaths puffing into the mist; she was superstitious and had seen a raven with a bloody beak fly over the cottage earlier in the day. It was a clear harbinger, so she said, that death would be coming to their door.

"Take the bairns an' get back inside," he ordered quietly. "Tell ma sister tae ready the trapdoor."

"Holy mither, ye dinna think it's the English sojers, dae ye?"

The thought had occurred to him, but he dismissed it almost as fast. Nearby Inverurie Castle was a Jacobite stronghold and the *Sassenachs* had not proven to be stupid enough to wander too deeply into the thickly wooded glens thereabout. Moreover, with news of Wade and Cumberland's forced delay, most of the government troops had been withdrawn to Edinburgh.

"Just get inside an' be ready tae stow yerselves in the hidey-hole if need be."

He waited until she had gone, then edged closer to the corner of the low-slung roof of his clachan. His firelock was hidden beneath the thatch, an arm's reach away, as was his *taugh-cath*, an ax forged in the hills of Lochaber. The musket was kept loaded, but it had rained earlier in the day and the powder would be damp. Or it might be just dry enough to misfire and take out his eye; then how well would he be able to protect his wife and family? Only last week he'd heard of a good woman raped by the English and left naked for her husband to find when he came home from the fields. And just last month he'd had to bury a brace of *Sassenachs* in a nearby bog after they had insultingly offered his sister a penny to spread her legs for them. The slut had been willing and the penny would have been welcomed, but he reasoned their purses would yield more if they were dead.

This sounded like far too many for the bog to hold.

Perhaps whoever it was would ride past. His sod clachan was built into the hillside and was difficult to see even in bright sunlight. Perhaps there was no one out there at all; no one in human form, at any rate. . . .

As if the druids had read his mind, the enormous rumbling slowed, then stopped altogether.

Something detached itself from the main body and plodded slowly forward. The gray of the mist took on the sickly yellow tinge of a torch that throbbed and bloomed into a larger circle, pushing great swirls of mist forward, bathing Colin's face with the wet stink of pitch.

His hand inched upward toward the thatch roofing.

"Is this the home of Colin Mor?"

The sound of a woman's voice froze his hand, froze his mind.

"Colin Mor of Dalziel?"

His lips parted, but no sound came forth as a huge black-eyed monster began to emerge from the banks of gray swirling mist. He held his breath as the beast took on the shape and substance of a huge mottled gelding; his eyes widened almost beyond their limits when he saw the woman perched high upon its back. She wore tartan trews and a green velvet short coat trimmed with gold lace. Her hair was red as hellfire, braided into a long tail that snaked over one shoulder, and on her head a bonnet with an eagle feather pinned on the crest. At her waist she wore a brace of claw-butted dags and, slung across her lap, glinted the metal barrel of a Brown Bess.

Colin's jaw dropped farther.

Word had spread throughout the bens and glens that Lady Anne MacKintosh had taken it upon herself to raise her clan to fight for Prince Charles. No sooner had her husband departed for Edinburgh to fight for the English than she was riding about the countryside, carrying her petition to every laird within the confederation of Clan Chattan.

His gaze flicked to the pulsating orange and yellow glow behind her. There were three more riders, two of whom held torches aloft, the flames causing the suspended droplets of mist to sizzle and hiss. He looked at the two bearded faces, identical in almost every way, and surmised they must be the infamous lady's cousins from Monaltrie. The third man, the great blond giant who halted his steed alongside Lady Anne's, needed no introduction either, and Colin felt a ripple of raw excitement flare through his loins.

"Colin Mor?"

"Aye," he rasped. "Aye, that I be."

"You know who I am?"

"Aye." Awe rended his answer all but inaudible.

"We have been riding since dawn, Colin Mor," Anne said. "And we would be grateful for your hospitality if we could camp in your pasture for the night."

Colin's chest swelled with pride. "God's truth, an' the

honor would be mine, Colonel Anne. I've nae much tae offer, but there's stew left frae supper—hot an' hearty—an' a cask o' ale, fresh brewed."

"Our men have food enough," Anne said, smiling her thanks. "But if you could spare a seat by your fire until the tents are raised, I would not refuse the warmth."

The crofter shed his timorousness upon the instant and hastened forward, wiping his palms dry before he took hold of the gelding's bridle. "Ye'll nae sleep in any paucy tent this night, ma lady. No' while I've a roof an' a bed tae offer. Aye, an' there's room on the floor f'ae the rest o' yer men, sure."

The MacGillivray swung his leg over the saddle and dismounted. He strode toward Colin, his hand outstretched, and the clansmen felt his fingers crush together, his knuckles crack with the heartiness of the greeting.

"Ye've room for six hundred men on yer floor?" he asked with a leonine grin.

"Six . . . ?"

MacGillivray laughed at the crofter's stunned expression and turned long enough to bark an order to make camp. The order was relayed mouth to mouth, traveling back like an unending echo.

Colin Mor could count no higher than the twenty-three sheep he penned each night, and even that required using some imaginative appendages for keeping track, but he thought, by the sound of it, he might have to crack open two kegs of ale.

MacGillivray reached up to assist Anne out of the saddle. Though she would have torn her tongue out by the root before admitting it, her rump felt like lead and her thighs ached so badly she prayed she did not humiliate herself by walking with permanently bowed legs. They had been on the road for two days, battling every element nature could throw at them: high winds and bitter cold in the mountain passes, rain and mud on the moorlands. The mist had started closing in an hour ago, and for the past mile or so, they'd been riding blind, guided only by sheep tracks leading through the glen.

Through it all, the men sang and laughed and joked

amongst themselves. At each crossroad, each cairn they passed marking the miles from Inverness, there were more men waiting to join them, all eager and spoiling for the long-awaited chance to fight for Scotland's honor.

With MacGillivray by her side, Anne had carried her petition to every laird within Clan Chattan. A few were understandably reluctant to openly defy their chief, but in the end, she had come away with ninety-seven signatures, shy of the requisite hundred by only three. Scores of tents and campfires had littered the open fields around Dunmaglass, for MacGillivray's stronghold had become their headquarters and gathering place. Out of necessity, Anne had left Drummuir House and taken up residence at Dunmaglass, surrounded and protected by a personal guard that included John, Gillies MacBean, at least two of her three cousins—the third, usually Eneas since the twins did not like to be separated for long, rode back and forth to Aberdeen conveying messages to and from Fearchar—and never any fewer than twenty armed clansmen bristling with weaponry.

The wound in MacGillivray's shoulder had healed remarkably swiftly, with no apparent lingering stiffness. If anything, she marveled daily at his strength, watching him practice in mock battles with his men in the mornings, slashing the great steel blade of his to and fro until his face ran with sweat. Afternoons were spent going farm to farm assuring the other lairds he was more than capable of assuming a battlefield command. Evenings he supervised the small armory that had taken over the main room of Dunmaglass. Guns, targes, and swords filled every inch of empty space, with men hunched over long trestle tables day and night working with lead molds to make shot, others with casks of black powder to measure and fill paper cartridges.

Most men had come into the glen with swords and pikes, some with muskets and Lochaber axes, but there were those who came with just their hearts and their pride, and to supply these men, Anne had emptied the strongbox at Moy Hall. MacGillivray had put each coin to good use, and when there were no more guns or casks of powder to be purchased through his fellow smugglers, he had slipped away in the dead of night with a dozen of his best men, returning before morning with wagons filled with kegs and crates stamped with the seal of the British army quartermaster.

He never seemed to sleep, never even looked tired. If anything he appeared to be more relaxed, as if the weight of the responsibilities he carried now was not half so oppressing as the weight of being able to do nothing at all.

Anne, on the other hand, came to know exactly how her grandfather felt when the burden of holding her eyelids open for one more moment became a near impossible task. Sheer necessity had bade her move from Drummuir House to Dunmaglass, but it was not a house accustomed to female residents. The furnishings were spartan at best, the only bath a large wooden barrel cut in half. She had clothes sent from Moy Hall, but it soon became evident that skirts and a corset were a definite hindrance. She had not felt a scrap of silk against her skin, nor plied a pair of tongs to her hair since she had departed the dowager's house on Church Street. She was surrounded day and night by burly men who had taken to addressing her as Colonel Anne, and she had begun to answer without pause.

In truth, the first few days had been exhilarating. Riding out with MacGillivray and her cousins had brought back all the adventurous memories of her reckless youth. But now, a fortnight later, the days had simply become exhausting and dirty. The coarse woolen trews itched at the most inopportune times and in the most inconvenient places, and while men appeared to have no qualms about scratching whenever, wherever, she was forced to suffer in squirming silence. Similarly, she had never given much thought to Angus's reluctance to intrude on her when he was fresh from the stable smelling of horse, leather, and sweat. Now she noticed everything—the smell of unwashed wool when it was wet, the tang of sheep offal on a carelessly placed shoe, the pungent blend of body sweat, peat, and woodsmoke that clung to common clansmen who might think to bathe only once in a twelvemonth.

That was possibly why she had begun to notice MacGillivray's distinctive scent. While he was by no means as fastidious as Angus with hot water and soap, he was not hesitant to strip down after a morning of exercising with the men and dump a bucket of water over his body to rinse away the sweat. Anne had happened by a window once when he was in the process of doing just that, and it had caused her to stare so long and hard her eyes burned from the dryness. The fact there had been a dozen men stripped naked and standing in the snow tossing water at each other had hardly left an imprint on her mind. It had been the sight of John MacGillivray, tall and sleek with muscle, his face tilted upward and his hair streaming golden and wet down his shoulders, that had warmed her cheeks and left her body tingling in all the wrong places.

It had been equally difficult not to remember how he had looked naked and sprawled out in the candlelight, or how those brawny arms had felt wrapped around her, pinning her to the bed. Harder still not to recall all that heat and strength crowding her against the wall of a booth at the fairground, his hands pressing boldly between her thighs, daring them to open that she might feel what else he had to offer.

It did not help her concentration either that he was rather cavalier about his dress. In the comfort of his own home he favored little more than a long, loose fitting shirt and short breacan kilt. The former was often left unlaced, the edges parted carelessly over the reddish gold mat of hair that covered his chest. Nor was he reluctant to slip one of his large hands beneath the cambric and scratch absently at a rib or breast while he was engaged in a conversation with his men, and she suspected he was completely unaware of the effect when he raked his fingers through his hair and left the golden mane scattered and boyishly disheveled.

He smelled wonderful as well, for it was a rare occasion that found John MacGillivray without a cigar clamped between his teeth. Pipes were as commonplace as dirks and dags in a man's belt, but cigars were an extravagant luxury, one of the few he indulged himself as a reasonably wealthy laird. It was also one he kept to himself despite the often blatant hints from the Farquharson twins that they might enjoy a draw with their evening tankards of ale. He ignored any and all appeals to his sense of hospitality, and in spite of a thorough—and decidedly ill-bred—search of the cabinets and cupboards of Dunmaglass, the lads could not discover where he hoarded his supply.

Anne found the scent heady and at times uncomfortably arousing, especially if he happened to be seated at the table while engaged in a debate, his chair tilted precariously back on the two hind legs, a glare on his face like that of a lion contemplating his next meal. Or when he leaned close to look at something over her shoulder and she could feel the silk of his hair on her cheek, the warmth of his breath on her skin.

Or when she was cold and tired and her legs ached with cramps from riding all day, and he stood beside her, his arm remaining around her waist for support while she wobbled and chose to lean against him rather than slide into a heap on the ground.

"If ye'll come this way, Colonel Anne," said Colin Mor, bowing awkwardly as he held a hand out toward the door of his cottage, "ma wife Rose will be glad tae pour ye a dram o' hot broth tae warm yer bones."

Anne started and looked guiltily away from the smile that had begun to cross MacGillivray's face. How long had she been staring up at him? Had she had another "Fearchar" lapse in concentration? The big Highlander was proving to be every bit as adept as Angus in reading her thoughts, and while it could sometimes be a wonderful thing for a husband to know when his wife was craving certain . . . attentions . . . she did not think it was particularly wise to pique MacGillivray's interest.

Her hands, she noticed, were braced with easy familiarity on John's chest and she lowered them quickly before turning to follow Colin Mor into the cottage. His wife had already re-lit the lamp and a couple of thick tallow candles; she stood nervously back in the shadows, the children still clinging to her legs, peeking out from behind her skirts. A second woman, a year or so younger, was standing against the wall. She bore such a strong resemblance to Colin Mor it came as no surprise when she was introduced as his sister Glenna.

The clachan was like a thousand others that dotted the glens and nestled into the hillsides. A bare earth floor supported timber walls fortified with muck and peat, and a steeply canted roof from which hung strips of dried, salted meat and fish. There was the usual assortment of household trappings. A rough straw divider at one end separated the narrow sleeping pallet used by Colin's sister from the larger one he shared with his wife and children. The cooking fire was in the center of the room and on it, a tripod from which hung a black iron kettle. The Mors were better off than most, for in addition to several woven rag rugs, they had a table and two benches. In one corner a pen held chickens, and in another a milk goat was tethered to a post.

"A thousand pardons for disturbing your evening, goodwife," Anne said in Gaelic. "We were told your glen had a sweet burn running through it that would lead us right the way to the river. Unfortunately, we could not find the burn in the mist and were afraid our wagons would find the river without any warning. We smelled the smoke from your fire, and . . ." She waved a hand to indicate the natural progression of events, but the woman just stared.

"I ken who ye are," Rose whispered, her initial awe over their guests replaced by the more practical emotion of fear. "An' I ken why ye're here. Ye've come tae take ma Colin awa' tae war."

"No," Anne said carefully. "We've not come to take him away. He is free to join us if he wishes, but we will not force any man to come with us. Each must listen to his own heart and decide the best way to serve his family, his clan, his honor."

"Aye, well." The girl bit her lip and glanced down at the wooden cradle. "Ye put it that way, he'll no' be able tae refuse, will he?"

She turned her back, startling the two smaller children into scrambling to reposition themselves as she leaned over to pick up the fussing baby and settle it back over her hip. "Will ye have broth, or a mug o' ale? There's rabbit stew as well. Glenna can fetch it f'ae ye, if ye're of a mind."

"A cup of broth would be very welcomed, but I do not want to put you to any trouble."

" 'Tis too late f'ae that now." She paused and glanced past Anne's shoulder as MacGillivray ducked his head beneath the low lintel and came into the cottage, followed closely by the Farquharson twins. "Ye've brung the trouble wi' ye."

Seeing the handsome trio, Glenna Mor showed a reaction for the first time, straightening and squaring her shoulders so

that her breasts pushed round and full against her bodice.
There was an inordinately large amount to push, and the
twins' gaze stalled there long enough for John to give them
both a clout on the shoulder.

"Like I said," the wife muttered. "Looks like ye've brung
the trouble wi' ye."

Anne had been determined to repress all memories of the incident in MacGillivray's bedroom. The kiss had meant nothing. Nor had it in any way been a conscious effort on his part
to seduce her. He had still been half drunk from the previous
night, scarcely accountable for his actions. Yet it was difficult
to ignore the effect his presence had on other women. The
trull, Glenna Mor, all but fell over herself to serve him his ale
and ladle the choicest bits of meat into his wooden bowl. The
lacings on her bodice miraculously loosened from one turn to
the next so that each time she leaned forward, he had an impressive view of her breasts. And being a hot-blooded male,
he noticed. More than once, Anne caught him staring un-
abashedly at the succulent offerings, his one brow slightly
raised in speculation, his mouth curved in a lopsided grin.
Robbie was less circumspect. He practically had to keep his
hands in his lap to prevent his kilt from tenting each time she
brushed his shoulder or gave him a sly wink. While Anne had
no right to be angered by the innocent flirtations, she felt as
bristly as a hedgehog and found herself wanting to reach
across the table and slap them all silly.

It wasn't fair. She might have been able to abide the sloe-
eyed glances and smiles and swaying hips with somewhat
more tolerance had her husband been beside her. As it was,
each time the girl's bodice gaped, she felt her own breasts
chafing against the constraints of her cambric shirt; each time
the wench ran her fingers through her hair and flirted openly
with John or the twins, Anne thought of the tremors she had
felt in Angus's hands when he'd taken the brush and stroked it
through her own hair, the movements slow and sensual, the
effect as thrilling as the tiny crackles of static the motion produced. She thought of his body, hard and straining into hers.
She remembered the heat of his skin, the warm smell of him,
the way his head arched back and his eyes smoldered with

pride when she shivered around him time and again and refused to let him go.

He had lied for her. He had not exposed her part in the theft to Forbes or Loudoun or Worsham, but what did that mean? What *exactly* did that mean? If he cared for her enough to put himself in such a precarious position—surely he would have been arrested and treated to the same prison hospitality as Anne, had they caught him in the lie—why had he not swept her into his arms at Drummuir House and told her so? Why had he deliberately kept himself at arm's length?

No, it wasn't fair. And it wasn't fair to be in the constant company of a man who seemed to know she was not always squirming and red-faced because her trews itched.

"Ye look as if ye've fought a battle already, lass." MacGillivray's quiet voice came over her shoulder, startling Anne into looking up from the fire. She had moved there when Robbie had started laying pats and pinches on Glenna Mor's bottom and the girl's incessant giggles had begun to shred Anne's last nerve. She wasn't sure how long she had been staring at the low ripple of flames, but there were snores coming from the family pallet, and more than one figure lay bundled in plaid on the dirt floor.

She was seated on a three-legged stool, and without waiting for an invitation, MacGillivray lowered himself onto the floor beside her, sitting cross-legged, cradling a cup of whisky in his hands.

"'Twas a long day. We started out before dawn, did we not?"

"Aye, that we did. An' we'll start out afore dawn on the morrow, too, so ye shouldna be squanderin' what little time ye have to rest by thinkin' on things that have no answer."

She studied his firelit profile for a moment before scowling. "You cannot possibly know what I am thinking, John MacGillivray."

"No? Then I'll gladly apologize if I'm wrong, but ye've the look of a wife worryin' after her husband."

She just stared until he looked up and grinned gently. "'Tis a look we've both seen often enough these past weeks, each time a man kisses his wife an' bairns an' promises he'll be back after we've driven the *Sassenachs* back to England."

"Even so, I will accept your apology," she said archly, turning her gaze back to the fire, "for you are wrong; I wasn't thinking of Angus at all. He made his choice, I made mine, and we both knew we would have to live with the consequences. In truth, I wasn't thinking of anything at all. I was just enjoying the sensation of having warm toes and fingers."

She was aware of his smile, but since she did not feel like compounding her foolishness by having her bluff called, she did not look his way again.

In the end, he sighed affably and stretched his hands toward the heat. "A worthy pleasure," he agreed. "For the rest of the body as well."

She watched his hands as he turned them this way and that, noting the width of the callused palms, the length of the strong, blunt-tipped fingers. Angus's hands were smoother, far more elegant than they were powerful, more comfortable holding a quill than a *clai' mór*. They were gentle and tentative when they reached for her, and she could not imagine for a moment Angus Moy lifting her against a wall at a public fairground and threatening to take her there and then before God's eyes if she did not give him a kiss.

"Jesus God and all the saints," she whispered, bowing her head with a small shake, wondering what it would take to rid her mind of such unwanted images.

"Ye have need of a special prayer?" MacGillivray asked.

Unaware she had invoked the heavenly powers aloud, she felt all the more foolish for it and smiled wearily. "An exorcism, perhaps. But you were right. I should make my bed while I have the chance."

She started to shift forward, to push herself off the stool, but her legs had become locked in the folded position and refused to budge.

John's grin came back, tempered by a cluck of his tongue. "Did ye not use the unguent I gave ye, lass? It will ease the stiffness out o' yer muscles each night an' let ye ride in comfort in the mornin'."

"It smells dreadful, like camphor and turpentine and something else I cannot fathom."

"A virgin's piss gathered fresh in the mornin'." He laughed when he saw her startled expression, and sprang to his feet so easily she wanted to kick him. Reaching down, he grasped her around the waist, bringing her up slowly, letting her legs straighten and uncramp with a minimum of strain. It took a full minute or more, with Anne's hands resting on his chest all the while, her fingers splayed over the solid bulk of muscle beneath. His head was bent forward, bringing the musky scent of smoke and whisky closer than was probably wise at that precise moment, but his next suggestion nearly sent her toppling backward.

"Drop yer trews for me, lass: I'll ease what ails ye in no time."

Her eyes, blue and huge, locked with his long enough for the smile to fade from his face and his complexion to grow ruddy.

"I meant the salve," he murmured. "Ye need to rub it in hard for it to work best."

"I can manage it on my own."

"Aye, of course ye can." He lifted one of her arms above her head and snorted when she did not have the strength to hold it there without wincing. "Now get on over to yer blanket, drop yer breeks, an' cover whatever ye dinna want me to see."

Anne glanced around the room to see if anyone was paying attention, but they had kept their voices low enough not to disturb the sleeping forms. She went over to her pallet of blankets and gingerly unfastened the waist of her trews, pushing them down past her hips and sliding them, with difficulty, to her ankles. She was wearing one of Jamie's cambric shirts, the hem of which fell almost to her knees and could be tucked between her legs to spare her more tender parts the worst of the chafing.

MacGillivray scarcely seemed to notice as he fetched the jar of liniment from his saddle pouch and rounded the fire. When she was lying facedown on the blankets, he smeared a healthy dollop in his palms and rubbed them together, warming the oily mess first before he knelt beside her.

His first strokes were gentle, smoothing the slippery concoction into her skin and working it into her thighs and calves. He added more, warming it each time, and when he judged her slick enough, he began to knead the muscles with the vigor of a biscuit maker. The heat of his hands combined with the heat of the camphor started a not uncomfortable burn down the length of her legs, and when he paused to nudge the hem of the shirt up to the crease of her bottom, she did not object.

"You've not said much about Elizabeth," Anne murmured.

"Ye havna said much about Angus," he countered.

"You are going to marry her, are you not?"

MacGillivray's sigh was extravagant. "We have talked about it, aye."

"Just . . . talked about it?"

"Aye. I'm a great talker, have ye not noticed?"

Whether she would have pursued the topic or not was cut short on a gasp as he lifted the shirt higher and sent his hands sliding all the way up to her shoulders. Her teeth clamped down over her lower lip and her fists curled tighter around the little hillocks she'd made in the blankets, but the massage felt so good and the heat produced by his big hands was so comforting, she stopped thinking of her bared bottom after the first few strokes.

MacGillivray felt her shock and saw the clenching of her fists, but it was the only way he could think to end the conversation. He did not want to talk about Elizabeth of Clunas, or of his impending marriage, not while his hands were doing what they had ached to do for so many years. The pleasure of feeling her skin all sleek and warm and bared to his touch was so intense, it stirred sensations that had no right to be stirred, arousing needs that had no right to be aroused.

He may well have been half sotted the last time their lips had met, but he remembered all too well how she had tasted, how she had felt, how she made those tiny sounds deep in her throat when he had kissed her. God's truth, he had dreamt of them lying together so many times, he imagined he knew exactly where and how to caress her until she was trembling with the madness of wanting his flesh inside her. And once there . . . once there, by God, he knew she would be as insatiable as a nymph, rising against him, engulfing him so completely with her own orgasms he would scarcely have need to worry about his own. But of course he would. He would feel her flesh sliding over his, feel it squeezing him, working him like little fists, and the climax would be cataclysmic.

Wild Rhuad Annie. How many times had he regretted not taking her that day in the fairground? She had been willing. She had been more than ready. She had kissed him as if her soul had been in her mouth, his for the taking. But he had stopped himself, had slapped himself down, not wanting to risk tarnishing her reputation until they were well and properly married. He had known about the betrothal arrangement pledging her to Angus Moy, but when her fiancé had become the vaunted chief of Clan Chattan and it looked as though the agreement might be nullified, he had felt confident Fearchar would accept him, John Alexander MacGillivray, as a worthy alternative. The day—the very bloody day—before he had decided he could wait no longer to offer for her hand, he was told the wedding to The MacKintosh was to proceed as planned.

The day of Annie's marriage, he had gotten so drunk, it had become necessary for Gillies to tie him down to keep him from tearing Dunmaglass apart plank by plank. He had stayed drunk for a month and sought to ease himself on every whore within ten miles of Inverness.

After four years, the ache was still a living thing in his belly. It sent tremors through his arms, down his legs; it sent rivers of heated blood flowing into his groin, swelling him to almost unbearable lengths.

He had helped Anne to her feet a while ago, but who would help him now? Who, for that matter, would stop him if he turned her on her back and plunged himself between her thighs? He could take her and damn them both to hell without a qualm. He had seen her watching him surreptitiously from a window at Dunmaglass, and he had lost count of the number of embarrassed little glances he caught her sending his way ever since. A kiss would silence her. She was vulnerable, aching with a need Angus was not here to satisfy and had been too foolish to see how precious a thing it was.

The tension in John's body became as palpable as the heartbeat thundering within his chest. His hands skimmed downward, slowing when they smoothed around her ribs. His fingertips brushed against the pillowed curve of her breasts and he bowed his head, cursing his own damning weakness.

Angus Moy was his friend as well as his laird. Not only that, but he had come to Dunmaglass the day before he left for Edinburgh and asked John to look out for Anne while he was gone. He had said he knew his wife was too stubborn to stay at home with her needlework, and if she managed to get herself thrown in gaol for spitting on the Lord President, would John mind blowing up the courthouse to break her out?

The irony had almost choked him then, for had her husband come an hour earlier, he could have seen Anne standing there brazen as brass announcing she was going to call out the clan and march to war.

It choked him now when he thought that if he had gone to Fearchar a day earlier, if he had, indeed, stolen more than a kiss that day at the fair, if he hadn't been so damned arrogant in thinking she was too wild and spirited for anyone else to want to try to tame . . . ?

"Ye'll be the sorry death o' me, lass," he whispered. "Ye ken that, do ye not?"

When there was no answer, he leaned forward and looked at her face. Her eyes were closed, her lips slightly parted. She was fast asleep and he did not know whether he should feel relieved or disappointed.

He straightened her shirt and drew a bundle of blankets up over her shoulders, tucking her in as gently as he would a child. At the last, he could not resist bending over and pressing a kiss into the gleaming red crown of her hair, for he knew it would be the last time he could risk doing such a thing. He loved her far too much to see her hurting any more than she was now, and to put the horns to her husband would surely tear her apart.

He stoppered the jar of unguent and pushed to his feet, glaring balefully down at the enormous bulge in the front of his kilt. There was little likelihood of his being able to sleep himself this night, he thought grimly, not with his body as tense as a cocked pistol and his mind full of what-ifs and why-nots.

He fished a Carolina cigar out of his sporran and bit the

end. While he was leaning over to light a taper he caught a movement out of the corner of his eye and glanced sharply at the darkened corner where Glenna Mor made her bed. She was there, sitting back on her heels, her eyes large and round and dark in a face framed by a tousle of curls. How long she had been watching them, John did not know, but as he stared at her now, she tipped her head and raised her hands to her bodice, peeling the cheap wool aside to show him that her breasts were ripe and lush, her nipples hard as beads.

Her hands moved again, sliding down into the juncture between her thighs. She seemed to purr and stretch with the sensation and this time, when she tilted her head, she did so in the direction of the door.

John narrowed his eyes against the flare of the taper. He held it to the end of his cigar and through a thin blue cloud, watched the girl snatch up her cloak and move toward the door.

Once there, she paused and looked back over her shoulder, smiling an invitation before she slipped outside. With wisps of smoke trailing behind him like a Medusa, John stalked after her, but no sooner had he closed the door behind him when another short, stocky shadow loomed up out of the mist.

"I were just comin' tae fetch ye," said Gillies MacBean. "We found a camp down by the river. Forty *Sassenachs* wi' three wagons saggin' wi' what looks like barrels o' grain an' casks o' ale. The men were thinkin' we might have more need o' such things than Thomas Lobster."

MacGillivray cast around. There were enough campfires blazing to provide a weak, watery kind of light through the fog, and he could see the girl's silhouette paused by a patch of soft green grass a discreet distance from the house.

"Aye," he said. "Bring the horses. We could use a little diversion."

Gillies followed his glance and saw the waiting shadow. "I could take the men out maself if ye've more pressin' needs tae tend tae."

John stuck his cigar in his mouth and clapped a hand around the shorter man's shoulder. "Ye're a good friend,

Gillies, but ye've likely just saved me from a fine case o' the pox."

Gillies grinned. "Dinna tell Robbie that. She wrung him out in the haystack no' an hour gaun. He's lyin' there still, drained tae the bone, weak as a saplin', declarin' undyin' love."

"Love," John snorted. "Almost as bad as the bloody pox. Let's away. It'll be dawn in a few hours, an' ye've given me a taste for fresh bannocks."

Chapter Eleven

$\mathcal{N}$inety miles directly to the southwest, Angus Moy had such a foul taste in his mouth, no amount of claret, whisky, or French brandy was proving able to remove it. It was not the lingering effects of the meal he'd had earlier, for the salmon served that evening at Holyrood House had been succulent, the venison tender enough to cut with a fork. It was the company that was wearing on his patience, souring his disposition, a condition that seemed to be becoming increasingly frequent with each passing day. Even with his own men, he found himself snapping their heads off with little provocation other than a sidelong glance or a heartbeat of hesitation. He had, to his utter personal disgust, even ordered a man flogged for failing to groom his horse properly the day before.

The harshness of the penalty had, perversely, won him respect from another quarter. General Henry Hawley was a seasoned campaigner, a veteran of the wars in Europe. He was a particularly cruel commander, a harsh disciplinarian beloved by no one, respected only by those who shared his penchant for floggings and hangings. Every day without fail there were entries made in the Order Book, names of men sentenced to the lash who received any number from the minimum of twenty-five strokes to the maximum of three thousand. Gibbets were one of the first structures erected when Hawley made camp, and the more prominent the location, he reasoned, the better for maintaining the proper morale. In Edinburgh, he had chosen the town square, for his occupational powers were not limited to soldiers; there were a number of townspeople he felt were deserving of lessons in constancy.

Businessmen known to have willingly provisioned the Jacobites with weaponry or munitions were fined into bankruptcy and locked in public stocks to be spat upon and pelted with rotted garbage. Those found guilty of participating in acts of sabotage or suspected of causing general mischief were either lashed to within an inch of their lives or hanged by way of example alongside soldiers accused of cowardice or sedition. Women fared little better. Doxies who stated their preference for men in kilts were treated to the whirligig; they were strapped into a chair and raised off the ground, then spun at such length and with such vigor, the nausea and vomiting lasted for days.

Following Cumberland's example, Hawley had forbidden gambling and banned women from the company tents. A man with an urge had to either ease it with his own hand or risk the lash by bribing his way outside the picket lines to the wagons of the camp followers—none of whom suffered a lack of steady custom despite the restrictions.

Naturally these rules did not apply to officers. Many of them traveled with wives or mistresses, and to judge by the resplendent array of silks, the glittering splash of jewels, the sweeping décolletages and seductive come-hither smiles, one would be hard-pressed to believe the country was in the midst of a rebellion. No common barracks for these fine officers, either. The lavish homes of the burghers and bankers had been appropriated as billets, the wine cellars and pantries accessed freely, with only the vaguest promises of compensation.

Angus had been assigned a lovely gray brick home with a spectacular view of the spires and steeples of the ancient royal city. From an upper window he could watch the effects of the sunrise against the massive edifice of Edinburgh Castle, the battlements braised gold and orange, shrouded in sea mists that gradually burned away to reveal the glinting mouths of the cannon that looked down over the streets. Old Colonel Guest had stubbornly refused to surrender the castle throughout the three months of Jacobite occupation, and had even threatened to fire his heavy guns on the city should any attempt be made to breach the walls. Fortunately for the townspeople, Charles Stuart had had no siege cannon in his possession at the time, and the castle was left unmolested.

Upon the hasty departure of the Jacobite forces, the gates had swung open with great pomp and ceremony to welcome General Hawley when he reclaimed the capital city. Hawley, in turn, had relieved the beleaguered troops and paraded Colonel Guest from the inner courtyard of Crown Square along the Royal Mile to opulent lodgings at Holyrood House as if he had single-handedly preserved the crown's possessions in Scotland.

Since Angus was, in effect, a bachelor during this sojourn, he had been billeted with Major Roger Worsham. He had little doubt the pairing had been on purpose, so that his comings and goings could be closely monitored; to that end, Worsham was, if nothing else, efficient to a fault. If Angus went for a stroll, he was afraid of stopping too quickly lest the major walk up his heels.

As far as his personal habits went, the man was a lecher and a boor. He had convinced Adrienne de Boule to come away from Inverness, and while she was officially housed in another area of the city, there were nights Angus could hear them laughing and carrying on in Worsham's room at the end of the hall. Several mornings, whether by accident or intent, he had emerged from his room to find Adrienne in various stages of undress, either accompanying the major down to breakfast or trying to entice him back to bed. The first couple of times she had seemed genuinely embarrassed. After that, she only laughed at his shocked expression.

Angus, on the other hand, had not heard from Anne since he had left Inverness. She had not written, had not even troubled with the courtesy of informing him she had left Drummuir House. Indeed, he might not have known at all had his valet, Robert Hardy, not let it slip that he had sent for some of Angus's personal possessions and been informed by the housekeeper that not only had Anne left the dowager's house, she had removed her things from Moy Hall and taken up residence at Dunmaglass as a guest of John MacGillivray.

When he had first heard this, Angus had been dumbfounded. He had known she was upset over his departing for Edinburgh, but he had not foreseen the possibility of her being so repulsed she would move out of his home and into that of another man.

Generally speaking, his insights into the workings of a woman's mind were limited, but with Anne, who never saw any reason or use for pretense, he felt reasonably sure he knew where he stood in her estimation at any given time. If anything, it had been her inability to conceal any of her emotions that posed the greatest threat to her safety these past months. The daggers in her eyes were real; anyone foolhardy enough to earn her wrath was impaled on the first glance. Angus himself had felt the flashing darts on many an occasion, but she had always stopped short of letting him bleed to death. And more times than he was proud to admit, he had used her obvious vulnerability to defuse a potentially explosive situation.

That vulnerability was her love for him, and as much as he wanted, needed, craved to see it in her eyes, hear it in her voice, feel it in her body when she shuddered in his arms, he could not let anyone else see it. He could not, for instance, let Forbes or Loudoun have the faintest suspicion that he would have forsaken everything, his clan, his titles, his wealth, his very life in order to protect her from harm.

The major had not mentioned the incident at Drummuir House again, but it was clear he had not believed for an instant that Angus and John MacGillivray had been drunk together that or any other night at Moy Hall. Whether or not he believed Anne had merely been walking off a cramp in the hallway was doubtful as well, but without proof he could do nothing more than speculate over who had stolen the dispatches and how they had eventually made their way into Lord John Drummond's hands. It had been an astonishing coup by the Jacobites, and part of Angus was as yet unable to grasp the fact that his wife had been singularly responsible for sending six thousand crack troops back to Holland.

There had been further rumors that the Farquharson trio had been riding around the shire attempting to foment rebellion within the clan, and reports that MacGillivray and

MacBean had been raiding the quartermaster supplies at Fort George, but again there was no proof, and half of what the Jacobites had accomplished thus far—including the panic over the imminent landing of a massive French fleet—had been achieved by fabrications and rumors. Until the actual retreat from Derby, the government had not even had a clear idea of how many Highlanders had marched into the heart of their country. Lord George Murray had been adept at subterfuge and confusion, sending out patrols ahead of the advancing army to warn the towns and cities in their path that a great hoard of ravenous Highlanders was descending on their countryside. Twenty and thirty thousand troops had been reported at various times, sending the population fleeing before them and allowing the few thousand Jacobites to enter the English cities unmolested.

The retreat had been as much of an embarrassment to the Hanovers as to the Jacobites, for when the news spread that there had never been more than five thousand Scots in the prince's camp, the Elector's generals were a laughingstock.

One would think they had learned a hard lesson, but General Hawley sat idling away his days and evenings in Holyrood House while the prince's forces regrouped and resupplied, growing stronger each day. The Stuart's main army was back to full strength at Glasgow, while Lord Lewis Gordon was welcoming fresh contingents to Aberdeen every day.

Despite receiving daily—sometimes hourly—reports of increased activity, Hawley appeared unconcerned. Angus suspected the general's own arrogance dictated that he wait until there were sufficient numbers to make opposing them worthwhile. How, he had been heard to proselytize, could sending his eight thousand troops to quash a disorganized rabble of twelve hundred be regarded as anything more than a hollow victory? Even twenty-five hundred posed no real threat. Charles Stuart was preparing to decamp from Glasgow and march to Stirling; defeating *him* would be a worthy challenge.

Angus listened to Hawley's boastings and only thought him the greater fool for his arrogance. He had surely read the reports after the battle of Prestonpans, wherein the officers stated that the sheer terror evoked by the sight and sounds of a Highland charge had scattered most of their men into a retreat without their having fired a single shot. The blond, pike-faced Hamilton Garner had been on the field that day. If anyone should be tugging on Hawley's ear, it should be Garner, for he had been among the few who had stood their ground and met the bloody onslaught, but at an appalling cost of over half the dragoons in his regiment.

"Ah, there you are, MacKintosh."

Angus cursed inwardly and took another sip of brandy. At the conclusion of the evening meal, he had removed himself from the smoke-filled drawing room and had hoped to steal away from Holyrood House before his absence was noticed. Waiting for the distraction of musicians and pretty women to take effect, he had temporarily taken refuge in the portrait gallery, a long, arched affair of marble and gold gilding.

"Admiring one of the royal ancestors, are you?" Major Worsham came up beside him and tilted his head to study the painting Angus was standing under. The walls were hung with tapestries and life-sized portraits depicting the royal house of Stuart in all its former glory; the one Angus had gravitated toward was of the prince's great-great-grand-mother, the Stuart queen known as Bloody Mary.

She had been a strikingly handsome beauty in her youth, and the artist had not spared the power of his brush to portray her. Her hair was as red as flame, her throat smooth and long, her eyes as blue as sapphires where they gazed seductively down from their lofty perch.

"There is certainly much to admire," Worsham conceded, "despite her penchant for murder and intrigue. I can see why you would choose her to contemplate over the others, how-ever; the resemblance to your wife is quite startling . . . around the eyes and the mouth in particular."

Angus turned, surprised and vaguely unsettled at the sight of another scarlet-clad officer standing behind him. It was Major Hamilton Garner, with the sloe-eyed Adrienne de Boule on his arm.

"I am afraid I don't quite see it," Garner said affably. "But then I only had the pleasure of making your lady wife's ac-quaintance the one time."

"There are some vague similarities," Angus admitted.

"Come now," Worsham argued with an airy wave of a

hand. "The hair, the eyes, the fulsome shape of her . . . upper form. The likeness is there. I am driven to inquire if you have ever had the Lady Anne sit for a portrait?"

"I have suggested it several times, but she always manages to find an excuse. I fear she imagines too many shortcomings, which would in turn lead to exaggerations on the canvas."

"Shortcomings? I was not aware of any."

"She thinks she is too tall," Angus murmured, looking up at the painting again. "And she believes her nose is violently crooked, whereas I have assured her it only tilts . . . ever so slightly . . . to the left."

"Gad. Most married men would not be able to tell you if their wives had blue eyes or brown. Never say that you find yourself missing her company, sir."

Angus caught himself and smiled wanly. "I confess there are times I miss the diversion."

"Even when there are so many others about?"

Angus glanced at Adrienne, as he was invited to do. Her hair was piled high and powdered as white as her skin, of which there was no lack on display. She was a tiny, slender creature to begin with, but her waist had been pinched even smaller, and her breasts pushed so high there were two faintly pink rims of nipple showing above the rich burgundy silk of her gown.

She saw him staring and smiled.

"Your wife," Garner said casually. "I understand she has been diverting more than her fair share of attention these days."

"I beg your pardon?"

"You've not read today's crop of dispatches?"

Angus looked into the jade green eyes and had the sensation of being lured out onto ice that was too thin to bear his weight. "I have been conducting musket drills in the field with my regiment all day, and I confess the thought of a hot bath was more appealing than wading through a small hillock of parchment."

"Then you know nothing of your wife's activities in your absence?"

"You make it sound as if she has stormed London and taken the king hostage."

Garner's laugh was a brief exhale from the back of his throat, as phony as the air of friendly camaraderie. "I would suggest, sir, that this is no jest. It seems your wife has been making quite the spectacle of herself. We have it on good authority that she has been gadding about the countryside in secret, aspiring to incite rebellion amongst your clansmen. To be more precise, she has declared for the prince and spent the last three weeks collecting signatures on a petition that would give her the necessary leverage to assume leadership of the clan in your absence."

Angus looked at him in astonishment. "I don't believe it."

"The source is reliable," Garner added, watching Angus's face intently. "Lord Loudoun himself questioned a man they recently arrested and who was . . . persuaded . . . to reveal what he knew about a flurry of rumors we had been hearing for the past fortnight. In all honesty, it must be said there was a suspicion in some quarters that you might have sanctioned, even encouraged her activities, but"—he held up a hand with the arrogant negligence of someone accustomed to offering insults without fear of reprisal—"Lord Forbes has personally vouched for your loyalty and has assured the general your commitment to King George is firm."

Angus set his glass on a nearby table and clasped his hands behind his back. "My commitment to Scotland is firm, sir. To do what is best for her and her people."

"An admirable sentiment, I'm sure, but as you know there can be no room for sentiment on a battlefield. As a fellow officer I am more concerned with knowing that when my dragoons charge the field, your infantry will be behind us to offer their support."

"So long as your men are charging in the right direction, Major, you have no need to concern yourself over the whereabouts of me or my regiment."

The green of Garner's eyes darkened, and Angus could feel the ice cracking beneath his feet. It was well known throughout the ranks of the military that Garner was both a master swordsman and an expert marksman. To date, there had been only one cloud dampening a perfect record of duels fought and won.

"You take liberties with my humor, sir," Garner said stiffly.

"You take liberties with my country, my family, and my good name. I do not know who this 'reliable source' of yours might be, but I can assure you my wife is not gadding about the countryside. She is in Inverness, the guest of my mother the dowager Lady MacKintosh, and if there are rumors, I suggest they are unsubstantiated at best, unmitigated folly at worst."

"And of course you can offer proof she is at Drummuir House?"

Angus's eyes cut swiftly and coldly to Worsham. "I should not have to prove any such thing, sir."

"But if you did," the major countered, his eyes glinting.

"If I did," Angus said, "I have letters from both my wife and my mother. Long, boringly detailed letters about how they have been spending their long, boring days. How can you be certain the woman riding about the countryside creating havoc is my wife?"

"Various reports have mentioned a tall, red-haired woman in the company of John MacGillivray," Garner said. "They place her at his house as well, at Dunmaglass."

"Various reports swore the prince's army was fifty thousand strong. If the proof you offer is that this woman has red hair, I suggest you try to find a farm, a village, a city tavern lacking someone who fits the same description. At the very least, I would suggest you make the acquaintance of John MacGillivray's fiancée—a very tall, very striking woman with a veritable cloud of long red hair—before you offer insults against my wife."

Garner's eyes narrowed. It was a safe bet the major had not met Elizabeth Campbell, or even if he had, that he would not remember she was short and dark-haired. In any case, Angus braced himself, wondering where his best chances lay in a duel—with sabers or pistols.

But it was Adrienne de Boule's much-put-upon sigh that ended the tense standoff. That and a snap of her fan that sounded like a gunshot in the silence.

"Come now, gentlemen," she scolded prettily. "Must we spoil a perfectly lovely evening by scowling at each other?

Captain MacKintosh, you promised me a set, and I can hear the musicians tuning."

"You will have to forgive me if I find I am suddenly not in the mood for dancing."

"That was the excuse you used last night and the night before." She gathered the folds of her gown and moved daintily over to stand by his side, draping her free hand through the crook of his arm. "Refuse me again, my lord, and I shall be left with no alternative but to toss myself out of a window in despair."

Angus frowned down at her. His first instinct was to offer to open the nearest pane of glass. His second, arrived at when he felt the points of her nails dig into his arm, was to acknowledge the warning gleam in her eyes.

"Naturally," he said haltingly, "I should hate to be responsible for such a waste."

"*Bien!*" She smiled at Garner and Worsham. "If you gentlemen will excuse us, then?"

The two scarlet-clad officers watched them walk along the length of the gallery and Angus could feel the heat of their glares burning between his shoulder blades.

"Do you have a death wish, Captain," she murmured when they were out of earshot, "or are you just an idiot?"

He started to draw to a halt but she maintained her grip on his arm and kept him moving forward.

"The pair of them would like nothing better than to goad you into a fight. Garner, in particular, is as bloody-minded as they come, and Worsham . . . well. He attempts to compensate for his shortcomings in other areas by strutting around like a bandy cock."

"Mademoiselle de Boule, while I appreciate your stepping in to defuse the situation—"

"The green-eyed one would cut you down without expending a bead of sweat," she said bluntly. "I have heard he toys with his victims as a cat toys with a mouse, and when he tires of the game, he ends it. As simply as that."

"Your opinion of my potential skill is heartening," he said dryly.

"I am a realist, m'sieur. I have also seen you practicing in the exercise yards."

"Now see here—"

"No. You listen to me. You have no idea how close you have come on several occasions to being arrested. The only reason you have not been before now is that although the major is convinced you are passing information to the Jacobites, he has not been able to catch you at it. Until he does, he would not dare go against the guarantee Lord Forbes has proffered on your behalf."

"How do you know about that? And why the devil would they think—?" He stopped as they entered the ballroom and Adrienne's skirt was snagged on the saber of a passing officer. First and always a flirt, she assured the handsome young man there was no damage, then for the two full minutes it took for the guests to assemble and form lines for the dance, she teased him about the size of his weapon and the hardness of his blade.

The music commenced and she came forward, bowing in front of Angus, low enough for him to whisper urgently over the top of her head.

"Why the devil would they think I have been passing information to the Jacobites?" he hissed.

"Because your wife is one of them, m'sieur, and I, too, saw the look of longing on your face when you were studying that portrait in the gallery."

"Politics aside, Anne has better sense than to involve herself in something so dangerous."

Adrienne straightened and gave him an odd look, then swirled away in a graceful circle, the burgundy silk of her wide, ruffled skirts flaring out in perfect symmetry with the dozen other colorful skirts on either side. When they were close enough again, she smiled and barely moved her lips as she spoke. "You foolish man. Do you really believe she is languishing at Drummuir House?"

"I do not know what you are implying, but—"

"You *really* do not know?"

"Of course I bloody don't—" They parted, and Angus had to bite his tongue until the next pass.

"Your wife is a day's ride from Aberdeen," Adrienne said, sweeping forward to execute a graceful measure. "She has brought eight hundred of your clansmen with her, all armed, all wearing the Stuart cockade."

Angus stumbled. He bumped into the gentleman beside him, who accepted his hastily murmured apology before the couples parted and moved into the next pattern of intricate steps.

Eight hundred men!

That could not possibly be true!

Good God, if it was . . . What was she thinking? No, obviously she wasn't thinking at all, but . . . *eight hundred men!* He, the chief of Clan Chattan, had barely managed to muster six hundred to his command, and by the time he had arrived in Edinburgh, all but forty had melted away into the night, refusing to raise arms against the prince.

Adrienne swept back in a crush of burgundy silk. "They have even accorded her a rank," she said sweetly. "They call her Colonel Anne. She has appointed officers to serve under her, of course; most notably Captain John Alexander MacGillivray."

This time Angus stopped. His hands hung limp at his sides and he was oblivious to the stares and hissed rebukes of the surrounding gambollers. The vast amounts of alcohol he had consumed throughout the evening seemed to catch up to him all at once, swamping his senses, leaving him light-headed, his mouth dry, his palms wet. Seeing the color drain swiftly out of his face, Adrienne quickly took his arm and guided him through a set of open doors that led out onto a stone terrace.

At her prompting, he took several deep gulps of cold air, which helped considerably. At least he was in no danger of dropping to the floor like a sack of grain. Adrienne disappeared for a few moments, then was back pressing a glass of undiluted claret into his hand.

"Drink it," she ordered. "All of it."

"How do you know these things about Anne? How do you know they're true?"

"My sources are better than Hawley's," she said simply. "I expect that situation to change any day now, however. As soon as your Colonel Anne arrives in Aberdeen, it will be difficult to convince anyone that she is at home writing letters."

Angus rubbed his temple. "I . . . don't understand. I mean, I know she is spirited and headstrong, but this . . . this goes far beyond anything she has done before."

"Yes, well, we all of us do things from time to time that go far beyond anything we have done before, especially in times like this. Sometimes we even surprise ourselves by pretending to be something we are not. By pretending, for instance, that we enjoy being pawed and fondled when we can barely endure the touch of a man's hand. That particular man, at any rate."

His frown deepened as he looked at her. "Worsham?"

"He is a pig, m'sieur. A cruel, mean pig, and I scrub myself raw each morning after I have been with him."

"Then why . . . ?"

"Because he is a poor reader," she said, smiling slyly. "He often has to sound words aloud to understand the letters that he sees on the paper. And this he most often does at night in his room, when none of the other officers can see him and perhaps laugh at his inability. At first he was careful in my presence and only moved his lips, but then he found something he thought would entertain me and when I told him it only bored me and put me to sleep, he started doing it just to annoy me. It amuses him, you see, to annoy and torment. The more I ignored his dispatches and charts and memoranda, the more he began to read aloud, and because I have a very good memory, I am able to write down these same words later and pass them on to men who know how best to use the information. It is not as valiant as donning a sword and riding about the countryside calling men to arms, but my talents are severely limited. Specialized, even, you might say. This was something I could do, and do well."

"You're a *spy*?"

"I prefer to call myself a loyal Jacobite, m'sieur. And perhaps the next time you see me in the hallway coming down to breakfast, you will remember the extent of my sacrifice and not scowl quite so darkly?"

Angus was speechless, but she only laughed and shook her head at his naiveté. "Now then, my bold captain—whose confidence I assume I may trust—these letters from your wife that you spoke so gallantly of, I do not suppose they truly exist?"

"Surely Worsham will not ask to see them."

"No. But he will have your room searched, you may count upon it."

He spread his hands in a gesture of impotence.

"Long and boring?" she asked with an exaggerated sigh. *"Bien,* I have a maid, Constance, who enjoys talking so much she forgets to take a breath. I shall sit her down with a quill and a sheaf of paper and by morning, you shall have your letters. Dozens of them, for she is creative enough you could well end up with a penny novel. Be sure you read them, in case you need to know what they contain."

"Is that not a horrendous risk to your own safety?"

"Yes, it is." She rose up on tiptoe and put her mouth to his ear. "And you shall owe me an outrageous favor in the future."

Her lips brushed his cheek, then his mouth, then she was gone, stepping back inside the ballroom with a coy snap of her fan.

Chapter Twelve

$\mathcal{T}$hree days later a courier arrived at General Hawley's head-quarters informing him that the prince had decamped and was heading east. At the same time, Lord Lewis Gordon had left Aberdeen with upward of thirty-two hundred men and was headed west, hoping to unite with the main body of the prince's army before it reached Stirling.

On January 13, unable to ignore the threat any longer, General Hawley sent his second in command, Major-General John Huske, marching from Edinburgh. Two days later, Hawley himself marched, reuniting with Huske's troops outside the city of Falkirk. There he was joined by an additional twelve regiments of Argyle militia, bringing the royalist strength up to eight thousand. For the first time since the conflict began, the numbers were equal on both sides, and both sides were spoiling for a much-needed victory—Hawley to avenge the poor performance of the Elector's troops thus far, Charles to restore the confidence lost on the retreat.

"Will ye take anither dram, lass?" The question was bellowed over the din as Archibald Cameron lifted a freshly opened crock of *uisque baugh* to his shoulder. "Yer eyes are barely crossed, an' we've still a blather o' toasts tae make tae both yer courage an' yer beauty."

Anne laughed amidst much banging of mugs and cheers of approval. Her eyes might not have been crossed, but her senses were fuddled—wonderfully, dizzyingly so—and she raised her cup for another splash of whisky and a raucous round of support.

She was the sole female in a tavern filled to capacity with brawny Highlanders who had marched to the heart of England and back; brave men all, who had not only been fore-warned of her presence in Aberdeen but knew the role she had played in removing the Dutch from England. The two fac-tions of the army had come together near Stirling; easily half the prince's men had lined the approach to the city to wel-come Lord Gordon, doffing their bonnets and spinning them overhead like dervishes.

Anne, for one, had never seen such a spectacle, let alone been part of it. Yet there she was, sitting high and proud on her massive gray gelding, fighting hard to keep her eyes dry and her heart from flying out of her chest.

Riding by her side was the golden-maned John MacGillivray, as fierce as ever a black-eyed giant there was, his hair combed into a tail, his personal body armory of guns and dirks and swords glittering in the sunlight. His lieu-tenants, Robert, Jamie, and Eneas Farquharson, followed, and between them, his face streaked with unabashed tears of joy, the grizzled old warrior, Fearchar of Invercauld. Gillies MacBean rode at the head of his MacBeans, his pipers com-peting good-naturedly with pipers from the Shaws and Davidsons, MacDuffs, MacPhersons, and MacKintoshes, all of whom marched in strength behind the standard of Clan Chattan.

Charles Edward Stuart, a princely figure in tartan trews and a blue velvet jacket, had been waiting to welcome them personally. A boyishly handsome man of four-and-twenty years, he had greeted each laird in turn, announcing their names aloud to the throngs of cheering Highlanders. When Anne had come forward, he had stopped her from offering a curtsy and bowed gallantly over her hand instead, addressing her as *"ma belle rebelle"* and causing such a roar to rise into the crisp winter air that casings of ice on the tree branches overhead cracked and fell to the ground.

Behind her, she could hear her grandfather bawling like a child as she was welcomed with an equally unceremonious hug by Lord George Murray. MacDonald of Keppoch kissed her hand, then chucked her on the cheek. Donald Cameron of Lochiel was looking over her shoulder at John MacGillivray, obviously impatient to meet the fighting men and judge their caliber, but he offered a formal bow and took pains to introduce his brothers, Dr. Archibald and—as if she were not already faint enough from having her heart stop so many times—the man around whom the word "legend" was used with genuine awe, the *Camshroinaich Dubh*: Alexander Cameron.

Anne had listened raptly to the stories told and retold around the campfires in Aberdeen about the bravery of the Camerons and the MacDonalds and Lord George's Athollmen, and the courageous roles they played in defeating the might of the English army at Colt's Bridge, then later at Edinburgh and Prestonpans. How she had wished Angus could be counted among them, fiercely steadfast in their loyalties, intrepid beyond measure, willing to forsake all—not the least of which was their lives, properties, and fortunes—in defense of their king and country.

And how she wished he could be here now, in this cramped and airless tavern on the outskirts of St. Ninians, a stone's throw from the sacred field of Bannockburn. How she longed to share with him the excitement of the pipers skirling in the background, the clansmen singing and pounding the tables with their tankards, and men like MacGillivray and Alexander Cameron joined together in toasting the prince's future success.

Easily as tall and broad across the chest as MacGillivray, the Dark Cameron had spent the past fifteen years in exile on the Continent fighting other men's wars. He had returned to his beloved home at Achnacarry only to find his country on the verge of rebellion, and since then had ridden at the right hand of Lord George Murray. It was rumored that he had brought an English wife with him, which did not set well with a clan whose elder statesman, Old Lochiel, had been with the exiled court of James Stuart since the failed uprising of 1715. But it was also said that his *Sassenach* bride had adamantly refused to remain in safety at her English home and had joined her husband when the prince's forces retreated from Derby.

Another roar sent Anne's gaze to the end of the table, where a mountain of a man had been called forward by the boisterous Dr. Archibald Cameron. His name, Anne recalled, was Struan MacSorely, and as she watched in amazement, he lifted a quart-sized pewter tankard to his lips and began to drink. Eight, nine, ten loud swallows were counted off by the men, after which a hearty clamor saw the good doctor clapping him on his back, then issuing a challenge from a pair of narrowed blue eyes to their prey at the opposite end of the table. Anne leaned forward, grinning when she saw Gillies MacBean push to his feet. Jamie and Robbie stood on either side of him, good-naturedly massaging his shoulders, neck, and belly, and when a brimming double tankard was set in front of him, the twins stepped solemnly back and crossed their arms crookedly over their chests, watching him like a pair of half-sodden bear handlers.

Gillies emptied the cup with nary a batted eye and set it down with a flourish. The crowd went wild for a moment; in the next, like magic, bonnets came off heads and wagers were taken from all quarters.

"I would hate to embarrass our compatriots by robbing of them of all their coin on the first night in camp."

Anne glanced across the table and smiled at the speaker, Alexander Cameron.

"Indeed, sir, I was thinking somewhat the same thing, only wondering what your reaction would be to our stripping you of all *your* coin our first night here."

Cameron leaned back, his midnight blue eyes gleaming. Beside him, his clansman Aluinn MacKail guffawed and fished in his pocket for a gold sovereign. A third gentleman, a flamboyant Italian count in a beribboned doublet and feathered musketeer hat, brought his hand down on the table in a flutter of cuff lace and deposited a second coin just as quickly.

"I'm-a know from-a the first night I join-a this troupe of-a madmen, that you need-a the iron gut to stand-a with MacSorley."

"As I recall, Fanducci," MacKail said over his shoulder, "you outlasted him."

"*Ah, sì, sì.*" Another flutter of lace brought a modest hand to the count's breast. "But I'm-a no ordinary madman. I was-a given wine before-a the breast."

MacGillivray, seated beside Anne, dug two gold coins and a fresh cigar out of his purse. When he saw the way the midnight eyes followed the latter rather than the former, he grinned and clamped the one cigar between his teeth while withdrawing a second one and setting it down alongside the coins. "We'll wait an' see who is still standin' at the end o' the hour, shall we?"

Cameron tipped his head to acknowledge the Highlander's wisdom, then withdrew two thin black cheroots from his own breast pocket. The one he moistened and placed thoughtfully between his lips, the other he laid alongside the fatter, more coarsely rolled Carolina.

Gillies and MacSorley, in the meantime, had downed their second full tankard apiece and were both standing rock solid at their respective ends of the long oak trestle. Dr. Archibald Cameron was now up on a chair—which put him on an equal eye level with his champion—and the twins, not to be outdone, dragged an empty keg over for the stocky Gillies to stand on.

"Your wife is very brave to accompany you, sir," Anne said to Alexander Cameron across the din.

"Aye, that she is, Colonel. Brave and stubborn. Not unlike someone else seated at this table." He lifted his mug in a salute. "And the name is Alex, not sir."

"Then you must call me Anne. I fear the rank is only for decoration anyway."

"Would you prefer '*ma belle rebelle*'? Or perhaps 'that red-haired Amazon'?"

She laughed and shook her head. The latter appellation had come as a result of a small but vicious skirmish along the road to Stirling. The vanguard of the Argyle militia had crossed Blairlogie just ahead of Lord Gordon's forward guard, and because the latter had consisted mainly of MacKintosh men, Anne had been in her usual place alongside MacGillivray. There had been no time for her to fall back when the Argylemen had attacked, and she had found herself in the thick of things. The Campbells had hoped to slow or delay the Jacobite column, but instead they had encountered such fearsome opposition, they were lucky to escape with only a handful of casualties. One of the fleeing clansmen had spotted Anne, her bonnet gone, her hair streaming around her shoulders, her magnificent gray gelding rearing as she wind-milled a saber overhead.

Word of a "red-haired Amazon" in the Jacobite ranks had spread like butter on a hot pan, even making its way into a report from Hawley's camp that was intercepted on its way south to London. It only brightened the already glowing aura that had begun with her audacious theft of Duncan Forbes's papers, and it made nearly every man present in the tavern that night want to fill her tankard and offer a toast.

". . . Seven . . . eight . . . nine . . ."

The crowd howled and she leaned forward again. Gillies was on his fourth tankard, and while the swallows were coming slower, they were still deep and steady, and the emptied vessel met the tabletop with the same resounding thud of satisfaction as MacSorley's had done moments earlier.

"By Christ's holy beard," Archibald declared, swaying unsteadily on his perch, "he's that good, is Struan. Mayhap we'll be needin two casks soon—one tae drink out o', the ither tae piss intae."

"I believe I can lead a full life without witnessing that landmark event," Anne said, her head already too light by far. She pushed to her feet, bidding the men to remain seated when all would have risen with her. "It has been a very long, tiring day—" She paused as Archibald Cameron pitched forward off his chair and fell unconscious, plunging facedown into a net of waiting hands. "And I certainly would not want my presence to hinder anyone's more manly pursuits."

MacGillivray, who had not obeyed her instruction to remain seated, settled his bonnet firmly, albeit askew, on his head.

"There is no need for you to leave, John," she said, laying her hand on his chest.

He glanced down at her hand—as did nearly every other pair of eyes within a ten-foot radius—then smiled the kind of smile that, if seen in polite society, would have sent a bevy of chaperones into a dead faint.

"I'm no' bothered. I've every faith in Gillies. So much so in fact," he added, leaning over to pluck the black cheroot off the table, "I might as well take this now an' enjoy it on the walk back to ma bed."

Cameron reached for the fat Carolina. "And I've enough faith in Struan to savor this now and collect another come morning."

MacGillivray glared down for a moment, then bared his teeth in a wide grin. " 'Tis a good thing we're on the same side, you an' I. Ye might vex me enough I'd have to reshape that fine nose o' yourn."

"And you have far too many teeth for my liking; I'd be bent to put a few of them in your pocket."

The two men exchanged grins and clasped hands. After bidding all a good night, John led the way through the shoulder-to-shoulder bodies, parting them by sheer brute strength. Outside in the clear, cold air, he set the unlit cheroot between his lips and stretched his arms to the side and back before falling into step alongside Anne. At his insistence she had taken lodgings in a cottage that had been made available for her comfort, and since the entire length of the village was no more than a quarter mile, she preferred to walk rather than force herself up into a saddle again.

"Well?" she asked, drawing her plaid around her shoulders.

"Well what?"

"What do you make of it all so far?"

"I've no' had much chance to weigh *all* yet, but they seem to be a braw lot o' men back there. More than willing to follow Lord George anywhere he leads."

Anne noted that he did not cite the prince's powers of leadership and wondered at the tension she had sensed herself between Charles Stuart and his commanding general. She was told that in the days following the retreat from Derby, when Lord George's logic had prevailed over the prince's passion, they were barely on speaking terms and communicated through brisk, formal notes.

The situation had hardly improved on the march from Glasgow to Stirling. Indeed, Lord George and two hundred of his Athollmen had left that very afternoon for Linlithgow under the auspices of intercepting any supply trains bound for Hawley's camp.

"How far is Falkirk?" Anne asked.

"A glen, a ben, an' a bog," he replied. "About ten miles that way," he added, pointing off into the darkness.

"Do you suppose the English know we are here?"

"They'd be a ripe daft lot if they didna. I warrant we could climb up the top o' the nearest hill an' see the glow from their fires in the distance, just as they could as like see ours."

"Do you suppose they are making plans to attack?"

"I doubt they're makin' plans to dredge the river, lass." They walked in silence, listening to their own footsteps crunch across the frozen ground. The echoes of a dozen pipers reverberated along the throat of the glen, for it was a fine, clear night, the sky blanketed in stars. The surrounding slopes sparkled with a hundred bonfires and tents too numerous to count. They were pitched in a wide swath from here to the meadows of Bannockburn, and even beyond to the banks of the Forth. The camp had been spread thus in the hopes of deceiving the English scouts into vastly overestimating their strength, a ploy that had worked so often in the past, it was almost ludicrous.

" 'Tis no sin to be frightened, ye ken."

Her steps slowed. "I'm not frightened. Not really. Not if I don't think about it anyway."

"An' if ye do think about it? What then?"

"Then . . . I feel like the world's biggest coward, because I just want to run and hide somewhere and hope that no one will ever find me."

"Bah!" He put a gentle hand on her shoulder and, although he had not intended them to do so, his fingers found their way beneath her hair to the nape of her neck. "We all feel that way sometimes. Ye think I've never lain awake at night wonderin' how it would feel to have the wrong end of an English bayonet in ma gut?"

"I don't believe that," she said on a wistful sigh. "I do not believe you are afraid of anything, John MacGillivray."

"Then ye'd be wrong," he said after a long, quiet moment. "Because I'm dead afraid o' you, lass."

Anne slowed further, then stopped altogether. She became acutely aware of his fingers caressing the back of her neck. She knew it had been meant as a friendly gesture, nothing more, and yet . . . when she looked at him, when she felt the sudden tension in his hand that had come with the hoarse admission, she knew it was not the caress of a man who wanted only to be a friend.

Perhaps it was the closeness of his body, or the lingering effects of too much ale. Perhaps it was because there were too many stars, or because the skirling of the pipes was throbbing in her blood. Or perhaps it was just because they were alone for one of the few times she'd permitted such a lapse in judgment, knowing all too well how the tongues were wagging about them already.

Perhaps it was for all those reasons and more besides that she reached up and took his hand in hers, holding it while she turned her head and pressed her lips into his callused palm.

"It's yer eyes, I think," he said, attempting a magnificent nonchalance. "They suck a man in, they do, so deep he disna think he can ever find his way out again. An' it makes him wonder . . . about the rest. If it would feel the same."

Anne felt the rush of heat clear down to the soles of her feet, and she bowed her head, still holding his hand cradled against her cheek. An image was in her head, so strong it sent shivers down her spine, of this hand and the other moving over her bare skin, sliding over skin slicked with oil and warmed by his body heat. Another heartbeat put her against that damned wall at the fairground again, and she knew what he had to offer, knew what he could offer her now if she but gave him a sign.

"It would be wrong," she said softly.

"Aye. It would."

"I love my husband," she insisted, not knowing whether she was trying to convince him, or convince herself. "Despite everything that has happened, all the harsh words, the terrible disappointments . . . I do still love him."

"Then ye've naught to worry about. Ye need only leave go of ma hand, walk straight the way into yer cottage, into yer own bed, an' we'll pretend this conversation never happened."

"Can we do that?"

"We'll have no choice, will we?"

Was he asking her or telling her? She tilted her face up, meeting eyes that were black as the night, burning with an emotion she did not even want to acknowledge, for if she did, she would reach out to him with her body and her soul, and they would both lose the battles they were waging within themselves.

"It would be for the best," she agreed.

"Aye. It would."

She lowered her hand. He lowered his. And they each exhaled a steamy puff of breath.

Suddenly cold, Anne hugged her arms and drew her plaid tighter around her shoulders. They had stopped at the end of the neat little stone path that led to the front of the cottage; a lamp had been left in the window, the latter made of pressed sheets of horn so that the glow was diffused and did not reach past the overhanging thatch on the roof.

It was simple, one large room with a pallet in one corner, a table in the other. There might have been more furniture—a chair or a stool, and pots on the wall—but at the moment, Anne could only recall the bed.

"I'd best leave ye here, then," John said, his voice tense with the conflict between loyalty and desire. "Ye'll be all right?"

"I'll be fine. John—!"

He had turned to leave, but at her call, he looked back—so quickly she almost took an instinctive step toward him.

And would that be so terrible? The English army was half a day's march away. MacGillivray would be leading the MacKintoshes into battle. He would be in the front line, the first to step onto the field, the first to break into the charge, the first to meet the awful fusillade from a thousand English muskets. It was true the English stood in disciplined lines like a row of child's skittles, but it meant they could fire, load, and fire their weapons again over and over in the time it took for the Highlanders to rage across an open field to meet them. John would be there, in the front ranks, through every deadly volley, for it was not the Highlander way to crouch behind rocks or wait in ambush. Honor and tradition sent them charging headlong to meet their fate with the battle cry of the clan screaming from their lips.

Anne would be forced to stay well back out of range of any stray shots or cannon shells. If she saw her brave golden lion go down, would it seem so important that she had remained faithful to the man who might well be the one who fired the fateful shot?

It isn't fair, Anne thought. *Not to John, not to me, not to Angus.*

"Thank you," she whispered. "For walking me back."

The ache was still there. The agony of indecision, of knowing right from wrong but still wanting . . . even if it was just for the one night . . .

"I'll send one o' the lads to fetch ye in the mornin'," he said. "Try to get some sleep."

She nodded, unable to tell him how absurd a hope that would be, unable to speak at all for the tightness in her throat. His footsteps made a sound like that of crushed glass on the frozen earth, and as she watched him stride away into the darkness, she thought it sounded a little like the brittle cracking of her heart.

With a sigh that seemed to come from the bottom of her soul, she entered the cottage and looked around. Small. Nondescript. Desolate. Exactly the kind of cottage in most respects as the one she had called home throughout most of her life. She was never meant to be the chatelaine of a grand estate like Moy Hall. She was never meant to wear corsets and fine silk, or to have upward of seventy servants look to her for instruction.

She tipped her head back against the wood of the door frame. Would it have been so terrible to forget she was that grand chatelaine for just one night? The loneliness was like a palpable thing inside her, but so were the feelings and emotions of Wild Rhuad Annie. MacGillivray wanted her; the heat was in his every breath, his every unguarded glance. What woman with any manner of grip on her wits would send him away, he to his cold bed, she to hers? What warm-blooded woman in her right senses would not want to feel those arms around her, hear that voice trembling in her ear, feel that naked body pushing slowly into hers?

She groaned softly and closed her eyes.

Was it possible to love two men at the same time? Would her soul burn in hell for even daring to ponder such a thing?

The sound of a quiet knock on the door sent her jumping forward. She turned and stared at the scarred timber a moment, wondering if John had been thinking the same thoughts. If it was him, if he was standing there, his bonnet in his hand, a curse on his lips, and a careless disregard for eternal hellfire burning in his eyes . . . then, in fairness or not, the decision had been taken out of her hands.

Chapter Thirteen

After her initial gasp of surprise, it took a further moment to recognize the shadowed figure who stood in the entryway. The collar of his cloak was up, his hat was pulled low over his brow, and the weak lamplight barely touched on the shape of his nose or the grim, flat line of his mouth.

"Angus?"

He reached up and pulled the bonnet off his dark hair, and if not for the fact she was still clutching the door, she might have staggered with the shock. As it was, she was thankful she had something to hold on to, to support her for the ten seconds it took to blink the whirling black dots out of her vision.

"Angus?" she whispered. "Is it really you? Where . . . where on earth have you come from? How did you find me? Good God, you look like a block of ice! How long have you been out there?"

"I am not sure. A couple of hours, I suppose."

"A couple of—? But . . . where? Why—? How—?"

She knew her questions were incoherent as well as incomplete, but her tongue did not seem able to catch up to the wild tumbling of her thoughts. Flustered, she pulled him inside, only thinking at the last moment to glance out into the darkness before she pushed the door shut.

"No one saw me," Angus said. "I was careful."

"But where have you come from? How did you find me?"

"I've come from Falkirk," he said. "And, in truth, it was Hardy who found you."

"Hardy?"

"I did not think it would be particularly prudent for anyone to see me roaming around the enemy camp. Besides, I was not entirely certain I would be welcome."

"Not welcome? You are my husband, of course you would be welcome." Then, as if her mind was just catching up with the previous answers, she released his gloved hand and withdrew a step. "Falkirk? You are here with the king's army."

It was not a question and it did not require an answer. Now that he had loosened his cloak and lowered the woolen collar, she could see the blazing red of his tunic, the blue facings on his collar and cuffs.

He saw her staring and blew out a soft breath by way of a wry explanation. "Not particularly wise to be seen leaving the government camp out of uniform, either."

Her eyes locked briefly with his before cutting away to the droplets of melting ice on his face and hair.

"Come." She backed up toward the hearth. "Sit and warm yourself by the fire. It will only take a moment to build it up hot again. Or . . . can you not stay?"

"I can stay. For a little while."

Anne turned away, a tiny sliver of panic running down her spine. Her husband was here. She hadn't seen him in nearly a month, and the last time they had been together at the dowager's house . . .

The whole ugly scene came crashing back in a series of disjointed images and angry echoes. They had not exactly parted on happy terms; since then, she had openly thumbed her nose at his authority both as a chief and a husband, and only moments ago had been contemplating bedding another man.

She pushed *that* thought out of her mind as best she could and bent over the fire to add fresh, dry wood to the bed of glowing coals.

"You are well?" she asked lamely, glancing over her shoulder. "You look well."

He had not moved from the doorway. Had not moved at all except to take off his gloves and comb his fingers nervously through the dark waves of his hair.

"I am well enough. And you? You look . . . fit."

She followed his gaze to her trews and tall knee boots, the thick bulk of her doublet and shortcoat, the casually plaited coil of her hair where it hung over her shoulder.

"Please," she said, pointing to a stool beside the hearth. "Come closer to the fire. Warm yourself."

He seemed to hesitate, as if by admitting he was indeed chilled to the bone he would be admitting some other inadequacy.

Anne unwrapped her own plaid and rubbed her hands together to warm them. "I've just come in myself. We were at the tavern. We actually just arrived in camp this morning. Around noon, really."

Now she was talking just to make noise. Beside her, the dry tinder caught and a flame flared along the lengths of the fresh logs, crackling loudly enough to make her jump. To cover her nervousness, she fetched a bottle of wine from the table; after filling two mugs halfway, she added some steaming water from the kettle that hung over the grate.

Angus moved stiffly, grudgingly, but he took the offered mug, wrapping his fingers around the heated metal and cradling it to warm his hands. After another awkward moment, he accepted her invitation to sit, lowering himself gingerly onto a stool while Anne sat back on her heels beside him.

She took a single sip of her wine to unstick her tongue from the roof of her mouth, but set it aside almost immediately, not wanting to risk numbing her wits more.

"When I saw you standing there, I thought . . . well, I hoped . . ."

"You hoped I had finally come to my senses and decided to join you?"

"Something like that," she acknowledged softly.

"Well, I haven't. Come to join you, that is. I have, however, come to ask you what the bloody hell you think you are doing. You and those damned cousins of yours."

He asked the question so casually, kept his voice so mellow and low, they might have been sitting in front of a blazing fire at home discussing the next crop of apples.

"None of us made the decision lightly," she began. "Or entered it in haste."

"No. No, I understand it took you nearly three weeks to gather the signatures of enough fools willing to follow you to Aberdeen. Oh, yes, I've heard all about your petition. I can even tell you who signed it and what threats were employed to get them to do so. What I do not understand is why you can't see that they are using you—Fearchar, your cousins, all of them. They used you to get to MacGillivray, for there was no other earthly way he would have broken his oath to me."

She felt another shiver, one that had nothing to do with the cold and everything to do with the frost in his eyes.

"As to that," he asked quietly, "was it not enough to have humiliated me by taking control of the clan? Did you have to fashion horns for me at the same time?"

"Horns?" Her voice was a bewildered tremor. "I don't know what you—"

"That was quite a touching scene I just witnessed between you and MacGillivray. It must have been so much more convenient for the pair of you while you were living with him at Dunmaglass."

A second log caught fire, throwing more light across his face, and for the first time Anne saw that there was more than just anger rendering his face gaunt and tight. There was pain as well. Deep emotional pain, so naked and vulnerable on a man who prided himself in his composure that she felt her heart begin to wither and crumble into a heap of dust.

"Angus . . . John has never been anything other than an absolute gentleman in my presence. Not by word or deed has he ever sought to offer more than his hospitality and friendship. I moved out of Moy Hall and into Dunmaglass, yes, but only as a guest and only to avoid having any taint that might become attached to my name or actions spill over to yours. Dunmaglass was as much an army camp as Bannockburn is now, and I sorely doubt we could have found a private moment together to do so much as touch hands, let alone touch anything else, even if we had been so inclined. Which neither of us was. I never forgot I was a married woman, and neither did he."

"That did not seem to be the case a few moments ago. Not when you had your heads together at the end of the path. And not by the way you said his name when you opened the door just now."

She bit the edge of her lip. She hadn't realized she'd gasped out John's name, just as she wasn't completely sure what she would have done had it been he and not Angus standing on the threshold. But it was Angus who was here before her now, with more than just his husbandly pride bruised. She had gone behind his back and she had usurped his authority within the clan, but what choice had he given her? What choice had he given his clansmen? It was obviously one they had not wanted to make, for she had seen reports as well. There were spies and couriers going back and forth between the enemy encampments like a trail of ants. Angus had left Inverness with six hundred clansmen, but by the time they arrived in Edinburgh, most of them had quietly slipped away and either gone back home or crossed over the moor to join the prince. But she would not throw that in his face. As for his assumption that she had moved into Dunmaglass so that she and MacGillivray might carry on some wild and passionate affair . . . !

"I have had far too much wine tonight," she admitted shakily, "and I am really not strong enough to do battle with you, Angus. I am certainly not strong enough to lie to you. If you choose not to take my word for it, then you are going to believe the worst and nothing I can say or do will change your mind. But I swear I have not been unfaithful. I'll not insult either one of us by saying I have not had thoughts and dreams . . . some of them vivid enough to keep me awake through the night. I will also freely confess that I have been lonely and frightened and perhaps even a little desperate to have someone hold me and treat me like a woman. I have feelings for John, yes, but I don't know what they are and I have never acted upon them. What you saw outside was a man putting his heart into my hands and my refusing it because I care too deeply for another. Simply that and nothing more. As for the rest, I am only too well aware that Fearchar used me as a means of getting what he wanted, but so has everyone else at some time or another, including you."

"Me? How the devil have I used you?"

"Oh, please, Angus. Why else would you have agreed to marry me if not because you hoped it would win Fearchar's support away from Cluny MacPherson as clan chief? Why else, if not because you thought that marrying a Farquharson would prevent the clan from splitting apart, exactly as it has done now?"

A shadow flickered briefly behind his eyes. "That was not why I married you."

"It never occurred to you, not even when you hesitated at the altar and it was so obvious you wanted to be anywhere else, with anyone else but me, that you were doing it strictly and stoically for the good of the clan, that it was just another thankless part of your duty, another tiresome and unwanted burden you inherited along with the title?"

"Anne . . ." He was genuinely appalled. "I never thought that. Not once."

She passed a hand in front of her eyes as if to ward off the futility of any more lies. "Fearchar told me he had to practically threaten you to honor the agreement. He also told me that you, in turn, demanded the dowry money because you knew he did not have it, and he would have had to forfeit the contract if he could not raise the stipulated amount."

"It was five thousand pounds," Angus murmured. "And if I truly had not wanted to go through with the marriage, Anne, I would not have been in that chapel at all."

She started to turn away, clearly disdainful of his efforts to patronize her, but he quickly set his wine aside and caught her shoulders, forcing her up onto her knees before him, bringing their faces so close she had no choice but to look up into his eyes.

"While Fearchar was telling you these fables, did he happen to mention where he came by the money for the dowry?"

"He said he was forced to sell off a valuable parcel of land."

"Valuable?" Angus snorted. "It was a stretch of bog along the edge of Meall a'Bhreacraibh that sits under three feet of water for nine months out of the year."

"Meall a'Bhreacraibh? But . . . you have land adjoining that moor."

"Aye, and my agent thought I was mad for buying more at such a ridiculous price, but he did as he was told and paid for it in cash, and never told Fearchar who the simpleton was who paid so much for something so worthless."

"*You* gave him the money?"

"Call me the biggest fool for it, if you will, but I thought the price well worth it."

Her lips parted slowly, and her shoulders lost some of their stiffness. "You did?"

"Then"—he seemed to stall over the words for a moment—"and now. I never regretted my decision for a moment, Anne. And if I appeared to hesitate in the church that day, it was because I was afraid if I moved, I might wake up and the dream would shatter. You see, I knew even then that MacGillivray would have been your likely choice had the two of us been standing side by side. Fearchar told me you and he were lovers—"

"We were *never* lovers," she began.

"I knew that on our wedding night, and you can have *no* idea how thankful I was you were a virgin—solely because you would not know how much terror I was feeling that you might think me an inadequate lover compared to John."

Anne felt the particles of dust in her chest stir and begin to take shape again. "Yet you married me anyway?"

He brought his hands up from her shoulders to cradle each side of her face, then bent his head forward until their brows touched. "I had seen you out riding on that great beast of yours and I swear my heart stopped from the sheer beauty of the moment. Your hair was wild, your skin was flushed from the wind, and your laughter . . ." His hands tightened and his eyes closed. "I thought if I could just hold that moment in my heart forever, it would be enough. But then I found the betrothal papers, and I knew I could hold so much more."

Anne said nothing; she just stared. His lashes were dark against his cheeks, and his mouth looked so grim it took all of her willpower not to simply fling her arms up around his neck and crush his lips beneath hers.

But she resisted. She moved her hands slowly instead, lifting them to touch his cheek first, to brush aside an errant wave of hair, then to thread her fingers deep into the silky brown locks. She tipped her mouth up to his, her eyes wide open, her body edging closer, and felt the tremors in his hands as they slipped down to her neck, then her shoulders again, and for the length of two, three pulse beats she feared he might still push her away.

Her lips pleaded silently for forgiveness, begging his to respond. And when they did, parting around a harsh groan of abandoned pride, his arms went around her and gathered her close, so close she feel his heart thundering within his chest. The air was driven from her lungs on a cry of unabashed relief, but his mouth was there to capture it, to share it, to revel in the mutual banishment of any lingering fears and hesitations. He brought her up hard against him, devouring her in the punishing caress of a man who had allowed himself to think the worst even though he had been desperate to believe it could not be so.

Anne responded with pure carnal joy. It trembled through her arms and quivered the length of her body, turning her blood to liquid fire. She drove her hands deeper into his hair and refused to let him break away, not even to grasp at a mouthful of air or plead for a moment of space to accommodate the sudden pressure swelling at his groin.

A rough curse brought him swiftly to his feet, dragging her with him. His mouth stayed fastened over hers but his hands flew down to tug at her coat, to tear aside her doublet, to fumble with her shirt, and finally, with a curse that voiced his impatience as well as his lust, to rip it from neck to hem in his haste to expose her flesh to his hungry lips. Anne arched her head back, groaning like a wounded animal when she felt the suckling heat close around her breast, but when he would have picked her up into his arms and carried her to the bed, she stopped him with a shallow cry.

Wide-eyed, panting lightly through swollen lips, she pushed out of his arms and backed up against the wall. When she could retreat no farther, she unbuckled her belt and kicked her way out of her boots and trews, then stripped off the loosened upper garments, all save for the shirt, which she left hanging open over her breasts.

"I want you to take me here," she said huskily. "Right here. Against the wall."

He was not entirely certain he grasped what she was asking, or that he could walk that far unaided. "Right there?"

"Here." She nodded. "I have a demon that needs exorcising, my lord, and I want to burn this into my mind so that when I close my eyes, this will be all that I see and feel."

Something in the timbre of her voice turned Angus's bones to jelly and his flesh to iron. He had not planned on this, not at all. In fact, when he had seen her standing out under the starlight with MacGillivray, the pair of them exchanging whispers like lovers, he had almost walked away and not looked back.

Now there she stood with her coltish long legs bared, her body lush and ripe, challenging him to take her in a way that sent the blood pounding into an erection that was already perilously close to causing him permanent damage.

"You won't mind if I remove some encumbrances first," he murmured, his voice low and fierce, his cloak already hitting the floor. He ripped at the brass buttons on his tunic and waistcoat, tearing them off as one garment, casting them aside without a care as to how close they came to the fire grate. Toe to heel he removed each boot and kicked it aside. His shirt was tugged free of his breeches and pulled over his head; the buttons over his codpiece were released, an action that caused his flesh to surge forward, rigid and tall against his stomach before the unwanted garment was shoved below his hips.

Anne stood perfectly still against the wall, her body drowning in alternating waves of heat and icy anticipation. Her eyes were all that moved, avidly devouring the glorious lines of his naked body. There were some subtle changes, she noted. The muscles in his arms seemed to be more defined, his thighs thicker with sinew, and there were more distinct ridges of power sculpted into the lean bands across his waist and belly.

"You have not been sitting idly around the barracks," she said, as breathless as if she had been running.

"There are a few muscles I've not had the opportunity to exercise," he murmured, beginning to close the gap between them.

Because she could not help herself, she stared openly at his erection. "They do not appear to have suffered."

"Believe me"—he drew a breath and exhaled it slowly— "they have suffered."

He stopped just shy of touching her and let his gaze roam down the torn seam of her shirt. It was as bold as a physical caress and Anne felt the cloth quivering to echo her body's needs. She moistened her lips and saw his eyes flicker upward, saw his flesh take a small leap even as his hands came forward and slowly, deliberately peeled the edges of cambric aside. The fingers of one hand skimmed upward to capture a breast, the other went lower, brushing lightly over the tangle of coppery curls before slipping between her thighs.

Anne pressed her head against the wall. She was trembling, slippery with the heat of wanting him, and she heard him suck in a slow breath at the discovery. He stroked again, deeper this time, his finger tracing along the folds of her flesh, probing the silky rifts until he heard her imploring whimper and felt her thighs tighten around the intrusion. He moved forward again so that it was no longer his fingers sliding to and fro into the wetness, no longer just a teasing threat.

When her hips started to curl upward to meet him, he bowed his head, his mouth nuzzling her neck, his tongue painting rivers of fire along her throat and across her shoulder. His hands smoothed over her breasts, his thumbs toyed with the stiffened peaks of her nipples, making short work of the rest of her patience.

Cursing softly, Anne brought herself up onto the tips of her toes, pressing her bared breasts against him. She reached down and grasped hold of his flesh at the base, refusing to let him thrust forward again without knowing some of the torment he was evoking. A groan brought him sliding into the tight sheath of her fist, his flesh hot and sleek with her moisture. She squeezed her fingers and held him there, rubbing herself over the smooth, engorged head until the pressure became exquisitely focused and his hips bucked with his own urgency.

"I don't know," he gasped, "if this can be done gently."

"It just needs to be *done,*" she countered.

The teasing was over.

He brushed her hand aside, parting her thighs with a hunger that elevated desire to raw lust. Greedy for the feel of her, he lifted her and settled her over his flesh in the same fluid motion that saw him thrusting upward as deeply as the angle of penetration would allow. He staggered a moment, nearly undone by the ferocity of sensation that poured around and through him, but the climax was a small one, controllable. It even helped to temper the overwhelming need he felt just to slam into her for quick gratification. She had already wrapped her arms around his shoulders, clutching at any means to give her leverage and bring her closer, but at his ragged command, she hooked her legs around his waist and locked her ankles behind. He bent his knees, putting all his power into the next upward, inward thrust, reaching a depth even he had never dreamed possible before.

Anne's head arched back and she cried out. He stopped on a panted oath, fearing he had hurt her, but her hands clawed into his back and her nails gouged into his skin and her body strained so feverishly against him that he gave her what she asked for and did not hold back again.

Anne's pleasure was explosive. Her orgasm began at the first stroke of his flesh and did not relent until long after he had shuddered through his own release. Even then there were shivers and tiny quaking spasms of pleasure that kept her arms locked tightly around him. She doubted she could have moved anyway, for he still held her braced against the wall, his legs trembling, his chest heaving in a ragged effort to catch and hold a breath.

Anne did not care if they remained there forever. Nothing mattered, not the war, not the prince, not the fact she was pinned like a starfish against the mudded timbers of a small, dusty cottage. All that mattered was that she was in her husband's arms, that those arms had been shaking with the force of his pleasure . . . and were doing so now with the startling, surprising sound of his laughter.

"Sweet God above," he gasped. "Grant me mercy and tell me why, tell me how you manage to do this to me. I was ever such a sane man. Sane, confident, noble, dignified. Look at me now."

Languid and drugged on passion, her thighs running slick with the proof of his fall from grace, Anne took his face between her hands and kissed him. "I do not have to look, my lord husband. I can still feel you inside me and I detect no lack of confidence there."

"And this demon you sought to exorcise?"

"He is well and truly gone." Anne smiled and drew his mouth back down to hers. "But just in case . . ."

Anne was wakened by the sound of a foot thumping gently into a boot to seat it. She raised a hand to rub her eyes and saw a shadowy figure searching around in the gloom for missing articles of clothing. He had found his breeches and his boots, but his shirt seemed to be eluding him.

"What time is it?"

"Dawn is not far off," Angus said. "I had hoped to be back in Falkirk by now. Hawley's pickets are a nervous lot."

"You are going back?"

He glanced over, then glanced away again as if the question caused physical pain.

"Angus—"

"Don't ask me, Anne. Please don't ask me to do something I cannot do."

"But why?" She sat up and curled her legs beneath her, heedless of her nudity. "Just tell me why. I know your heart is not with the English. I know it."

"Ahh, there it is." He snatched up his shirt and shook out the creases before shrugging it on over his head. A quick tuck into his waistband left wads of uneven linen here and there, but he donned his waistcoat anyway and buttoned it snug to his torso. His fingers served as a comb between adding layers of clothing—and as a means of avoiding having to look at the pale figure on the bed.

He could not believe he had allowed himself to fall asleep. Neither could he believe he had permitted himself to be lured to such recklessness by soft breasts, softer lips, and silky thighs. Robert Hardy would be beside himself, thinking his master had been captured. At the moment, with Anne sitting there in a waterfall of tousled red curls, it did not seem such a bad notion, but Angus pushed the thought aside and reached for his tunic.

"Just tell me why," she said again.

"I have told you a dozen times. I've given my word, my oath as an officer of the crown."

She watched him struggle with the brass buttons.

"You promised me not so long ago that you would never lie to me," she said evenly.

"I am not lying; I have given my word. Have you seen my gloves?"

The cold efficiency was back. His movements were calculated and sure, his jaw squared against any suggestion that a few hours of exhaustive lovemaking could have changed the way the earth spun on its axis.

Anne looked down at her hands, for her world had certainly been sent on a spin. "They're on the chair, under your cloak."

He grunted his thanks and swung the enormous wool cloak off the seat and settled it around his shoulders. He stood there a moment staring at the top of Anne's head, at the white slope of her shoulders, at the lushness of her body. He actually started to pull on one of his gloves before he turned, suddenly, and threw both of them across the room. He would have liked to pick up the chair, the stool, the kettle of simmering water and hurl those as well, but there was enough chaos in his mind already without adding more.

"I came here last night with every intention of taking you away with me. Of *ordering* you, as my wife, to come away with me. If I had done that, what would your answer have been?"

She replied without hesitation. "I would have refused."

"And what reason would you have given me? What possible reason could you give for disobeying your husband, the man to whom you made a solemn vow to honor and obey? You would have said you had a previous, binding oath to another, one that had nothing to do with love or marriage vows, and for some unfathomable reason you would have expected that to be all the explanation I would need. Why, then, I would ask by imploring all the saints in heaven to give me the strength to understand, is it not enough of an explanation for *you*? Is *your* word worth more than mine because you happen to think your cause is more just? Or do you not see the contradiction, the pretension, the *irony* of your asking me to break an oath when you yourself would not consider doing so for an instant?" He spread his hands and dropped them in frustration. "You cannot have it both ways, Anne. Either I am a man of my word, or I am not. Which is it to be?"

"Your loyalty to the Stuart king should come first," she cried softly. "Your grandfather was a member of his council, your father fought in The Fifteen."

He expelled a breath and sat on the edge of the bed. The mattress was stuffed with thatching and hung on ropes stretched across a plain wood frame, all of which protested loudly, each in its own manner. During the night creaks and rustlings had amused them, now it grated on the nerves and made their surroundings seem cheap and tawdry.

"Anne . . . look at me." He waited a moment, then took up her hand and raised it to his lips. "I never swore an oath to the Stuart king. Never. Not here, not in Italy, not in France. My grandfather did, my father surely did, and perhaps my brothers, too, but *I* never swore allegiance to James Francis Stuart or his son, not even in absentia. Not even in a secret toast to the king over the water."

"What about your loyalty to Scotland? Do you want to see our country under English rule forever?"

"What I want and what is likely to happen are two very different things. Hawley has brought eight thousand crack troops to Falkirk. Well-armed, well-fed, eager for revenge. If there is a battle in the next few days—and I cannot see any way of avoiding one, shy of having the prince surrender under a white flag—the whole damned conflagration will be resolved one way or another, and my greatest fear is that this ... this reckless courage, this ... incredibly valiant display of honor and loyalty will all have been for naught. The prince will return to France, his army will go back to their farms and clachans, and in another twenty years we will have to go through it all again."

She was quiet, but at least she did not pull away from his touch as he smoothed a shock of red hair off her cheek and tucked it behind her ear.

"Will you come back with me?"

Her eyes were large and grew shockingly bright as she fought a suspicious sheen of wetness.

"I had to ask," he said helplessly. "Can you not see I am terrified to the bone at the thought of you being anywhere near a battlefield?"

"John has already threatened more violence than I could encounter in a battle with the devil if I do not stay well behind the lines with the prince and his royal guard," she admitted.

"And you will keep your word? To him and to me?"

"Dear God," she whispered, her eyes growing even rounder, wetter. "You will be in the front line, won't you?"

"I will be with my men, yes."

She closed her eyes and leaned forward, burying her face in the curve of his shoulder. She bit her lip against the hot flooding of tears, but the night had been too emotional, the pleasure too intense, the loss she might sustain too horrific to stanch the two wide streaks that flowed down her cheeks. Her arms went up around his shoulders and she pressed her body against him, ignoring the scratch and bite of wool and buttons. For his part, Angus held her as close as was humanly possible without crushing her half to death.

"I have to leave. Will you not, please, for pity's sake, reconsider and come with me?"

"Will *you* reconsider and stay?"

Angus held her a moment longer, then stood with great reluctance. Half blinded by something stinging hotly in his own eyes, he walked quickly over to retrieve his gloves. Knowing there was nothing more to say, he went out the door into the predawn chill and walked hurriedly toward the nearby woods.

He was not yet safely inside the outer rim of firs when a tall, tartan-clad figure with the golden hair of a lion stepped out of the shadows, cocked two steel-butted pistols, and aimed them dead center at his chest.

Chapter Fourteen

*A*ngus slowly raised his hands and stared into John MacGillivray's dark eyes for what seemed like half a lifetime. There was a slight breeze blowing, and it ruffled some of the long brass-colored hair that hung below John's bonnet, but other than that, the Highlander was still as a stone.

"Ye're that lucky I didna shoot ye for a thief," MacGillivray said finally. "Or a spy."

"I came only to see my wife, nothing more."

"Aye. So I gathered. I had men watchin' the forest an' they told me they saw someone sniffin' around the cottage. Ye'll be warmed to know there were twenty of us standin' outside the door, ready to break it down on the instant."

"What stopped you?"

"We found yer manservant shiverin' his teeth to nubs ayont the road."

"Hardy? Is he all right?"

MacGillivray scowled. "He's a damned sight better than he would be an he were still waitin' on ye in the cold."

The subtle *snick* of both hammers being uncocked eased the pressure in Angus's chest, but he was careful to wait for permission—which came in the form of a casual nod—before he lowered his arms.

"Where is he now?"

"We're keepin' him warm for ye. The horses, too. We were no' too sure how long ye'd be."

Angus heard the soft rustle of more footsteps and turned to see two more figures melt out of the trees beside him. He recognized one of them instantly, despite the suspended blue gloom of the air, for he had met Alexander Cameron some years before during his travels around Europe. Only slightly less unforgettable was his friend and clansman, Aluinn MacKail.

"Cameron." Angus nodded to acknowledge their presence. "MacKail. It has been a long time. Still tilting at windmills, I see."

"Call us hopeless romantics," Alex said. "Not too dissimilar, however, from a man who rides into the heart of an enemy encampment just to speak to his wife. Although"—he paused and grinned—"from the sound of it, you were enjoying more than just conversation."

Angus glanced at MacKail, who was also grinning above the tartan he had muffled around his throat. "Thatch roofing," he said. "Keeps the weather out, but I wouldn't trust it for keeping secrets in."

Angus expelled an angry stream of misty breath. "I trust you all enjoyed the entertainment."

"I have no doubt we would have," Cameron said, "had there not been other diversions."

He pointed behind them to the road. Dawn was beginning to smear across the horizon, lifting the gloom enough to reveal the sprawled bodies of several clansmen rolled in their tartans who had staggered away from the tavern and not thought the effort worthwhile to find their beds. Lying together in the middle of the road, the one draped across the other's chest, were Struan MacSorley and Gillies MacBean. The bigger man was laid out like a crucifixion, obviously the first to go down; MacBean looked as if he'd had time to sit and enjoy a laugh before he careened over.

Cameron clucked his tongue and removed a cigar from an inner pocket. "That's twice now, including Count Fanducci," he said, handing it to MacGillivray. "Struan will be as pleasant as a bear when he wakens."

Angus was the only one who did not laugh. "May I ask

what happens now? Am I to be marched to some puppet court as your prisoner?"

"Actually, we thought we would be neighborly an' provide ye with an escort back as far as Dunmore," MacGillivray said. "We wouldna want it on our conscience if ye were picked off by one of our own lads."

"You are letting me go?"

"If yer wife could no' persuade ye to stay, we didna think we'd have any better luck."

"Just like that? No questions, no appeals to my loyalties or honor, no attempt to get any information from me?"

"Ah, well, now." Cameron propped one booted foot on a rock and draped an arm over his knee. "Since you mentioned it, we were a little curious about a few things."

"I am sure you are. Just as I am sure you know that as an officer in His Majesty's service, I am not obliged to tell you anything more than my rank."

"Captain MacKintosh, is it not?" Cameron asked with an easy smile. "First Royal Scots Brigade under the command of William Keppel, earl of Albemarle. I understand your personal regiment has become somewhat depleted—fewer than forty men all told?—but they will likely be incorporated into the ranks of the Argyle militia. A prized command, since Albemarle and Hawley answer only to Cumberland himself. How is the earl anyway? Is his stomach dyspepsia still troubling him? He should not be so insistent upon eating so many raw eggs in the morning. Two dozen at a seating would have any man blowing sulfur."

Angus was irritably impressed, as he was meant to be. "Since you seem to be well informed already, I fail to see what possible curiosities might yet remain."

"That's exactly what we are, just curious. Mainly about why Hawley has not moved to establish his position yet. There are few places between here and Falkirk large enough to accommodate two armies. A prudent general would take the precaution of staking out the only high ground."

"One could make the same observation about the prince."

"One could," Cameron agreed, "if one was not aware of the four thousand men on the march even as we speak."

"Your army is on the move? Today? But I thought—" He

bit his lip and stopped, but the damage was done. He could see it in Cameron's widening grin.

"You thought we would behave like perfect gentlemen and wait for the general to amass all his supply wagons, artillery, and ammunition carts? You thought we would wait for him to address the time and place for the attack?"

That was precisely what Hawley had thought, Angus acknowledged inwardly. He had surveyed the high ground on the moor and pronounced it "suitable," but had taken no further steps to establish a royalist presence, apart from a few sentries and patrols. He had retired to his billet confident to the point of arrogance that the rebels would never dare initiate an attack. Moreover, he had dispatched a courier the previous evening with a message stating that he thought it uncivilized to plan any sort of military engagement that might spill over onto a Sunday, and if it suited the prince, Monday morning should do nicely.

"I don't suppose it would do any harm now to tell you our men were rousted two hours ago," Cameron continued. "The rest will be in their boots as soon as the sun is up. By noon Lord George will have the high ground as well as the weather gauge."

Angus felt a second chill trickle down his spine, this one far more ominous. If half the prince's army had left camp during the night and the other half was taking to the road before too long, it would set the stage for another surprise attack like the one at Prestonpans, when the Jacobite army had circled around behind the Elector's troops and launched their attack from the primordial ooze of a seemingly impassable swamp.

Hawley had vowed not to make that particular mistake again and, to guard against it, had camped with the choppy waters of the firth at his back and a sodden moor on his flank. But he had grievously underestimated his enemy's ability to rebound from a disheartening retreat that might well have demoralized any other army.

"If you actually do prevail at Falkirk," Angus said, "have you given any thought to what Cumberland's reaction will be? Despite your efforts to stymie him with nonexistent French fleets and Dutch treaties, he will be returning from London with over five thousand Hessian soldiers, all of whom are huge ugly brutes who sharpen their bayonets with their teeth."

Alexander Cameron's dark eyes glittered. "So Cumberland is in London, is he? We were wondering where he had gotten to, and since none of our people could seem to find him, we were worried he might have been creeping up on us by way of Rutherglen."

Angus's brow folded sharply.

"Moreover, if he is bringing five thousand troops back with him—and I thank you for the advance warning—it should put him at least two weeks out of the hunt. As to his reaction should Lord George Murray prevail yet again, I would say he would be pissed. Aluinn?"

"Aye," MacKail agreed amiably. "Pissed. John?"

MacGillivray nodded. "Aye, proper pissed."

Angus stared, realizing Cameron had effortlessly extracted exactly the kind of information he had so boldly declared he would not give them. Great care had been taken not to divulge the Duke of Cumberland's whereabouts, and the news of the Hessians had been delivered orally by courier with nothing trusted to paper.

"No need to fall on your sword," MacKail said, reading the look on Angus's face. "Alex does that to everyone. It's a knack. When you have been with him as long as I have, in fact, you expect to walk away scratching your head at least once a day."

"Yes, well, I would rather not be around long enough to test your theory, if it is all the same to you."

"Aye." Cameron shifted, squinting up at the sky. "I can smell rain in the air. You had best be on your horse and away from here before the weather turns."

Angus followed his glance and saw that what he thought had just been a reluctant dawn was in reality a low, dark ceiling of cloud hovering over the tops of the fir trees. The wind was beginning to gust as well, snatching at the wings of his cloak, driving the dampness straight down the nape of his neck.

"I'll show him the way," MacGillivray said. "I've an escort of MacKintosh men waiting."

"We'll say good-bye here, then." Alexander Cameron

straightened, and without the smallest trace of malice or
mockery extended his hand. "I wish you Godspeed and good
health, MacKintosh. It is a true pity you have chosen to take
your stand on the wrong side of the field, but I bear you no
personal ill will. Oh, and by the way, if you are looking for
General Hawley upon your return, I'm afraid he might have
overslept this morning. Since we knew he detested camp cots
and damp canvas so much, we persuaded the Lady
Kilmarnock to offer the hospitality of Callendar House for
the comfort of him and his senior officers. They threw a little
party in his honor last night, and the wine may have gone to
his head."

"I've seen Hawley drink a quart of whisky without batting
an eye," Angus commented.

"Laced with opiates?"

Angus shook his head. "May I ask why you did not just
poison him?"

"That wouldn't have been sporting, now, would it?"

Angus laughed despite himself and clasped Cameron's
outstretched hand, reminded once again that he was trusting
Anne's safety and well-being to the hands of these reckless
madmen. He did not want to dwell on the dangers she would
be facing in short order, but how could he not? She had promised to stay well out of harm's way, but how could he know
for sure she would honor that promise?

Deep in thought, he followed MacGillivray along a path
that would take them through the woods, but as soon as the
village was out of sight behind the trees, the tall Highlander
stopped and swung around.

"I just want ye to hear it from ma own lips that I never
touched her. I wanted to. I came damned close more times
than I care to admit, but she has never broken faith with ye
an' I'll no' hear it said from any man's lips that she did. No'
even yours."

"I believe you. I believed Anne last night."

"Last night? Last night we were both feelin' our *uisque*. I
was the more fool for lettin' slip something I've been carryin'
around on ma tongue like a glowin' brand, but it was damned
near burnin' me. Aye, I would have let it burn her, too, an' the

devil take you, Angus Moy, if she'd given me the smallest sign that she could live with herself afterward."

John stopped to take a heave of breath, the bulk of his shoulders and chest making him look as dark and threatening as the firs that loomed on either side of the path. Having made the comparison, it occurred to Angus that a body could be thrown under those trees and lie there undiscovered until the spring thaw.

"Aye," John said, reading the wariness in Angus's eyes. "Have ye any idea how lucky ye are? Do ye ken how many times I've thought just to take ye in hand an' crack yer spine over ma knee? Ye'd snap like a twig, ye would. An' then it would be over an' done, an' I'd not have to look into her eyes an' see the hurt ye've caused. I'd tell her every day how brave an' beautiful she was, an' if she once . . . *once* looked at me the way she looks at you . . ." He had his hand raised for emphasis, but when the words and all their unspoken possibilities failed him, he curled his fingers into a fist and looked away, looked anywhere but into the face of the man whose betrayal had made Anne cry herself to sleep nearly every night at Dunmaglass.

In the end, he settled for spitting an oath into the ground as he turned away.

"John, I know how you feel. And I know how Anne feels, but you don't understand—"

The fist came up again in warning, still clenched, though the Highlander did not look back. "Enough. Ye've said enough. Another word, I might just as well spare the clan the shame of seein' ye across the battlefield wearin' Hanover colors."

"Then that is what you will have to do, because by God"—Angus raised his voice to compensate for the distance MacGillivray's huge strides were putting between them—"I have stood here and listened to you declare your love for my wife; the least you can do is hear me out. If not as your chief, then as someone who was once your friend."

MacGillivray stopped. His upper torso swelled as he sucked in a deep breath, then he reached up and snatched the bonnet off his head, throwing it down with another curse. He shrugged off the length of plaid that had been wrapped around his shoulders, and reached up with two hands to grasp the hilt of the *clai' mór* he wore strapped across his back. The sound of five feet of honed steel sliding out of its studded leather sheath shivered through the cold air and sent Angus's hand to the hilt of his own slim saber.

He did not draw it, however, knowing it would be like matching a sapling against an oak tree, and when MacGillivray stalked back, close enough to touch the point of steel to the hard ridge of Angus's windpipe, the hesitation was mocked with a sneer.

"Ye want to say yer piece, say it."

"As simply as I can, then: The reason I will be standing on the opposite side of the battlefield today is not that I want to be. It is because Forbes gave me his word . . . in writing and stamped with the royal seal . . . that as long as I served in King George's army neither Anne nor my mother would be in any danger of arrest. It was a guarantee of immunity, and had I not agreed to the terms, the opposite result would have been the immediate signing of warrants for them, for you, Fearchar, MacBean, and about two dozen other lairds of Clan Chattan. He was not going to give me any choice in the matter, just as he had not given much choice to other lairds in my position. Luckily, I was warned ahead of time and managed to convince him my years in Europe had left me indifferent to the political intrigues of either side. To my shame, I even led him to believe I was indifferent to my marriage as well, that Anne's arrest would be more of a blot against the noble name than anything else. Unfortunately, I seemed to have played the part too well, for she began to believe it herself, and for that damning cruelty, if you still want to take my head off my shoulders, do it now, for the pain of eternal silence would be less than what I have had to endure these past few months! Here! I will even make it easier for you! A clean stroke should free us both."

Angrily, he tore at the fastening of his cloak and ripped it aside along with the underlying edges of his tunic and waistcoat. So vigorously did he yank open his shirt and invite a quick end, he scraped a peeling of flesh from his chest, deep enough that it turned instantly red with blood. There he stood, his legs braced apart, the wind against his back, the dark locks of his hair blown forward over his cheeks, and waited for his fate to be decided in MacGillivray's eyes.

It seemed to be a long time coming, but in the end, John slowly lowered the point of his sword. His eyes were narrowed, glittering like two shards of black glass, and his eyebrows drew together in a deep V that only grew deeper and darker as he absorbed what Angus had said.

"Immunity? Ye've whored yerself to the *Sassenachs* to win us all a promise of immunity?"

"Bluntly put, as always. But yes. I thought it worth the price to safeguard my family. At the same time, it left you free to carry on your smuggling and blockade running, neither of which has sat well with Forbes, I might add, especially when he had the means and proof to arrest you half a dozen times over in the past months."

MacGillivray glowered a moment longer. "Why, for the love o' God, did ye not tell me? Or Annie, for Christ's sake. Ye've put her through royal hell, ye bastard."

"I thought I could protect her better this way," Angus said lamely. "Her contempt for me had to be genuine if for no other reason than to help convince Loudoun and the others that greed was my only motive, nothing else. It was not the kind of act I thought she could sustain over several months."

"But you could?"

"My entire life has been a performance; I was raised to wear a mask at all times."

"Aye, well. Ye wore it well enough ye nearly sent her into the arms of another man."

"It was a chance I had to take. Can you imagine the leverage Forbes would have had if he knew how desperately I loved my own wife?"

The admission, as much as the raw honesty in Angus's voice, set MacGillivray back another step. "Still an' all," he said after a moment, "she willna thank ye when she finds out."

Angus shook his head. "She mustn't find out. I want your word on that, John."

"Why the devil would ye want me to swear to such a thing? If she knew why ye were doin' this—"

"She would only feel twice as guilty and hurt as before."

"What about the others? Gillies? Fearchar? Do they no' deserve to know why their laird is wearin' the Hanover cockade?"

Angus released his grip on his torn shirt and drove his hands through his hair. "No. No, it has to be this way, and if you don't believe me, just look at yourself. Ten seconds ago you were ready to split me open like a melon. Now you have that same noble look on your face that you had when we were boys and Ranald MacFeef threw me in the bog. You were five years younger than I, but I was the one lying there sobbing over the stains on my brand-new satin breeches while you were standing over me like a bloody great wolfhound daring them to laugh or pelt me with another plug of dung. Tell me, if you can, that you would not come straight back to Falkirk with me now if I asked you to guard my back?"

MacGillivray glared. His lip curled as if he were about to deny the charge, but in the end he only spat out an oath. "Ye could always just turn around an' go back to the cottage. Then I'd guard yer back through the gates o' hell if need be. If we win today, I'm of a mind Loudoun's guarantees will no' be worth the paper they're written on, anyway."

Angus cursed his way through a sigh of exasperation. "But if the British win, they might be worth the weight of every insult and affront I've had to endure."

"In other words, yer lack o' faith in us hasna been entirely an act."

"It has nothing to do with faith, my friend, and everything to do with artillery, cavalry, and thousands of infantrymen who have been fed nothing but a steady diet of drilling and discipline. Suppose—just for the sake of argument, if you will— that the prince is captured or slain today, and his army is driven from the field in defeat. Anne's cousins safeguard her as they would a younger sister, and I've no doubt that every man who sees her riding before them like a Celtic Jeanne d'Arc would sooner drive a red hot stake into his own eye than be caught looking upon her with anything other than pure, honorable thoughts. But if the British win, they will not stand on ceremony. Men will be hanged, executions will be rife, and any woman found wearing the white cockade, regardless of who she is or what noble quest brought her to the field, will be treated like spoils of war."

"That will never happen," MacGillivray said, his hand tightening around the hilt of his sword again.

"Can you guarantee it? Can you absolutely guarantee you will walk off the field alive, victorious, and in total command of an army drunk on blood lust? If so, you are a better man than I, for I've seen a full British volley, and I've seen a battalion of cavalry at full charge, and I'll not be foolish enough or arrogant enough to predict my own odds of survival at the end of the day. But if I do come through this alive, I've a better chance of stopping my wife from being raped by a corps of triumphant dragoons than you would with your pride bloodied and your sword surrendered."

MacGillivray bared his teeth in a snarl and started to say he would never surrender his sword, not while his body still drew breath, but another, calmer side of him could see Angus's reasoning. Much as it galled him to think of the consequences of defeat, after they had waited so long to take part in the rebellion, he had to admit the possibility was abhorrently real. He also knew full well how murderous a British volley could be. Anne believed he was immune to fear, but he was not; he simply pushed it to the back of his mind and refused to look at it too closely.

A cold, fat droplet of rain splashed on his face. The sky was as light as it was likely to get and he could hear the distant cacophony of pipers skirling the men awake, bolstering them for the long day ahead. With the camp spread so far, the sounds came from all directions, pipers from each clan playing their distinct *piob rach'd* to stir the blood. The MacGillivray's personal contingent comprised about eighty men, all of whom would be in the front ranks on the field of honor.

"All right," he said with a grim, reluctant nod. "Ye have ma word I'll not say anything to Annie about this. I'll not even tell her we saw ye or spoke, because then she would be hangin' off ma collar wantin' to know exactly what was said, word for word, and I'm no' sure I could lie to her. It will be enough of a trial just gettin' her to stay off the field."

"You will do it, though. You *will* keep her away from the

battlefield at all costs! In this, I do not care if you have to tie her hand and foot to a tree somewhere. In fact, I would almost prefer it."

John resheathed his sword and fetched his bonnet from the forest floor. "She's no' completely daft. Besides, she's the only one who will be able to keep Fearchar off the line."

"Good God, you aren't suggesting—"

"Aye. Barely strong enough to lift a dirk without topplin' over from the weight, but he's insistin' on standin' in the front rank. It will be up to Annie to see him safe away where he willna be trampled to death in the charge. If she canna do it, or willna do it, I'll be after findin' enough rope for the pair o' them."

Chapter Fifteen

*A*nne was in no fit mood for company when Robbie and Jamie Farquharson came pounding on her door shortly after dawn. Angus had been gone perhaps an hour, and she had spent the time sitting alone in the dark, wrapped in a blanket that still held the scent of his hair and body. At first she had only felt abysmally sorry for herself. But knowing that would never do, she allowed anger, then resentment to flood into the empty spaces Angus had so recently filled with hope and promise.

Try as she might, she could not be entirely angry with her husband, for he had made the point well when he asked if his honor was worth any less than hers. It wasn't, of course, and she supposed she had known it all along; it had just been difficult to accept. Oddly enough, it brought some measure of relief, in a way, because she knew she no longer had to question or justify her love for him—to herself or anyone else. He was every bit as honorable as Fearchar or John MacGillivray or Alexander Cameron, and what was more, he loved her despite their opposing politics, despite their different backgrounds, different temperaments, and that was far more than most wives could ever hope to have in their marriages.

The pounding on the door startled her out of her reverie

and she answered it with an irritated yank. "I am awake. No need to bring down the—"

The appearance of the twins stopped the breath in her throat, for they stood under the glowering gray sky and looked more fearsome than usual, with muskets in their hands and broadswords strapped about their waists. They both wore pistols and dirks thrust into their belts, another dirk tucked into the garter on their right calves. They carried targes of wood and leather studded with nails, and even though it clearly threatened rain, they were not encumbered by extra lengths of plaid around their shoulders. Their bonnets had been brushed clean, and new sprigs of red whortleberry—the clan badge—were pinned to the crest. Whatever weariness they might have been feeling from the debauchery at the tavern had been replaced with the hard, bright sparkle of excitement.

"Well?" Jamie demanded. "Ye're starin' at us like as we've got three heads, no' two."

Anne glanced over their shoulders and saw more men on the road, all of them bristling with guns and swords, pikes and axes. One of the MacCrimmon pipers was coming from the direction of the main camp, leading a hundred or more of his clansmen in a brisk march through St. Ninians. The revelers who had fallen asleep by the roadside were sitting up slowly and scratching their heads, but they seemed to know exactly what was happening and within moments staggered to their feet and were running in the opposite direction, grinning and shouting at their comrades not to kill all the English before they could arm themselves and return.

"What is happening?" Anne asked. "Where is everyone going?"

"Lord George says if the bastard willna bring the fight tae us, we'll damn well bring it tae him. The MacGillivray gave us orders we were tae come fetch ye. We'll be marchin' in the second column alongside the Camerons, by Christ's bonny blood!"

"Aye," Robbie nodded eagerly. "We'll be wi' them on the field too, an' that's the best place a fightin' mon could hope tae be! Come on, come on, lass! Ye dinna want tae be left ahind, do ye?"

Anne whirled around and flung off the blanket she had been holding around her shoulders. She had swum naked with her cousins more times than she could recall—albeit mostly in their youth—and thus had no reservations about running to and fro in various stages of undress while she found and pulled on the layers of her clothing. She donned trews and a heavy linen shirt, then slammed her feet into stockings and boots. Ignoring an impatient shout from Robbie, she shoved her arms into a long skirted waistcoat quilted in satin, embroidered with sprigs of whortleberry, and added a fine lace jabot around her collar. There was no time to brush her hair properly, but a few savage strokes allowed her to divide it into three thick sections and plait it quickly over her shoulder. When the plait had been pinned, tucked, and crammed under a bonnet, she donned a blue velvet coat with gold buttons and lace on the cuffs, and strapped on two leather belts—one that held her pistols, the other a sword and dirk.

She doubted she had ever dressed faster in her life, but the twins were pacing back and forth like cats with turpentine up their tails. The three of them hastened down the path to where some clansmen were waiting with Robert the Bruce—her heroically and hopefully portentously named gray gelding—but before she put a toe to the stirrup, she gasped and ran back to the cottage. Finding the common clothes she had worn the previous day, she searched an inner pocket and withdrew the cameo locket she carried, with Angus's picture inside. After pinning it over her breast, she drew on her leather gloves and went back outside.

The three Farquharsons mounted and rode off at a quick trot to rendezvous with MacGillivray and the rest of the men from Clan Chattan. The fields were swarming with men, some already formed into companies, brigades, and regiments. The sixty-seven-year-old Lord Pitsligo saw Anne and waved, as did the younger Murray of Broughton standing at the head of his splendidly attired hussars, the latter distinguishable by their fur caps and black leather cross straps. Lord Elcho's company of Lifeguards was composed of gentlemen, all of great fortune; their uniforms were red and blue, and to a man they were well mounted on horses that would not have looked out of place at a race ground.

For the most part, however, the clansmen wore their kilted plaids, warm bullhide doublets, and tartan coats. On their bonnets was the badge that identified their clan, and on their lips the *cath-ghairm* that rallied them for battle. Every clan had their piper to stir their blood to fever pitch and, hopefully, strike a note of terror into the enemy who faced them across a field. The chiefs brought along a bard as well, who would record the day's events in exacting detail so that the valorous acts of bravery would be set down for posterity and the glory of the clan. These were usually men of meticulous memories and sonorous voices who would later compose the songs and poems to be retold around the campfires.

Anne's heart swelled with pride when they breasted the last hill and she saw the men of Clan Chattan. They were waiting for their colonel to lead them to the field, and when they saw her, a great cheer went up, louder than any skirling piper. Some would die this day, others would come away with dreadful, crippling injuries. But to a man they cheered, and half a dozen of them hoisted John MacGillivray onto their shoulders before depositing him on his horse.

MacGillivray was grinning as hugely as his men, his blond hair streaming back in the gusts of wind. He too had dressed with care, substituting for the plain woolen jacket he had worn away from Aberdeen a more regal one dyed a rich crotal blue. His hose and breacan were red with blue and black stripes; *brógs* had replaced his boots, the deer-hide worn fur out, and she knew this would be for ease of running. His bonnet sat on a jaunty angle on his head, the white Stuart cockade prominent beside the sprig of whortleberry. Strapped across his back was the basket-hilted *clai' mór*, deadly enough in his powerful hands without the need for the assorted pistols and dirks that bristled over all points of his body.

He tugged a burnished forelock as a sign of respect as he greeted Anne, then grinned even wider. "Lord George wanted ye to ride with the prince, but I told him we wanted ye here with us, Colonel. With yer men. At least until we reach the moor."

He said it loud enough to cause another roar of approval and Anne, blinking with her determination to keep her eyes dry, proudly took her place at the head of the long column of men. The Bruce seemed to know he carried someone very important that day, for his steps were high and sure, his tail held aloft in a fan of gray silk. Unlike other mounts that were unaccustomed to so many men and drums and pipers, he neither flinched nor broke out of line as the prince's army marched to war.

Twelve miles to the south, Adrienne de Boule lowered the delicate china cup from her mouth, leaving a small bead of chocolate on her lower lip. Without preamble, Major Roger Worsham leaned over and licked it away, his tongue continuing the sweep by snaking between her lips and embarking on a deep, prowling kiss.

He had no idea of the time, for the light that came through the window was dull and gray. The wind was gusting, spraying the glass with spatters of rain that seemed to justify a leisurely stretch and subsequent snuggling down onto the soft cushion of her breasts. His head was still fuddled and thick from the wine he had consumed the previous evening—a fact he considered odd, since he could have sworn he only had two, perhaps three glasses. And although he could not recall with any certainty how well he had performed, he assumed he had not left the company flags unfurled, for the minx looked tousled and smelled deliciously of sex.

He let his hand wander along the satiny smoothness of her body, marveling for the thousandth time how such a beauty had come to choose him over the scores of others competing for her attention. When he curled his fingers between her thighs he was rewarded with a sultry purr, and wondered if there was enough time before the rest of the household stirred.

Two doors away in a bedroom decorated in purple damask with pale yellow accents, Major Hamilton Garner was groaning. He was lying facedown on the bed, his arms and legs sprawled, a spidery thread of saliva trickling from his open mouth. The woman beside him moved carefully to extricate herself from the tangle of covers, desperate not to waken him. Her thighs were bruised, her breasts were scratched as if some wild beast had savaged her, and every orifice of her body ached so badly she wanted to weep.

Accompanying one of the British officers to bed had not been intentional on her part, and she only had herself to blame. The major had been so handsome, his green eyes so boldly seductive, she had been flowing like a fountain all through dinner and could barely wait to feel his hands, his mouth on her body.

Now she moved as quietly and quickly as she could, gathering up her clothes like a frightened mouse collecting crumbs. Not until she stood at the door did she turn and glare at the major's milk-white body. He was groaning again, thrashing out at some unseen enemy. It had been her mistake to waken him after one such nightmare last night, and she had paid dearly for her compassion. He had lashed out at her, calling her "Catherine," and forced her to do things that made her yearn to take a knife to his body and carve away the offending parts. She felt nothing but disgust now as she gave her long blond hair a toss, bidding him farewell with a crudely upthrust middle finger.

In the morning room, General Henry Hawley sat at the breakfast table, his head aching, his tongue coated with a sour fur that no amount of chocolate seemed to remedy. He felt groggy and stupid and was certain he was overlooking something vital in his dictations to the aide-de-camp who sat beside him.

"I shall want the linens and the bedding—once it has been laundered, of course—and I imagine the Earl of Kilmarnock must have a respectable wardrobe of clothing. I noticed a very fine library as well; take care to pack the books in sturdy crates, for I should not want them to suffer during transport to Edinburgh. There is a rather handsome repeating clock in my bedchamber, and I am particularly fond of that japanned board—" He paused and indicated the inlaid cupboard on which pots of chocolate, tea, and coffee sat. "Might as well include the china and silver plate. It will make a pleasant gift for my sister-in-law, who puts great store in such things. And check the larder. There seems to be an ample supply of salt beef, sugar, ham, and whatnot for the lady to spare enough victuals to make the journey back to Edinburgh palatable. Devil me, for that matter: Take the lot. Have the extra sent in care of myself to Holyrood House."

"Yessir. What shall I tell the Lady Kilmarnock with regard to compensation?"

"Tell her what we tell them all: After we have gone, she may apply to the offices of the Judge Advocate if she wishes an accounting. Her generosity has not fooled me in the least, I say, not in the least. She claims her husband is away on business, but I suspect that business is being conducted in the company of the Pretender's camp. She should therefore count herself lucky we do not confiscate every scrap of furniture and every grain of salt, and peel the silk off the walls as well."

"Yessir."

"Which reminds me—" He sipped and pointed. "Those curtains—?"

"Yessir. I shall see to it."

A delicate peal of laughter from the hallway made Hawley wince as he turned his head. Grudging the effort, he lowered his boots from the corner of the table and stood as their hostess swept through the open doorway. Lady Kilmarnock was young, with a lively eye and a ready laugh that she used freely with guests and servants alike. She dismissed the maid to whom she had been giving instructions, then smiled and dropped in a gracious curtsy when she saw the general.

Hawley's thin-lipped response was somewhat less genuine. He had bought his first commission in 1694 and spent most of his life in the army. Approaching his seventh decade, he was unmarried and biliously unattractive. Lady Kilmarnock had not had to worry about the sanctity of her own boudoir in the absence of her husband. The general was as particular about his companions as he was his accommodations, and there was no one in Callendar House who might have enticed him save for the cook's daughter, who was barely above nine years of age and plump as a dumpling.

"Good morning, General. Good heavens, can it really be nearing noon? I trust you slept well?"

"In truth," he scowled, "I barely recall. My head feels a treat and I have stayed abed much later than my normal hour—a fit of sloth that appears to have affected some of my officers as well."

"It must be the sleeping draught I put in the supper wine."

Hawley looked startled for a moment, but when she tipped her head and laughed, he saw the jest for what it was and nodded. "I prefer to credit my lethargy to my berth, madam. Would I could fit such a comfortable bed in my tent—I should do so upon the instant." He thought about that statement a moment and looked inquiringly at his aide-de-camp, who nodded and scratched another notation on his writing tablet. When he was done, the general dismissed him with a wave of his hand. "That will be all for the time being, Corporal Martin, thank you. Please inform Majors Worsham and Garner that I expect them to be occupying those two chairs"—he pointed to opposite sides of the long table—"in five minutes, or they risk court-martial."

The aide snatched up his cap and offered a smart salute, then departed, leaving the general and Lady Kilmarnock to their breakfast. Hawley's plate was heaped high with sliced ham and beef tongue, cheese, and sweetmeats swimming in a robust gravy, none of which had appealed to him thus far, but when he heard the lady order a rasher of bacon and sausage, he signaled to the manservant to fetch two.

"I admire a female with an appetite," he said. "None of this picking at bits and slivers."

"My husband accuses me of eating like one of the cattle, though if you met him, you would see he has no shy hand at the table himself."

"Ah, yes, the cattle. We will have need of your livestock, madam, in the days ahead. There will be prisoners to feed over and above the requirements of my own men."

Lady Kilmarnock smiled. "You sound confident of victory, General."

"I am confident of the resolve of my men, dear lady. Oh yes, I know their discipline is wanting and their valor has been precarious in the past, to say the least. But"—he waved a fork with a piece of ham impaled on the tines—"a more magnificent sight than the British army standing at the ready in full battle dress is not to be found anywhere. Imagine it. Eight thousand men lined up straight as arrows. A field of scarlet, with drums beating and flags snapping overhead. It almost brings a tear to the eye, I say it almost brings a tear! What it will do to an ill-trained band of skirted rabble, well, it only remains to be seen."

"I have been told," she said carefully, "that ill-trained rabble can be quite intimidating."

"Grown men in petticoats?" The general guffawed, spitting a morsel of cheese across the table. "I should think a strong wind up the backside would render their appearance somewhat more farcical than intimidating. A most despicable enemy, I assure you. Unmannered, unprincipled. Undisciplined in the extreme, with a want of military acumen that simply stupefies the mind. Why, they have left the Pretender's standard flying in plain view these last two days on a small moor to the south and east of Bannockburn, as if that should entice us to panic. Panic? Faugh! I have been tempted to send a man on foot, on foot I say, to retrieve the damned thing for a trophy."

Lady Kilmarnock set her jaw but glanced at the door where a butler had suddenly appeared.

"My apologies for the interruption, my lady. A courier has arrived from the general's field headquarters. A most agitated young man. He insists on seeing the general at once."

"Insists, does he?" the general asked, frowning. "Tell him I am engaged and will see him when it is convenient."

The butler glanced surreptitiously at Lady Kilmarnock before apologizing to the general again. "I have already told him you were indisposed, sir, but he is most obstinate."

"Tell him to wait," the general said, pronouncing each word as if it were ten syllables long.

"Yes, sir. Very good, sir."

Hawley sucked a shred of ham out of his teeth and glared along the table at Lady Kilmarnock. "You must excuse the lack of manners in my men, dear lady. Most are villains recruited straight out of the brothels, and with little more than a sworn oath of their being Protestant and without rupture, they are entrusted with a musket and sixpence a day. They complain about the climate, they complain about their rations of biscuit and water—" He paused to shovel another forkful of dripping egg into his mouth. "I vow, some days my head aches from the sound of the lash."

"As you say, however, they do look magnificent on the battlefield," Lady Kilmarnock murmured.

Hawley's lip twisted, but before he could address her comment, the butler was back, coughing anxiously into his hand.

"Yes, Donald?" Lady Kilmarnock arched an eyebrow.

"It is the courier, my lady. He is quite beside himself. He is threatening violence unless he is brought before the general at once."

"You see, m'dear?" Hawley spread his hands in a gesture of futility. "Self-aggrandizement. Oh, very well. Show him in, show him in."

The butler stepped aside and nodded disdainfully to a figure out in the hallway. A corporal hurried past, his hat under his arm, his hair and clothing shedding rainwater as he crossed to the general's side and, without waiting for leave, leaned over and murmured a few taut words in his ear.

The general stopped chewing. "What? What's that you say?"

The corporal bent forward again.

"On the moor! Impossible! The morning report said they were twelve miles to the north and west."

"I assure you, sir, there is no mistake. They may have marched north and west, but only in order that they might circumvent Torwood and cross the river Carron at Dunipace. The rebels have taken Falkirk Moor, sir, and they look to hold it."

"Look to hold it? The devil you say!"

Hawley scraped to his feet. He strode to the door without so much as a nod in Lady Kilmarnock's direction, his shouts echoing along the hallway, startling both Major Garner and Major Worsham as they were descending the staircase. Screaming obscenities, he called for his horse and guards. At the main door, one of his aides flung his cape around his shoulders, dislodging his wig. Another scrambled to pick it up, but the general was already gone, hatless and hairless out into the rain, his napkin still tucked into his collar.

Back in the morning room Lady Kilmarnock lifted her cup and took a sip of hot chocolate. She closed her eyes a moment to savor the sweetness, then set about enjoying the rest of her meal.

Chapter Sixteen

*A*ngus Moy arrived back in the Hanover camp in plenty of time to see General Henry Hawley riding hell-bent across the field, the large white square of what looked to be a dinner napkin flapping at his throat. Close on his heels were Majors Garner and Worsham, neither of whom brought his horse to a complete halt before they veered off in opposing directions to join their regiments.

The entire camp was in an uproar with men running hither and yon, yelling for horses, for muskets, for saddles, fastening buttons and strapping on leather neck stocks as they ran past. Rain was adding to the confusion. The storm had descended with a fury, bringing high winds and torrents of freezing rain throughout the morning. As the layer of snow on the ground turned to ice, the slopes became ever more treacherous, slippery with dead grass and bramble.

Earlier, MacGillivray's escort had left Angus a mile from the moor; it had taken him nearly two hours to struggle over the uneven terrain from there to the camp. Having been shocked by the sight of Highlanders pouring through the ravines and clambering up the slopes, he had been forced to periodically find cover while the men led by Lord George Murray had taken command of the high ground. Accomplishing the deed without firing a single shot, three regiments of men from Clan Donald had held the road open for the rest of the advancing Jacobite army to snake their way onto the moor, and by noon, with the Elector's troops still scrambling to button their stocks and find their ammunition loaves, Prince Charles was erecting his standard at the rear of the field. With the pipes skirling, the MacDonalds took their traditional place on the right of the battle line with their flanks protected by a morass of bogland. Occupying the far left were the Appin Stewarts and, in between, the Camerons, Frasers, MacPhersons, MacKenzies, and the lustily cheering men of Clan Chattan.

The second line was made up of seven more battalions, including Lord Elcho's Lifeguards, and three of Lord George's Athol Brigade. Lord John Drummond's men formed up behind them in reserve. The only part of the master plan that had not gone according to dictates was the positioning of the heavy artillery. Led by the flamboyant Italian, Count Fanducci, the guns sank up to their axles in the mud as soon as they left the road, and could not be coaxed up the unstable slope in spite of a steady stream of colorful invectives.

When Angus heard the haunting strains of the MacKintosh *piob rach'd,* half of him wished he were standing alongside the golden-maned MacGillivray.

The other half prayed.

He had searched the moor, the ravine, the surrounding slope for a glimpse of Anne, but he had not seen her—not until the very last, when Hardy, at his wits' end, had been about to drag his master from the field to avoid being seen and shot out of hand.

Anne had arrived with the men of Clan Chattan, but after securing their position on the battle line and delivering some words of encouragement, she had ridden reluctantly to the rear, where the prince stood with his royal guard. Angus prayed harder than he ever had in his life that she would remain there, surrounded by a phalanx of Highlanders whose sole responsibility it was to protect Charles Stuart and his entourage with their lives.

Three regiments of dragoons gained the moor first, followed by twelve battalions of Hawley's veteran frontline troops, with

the general's artillery lagging well behind. Despite the far superior firepower of their heavy guns, they were able to haul
only two four-pounders and one smaller "grape-thrower" that
might just as well have been left in the bog with the others.

The infantrymen were hardly better off. The rain soaked
through their paper cartridges and wet their powder, so that
when it came time to unleash their first volley, one in three
muskets misfired.

Hawley was furious but not daunted. He put his faith in
his dragoons and ordered the drums to beat, sending nearly
three hundred mounted Horse into a full charge.

Facing them down, their lines holding steady, the
Jacobites nervously fingered the triggers of their muskets, one
eye on the thundering wall of approaching horseflesh, the
other on Lord George Murray, who walked up and down the
line encouraging the men to hold their positions, ordering
them not to fire until he gave the signal. He, like every other
clan chief, was fighting on foot that day.

He waited until the screaming dragoons were ten yards
away before raising his musket and signaling the steady line
of clansmen to fire. In the deafening noise and smoke-filled
discharge of a thousand guns, the dragoons balked. Their
lines broke apart in wild confusion, with half their number
dead in their saddles. Those who kept coming forward discovered why the Highlanders had remained so calm: Not
twenty feet in front of their lines there was a deep rift in the
ground that the rain and mist had obscured and where, lying
in wait at the bottom of the trough, there were more Highlanders with pikes and *clai' mórs* ready to slash at the exposed
undersides of the horses.

Hearing the screams of the startled soldiers who were
pulled down out of the saddles and slashed to bloody ribbons,
what was left of Hawley's cavalry turned and fled the field.
Major Hamilton Garner, hatless and splattered with the
bloody brains of a fellow officer, managed to turn a handful
back through the threat of his own screams and slashing
sword, but for the most part it was a repeat of their shameful
performance at Prestonpans. So eager and desperate were the
dragoons to clear the field, they trampled back through the

advancing ranks of their own infantry, causing an even greater crush of confusion and panic.

On the left, the Highland regiments led by the Camerons, the Appin Stewarts, and the MacKintoshes took aim and discharged their muskets in response to the first full volley of the opposing divisions of Hawley's infantrymen. As the general had boasted, the line was impressive, once assembled. Their tunics glowed scarlet through the haze of rain, providing well-marked targets between the stiff white leather of their neck stocks and the tall white spatterdash gaiters.

By contrast, the Highlanders in their muted plaids and plain woolen coats blended into the browns and grays of the surrounding moorland, and with nothing to aim at, most of the royalist volleys went wild.

As was their habit, the clansmen threw down their spent weapons and ran forward, the air filled with centuries-old battle cries that had carried their ancestors to meet their fate. When what remained of the Hanover front line saw them charging out of the mist and smoke, their broadswords raised overhead, the infantrymen were not far behind the dragoons in breaking rank. As they ran they took the second line with them, and General Hawley found himself staring aghast at a sea of red uniforms spilling down the slopes and rushing down the road toward the camp.

They ran by forties and fifties, fleeing without a care for the muskets they left behind, the ammunition packs they flung from their belts, the stocks they tore off and cast aside. They ran for safety in the streets of Falkirk, and when that was not deemed to be far enough, they kept running, all the way to Linlithgow, ten miles away.

Not everyone fled the field in a panic. Lord George's Athollmen, with the Camerons and MacKintoshes fighting alongside, encountered several regiments who were determined to stand and fight. A squad of government troops attempted to circle around behind Lord George in a flanking maneuver, hoping to catch his men in a crossfire. MacGillivray saw this and shouted the rallying cry of "Loch Moy," calling for the men of Clan Chattan to veer off and charge to the rescue.

His long legs scything through the bramble and frozen grass, MacGillivray led his men into a headlong confrontation with the Elector's troops. He went in with his *clai' mór* at the ready, hacking and slashing in great sweeping motions that sliced through flesh and bone as if neither was of any substance. A pocket of infantrymen had the presence of mind to mount a volley and John felt a prick in his thigh, two more in his calf and rib. He shook them off as annoying stings, but something else caught the corner of his eye and took him by such surprise he tripped over a fallen clansman and went tumbling down into a shallow ditch.

Robbie Farquharson saw MacGillivray pitch headlong and bloodied into a culvert, but he had no time to stop. He ran alongside his twin, their two swords carving a fearsomely gory swath through the English lines. Eneas was close on their heels, as was Gillies MacBean, the stocky Highlander spattered in blood and mud from head to foot.

The English faltered, turned, and found the Camerons closing down on them like a swarm of demons from hell. In a body, the Elector's troops threw down their muskets and thrust their hands high in surrender, some of them squeezing their eyes tightly shut and bursting into tears in anticipation of feeling limbs hacked from their bodies.

Alexander Cameron shouted in time to stop his men from doing exactly that, but it did not prevent them from slapping out with the flats of their swords, spitting and hurling insults, especially when it was discovered that some of the captured troops were in the Royal Scots brigades.

With the lot of them surrendered and surrounded, Gillies MacBean doubled over at the waist to catch his breath. He was not yet fully recovered from his drinking contest with Struan MacSorley the previous night and when he turned green enough that it looked as if he might actually vomit, it gave the other men a reason to laugh.

All except Robbie, who turned and stared back into the sulfurous mist.

"What is it, lad?" Aluinn MacKail asked, clapping him soundly on the shoulder. "The bastards are in flight. We've won the day. Why are you wearing such a long face?"

"It's The MacGillivray. He were caught in that last cross-fire, God preserve him, an' now it's that balky he could bleed tae death afore we find him."

"Aye, well, God preserve yerself, lad," MacGillivray said, limping up out of the mist and rain. "I've no need of His aid just yet. Someone else might well beg it though, by the by."

He dragged his arm forward, sending Anne Moy MacKintosh sprawling across the wet ground. As she had lost her bonnet, her braid hung wet down her back, and her fountain-ous lace jabot had been flung away in the mud. There was blood on her face, on the gleaming length of her sword.

"What the bluidy Christ—?" Eneas pushed his brothers aside and strode forward, offering his cousin no helping hand as she clambered to her feet again. "Where did you come from? Were ye not told tae stay back wi' the prince's guard?"

"You really did not expect me just to sit and watch," she said, her blue eyes sparkling with defiance. "Not when I can outshoot, outfight, outride the lot of you!"

MacGillivray snatched up a fistful of her jacket and spun her around to face him. He had caught a glimpse of her through the downpour and not been able to believe his eyes. Even worse, when he had gone down, it was a shot from Anne's pistol that had stopped an English soldier from plunging a bayonet into his unprotected back.

"Ye're the wife o' the clan chief, for God's sake," he hissed.

"Aye, that I am. I am also colonel of this regiment, and I'll not sit comfortably under a canvas tent sipping wine and nibbling on sweetmeats while the brave men of my clan fight and die!"

John tightened his fist, drawing her so close she could feel the heat of his steamy breath on her cheek. He was angry enough to throttle her, a sentiment obviously not shared by her cousins, who whooped and tossed their sodden bonnets in the air, giving their answer plain enough, praising her courage. They scooped her out of MacGillivray's clutches and propped her on their shoulders, prancing around in maniacal circles until she grew dizzy from laughing and called for relief.

None of the Englishmen were amused. Huddled together in a forlorn clump, they had burned hot enough with shame without discovering there had been a woman on the battle-field. They had heard rumors of a flame-haired Amazon travel-ing in the prince's camp, but until now had assumed it was just that: rumors. Knowing no decent Englishwoman would be caught within several miles of a battlefield, they reasoned this one must be half man, half whore, but it still did little to soothe their battered pride.

They would remember her.

To a man, they would remember her.

The memory was to be embellished and emblazoned on the minds of a good many more prisoners when Anne rode through the British camp and surveyed the havoc. The prince had arrived a few moments earlier and had not only comman-deered Hawley's tent but had found the general's personal valet cowering in a corner and ordered him to fetch wine and victuals from the officer's private stock in order that they might celebrate the full extent of their victory.

The royalist army, in full flight, had abandoned their camp, leaving nearly all the tents and equipment, fourteen heavy artillery pieces, and a considerable quantity of ammu-nition, all of which was in short supply in the Jacobite army.

Charles Stuart, suffering the lingering effects of a terrible chest cold, was happiest to discover Hawley had a fondness for French brandy. He was on his third glass when Anne and MacGillivray rode up, leading their prisoners in a straggled column behind them. Only Lochiel and Lord George had proved tardy thus far in joining the prince to celebrate; they were still snapping at the heels of the fleeing English, insist-ing the victory would be moot if Hawley's army was allowed to escape and reappear another day.

Charles Stuart's soft brown eyes widened, however, when he saw his *belle rebelle* enter the crowded tent, her clothing rain-soaked and spattered with the evidence of her further re-bellion. He had been so involved in watching the battle unfold from his vantage point on the moor that he had not noticed her slip away.

"Good God," he declared when she rose from her curtsy. "Do you mean to say you disobeyed a direct order from your prince?"

"You never actually ordered me to remain by your side, Your Grace," she demurred. "I could clearly see the battle had turned in our favor"—a statement that won a glare from MacGillivray—"and thought only to be with my clansmen at their moment of triumph."

The prince started coughing into a lace handkerchief. Although his face flushed a dark red, he waved away the concerns of his two advisors, O'Sullivan and Thomas Sheridan, neither of whom had ventured out from beneath canvas coverings long enough to dampen their wigs.

When the fit passed, he sank back into Hawley's wooden camp chair and took a long draught of brandy.

"If this is what victory feels like," he gasped, only half in jest, "I should hate to envision defeat."

"Your Grace—" O'Sullivan began.

"Yes, yes, I know. This infernal dampness does not improve matters overmuch, and I should find my way back to bed at once. But dammit, man, there are certain pleasures we cannot set aside simply because we do not feel up to indulging in them. Our evening meal, for instance, will be at Hawley's table with Hawley's food served on Hawley's china plate. A petty gratification, perhaps, to gloat at the table of the man who declared me an incompetent wastrel, but there you have it." He glanced up at Anne, sparing a flicker of the eye to note the clods of mud attached to her boots. "And you, my dear. Apart from a hot bath, what would give you the greatest satisfaction at this moment?"

"Me, Your Grace?" She shifted her weight self-consciously from one foot to the other. "I am content enough to know your pleasure, Sire. However, I would beg one small favor if I may."

He waved his hand. "Name it."

"I would ask of your officers if they have had word of . . . of my husband's regiment." She looked around at the gathering of chiefs, most of whom had come bloodied from the field, and thought she saw one or two of them smirk in contempt. By the time the prisoners had been disarmed and marched back to camp, it had been too late to search the moor. If Angus had fallen, if he lay bleeding on the cold, wet ground, morning might come too late.

Angus's regiment had been attached to General Keppel, and they had been directly across the field from the MacKintoshes.

"I would beg your leave to go back and search, if—"

The prince held up his hand, cutting off her plea. While the royal hand was still upraised, he wiggled two of the slender fingers at someone standing beside the door of the tent. Anne turned in time to see Alexander Cameron smile and lift the flap of canvas. He stepped aside to let another man come in out of the rain—this one with dark chestnut hair plastered flat to his brow and neck, and clear gray eyes that sought Anne's at once and held them fast.

Aware of the warlike chiefs watching her every move, she did not run and fling herself into her husband's arms as she so longed to do. Instead, she kept her face clear and her movements calm as she walked slowly toward him, her gaze sweeping the length of his body long enough to note both arms and legs were intact, and he was in possession of all his appendages. There was a gash on his chin that stalled her breath for a moment, but his eyes were clear and steady, locked on hers with the same intensity she suspected was in her own.

"Your servant, Captain," she said softly.

A muscle shivered in Angus's cheek before he squared his shoulders and slowly withdrew his sword. Holding it flat by the blade and hilt, he presented it to his wife in the acknowledged manner of a formal surrender.

"It would appear that it is I who am your servant . . . Colonel," he murmured, adding almost under his breath, "and may I say: very happily so."

"Quite right," said the prince, his voice petulant. "And now if you will offer me your parole, sir, I will accept it and we may get on with more pleasant matters."

Angus hesitated fractionally before stepping past his wife and approaching the royal scion. He went down on one knee and bowed his head. "I do offer you my word, Sire, not to take up further arms against your cause."

"I confess you were a great disappointment to me, MacKintosh. I had hoped I could count you among my dearest friends." When Angus made no response, he waved his hand again. "Rise. Your word as an officer and gentleman is accepted."

"May I beg leave, Sire, to tend my husband's wound?" Anne asked.

Another flutter of the lace handkerchief dismissed them and they exited the tent together, neither one exchanging a word as they mounted their horses and rode back through the camp. The rain had turned to snow; by the time they returned to St. Ninians, it was full dark, and they were both chilled through to the bone. The escort of Highlanders left them at the cottage and took the horses away to be fed and stabled. The fire had been left untended, the ashes were cold and gray, but before Anne could even divest herself of her jacket, the slamming of the door behind her brought the heat of a blush to her cheeks.

Angus was leaning against the door. He was hatless, and had been during the entire ride from Falkirk. His ears were as red as his nose; the dark locks of his hair were scattered every which way, some curling forward over his cheeks, some trailing down over the collar of his tunic. The icy, appraising gray of his eyes held her steadfast, breaking away only once in the ensuing small eternity of ticking seconds to stare at the floor a moment before looking back up.

"I was under the impression, when I left here this morning, that I had your promise, your word of honor, if you will, that you would not set foot upon the battlefield."

Trying the same tack she had used with the prince, Anne moistened her lips and attempted to defuse her husband's quiet wrath. "I never actually gave my word, not in so many words."

"And you think that absolves you of any blame for your actions?"

"It is the same absolution you sought in explaining why you did not declare for the prince."

"Do not attempt to use my own words or logic against me, madam," he warned, pushing away from the door. "Or to twist them to suit your own purposes. You know damned well your place was not on that field today. You know damned well what could have happened."

"Indeed," she answered calmly. "John might have been killed. I thought the risk worth taking."

Angus's chest swelled as he took several measured breaths. His hands clenched into fists and the knuckles turned pink, then white, as he debated whether or not to strangle her now and be done with it. In the end, he came forward and took her face between his hands, drawing her into a hard and forceful embrace that lasted far longer than reason or sanity decreed. His mouth was bruising, almost brutal, his body clearly too aroused to even contemplate denying him anything, not even when he scooped her into his arms and deposited her summarily on the bed.

With their mouths still joined, his hands fumbled at joinings and closures and in a few feverish moments, his kilt was raised, her trews were stripped away, and his arms were hooked beneath her knees, lifting them, raising them so that she was completely open to the heat and hardness of his body. He plunged savagely and repeatedly between her thighs, thrusting deep enough to shock them both into stiffening as the heat poured from his body into hers and kept pulsing, strong and swift, until there was nothing left but the quiet pants of repletion.

"You realize," he gasped when he could, "that I would be more than justified in beating you blue for disregarding the orders both MacGillivray and I gave you. I could tie you hand and foot to a wagon and send you home with ten men strong enough to keep you locked in a turnip bin if need be."

Anne swallowed hard. She was bent almost in half, her knees pinned to her shoulders, and the image of being stuffed into a vegetable bin struck her as being a terrifyingly funny threat after all she had been through that day.

"Have you nothing to say? No clever witticisms? No sarcastic rebuttals?"

She curled her bottom lip between her teeth and shook her head. The rest of her body began to shake as well, bringing Angus's head up off her shoulder.

"Are you mocking me, madam?"

A great, glorious peal of laughter burst from her lips. "Never, my lord. I would never mock you for thinking of turnips at a time like this, not when my leg is cramping and the buttons on your damned *Sassenach* uniform are leaving imprints of the Royal Scots battalion crest on my belly."

Cursing softly, he carefully extricated himself and sat upright. There he was, chastising her for her outlandish behavior, yet his own had undergone so many changes of late—many that were so astoundingly out of character he did not know whether to be disgusted or amused by this latest display of crudeness.

"I'm sorry. I . . . I don't know what came over me."

"The same thing that came over me last night," she said, touching his arm. "I believe the common folk call it lust."

He leaned forward and cradled his head in his hands. "Is that supposed to make me feel better, knowing I have lost *all* saving grace?"

She rose up onto her knees beside him and rested her cheek on his shoulder. "Why should you be any different from me, my lord? You need only smile or crook your finger at me and I can barely stand."

He stopped short of snorting, but only just. *"Me* crook *my* finger? One look from you, madam, the smallest touch, the faintest scent of your hair or skin, and I am reduced to a randy schoolboy stumbling about on three legs. Even now, as angry as I am, as angry as I should be, all I can think of is being inside you again. It is as if I can't get enough of you. As if I am afraid I will never get enough of you."

Anne smoothed a dark lock of his hair off his cheek, tucking it tenderly behind his ear. She cupped his cheek in her hand and gently forced him to turn his head, to look at her. "I wonder: Will you still feel that way a dozen years from now?"

"Those words will be on my lips with the last breath I draw on this earth," he whispered tautly, "and the first I take in eternity."

Trembling, Anne drew him down onto the bed again. "I am so very glad, my lord, for I will never tire of hearing you say them."

———

At almost the same time Anne was welcoming Angus back into her arms, General Henry Hawley raised his sword and brought it slashing down with out preamble or sentiment. He was trembling as well, but out of rage, not pleasure; with contempt, not anticipation. He stood in the market square of Linlithgow, the snow falling thick as wool shearings over the bowed heads of every officer who still possessed enough sense to have answered the general's summons. To Hawley's immediate left was a long, sturdy tree trunk that had been chopped down and denuded of its branches before being suspended from the corners of two buildings. From this makeshift gibbet the bodies of fourteen men jerked and twisted at the ends of their ropes, their lives forfeit on the downstroke of Hawley's blade.

Most of them were dragoons whose names had been put forward by a choleric Major Hamilton Garner. Another score waited hatless, their tunics stripped of any identifiable rank or rating, their hands bound behind their backs. When the macabre dance of their comrades ceased, they too would be summarily hoisted above the solemn crowd by way of demonstrating the extent of Hawley's outrage and disgust.

"Cowards!" he screamed. "Cowards and curs! Look well on these fornicating dogs, for they are no better than the dung they left behind in their haste to desert their posts! Was there ever an army so rife with poltroons and miscreants! Was there ever a general so cursed, so shamed, so humiliated, so completely appalled by the character of his troops! Hang them! Hang them all, by God, for they are not worth the powder it would take to shoot them! Powder, I might add, that we no longer have in any adequate supply since *every godforsaken piece of equipment, fourteen heavy artillery pieces, and ammunition was left behind for the enemy to enjoy!*"

Winded by the fury of his diatribe, Hawley paced to the end of the raised boardwalk and, having no other immediate outlet for his rage, broke his sword over the head of the nearest man.

"I want names," he raged, his chest heaving, his mouth flecked with spittle. "I want the names of every man in every regiment who turned and ran. I want them flogged! I want their skin flayed and hanging in shreds, and I want them left on the racks so that every soldier who sees them will know the consequences of cowardice in my army! I want them to *know*," he screamed, "that in future, death on the battlefield will be a thousand times preferable to dereliction or dishonor! Never think . . . *never think for one foolish moment* that I will hesitate to hang the lot of you if you fail me again! Now go! Get out of my sight! You disgust me!"

He strode off the end of the walk and stormed away into the darkness, leaving the officers shaken and silent enough to hear the heavy flakes of snow falling around them. As the bodies of the first hanged men were cut down and new ones pushed forward to take their place, those who had been lucky enough to avoid the worst of Hawley's wrath began to slink away.

Garner was one of the few who lingered, as was Major Worsham, both of whom had found redress on the battlefield following their inauspicious departure from Callendar House.

Both men were wounded. Garner stood with his hand bracing two broken ribs, his face gray with the pain, his jaw set against the nauseating sound of the bones grinding together. Worsham's cheek had been sliced open to the bone and his left arm hung limp and nerveless by his side; his injuries had been hastily bandaged by a surgeon stained to his elbows with other men's blood, but he dared not have them properly stitched until the general's spleen had been vented.

The opening Jacobite volley had shattered the resolve of the dragoons; less than half an hour later, the government forces had been in full flight. It was impossible at this time to even begin to know the tally of dead, wounded, or captured, for there were surely those who were still running and would keep on running until they were certain they would never be found again.

Worsham had no qualms about punishing deserters or cowards. It was a harsh fact of army life that any man who signed his name to the roster was giving his oath to obey the orders of his superiors regardless of whether he agreed or disagreed with the execution. Any man who violated that oath did so at his own peril.

And then there were the men who'd had no intention of fighting at all. They had formed up in their ranks and they had marched onto the field, but once there, they had crouched down to avoid the heated fusillades and, when those had passed, had run across the moor and joined their Highland clansmen. Worsham had shot one such man just as he was about to hand off Pulteney's regimental colors to a kinsman in the Jacobite ranks.

The MacKintosh contingent was a fine example of this attrition. Most had deserted on the march from Edinburgh, but of the handful who remained to take the field that day, not one had returned to his regiment. Their chief, Angus Moy, had not been seen since forming up on the field, and Worsham sincerely hoped, for the bastard's own sake, that he was lying among the dead on Falkirk Moor.

He closed his eyes against the sharpening agony in his arm and reached into the pocket of his waistcoat for the small packet of powder the surgeon had given him to dull the pain. He had only taken a few grains the first time, cautioned that too much would render him so free of pain he would be unconscious. He measured out more this time, holding it on his tongue until he could reach one-handed for a flask of wine confiscated from one of the condemned men. The powder was bitter and it required several swallows to wash away the worst of the taste. What remained was a dry metallic taint that coated the back of his throat, not unlike the taste of blood.

And, oddly enough, not unlike the aftertaste left by the dinner wine served to them the previous evening at Callendar House.

He dismissed the thought, attributing it to his own state of near exhaustion. He looked into the swollen face of one of the last men to stop twitching and recognized him as the young corporal who polished his boots each night.

Now that was a genuine waste, for he had been the only man able to polish the boots to a high gloss.

Chapter Seventeen

*U*pward of three hundred Hanoverian prisoners were taken at Falkirk; nearly twice that many lay dead or wounded. On the Jacobite side, there were fewer than eighty casualties all told, but with the weather turning sour and Hawley's army retreating hastily to Edinburgh, it once again became incumbent upon Lord George and the chiefs to convince the prince his force was still vulnerable.

Lord George had implored Charles Stuart to send his troops after the English, but the prince, taking the advice of O'Sullivan instead, decided that the retaking of Stirling Castle, which had been under siege since the Jacobites had departed Glasgow, would be far more beneficial to morale than chasing after a defeated army. Better, he said from his sickbed, to consolidate their victory at Falkirk by driving the rest of the government troops out of Stirling and Perth, thereby reclaiming control of the Lowlands south of the Grampian mountains.

Lord George disagreed as violently as he dared, but to no avail. He could only vent his frustration in private, then get reeling drunk at the squandering of such a hard-won opportunity to crush their enemy—one that might not come again without paying a much steeper price. He understood, where the prince and his insufferable Irish advisor did not, that the

Lowlands had never been receptive to the Stuart cause. They could waste weeks trying to take the impregnable castle at Stirling—weeks that would be better spent in the Highlands, where most of the clans were sympathetic to the prince and it would be possible to strengthen their army, not weaken it.

Moreover, the vast tracts of mountain ranges cut by lochs and hostile sweeps of frozen moorland would not appeal to the English for a winter campaign; weather and terrain would discourage pursuit until at least the spring, when the Jacobites would have had time to regroup.

For Anne's part, she was disappointed to say the least, having come this far only to be told they were likely turning around and going back to Invernesshire. At the same time she was elated and vicariously delighted at the thought of marching home with an army of thousands to oust Lord Loudoun and reclaim the capital city for the prince.

The rest of the clan chiefs, men like Lochiel and the MacDonalds of Keppoch, had their own reasons for wanting to return to the Highlands. In their absence, the English had strengthened their positions at Fort William and Fort Augustus, placing heavy garrisons at either end of the Great Glen, and with the ancestral homes of the Camerons and MacDonalds located in the middle, it was urgent to send relief. News from the remote regions of Lochaber had been sporadic at best, but the effects of such a harsh winter could prove devastating. Many of the clansmen had been away from their farms since the previous July; they needed to assure themselves that their families had not starved and would not starve if the war dragged on through another long summer. Despite the snow and frigid winds that kept the prince hemmed in at Falkirk the latter two weeks of January, at the first sign of a thaw, fields would still have to be plowed, crops planted.

That was the trouble with raising an army of farmers and shepherds. As brave and loyal and valiant as they might be, if they had no land, no homes, no crops, no herds to go home to, what was the point of fighting at all? The chiefs would demand their rents and tithes regardless if they won or lost, and while the grand castles at Achnacarry and Blair Atholl might suffer from a lack of wheat for fresh *uisque*, they had stood for centuries and would stand for centuries more, supported by the sweat and toil of the common tacksmen. In the feudal system, it was the crofters who would starve from the lack of bread, and when they could not pay their rents, they would find their meager sod cottages torn down or burned and the land taken over for cattle.

The prince turned belligerent. He had forbidden Lord George to pursue the English farther than Linlithgow, but when he heard Hawley had escaped to Edinburgh, he did an about-face and laid the blame squarely on Murray's head. To make matters worse, news arrived in the Jacobite camp on the last day of January that Cumberland had left London and marched his army to Edinburgh in near record time. He had brought reinforcements of cavalry and infantry, as well as a fresh artillery train to replace the heavy guns lost at Falkirk— guns that took a week to haul and position to best advantage around Stirling, and that fired no more than two rounds apiece before they were blown off their carriages by the superior firepower of the English gunners on the walls.

Lord George, with his last nerve snapped, ordered the ineffectual siege to be abandoned and dragged the remaining cannon to the nearest cliff, where he had them spiked and rolled over into the churning waters of the firth.

The prince did not take either the news of his cousin's arrival or the departure of the artillery well. He ranted against Lord George, believing now more than ever that his general was determined to sabotage his every effort to win back the throne. He raged and banged his head against a wall until he staggered like a drunkard, at which time he retired to his wagon with two bottles of whisky and became one. With the prince mired in self-pity, it was decided to once again split the army into two divisions, the prince being escorted by the majority of regiments through the high mountainous passes that cut through the Jacobite territories of Blair Atholl, Dalnacardoch, and Dalwhinnie. Lord George would travel a more circuitous route by way of Aberdeen, hopefully to draw off any pursuit Cumberland might be mounting. The two divisions would reunite at Inverness, where they could then set about routing the government forces garrisoned at Fort George.

"Might I play devil's advocate a moment," said Angus

Moy, "and ask what the prince will be able to do with Inverness even if he does take it?"

The question was practical and forthright, greeted by the silence of a grim circle of men that included Alexander Cameron, Aluinn MacKail, and John MacGillivray. Angus had been surprised by the invitation to join the others at the tavern, but he had had his own reasons for obliging.

"The entire coastline is under a tight blockade," he continued, "and unless I've missed something in the thousands of dispatches I've read over the past months, the prince has no navy. Not one single ship. Loudoun, on the other hand, has fresh supplies delivered every day—meat, fish, vegetables, fruit, even tuns of French brandy confiscated by the revenue ships in the Channel. Their lead shot comes in barrels; they do not have to make their own in the field. If a musket fails or misfires, there is another in common stores to replace it. I have seen their warehouses; they want for nothing, whereas I have seen some of your men walking in the snow with rags wrapped round their feet."

Cameron's dark eyes assessed the two Highlanders seated across the table. Big John MacGillivray was a genuine throwback to a Viking warrior: Nothing seemed to slow him down. He had been wounded in three places on Falkirk moor, but had barely acknowledged his injuries long enough to allow Archibald to stitch and bandage them. The men were in awe of him; his experience as a smuggler and reiver made him doubly valuable to the prince's army.

As for the chief of Clan Chattan, he was a difficult man to read, not given to revealing too much either through his eyes or his expression. Perhaps that was what pricked Alex's instincts the most. Was the chief of Clan Chattan a more formidable adversary than he appeared to be? And if so, could it work to their advantage?

Alex twirled one of his thin black cigars between his fingers and glanced across the table at Aluinn, but there were no insightful glances coming back his way.

"Yes, well." Cameron cleared his throat. "You play the devil well, Captain MacKintosh, but you are not telling us anything we do not already know."

"What if I *did* tell you something you didn't know?"

"We might question the motive for your generosity," came the blunt reply.

"Of course." Angus smiled. "Then why don't we speak of motives first and clear the air, so to speak?"

Alex spread his hands. "You have our complete attention."

"Quite simply, when the army returns to Inverness, I want my wife sent back to Moy Hall. I care not how it is done or who does it, or under what pretense, but I want her sent home. I also do not want her to know she is *being* sent home, for if she believes that to be case, she will likely thumb her nose and tell you to break wind at the moon."

The midnight eyes narrowed further. "And in exchange?"

"In exchange I can give you detailed maps of Fort George, inside and out. I can tell you where the walls have recently been reinforced and where there are concealed batteries of guns. And I can tell you the weakest points in the fortifications, which, conversely, would be the best places to lay your mines—assuming, naturally, that you wish to avoid another comedic debacle like Stirling Castle."

"We would indeed," Cameron said after a moment, "but what if I told you your wife has offered us the same information?"

"It would be accurate . . . to a degree. At least one of her rapscallion cousins has spent time behind bars there, and her grandfather has been around long enough to have seen the original walls go up. But there have been changes in the past year I doubt even they know about. Loudoun has been cautious since he assumed command. In recent months, he has been nervous, too, to the extent that he has had details of enlisted men doing most of the work, digging, building gun emplacements, setting traps and the like."

"Traps?"

Angus nodded. "In the armory, for one. If you fail to reach it quickly, there are kegs of powder set with fuses that need only be lit by someone requiring ten minutes to exit through a nearby tunnel. If they blow, they will send half the fort to hell and gone—and anyone in it at the time."

The pause was noticeable as Cameron glanced once again at MacKail, who shrugged but looked intrigued nonetheless.

"It seems to be a fair exchange. It would also help if we

had precise maps of Inverness as well as any defenses in the
harbor and surrounding areas."

"Anne can give you that," Angus said. "She has a better
eye for detail and is more familiar with the moors and bogs.
Plus, it will occupy her time when I have gone."

"Gone? You're going somewhere?"

"Is that not why you asked to meet with me tonight? Because you want me to go back to Edinburgh with the other
prisoners when they are released?"

Alex tried not to look surprised—or excited. As had been
the case following the Battle of Prestonpans, it had been decided that all prisoners would be released if they agreed to
give their word not to take up arms against the prince again.
The number was vastly smaller than the fifteen hundred prisoners taken in their first victory, but with supplies short and
tempers frayed, the chiefs were more concerned with providing the bare necessities for their own men than catering to the
needs of captured soldiers.

"I will admit the thought occurred to us," Cameron said.
"The possibility of having someone close to Cumberland's
command is intriguing, and your name did come up several
times in various conversations."

"Now hold on a minute," MacGillivray began.

"You did not know this was what they wanted to discuss?"
Angus asked.

The big Highlander looked like he wanted to smash the
table in half. "I did not."

"As I said"—Cameron leaned back and gave his cigar another thoughtful roll—"Aluinn and I were only toying with
the idea. And it isn't as if you would be doing anything out of
the ordinary. No skulking in dark alleyways, no cloak drawn
over your face with a dagger at the ready. You would simply
have to do what you do already: read dispatches, follow troop
movements, let us know who is moving where and what their
intentions might be. Then it would just be a matter of—"

"Tying a cryptic note to the ankle of a carrier pigeon and
releasing it from a rooftop?"

Cameron smiled at the dry sarcasm. "Nothing quite so
dramatic. We have other people in the Elector's camp who act
as couriers."

"Like Adrienne de Boule?"

Cameron's midnight eyes flickered again. "Yes. Like Adrienne. Unfortunately, her access is somewhat limited and she cannot move freely around the camp every day."

"And if I say no?"

"Then it ends here, no harm done. You can leave or stay— which you would, of course, be most welcome to do. The terms of your parole would give you an honorable release from any obligations you might have had to serve the king, although I expect your wife's participation at Falkirk would render the terms of the immunity Forbes offered moot either way."

Angus turned slowly to glare at MacGillivray again, and this time the Highlander only glared back. "I was not goin' to die the only one knowin'. An' if ye've no' learned by the now that ye can trust these two men above all, then I'll send ye back to Edinburgh maself on the toe o' ma boot. Not"—he added gruffly, qualifying the endorsement by glowering at Cameron and MacKail across the table—"that I'm sayin' it's a good idea to send him back at all. We already know Hawley has nae fondness for Scots officers at the best o' times, an' if it's true he has already hung sixty-three of his own men for desertion an' cowardice, what makes ye think The MacKintosh willna be swingin' from a gibbet the instant he walks through the gates o' the city?"

"Because I don't imagine any of those officers or men were returning of their own accord, or that they were bringing back valuable information from the rebel camp."

Angus's mouth curled up at the corner. "I would be bringing back valuable information?"

Alex hesitated long enough to draw on his cigar. "I'm sure we can find something of merit. The prince has written enough memoranda in the past month alone to fill a warehouse. A few of them should prove interesting reading for Cumberland, if nothing else."

Angus's wry smile faded quicker than it had appeared, and he stroked his thumb down the side of the tankard, tracing patterns in the tiny beads of condensation. "In truth, I have not had too much of a problem dealing with Hawley. It's the other two, Worsham and Garner, who watch me as if they would like to take my gizzard for their next meal."

"Major *Hamilton* Garner?" Cameron asked with quiet curiosity.

Angus nodded, not looking up. "And Major Roger Worsham. Major headaches, the pair of them; both eager for promotion and favor within Cumberland's inner circle."

"I don't think you'll have a problem winning Garner's confidence," Cameron said, exchanging a glance with MacKail. "In fact, I would be willing to stake a considerable fortune on his becoming your closest friend and ally if you but tell him you and I spent time in the same room together."

Angus started to frown, then remembered. "Ah, yes. He and your wife, Catherine, were . . . acquainted, were they not?"

"They were engaged, actually, until I won her off him in a duel." He grinned through the smoking stub of his cigar. "Long story. In any case, let's just say that he and I have some unfinished business, and any information you bring him concerning my whereabouts will elevate you to the rank of champion."

"I haven't agreed to anything yet," Angus said.

"And you certainly do not have to, either."

The men looked up as Anne approached. She had come into the tavern so bundled in plaid, no one had paid her notice until she came near their darkened corner and pushed the tartan back to reveal the bright red hair beneath.

The men started to scrape to their feet, but she waved them down with an angry gesture that told Angus the flush in her cheeks was not all due to the cold.

"Did I hear you correctly? You want my husband to spy for you?"

"We have been attempting a little shameless extortion, aye," Cameron admitted.

Angus felt a sudden, unpleasant hollow sensation in his belly. Like the others, he hadn't noticed her come into the tavern, so he wasn't sure exactly how much she had overheard.

"And?" She put her hands to her hips. "Has he bowed to it?"

Angus indicated a place on the bench beside him, which she ignored. "They have asked. I have not yet given an answer."

"He might agree, Colonel," Cameron said. "If you can convince him it would be for the best."

"Me?" She unwound her scarf and shook off the glittering ice crystals—some of which hit Angus's cheek like tiny pellets. "Why on earth would I want to convince him to return to the Hanover camp?"

Cameron leaned back and folded his arms across his chest. "Because we need him there. He has Hawley's ear, he sees reports, he has access to information we can get no other way. We need to know Cumberland's intentions, the strength of his troops, where he plans to strike at us and when. Both MacKail and I have told your husband the information could be critical to the prince's safety and success, possibly even the deciding factor in whether we win or lose the Highlands, but"—the midnight eyes narrowed, their glitter rivaling anything Anne could lash back with in response—"we have also told him it is dangerous, and there is undeniably a great deal of risk involved. We can understand if he is reluctant to agree. Unfortunately, we often have to ask terrible things of people in times of war, but that is all we are doing. We are just asking. If the captain is uncomfortable or uneasy, or if he believes his return to Edinburgh would be seen as another betrayal . . . ?"

"My husband has never betrayed his clan," Anne said evenly. "If anything, he has done everything in his power to uphold their honor."

Cameron pushed to his feet and drowned the stub of his cigar in the inch of ale at the bottom of his tankard. "We all have uncomfortable choices to make. Sometimes we make the right ones; sometimes we don't. In this case, we are merely asking your husband to do what he has been doing all along: wear the Hanover cockade and take his brandy and cigars with the likes of Henry Hawley and William Cumberland. We cannot force either one of you to help us, and frankly, I don't have the time to waste softening you with trite words like 'life and death,' but that is very well what it could amount to. For all of us. On that pontificating note, I'll say good-night to you now, Lady Anne, Captain MacKintosh, Captain MacGillivray." He nodded at each as he pulled his tartan around his shoulders. "Aluinn . . . are you coming?"

MacKail blinked and stammered a reply in the affirmative as he quickly gathered his gloves and bonnet off the bench. MacGillivray caught the subtle glint in Cameron's eye and muttered some excuse about needing to check the pickets.

They exited in a group, leaving Anne and Angus alone, one standing, one sitting, neither moving so much as an eyelash for a full minute.

"I expect there is never any need to wonder where you stand with a man like Cameron," Angus said finally. "But he is right about one thing. While I have been enjoying some very excellent brandy and some very excellent cigars, they have fought and died and marched to Derby and back."

Anne reached forward and touched her fingertips to his shoulder. "That is not all you have done."

"No, it isn't." He covered her hand with his. "But he almost makes it sound like an act of cowardice to want to protect what you love most in the world."

"I'm sure he did not mean it that way."

"Perhaps not. Or perhaps he was offering me a last-minute reprieve. A way to redeem myself in the eyes of my wife and my clan."

"There must be another way," she cried. "You don't have to do this. You certainly don't have to let him—any of them—make you feel guilty about what you have done or not done."

"Not even you?"

"Oh, Angus—" She slipped around in front of him and slid down so that she was on her knees, her hands cold and trembling where they cradled his face between them. "I never meant to make you feel guilty."

"Yes, you did." He smiled tenderly and brushed her lips with his. "And you did a damned fine job of it, too, I might add. I am surprised I held out as long as I did, what with all the weapons you had in your arsenal. More than any ten armies, I can promise you."

"I never meant for you to feel *this* guilty," she protested with a shake of her head. "Not so much so that you would actually consider going *back*. Do you know what they will do to you if they catch you spying?"

"Probably the same thing they have done to a dozen other men who have thought the risk worth taking. And in this case, the potential benefits far outweigh the dangers. Anne . . . it isn't as if my heart hasn't wanted to do more all along. It is my damned head that has been too hard, and it has just needed an extra knock or two to get me to see things clearly. Cameron is right. They need someone in Cumberland's camp and I am a logical choice. I am privy to the kind of information that could help them prevent a disaster. And besides," he added, trying in vain to dispel some of the panic he could see shadowing her eyes, "while this is hardly comparable to riding onto a battlefield and slaying dragons, it is something I am infinitely qualified to do. Fine dinners at Holyrood House, comfortable billets in town houses where I can scratch out lists and copy orders in the dead of night. Even if the effort is coming at the eleventh hour, this is something I have to do, Anne. I'm not entirely convinced it isn't too late already, but if I can help—and not just for the prince's sake, but for the sake of preventing all of Scotland from going up in flames— then don't you see I have to try?"

"You're not just doing this for me," she said warily, searching his face for some weakness to attack, "or for any foolish notion of winning the approval of men like MacGillivray and Cameron? Because if so, you were only doing what you thought was right for the clan as a whole. You made your decision and you stood by it. There is no shame in that."

"I don't need their approval, but I would like to be counted among them, Anne, just for a little while. As for needing anything from you," he added softly, "your love, your faith, your trust is more than anything I ever hoped to call my own."

She shook her head again. "Then I am not letting you go back alone. I am coming to Edinburgh with you."

"Now that is definitely out of the question," he said gently.

"Why? I can play the part of the berated wife, humiliated into obedience, dragged away and threatened with beatings if I do not behave." She tightened her arms around his neck, pulling herself up so that her face was buried against his shoulder. "I'll be such a quiet, docile mouse you won't even know I am in the room, and . . . and I'll even pin a black cockade on my bodice and learn how to sing 'Up and Waur 'em a' Willie,' and if anyone asks I shall say I was kidnapped from Moy Hall and forced to ride with the clan as a hostage."

He stroked the gleaming red crown of her hair. "You know you cannot come with me, Anne. And not because I doubt for a moment you could charm the devil out of any ten dukes of Cumberland."

"Then why—?"

"Because the clan needs you here. They need a strong, fearless leader; one who has never wavered a moment in her faith or convictions."

"They have MacGillivray. They don't need me."

"Don't need you?" He cupped her face in his hands and tilted it enough to find her eyes. "Have you not seen the way the men look at you? Have you not heard the way they cheer when you ride past, the way their chests swell and they grin ear to ear with pride? Have you had one single man desert?"

She chewed miserably on her lip and whispered, "No."

"No. In fact, you have had more joining the ranks every day. I have recognized a hundred men who marched away from Inverness with me, but crossed the field when they saw you up on Robert the Bruce carrying the clan colors. You cannot abandon them now, Anne. They will need you more than ever when the army returns to the Highlands. They will need your leadership, your courage, your spirit." He kissed her tenderly to emphasize each enviable quality, lingering over the last until he could tighten the leash on his own emotions.

She studied his face another long moment before burying her face in his shoulder again. "It isn't fair. It just isn't fair! To finally have you here with me . . . and now you expect me just to watch you leave again!"

"Courage, my love," he murmured. "You have so much and I so little. Leave me what few shreds I have managed to muster about me, and do not make it any more difficult than it is already, I beg you. The prince is taking his army north to Inverness; if they cannot take the capital, then they cannot hope to survive the spring. We are going home, one way or the other, and we will be back together before the leaves are fully green on the trees, I swear it."

She was silent for so long, he started counting his heart-beats.

"You won't take any foolish chances?"

"I swear I shall be cautious beyond measure. I shall play the role of fawning milksop with such aplomb, they will think me part of the ornamentation on the walls. In return, I want a solemn promise from you."

"What kind of a promise?" She lifted her head again and sniffled through a frown.

"I want an absolutely sacred promise that there will be no more recklessness in the future. No more swords, no guns, no riding out in the middle of the night, no charging out onto a damned battlefield. I cannot even conceive of doing this thing if I thought I had to worry about what you were doing in my absence, and on this point there will be no argument, no debate, no bargains struck, no negotiable compromise. And no vague circumventions. I want you to give me your word of honor as a colonel in the prince's army, as a Farquharson, a MacKintosh, a woman, a wife, a lover . . . have I missed any possibilities? Left any loopholes open to your devious mind?"

Her frown was contentious, her sigh filled with resignation. "No. I expect you have covered everything."

"And?"

She looked up sullenly. "I promise. No more battlefields."

He studied her face a moment, wary of a too-hasty capitulation. "I would have you swear to undertake no more undue risks, but I suppose that would be beyond the pale, since you have already extended an invitation to the prince to be our guest at Moy Hall while his army takes Inverness."

Her eyes widened a moment with surprise, but he only shook his head and kissed the tip of her nose. "Cameron mentioned your generous offer earlier. Were you planning to tell me at all, or was it just going to be a surprise?"

"I was most certainly going to tell you. When—if—His Grace gave me an answer," she admitted softly. "I thought it only hospitable to offer the use of the Hall since it is so close to Inverness, and there is not another glen within ten miles large enough to encamp the army."

"Nonetheless, you might have asked," he murmured. "I am still the master of my own *home*, am I not?"

"Of course you are," she said. "When you are there."

He kissed her again, on the mouth this time, molding his

lips to hers, coaxing them gently apart and exploring the sleek surfaces with the tip of his tongue. When he released her, he watched her lick the moisture off her lips and almost forgot what they had been talking about.

"Do you remember the cave I showed you once? The one where my grandfather hid his entire family for two months, after the first uprising?"

She was staring at his mouth too, her own still tingling with his taste. "I think so. Yes, I do."

"The English searched day and night but could not find it. I doubt there are five men alive who even know where it is, myself included. I am thinking . . . it might be best if I leave Hardy here with you. If you need to take refuge there for any reason, and you're not certain of the location, he can show you the way. In any event, he can make himself useful, stocking it with food and supplies, lamps, bedding . . . whatever you feel might be necessary if the prince is forced to take flight. Besides, if I take him back to Edinburgh, he will only complain the whole way and beat me senseless with his clothing brush. I doubt he would bear up under questioning a second time, anyway."

Her gaze flicked up from his mouth. "What do you mean, a second time?"

"While you were leading the clan to Aberdeen, Hardy was swearing to a privately convened court of inquisition—namely Garner and Worsham—that you were still in Inverness at Drummuir House, the bored houseguest of your esteemed mother-in-law. He swore it could not possibly be you mentioned in the reports because you could not be in Aberdeen and Inverness at the same time, and he had taken delivery of handwritten letters from both you and the dowager to prove it."

A tiny wrinkle appeared at the bridge of her nose. "I did not write any letters."

"No, you didn't. But Adrienne de Boule was kind enough to have her maid write them for you."

The wrinkle deepened and was joined by another. "Adrienne de Boule was in Edinburgh?"

"She was there as a guest of Major Worsham."

"And she helped you write letters?"

"Four of them. On pink paper, I believe, with little red ribbons binding them. And a most exotic fragrance sprayed across the pages."

The blue of her eyes turned dark enough to cause the fine hairs along his forearms to stand on end. "How exotic?"

"Very exotic. The scent reminded me of a small white flower in India that opens only in the moonlight."

"That would be memorable indeed," she murmured. "And did it inspire anything else to open in the moonlight?"

"Oh, I am sure it did," he agreed affably. "But not, unfortunately, for my benefit."

"Unfortunately?"

Angus jerked slightly. He realized her arms were no longer around his neck but, as invigorating and liberating to his soul as these past fourteen days and nights had been, there was still something decidedly imprudent about a lady having her hands up a man's kilt in the middle of a public tavern.

That the two of them were temporarily alone was little comfort. There was no lock on the outer door, and an occasional scuffling sound marked the tavern owner's presence on the other side of a thin partition. The corner was dark, but the candle threw enough light to cause the flown wisps of Anne's hair to glow like a fiery red halo, and to cast a shadow on the wall beside them, mirroring the deliberate up-and-down movement of her hands.

"I assure you," he whispered, "you have nothing to be jealous about. Adrienne was just helping me out of a rather sticky situation. Stop that, minx," he added with a shaky grin. "Someone could come through the door at any moment."

"Someone could," she agreed, glancing over her shoulder. "But are you not the one who just said you wanted to start taking a few risks?"

"Well, yes, b-but—"

She pursed her lips by way of cautioning him to silence, then lowered her head.

"Dear . . . sweet . . . Jesus," he gasped. His hands were in her hair, but seeing what she was about, he moved them, sending one to grip the edge of the table, the other the back of the bench. His jaw clenched around a sound that was half shock, half pleasure, and despite the chill in the air, small beads of moral turpitude popped out across his brow. Every muscle in his body tensed into bands of iron, and because there was nothing he could do to prevent it, he felt the heat surge into his loins and pump into his chest, the blood pounding loud enough to drown out every last voice of reason. To his horror, he became dimly aware of the door opening and someone coming through, stamping the snow off his boots, but it was too late to do more than shoot out his hand and smash it down over the guttering candle. Soft white beads of wax spattered across the table and he groaned inwardly, steeling himself even as he clamped his fingers around the tallow shaft and squeezed it into a misshapen mass.

He remained that way, unable to move or even sweat for several exquisitely torturous moments. When he could, he sucked in a huge mouthful of air and glared accusingly at Anne, watching her as she rearranged the pleats of his kilt and slipped up onto the bench beside him. Demurely, she wiped her chin and took a sip of ale from his tankard; when she looked at him, he could see she was a breath away from laughing. Her eyes were still bright, but not with jealousy or envy. They shone with the lush certainty of a woman who knew exactly who her husband would be thinking about each night they were apart.

"Two can play such games, madam," he promised softly. "And you shall pay dearly for that bit of mischief."

"Is that a promise, sir?"

His hand slid up her thigh and he waited for her smile to lose some of its impudent edge.

"More of a warning, I should think. The promise, my dear, is that you shall not get one moment's sleep tonight."

Chapter Eighteen

Inverness

$\mathcal{T}$he retreat from Falkirk began on February 1, the day after a courier brought the startling news that Cumberland had unexpectedly moved the army out of Edinburgh and was marching to Linlithgow. The Jacobites decamped before sunrise; by noon, there was only trampled snow and a few broken carts mired in the garbage-strewn mud of Bannockburn to show they had ever been in the vicinity. In St. Ninians, the departure had not gone quite as smoothly. A careless spark had set off a series of explosions in the village church where the Jacobites had stored the kegs of gunpowder captured at Falkirk. Lochiel was nearly crushed under falling stones and, not surprisingly, Lord George was furious at the waste of valuable powder.

It took fifteen days for the prince's slow-moving column to cross the mountain passes. Half the time the howling wind blew snow directly in their faces, slicing through the layers of tartan, forming thick crusts of ice on beards and eyebrows. The other half of the time they were blinded by the vast whiteness and had to struggle to find the buried roads and tracts. The few cannon that had not been sent with Lord George Murray's column were spiked and abandoned in the

frozen drifts, and not one of the tired, ragged men who had
been hauling them over the impassable terrain was sorry to
see them left behind.

Cumberland, on the other hand, was happy to discover the
heavy guns Lord George had ordered drowned in the firth, and
thought it well worth a two-day delay to winch them back up
onto dry land. Hearing his cousin had taken the high road over
the Grampians, he wasted another three days trying to follow, but
the snow was able to do what the Jacobites could not: It turned
the king's son around and sent him scrambling east along the low
roads, nearly a full week behind Lord George.

Once over the crest of the mountains, the prince found the
going easier. The hills fell away sharply, rolling from one
glen to the next until the melting snow and mist emptied into
Loch Moy. The surrounding forests were thick with cypress
and cedar. Deer and game were plentiful, and the hills were
cut by sweet, fast-running burns that never froze. The glens
they passed through were still snow-covered, but by inches,
not feet. They were dotted with small stone-and-sod clachans
whose occupants came out to gawk at the slow-moving cara-
van of wagons and marching Highlanders. Some cheered and
offered what food and clothing they could spare. Others
turned and went back inside, closing doors and shutters
against the sight.

Meanwhile, Anne had ridden on ahead with MacGillivray
and the men of Clan Chattan to ensure the road to Moy was
clear, the glen secure, the estate as reasonably orderly as she
had left it six weeks before. Robert Hardy was with her, and
had barely dismounted before he was shouting at the household servants, ordering fires lit, bedding aired, floors
scrubbed, and the ovens stoked to capacity. Anne's first priority was a long, hot bath, a true and welcomed soaking
wherein the water was replenished three times, each time it
cooled. Maids were there to assist, and for once Anne did not
offer the smallest objection. She leaned back and let her hair
be scrubbed and rinsed and scrubbed again until it squeaked.
She welcomed the first few drops of scented oil to the water,
then snatched the bottle and poured so much, the smell of
lilacs permeated the entire upper floor.

Her joy at such small pleasures was dampened somewhat by the fact she had not heard one word from Angus since they had parted at Falkirk. There had been no word of an execution or even an arrest, so there was hope he had been accepted back into the ranks without consequence. And of course—as she reminded herself daily—he would have had the deuce of a time sending any letters to an army that was beating a hasty path across a snowy mountain range.

With that thought on her mind, she had ridden the last few miles to Moy Hall in a gallop and burst through the doors with enough anticipation to nearly tear the oak off the hinges. But there had been no letters waiting for her. Not even a message conveyed by word of mouth so that she would at least know he was alive and safe.

When a rider brought news of the advance guard approaching Moy, she chose a gown of pale blue satin with cascades of fine Mechlin lace spilling from the cuffs. Four layers of petticoats in varying shades of blue foamed from the parted V in front, and curled back like the wake of a ship when she walked to the door to greet her regal guests and proudly watch her glen fill with Highlanders. The MacKintoshes and Camerons occupied the slopes that bordered the misty waters of Loch Moy; Keppoch's MacDonalds camped to the west and the Appin Stewarts to the east, forming a tight protective circle around the prince. A lively black-and-white sheepdog marked the arrival of Charles Stuart's personal entourage in the glen, and despite the fact Anne had been in his company many times over the past weeks, she still found there were butterflies in her belly as she watched the royal scion dismount and stride up to the porticoed entrance of Moy Hall.

"Your Grace," she said, offering a deep curtsy. *"Cend mile failte."*

"Ma belle rebelle, a thousand thanks for your hospitality in return." As had become his habit of late, he held a scented lace handkerchief in his hand, its dual purpose being to wipe the constantly dripping moisture from his nose and to camouflage the smell of strong spirits on his breath. His cheeks were flushed with a slight fever he had been nursing

for the past day or so, and the splashes of color looked like pink paint against the absolute paleness of his skin. He was dressed for the weather in black breeches topped by a heavy leather doublet and wool coat. His stock was plain white cambric, not very clean, and his copper-colored hair was dull, plastered flat to his skull by the dampness of the battered wool bonnet for which he had acquired a fondness.

"I have a bath waiting and rooms prepared, Sire," Anne said, welcoming him into the elegant foyer of Moy Hall. "If it please Your Highness, my steward will show you the way and remain to tend to any further requirements you might have."

"My thanks, dear lady, but I do not wish to be of any burden. A bath and a bed are all I desire at the moment." He paused and coughed into his handkerchief, waving away a concerned aide who stepped instantly forward. "Perhaps a bowl of broth, however, very hot and salty. And some beef, or a guinea hen well cooked and dressed with mint, if that is at all possible. Oh, and I should dance a caper for a taste of venison simmered in a wine-and-onion sauce. And chocolate. Stirred to a froth with just a touch of sugar?"

"I shall speak to the cook directly, Sire; if I have it in my house, it is yours."

He smiled vapidly and nodded to Hardy, who then led the royal entourage up the stairs to the second-floor apartments.

There were more guests waiting outside the door. Alexander Cameron had at first declined Anne's invitation to stay at Moy Hall, but because his wife, Catherine, had seemed to succumb to the same exhaustion and listlessness that was affecting the prince, he had changed his mind and agreed that a warm room with a soft feather bed would be a welcome change from a damp, drafty tent. MacKail's wife, Deirdre, accompanied Lady Catherine and was equally happy to accept Anne's hospitality. Their husbands deposited them into Anne's care before they rode off to see to the placement of sentries.

Underneath several layers of grime, Catherine Cameron was a delicate blond beauty with the porcelain white skin prized so highly by the English. Her father, Sir Alfred Ashbrooke, was a member of the House of Lords, and not too very long ago she had been the toast of England's upper society. The gossips had not exaggerated when they said she had given up everything to be with her rogue Highland laird. Dressed in woolen trews and an oversized cambric shirt, she looked more like an orphan than the wife of a legend, but even so, Anne felt like a too-tall, thick-limbed Percheron disguised in blue satin, her skin weathered by the elements, her nose a crest of freckles, the thickness of her brogue a heartbeat away from what must be indecipherable Gaelic to a refined English ear.

"Lady Catherine," she began, articulating every word with care. "I am so pleased to have you and your husband as my guests. You as well, Mrs. MacKail. If you will follow wee Drena there, she will show you to your rooms."

"Please, just call me Catherine. I haven't felt like a lady for a very long time."

Her smile was genuinely self-deprecating and Anne felt the first wave of relief since hearing the sheepdog usher the riders into the glen.

"Then you must call me Anne and we can dispense with all the formalities, shall we?"

"I would like that, thank you. Have you met my brother, Damien Ashbrooke? He was delayed in joining us until we were breaking camp and leaving Falkirk."

A tall, darker version of Catherine stepped forward, his smile as infectious as his sister's.

"Colonel Anne. I have heard a great deal about you—your name has even made it into the news sheets in London—and believe me, the pleasure of this meeting is all mine."

Anne might have given her opinion of the London news sheets had Deirdre MacKail not given off a startled little cry. Catherine was swaying, a hand held shakily to her temple, and Damien had to move quickly to catch his sister before she slumped over onto the floor.

"Good gracious," Anne cried. "Is she hurt?"

"She's not hurt," Deirdre assured her, "she is merely exhausted and cold. She's not been getting the proper rest for several weeks now, and all this horseback riding . . . *astride,* no less . . . 'tis a wonder she hasn't miscarried!"

"Miscarried?" Anne looked at Catherine's pale face. "She's with child? Should I send for a doctor?"

"I'm fine," Catherine gasped. "It was just a little spell of dizziness. Damien, for heaven's sake, put me down."

He ignored her and obeyed Anne instead as she waved for them to follow her up the stairs to the bedchambers, where she stood aside and watched him set his sister gently down on the bed. "Is it not exceedingly dangerous to be riding around on horseback in such a condition?"

"I've tried telling her that," Deirdre said. "But she's as stubborn as a boil. If her husband knew, of course, he'd tie her hand and foot to a post and leave her there to rant about the unfairness of it all, but—"

"The *Camshroinaich Dubh* doesn't know his wife is pregnant?"

"She claims she has not yet found the right time to tell him."

"Perhaps a doctor would be a wise precaution, then. Just to make certain everything is all right. I would surely not want a man like Alexander Cameron angry with me should I be found wanting in my duties as hostess."

"No," Catherine called weakly, pushing herself up onto her elbows. "Please do not send for a doctor. I have already spoken to Alex's brother, Archibald, and he has pronounced me hale and hardy. I am truly just cold and tired. And since everyone under the sky appears to know my little secret now except for my husband, I expect I shall *have* to tell him before he hears the gossip from Cumberland's drummers!"

"Fine," Deirdre said, ordering Damien to the door with an imperious wave of her hand. "But in the meantime you'll take off those filthy rags and get yourself into a proper hot bath. If Lady Anne will tell me how to find the kitchen, I'll make you a nice hot cup of tea and fetch some bread to settle your stomach."

"Just tell Drena what you require and she will bring it at once," Anne said, beckoning to the maid. "In the meantime, I will leave you to rest. Please remember what I said: If you need anything, anything at all, just tell Drena."

The two women smiled their thanks. Anne hurried back

downstairs, for there were baggage carriers entering the front hall like a row of ants and servants everywhere, some attached to the prince, and others sent by lairds to make requests from the household. The hall quickly filled with noise and confusion, all of which might have grown to unmanageable heights if not for the sudden ominous thundering of a familiar voice.

Anne gratefully located the golden head belonging to John MacGillivray. He was standing in the middle of the foyer, his hands on his hips, his expression promising violence as he directed servants this way and that, dependent upon whether they were making inquiries, bringing deliveries, or were simply underfoot. He must have caught the splash of pale blue satin on the stairs, for he paused to grin up at her—a distraction that cost him in skin and blood as one of the porters scraped his bare calf with the edge of a wooden trunk and sent him dancing up onto one foot.

The prince, true to form, declared himself too feverish to take his meal in the dining room that evening. He begged Anne's pardon, sending his regrets along with a sheaf of dictated memorandums to Lochiel, Ardshiel, and Keppoch, the three chiefs who had been appealing to him to send contingents into Lochaber to oust the government troops from Fort Augustus and Fort William.

They were to get their wish. The prince had decided to dispatch them on the morrow with their respective clan contingents to blow both forts to splinters, if that was what was required to remove the Hanover presence from the Great Glen. Lord George Murray was due in Inverness at any moment and would undoubtedly, in his surly way, demand to know why the prince's forces sat idle. Charles had every intention of assuming command of the effort to take the Highlands, and despite a flurry of responses that came back from the chiefs advising him to wait for Lord George, he stood firm in his decision. Further, he ordered MacGillivray and the men of Clan Chattan to scout the terrain and determine the number of troops garrisoned at Fort George.

"The bastard is gonny put up a fight," MacGillivray said,

buckling on his heavy leather crossbelts. He had come to dinner along with nearly fifty other lairds, only to see the pinch-faced O'Sullivan handing out the prince's slips of paper. There had been no gracious word of thanks for hauling his royal personage safely through the mountains. No courteous acknowledgment of the trouble Anne was taking to meet his every comfort, or of the risk she was taking just letting him sleep under her roof. There was not even to be a full day's rest for the men, who would have appreciated a small respite after the draining march. "Or does he think Loudoun will just smile and hand him the keys to the gates o' the fort?"

Anne watched him struggle a moment with a knotted thong on his gunbelt, then gently pushed his big hands aside. "Just be careful. We cannot spare any men at the moment to come break you out of gaol if you are caught."

"I'll be fine. It's you I'm worried about. I'll say it here an' now: I dinna like the idea o' strippin' away nearly a thousand men to send them to Lochaber while ye're left here on yer own."

"Lord George will be arriving with a thousand more any hour now," she said, untying the knot and presenting him with both ends of the thong. "And I am hardly on my own."

John ignored the thong and took her chin between his thumb and forefinger, tilting her face upward. His eyes were so close it was like staring into a bottomless black well, and his gaze was so intense she actually felt a shiver of fear.

"This is no joke, Annie. We're ten miles from Inverness—no' even a hard ride on a good horse. Loudoun's men have not been sittin' idle while we've been away proddin' Hawley up the arse. And aye, ye're as good as on yer own here, with a sick prince, a pregnant woman, an' a handful o' men so tired they can barely keep their eyes open."

"Lord George is half a day's march away," she reiterated, frowning slightly.

"A half a day by whose say-so? That bluidy Irish futtrat O'Sullivan? He wouldna ken how to judge how long it would take to walk from here to the loch."

He let go of her chin and turned his attention back to retying the pouch that held his balls of shot. Anne continued to stare up into his face, distracted by a cut just below his ear that had not been there earlier in the day. She noticed it now because he must have rubbed it and reopened the wound, leaving a smear of blood on his neck. And she noticed it because it was not ragged, like a scrape. It was clean and even, as if it had been delivered by the slash of a knife . . . or the point of a sword.

She watched him tying the thong, his fingers still clumsy at accomplishing such a simple thing, and now she could see that the knuckles of his right hand were torn and red-raw, and that he seemed to be favoring the left arm, keeping it tight against his ribs.

"You've been fighting again," she said quietly.

"I fight every day. It's called keeping the men drilled an' primed for battle."

She reached out and took his hand into hers, flattening it so the full extent of the scrapes and bruising was evident. "You drill with your fists?" Her gaze flicked over to his ribs. "What would I see if I asked you to open your shirt?"

"A fine, braw stot of a man. What would I see if I asked ye to open yers?" When he saw her surprised glance, he blew his way through a Gaelic oath. "That was a ripe fine foolish thing to say an' I beg yer pardon, lass. It just fell off ma tongue."

"You're forgiven. As long as you don't lie to me. You were fighting again, were you not?"

His eyes came up to hers again. " 'Twas nothing. A wee disagreement."

"Not with one of our men, I hope?"

He hesitated. When he shook his head Anne knew better than to probe further. In the long march from Falkirk, she had heard of at least a dozen fights MacGillivray had either participated in or broken up. Her cousins had taken their fair share of bruises as well, most in response to an overheard insult or disparaging remark against the absent chief of Clan Chattan. Cameron had thought it best—safer for everyone concerned—to keep Angus's reasons for returning to Edinburgh confined to just a few people. John and Gillies knew. Her cousins and grandfather knew. Everyone else assumed he had done what many other English officers had done the moment they mouthed their parole: arrogantly gone back to his regiment and his command.

MacGillivray and her cousins had closed ranks, hoping to isolate her from the worst of the remarks, but that only made for raised hands and snickers of a different sort. More than once Anne had heard whispered speculation as to the exact nature of the relationship between herself and MacGillivray, and if she had had her full wits about her, she would have kept her distance. But with Angus gone, she desperately needed John's friendship, his strength, his courage. She knew, ever since that night outside the cottage in St. Ninians, that he tried his damnedest never to be alone with her, or if he was, never to allow the conversation to turn personal. But there were times it could not be avoided. There were also times, to her unparalleled shame, it even brought her comfort to know that if she ever cried out in the darkness, he would be there before the breath left her lips.

"Oh, John," she sighed. "I'm so sorry to be so much trouble. I'm sorry for everything—for getting you into this mess, for laying all my burdens on your shoulders. For everything. I just wish there were some way of going back and doing things differently. I wish—"

He touched a finger briefly to her lips, silencing her. "Wheesht, lass. What would ye wish different? Would ye wish no' to love yer husband as much as ye do? Or for him no' to love you as much as he does?"

"But if you and I—"

His finger pressed harder and his eyes glittered like two black beads. "Never say it. Never put that thought into words, for it's the words we hear and remember, no' the thoughts behind them. A dozen years from now, when ye're plump an' happy with a muckle o' bairns clingin' to yer skirts, ye'll not even remember ye once had a thought o' what might have been had ye done this or that different. But if ye say it aloud, the words will come back to nag at ye. Ye know damned well Angus is the right man for ye. We both know it, an' for all that, it makes it easier."

He ended his scold with a gentle chuck on her chin before lowering his hand and fussing with his belts again. And she almost believed him.

"What about the fighting?" she asked on a sigh.

"I didna say it makes it easy," he said with a grin. "Just easier. As for bashin' a few heads, well . . . I'd do the same if ye were ma sister. Speakin' o' which"—he paused and frowned his way through another soft oath—"ma sister Ruth thinks it's well past time I paid a visit to Clunas."

"To see Elizabeth?"

"Aye. Gillies thinks I should do it while I have the chance. I think mayhap I should, too, else her father will be after shovin' a musket up ma kilt."

Anne smiled. "Then you'd best go. 'Twould be a terrible shame to think of you gelded."

MacGillivray grinned. "Aye. Aye, it would at that. Then it's settled. I'm away to Inverness to peek through the hedgerows an' count bog-bins for the prince, then I'll be off to Clunas a day or so. I'll leave Gillies in charge o' the men. Ye'll be well protected."

"Don't worry about me. Don't worry about anything. Think about yourself for a change. And take her some flowers. She'll like that and forgive you all your absences."

"Flowers? Where the devil will I find flowers in the snow?"

Anne laughed and rose up on tiptoes to brush his cheek with a kiss. "That's why she will like it. Much more so than an anker of ale and a sheep's bladder full of blood sausage."

He did not look convinced, but returned her smile anyway as he crammed his bonnet on his head. "She'll like flowers more than sausage?" he grumbled. "What a strange lot o' creatures you women are."

Anne was still smiling when she climbed the stairs and made her weary way to bed. Candles had been left burning in the wall sconces for the benefit of the number of strangers sleeping under the gabled roof. Most of the bedrooms on the second and third floor were full, with a few spilled over onto pallets in the drawing room. As she walked quietly along the hallway, she could see by the light of her flickering candle the sleeping forms of servants hunched over in chairs outside their masters' doors.

She went into her own room and stood a moment at the
threshold, her gaze going—as it did almost every time she
came into the chamber—to the armchair in the far corner. If
she tried very hard she could see Angus's ghostly image sitting there, his feet stretched out in front of him, his shirt
glowing white against the shadows, a lock of dark chestnut
hair curling down over his forehead. Every time she looked
she hoped it would not just be an image she saw there. He had
surprised her once, appearing unexpectedly. He could do it
again, could he not?

If he was alive.

A draft tickled its way across her cheek and caused the
candle flame to splutter. The wind was gusting outside, hard
enough to cause a backwash in the chimney and send tiny
puffs of smoke and ash curling down over the grate. The fire
was high enough not to suffer for it; nonetheless the air
smelled of pine knots and charred memories.

"Angus." Her whisper sounded loud in the silence.
"Where are you? I know you are alive. I would have felt it if
you were not."

She pushed away from the door and walked into her dressing room, passing through to the adjoining chamber. Obviously Hardy had not thought it necessary to burn any lamps
or stoke the fire in his master's room, and Anne's candle cast
the only pinpoint of light through the darkness. It seemed
even quieter here. Colder. She closed her eyes and bowed her
head, and as she drew a slow, deep breath into her lungs, it
was there: the faint tang of sandalwood oil.

She felt the tears coming and did nothing to try to stop
them. It was all right. She was alone and it was all right for *la
belle rebelle* to cry. There was no one here to see her or to
judge her, no one she had to impress with her wit or her calm
demeanor. Here, she did not have to be strong or brave or
have all the answers. She did not have to hide the fact that she
trembled inside with fear and felt so helpless at times she just
wanted to scream. Nor did she have to hide the fact that she
hated herself for the envy she felt for Elizabeth Campbell of
Clunas, which was so completely unwarranted and unfair to
MacGillivray that she sagged under the added burden of
shame.

The candle started to shake, and became so heavy she had to set it aside. Blinded by tears, she crawled up onto Angus's big bed and dragged one of the huge velvet cushions to her breast, hugging it there, holding it there until she cried herself to sleep.

Chapter Nineteen

$Prince$ Charles rose from his sickbed long enough to give an impassioned speech to the Camerons and MacDonalds before they departed for Lochaber. Fort Augustus was the closest, located at the southern end of Loch Ness, a dark territory of thick mists and monsters. Fort William was another thirty miles south and west, verging on the vast area controlled by the Campbells of Argyle. At last report, Fort Augustus was maintained by a skeleton garrison of fewer than a hundred men and should pose no problem to the combined forces of Lochiel and Keppoch. It was Fort William, with a garrison of over five hundred men and a strong battery of heavy guns, that had to be taken in order to control the exposed underbelly of the Highlands.

Anne dressed brightly to wave the brave clansmen off. She rode Robert the Bruce to the far end of Loch Moy, then sat atop the highest knoll, smiling and returning the waves of the Highlanders who marched past. Once again the glen was filled with skirling pipes and tartans of red, gold, blue, and green. No more than fifty lairds and captains were mounted; the rest walked, as they had walked the countless miles from Glenfinnan to Edinburgh, from Edinburgh to Derby, from Falkirk to Inverness. Some of them sang as they marched. Most left the enthusiasm to the pipers who filled their chanters and squeezed out stirring *piob rach'ds* meant to strike terror into those who heard the distant, haunting echo.

MacGillivray had taken his men out before dawn, so Anne did not have another opportunity to wish him Godspeed. It was just as well. Though she had scraped snow from her windowsill and held it over her eyes, she knew he would have detected the traces of her tears, and she wanted nothing to distract him from the dangerous business he was about.

When the Cameron clan filed past, one of the officers pulled his big black stallion out of formation and trotted up the hill to where Anne sat. Alexander Cameron tugged on a forelock by way of greeting and drew up alongside her, watching the men tramp past and nod in their direction. Pride was blended equally with trepidation on his face; it did not take much to guess the cause of either one.

"I have come to shamelessly beg another favor of you, Colonel."

"I will take good care of your wife, Captain. As will she, in turn, take good care of your child."

The dark eyes crinkled at the corners. "I've promised I'll be back within the week, but she can get a bit of a temper on her if she is disappointed."

"Then you would be wise not to disappoint, sir."

He looked away a moment, then looked back, the crinkle turning to a frown. "You've still not heard anything from The MacKintosh?"

"No. But I was not expecting daily letters. We both agreed it would be safer all around if nothing passed between us. He might write something, or I might write something, that could put him in danger."

"Probably wise, aye. You might be interested, however, to know that there were some dispatches delivered into camp early this morning."

The change that came over Anne's face was like the sun breaking over the tops of the trees. "You have heard from Angus?"

"He informs us that Cumberland has declared the Highlands to be little better than a hell on earth. Apparently his men have no heart for our winters. On the first attempt to follow Lord George through the mountains, two hundred deserted. The second time, he lost nearer to four hundred. On the advice of his generals, he has decided to double back to Aberdeen and wait for the roads to become passable."

"They have retaken Aberdeen?"

"And Perth. But to reach us, they have to cross those." He gave a nod to the formidable blue-and-purple peaks of the Grampians that sprawled from one side of the horizon to the other. "Even if he waits for spring, he'll find all that snow has melted to fill the bogs and flood the moors."

"Angus . . . is well?"

Cameron looked back. "He is doing a very brave thing, Lady Anne. He has all but stretched out his neck and laid it on the execution block. This is why you should try not to be too hard on him when you hear he is on his way back to Inverness."

"He is coming here?"

"Well, not *here* precisely," he said, indicating the frozen beauty of Loch Moy. "Several regiments are being sent by sea to reinforce Lord Loudoun's position, his own among them. The news is five days old, but we have no reason to doubt its veracity. And, oh—" He paused and removed a letter from his breast pocket. It was written on pink paper, folded and sealed, bound with a red ribbon. "This came with the packet of dispatches he managed to smuggle out before his ship sailed. I imagine pink paper is difficult to come by in an army camp. Even an English army camp."

With those words and a handsome grin, he tugged his forelock again and wheeled his stallion around, descending the slope to rejoin his clansmen.

Anne continued to hold the letter in her gloved hand for a full minute without making any move to open it, her heart pounding so hard in her chest she was afraid it might fly out.

Angus was alive and on his way to Inverness. Cumberland's army would not be invading the Highlands anytime soon. She really did not need to know anything more than that, yet to judge by the thickness of the letter, he had a great deal to tell her.

A group of clansmen hailed her as they marched past and Anne responded with a dazzling smile. She tucked the letter into her belt and returned their waves, then glanced up at the sky, thanking the one who needed to be thanked the most for delivering the news safely into her hands. There was not a single cloud to be seen. The sun was warm and the snow glittered under its benevolent eye like a blanket of diamonds. Anne was as superstitious as any Highlander with good sense ought to be, and had the day been overcast and gloomy, she would have recognized it as a portent of ill fortune to come. But with the sun blazing from above and a letter from her husband pressing against her heart, she felt more confident about the future than she had in many long months.

"Are you certain your information is correct, sir?"

The speaker was Duncan Forbes, and the news was shocking enough to make him temporarily forget that his nephew Douglas was pouring him another whisky. He turned, pulling the glass out from under the decanter, then cursed roundly when the liquid splashed his hand, his leg, and the carpet in due order. With him inside the fortified walls of Fort George were Colonel Blakeney, newly arrived from Perth with fresh dispatches from the Duke of Cumberland; Lord Loudoun, who was pacing in circles like a bear tethered to a ring; and Norman MacLeod, Chief of Clan MacLeod and the officer in command of the Highland regiments at the fort.

"My source is above reproach, sir," Blakeney said. "We have a spy close to the prince, and he assures us the Pretender is right under your noses, gentlemen. Charles Edward Stuart lies drunk in a bed at Moy Hall."

Forbes took a hefty swallow of his whisky and shivered through the aftershock. "This man of yours also claims the bulk of the Pretender's army was there but now is not?"

"Lochiel and Keppoch removed their men this morning to Lochaber. Lord John Drummond is at Balmoral Castle, Clanranald is at Daless. At last report"—he paused to consult some notes he had scribbled on a piece of paper— "Lord George Murray is still struggling to cross the moors to Nairne. I would be surprised if he arrives any sooner than tomorrow noon. That leaves only Lady Anne's personal guard standing at the gates of Moy Hall."

"If by 'personal guard' ye mean MacGillivray," MacLeod said, "ye're talkin' about the Earl o' Hell himself, an' if he were standin' at the gates o' Heaven, Christ wouldnae get past."

"MacGillivray is at Dunmaglass," Loudoun said, briefly halting mid-circle. "He and his men raided some cattle from the quartermaster's stockyard earlier this afternoon, and were last seen driving them away into the hills."

"That's still too close f'ae comfort," MacLeod scowled. "Besides, are ye no' expectin' reinforcements from Edinburgh anytime now? I say we wait on them an' cut our losses by half."

"The troop ship, like everything else these days, appears to have met with some calamity off the coast. A storm or some such thing. They could arrive tomorrow, or the next day, or next week for all we know . . . assuming they have not gone down already or been smashed to bits on the rocks."

"Tomorrow or the next day may be too late," Blakeney insisted. "The time to strike is now, when the prince is vulnerable. The opportunity may not—most definitely *will not*—come again, and I say if there is a chance to capture the royal bastard, to take him with a minimum of bloodshed, then this entire tawdry affair could be over by midnight tonight. The will to stand and fight has gone out of his chiefs and council. They retreated from Derby, they retreated from Falkirk. Take away their only reason to remain steadfast to their oath and by this time tomorrow night, there will be no Jacobite cause, no army, no war—all to the greater glory of the men who had the foresight and audacity to bring it about!"

Loudoun swelled his chest with a speculative breath. "A bloodless victory would certainly pare Hawley's arrogance down a notch or two. I also expect the king would be generous in his rewards, were someone to save his son from the possibility of suffering the same ignominious fate as Cope and Hawley."

"How do you propose to do it?" Forbes asked quietly.

Blakeney smelled an ally and turned to the Lord President. "We have two thousand men in the garrison. Give me fifteen hundred."

"To capture one drunken, unprotected prince?"

"Merely a show of force to discourage any outside interference."

"To cover yer arse ye mean," MacLeod said dryly, "in case yer source is wrong."

"If he is wrong," Blakeney retorted, "a certain Corporal Jeffrey Peters will find his head impaled on a spike and set outside the citadel walls for the Jacobites to use as target practice."

Forbes exchanged glances with Loudoun and MacLeod, then nodded. "Very well. How soon can you leave?"

"The men can be mustered and on the road within the hour. Within two, three at most, we should be back here with the Pretender and his gracious hostess secured in chains."

"Lady Anne?"

"She is harboring an enemy of the Crown, is she not? That alone would be more justification than any military court would require to uphold a charge of sedition and treason. Personally, I have never hanged a woman before, but I'm told they bleat and squeal like little piglets—the same as some men I have lifted off their toes."

The sound of broken glass caused the four men to whirl and stare at Douglas Forbes, who stood all but forgotten in the corner of the room.

"I . . . I'm sorry, Uncle. The glass slipped. I'll . . . I'll fetch someone to clean it up right away. I'm sorry. Sorry, gentlemen. Do carry on."

He backed quickly out of the door, and when he was gone, the Lord President shook his head. "God knows my brother—may he rest in peace—was the same way. Turned pale if the conversation even hinted at violence. Though I do not imagine his reaction to be all that different from that of many. Hanging women is not what this is about, Colonel Blakeney, and would serve no purpose other than to make the young woman a martyr to the cause. Create martyrs and you create sympathy. No, Lady Anne is not to be molested in any way. Her husband is still a loyal officer in His Majesty's service, and I have given him the same guarantees I have given to others"—he looked pointedly at MacLeod—"to ensure his continuing *voluntary* support. If, as you say, there is a strong possibility of ending this whole sordid affair tonight, we will need The MacKintosh to pull his clan back under tight rein."

"What of The MacGillivray?" Loudoun asked. "I am of the opinion he has become a liability we cannot afford in war or peace."

"I gave no warranty against accidents," Forbes said. "And in the aftermath of hostilities, there are always . . . accidents." He looked at Colonel Blakeney, and the decision was made. "Bring me Scotland's prince, sir, and you shall have England's gratitude."

Douglas Forbes needed a few moments to catch his breath. He had stumbled out of Lord Loudoun's office and barely made it to a supporting wall before his knees gave way.

They were going to arrest Lady Anne! They were going to put her in chains and lock her away in a rat-infested gaol cell until a spectacle could be made of her hanging! It was too much. It was too damned much—and he could not allow that to happen!

Wary of the colonel's adjutant watching him, Douglas straightened himself and his clothes and strode as calmly as he could out of the headquarters and into the yard. Twilight was full upon them, and since the afternoon sun had been strong enough to melt most of the snow inside the fort, the myriad puddles shone like scattered pieces of broken mirror.

Feigning no great hurry, he called for his horse. When it was brought to him, he mounted and waved to the guards on the massive gates as he passed through. Inverness, a mile from the fort, was tiny by comparison to the other major ports of Glasgow and Edinburgh. Of the three thousand permanent residents, many had discreetly vacated their city homes to visit friends and relatives farther north in the more remote regions of Skye. If, as they feared, the final battle for possession of the Highlands would occur here, they would be faced with either a lengthy occupation by the Jacobites or the less than appealing military rule of Cumberland's army.

For all that it sickened Douglas to listen to the plottings and intrigues, he knew his uncle was right. Capture Charles Stuart, and Cumberland would have no reason to bring his army north. Inverness would be spared the reprisals of war, and her residents could return to their normal everyday affairs.

He had no quarrel with that reasoning. None at all. By the same token, however, he had become more and more convinced over the months that Scotland warranted better than being essentially a colony of England. The country was unique, the people were unique, and who were men like his uncle to decide what was best for them? England had surely fought hard enough to defend itself against French and Spanish attempts at invasions in the past, when a victory by either nation would have eradicated their way of life and imposed foreign rule. Why did they then feel it was their right to turn around and dictate to the Scots and the Irish and the Welsh how they should be ruled, whom they should pray to, and how their people should speak or dress?

Douglas realized these were all seditious thoughts, but again, when did pride and honor and a quest for freedom become sedition?

He pulled up sharply on the reins, not even aware of where he had been riding until he found himself at the end of Church Street. There, well back from the road, its windows winking at him through a long avenue of trees, was Drummuir House. The dowager would know what to do. She would know how to get a message to Lady Anne.

He spurred his horse forward and, after explaining to a liveried doorman that there was some urgency behind his unexpected visit, he was taken up the stairs to Lady Drummuir's private sitting room. The ten minutes he was forced to wait seemed interminable, but eventually he heard the rustle of silk petticoats and turned from the window to be greeted by his unsmiling hostess wearing a beaded black lace cap and voluminous bombazine sack dress.

"Well?" The dowager wasted no time on niceties. "I assume ye have a good reason for interruptin' my supper, young man. My soup is growing cold an' I've had to hold up the salmon tortierre, which will *not* please the cook, who cares more for her pots an' pans than she does her children."

"Forgive me, Lady Drummuir, but I did not know where else to go. I did not know who else might be able to help me."

Lady Drummuir's expression softened. "Good God, lad.

Ye're shakin' like a palsied leaf. Sit down . . . no, not there
. . . get yerself over by the fire. Aggie, fetch us wine, then
leave."

The maid who had followed her inside the sitting room
did as she was ordered. When she was gone, the dowager
nodded at Douglas, who then relayed as succinctly as he
could the conversation he had overheard in Lord Loudoun's
office.

"I am appalled my uncle would even consider arresting
Lady Anne. He gave his word of honor—" He raked a hand
through his hair in agitation. "Nay, he gave his oath as a guarantee against the safety of Lord MacKintosh's family and
clan, only to turn about now, when he no longer needs the
laird's cooperation, and conspire to hang the Lady Anne!"

"Guarantees? He gave my son guarantees?"

Douglas looked over. "Warrants of immunity, my lady, in
writing. I saw them myself, stamped with the royal seal of office."

The dowager turned and stared at the darkness outside the
window. "That would begin to explain much. The bloody-
minded fool, why he did not tell us?"

"Please, Lady Drummuir, tell *me* what I can do to help. I
have left my uncle's house, and I am yours to command as
you will."

The dowager's blue eyes searched his face for a long moment, debating the wisdom of trusting the Lord President's
own nephew regardless how smitten he was with her
daughter-in-law. In the end she reached for a small bell on the
table beside her and rang it hard enough to bring her maid
back into the room on the run. After calling for pen and paper,
she wrote out two notes. One she would send by courier to
Dunmaglass; the other she gave to Douglas.

"This should pass ye through any sentries that are posted
around Moy Hall, an' it should gain ye an immediate audience with Lady Anne. Tell her I have sent for MacGillivray,
an' if he is not halfway to Clunas already, he should be but an
hour or so behind ye. No, on second thought, dinna tell her
that. Tell her only that I've sent him word. Cut across the way
from Meall Moor, the ground should hold well enough, an'
get ye to Moy ahead of that poxy Colonel Blakeney. And

mind ye have a care, dammit. Ye've as good a chance at being shot for a spy at Moy as ye did comin' here from Fort George."

Anne was in the drawing room when Douglas Forbes was escorted inside. He was red-faced from the cold, and hatless, and he had been practically carried along the hallway by two of the burliest clansmen he had ever seen in his life.

Dressed in tartan trews, Anne was alone. An assortment of pistols and muskets were laid out on the table before her along with the supplies and implements necessary to load and prime them. The note the dowager had written was lying alongside a small keg of powder, and although she glanced up when Forbes was ushered in, she did not pause in her task but fed a lead shot down the barrel of a Brown Bess and packed it securely in place with an iron ramrod.

"So you have come to warn us about an ambush, have you?"

Douglas swallowed hard. The two stocky Highlanders remained beside him, their expressions as menacing as the muskets they held cradled across their chests.

"You are about twenty minutes late," she said without waiting for his answer. "One of the boys from the village overheard some whispers and ran straight here with the news. We managed to roust the prince from bed, and Mr. Hardy has led him, along with a few others, up into the hills. Can you load a pistol, sir?"

"I . . . I . . . yes. Y-yes, of course."

She indicated a dozen smoothbore muskets lying on the table alongside the powder, a canister of shot, and a length of silk waiting to be torn into patches for wadding. "I'm afraid we have more guns than men to shoot them at the moment, but best to be prepared."

"Is it true, then, my lady? You are without protection here?"

"My cousins, Robbie and Jamie, have gone to scout the road, taking the smithy and three of his apprentices along as reinforcements. There are perhaps a dozen ill or wounded men who did not have the strength to walk to Lochaber with their clans, but they have stumbled in here one at a time insisting they can be of help. There are a handful of servants who have perhaps *cleaned* a gun at one time or another, and two maids who come from a family of poachers." She laid down the one weapon and picked up another, standing it on end while she measured powder down the barrel, added the patch and shot, then tamped the lot in place.

Her hair tumbled loose around her shoulders as she did so, catching sparks of light from the score of candles that had been arranged in an arc around the table to render the working area nearly as bright as daylight.

"You are staring, Mr. Forbes."

He stammered another apology and quickly picked up an over-and-under double-barreled snaphaunce. "I just cannot conceive of there being so few men left to guard the prince. Where is his army? What madman sent them to Lochaber?"

"That madman would be the prince himself," she said wryly. "But I am curious to know what brought you riding out here tonight, Douglas. Surely the madness is not contagious."

"It was not a decision rashly made, my lady. I think my heart was ever more for an independent Scotland than it was for the pleasure of bowing to King George's court. My only regret is that I took so long to fall off the fence."

"Well, you will be bruised and bloodied soon enough," she said cheerfully. She cocked the last weapon to check the action of the hammer, then signaled to the two Highlanders to gather up the loaded weapons and follow her outside to where Fearchar Farquharson sat on an overturned bucket, giving instructions to the men and women who showed up in pairs or threes asking what they could do to help.

"Well, Granda'?" Anne looked around as she stepped out into the torchlight. "What is the count?"

"Ye've got twelve men on the road wi' Jamie an' Robbie, anither ten or so in the bushes ayont, an' mayhap the same in the house an' up on the roof. Half o' those are wimmin, more like as tae blow off their ain teats as soon as hit a sojer in the dark."

Anne leaned over and kissed his wrinkled brow. "Perhaps you should go inside and get behind the barricades, where you can watch them to ensure such a thing does not happen."

"Bah! I'm no' afeared o' any bluidy *Sassenach* sojers. I'll stay right here, never ye mind, an' ye'll see: Nowt a one will get past me. Nowt a one."

"Yes," Anne said grimly. "Not even if they are on our side."

"It were dark!" he declared. "He looked like a bluidy *Sassenach*."

"Corporal Peters *is* a bluidy *Sassenach*," Anne said gently. "And you recognized him easily enough this afternoon when he brought you a bag of sugared dates. It was only tonight, when he volunteered his help, that he damned near lost an ear."

Douglas Forbes was staring again. "Did you say . . . Peters? Corporal *Jeffrey* Peters?"

"Yes. Do you know him?"

"No. But apparently Colonel Blakeney does. He said they had a spy placed very close to the prince, and according to him it was a Corporal Jeffrey Peters who told him the manor house would be undefended tonight."

"There ye go," Fearchar snorted. "I told ye I didna trust the barstard. No' wi' them wee skrinty eyes always lookin' at the *Camshroinaich Dubh's* wife like as he could lick the skin clear off her bones. Where is he? Where is the barstard, I'll blow him open masel'!"

Anne looked out into the darkness, in the direction of the tall craggy peaks that rose above the tops of the fir trees. "Dear God, he's with them. He's with the prince and Catherine and the others."

Fearchar pushed to his feet. "Well, dinna just stan' there gawpin', lass! Get some horses. Get some men—!"

The rest of her grandfather's orders were silenced by the sudden popping of distant gunfire. It was sporadic at first, then came in volleys that echoed from side to side down the length of the glen.

"It's the English," Anne gasped. "They're here."

Chapter Twenty

John MacGillivray rubbed the nape of his neck, but the irritating prickle would not go away. If it were summer, he would have suspected an insect had crawled under his collar and was enjoying a feast of warm flesh, but it was the dead of winter and even the lice were too cold to forage.

He drew on his cigar and watched the last of the king's cattle being herded into the narrow chasm. The glen on the other side was a natural bottleneck, with a wide, grassy basin surrounded by sheer stone walls too steep for livestock to climb. Countless herds rustled by countless generations of MacGillivrays and MacBeans had been hidden here along with crates of untaxed cargo and black-market goods brought in by smugglers.

John had made a small fortune over the years, adding on to the tidy fortunes his father and grandfather had made before him. He was likely the first reiver with a conscience, however, for he knew these cattle would eventually go to feed the prince's army, and he would be lucky if he earned a smile by way of thanks.

How many fortunes could a man of simple means spend in one lifetime anyway? He had a good horse beneath him, warm clothes on his back, a full belly, and a roof over his head. With that and the right to come and go as he pleased, what more did he need, what more did he want?

Wild Rhuad Annie's face came unbidden into his mind and he clamped his teeth down over the butt of his cigar.

He had vowed not to think about her and, by God, he would not. In fact, he planned to finish up here with the cattle and ride straight on through to Clunas. If his horse didn't break its neck in a frozen bog hole, he would be there by morning, and by noon, if luck was with him, Elizabeth's legs would be around his waist and she would be helping him forget he loved another man's wife.

If only. Was that not what Annie had said? If only he had met Elizabeth first, for she was a lively, dark-haired beauty with a quick smile and a body that gave him no end of pleasure. Like him, she had no fondness for games or pretenses, which was why they usually had their clothes off within an hour of being in each other's company. He knew she loved him. He'd been her first and only lover, and it shamed him that he had waited so long to speak to her father. What had he been waiting for—a miracle?

Elizabeth would make a fine wife, give him fine handsome sons, and he would never give her any reason to doubt she was the most important woman in his life. The *only* woman in his life. And she would be.

"John! Alloo, John!"

He frowned, looking over his shoulder at the sound of pounding hoofbeats, and recognized Gillies MacBean by the stocky upper body and low silhouette in the saddle.

"Gillies, I told ye to take the men to Moy Hall. What the devil are ye doin' back here?"

"Aye." Gillies gasped and clutched the knot of reins to his chest as the horse skidded to an icy stop. " 'Twas the devil. A devil by the name o' Blakeney. He's taken the whole bluidy garrison out o' Fort bluidy George an' gone tae attack Moy Hall. He aims tae take the prince by surprise."

He gasped out more, but MacGillivray had already dug his heels into his horse's flanks and was tearing hell for leather back across the moor. The roar of rage was like thunder in his throat, startling the men who were driving the cattle, causing most of them to stop in their tracks and race after him.

They were half an hour from Dunmaglass, another half an hour from Loch Moy.

MacGillivray roared again and bent his head forward over the stallion's neck, his blond hair streaming back like a second mane.

Colonel Blakeney's men had been nervous from the outset. They had all heard the rumors about the huge Jacobite army descending on Inverness, and not one of them believed a commanding general like Lord George Murray would leave his prince alone, unprotected at a country estate less than ten miles from a sizeable garrison of government troops. Some of them had been with Cope at Prestonpans and knew firsthand the treachery of the Highlanders. They knew if a report said a hundred Scots were on the road, it usually meant a thousand. If it said they were in Edinburgh, they could as likely be knocking on the gates of London. Lord George was a master of deception, a brilliant strategist, and his men would walk through hellfire on his orders. Moreover, they did not fight like proper soldiers. They lurked in trees and crouched behind bushes; they waited in the darkness and the mist, then came screaming out of nowhere, their great bloody broadswords aimed straight for the heart.

Fully half of Blakeney's men were English. They suffered from the cold and the damp; they thought the food loathsome and the townspeople hardly less barbaric than the savages they had been sent to fight. The other half were Scots, a goodly number raised by the chiefs who supported the Hanover monarchy, yet they were not eager to fight their own kinsmen. Names like Cameron and MacDonald held a special terror for them; they knew the swords of these impassioned warriors cut deepest into Highlanders who wore the black cockade, and would show no mercy.

"Why have ye stopped the column now?" demanded Ranald MacLeod. Like his father, he had square, blunt features and found it difficult to keep the mockery out of his voice when he spoke to the English officers. "Are ye seein' mair bogle-men in the bushes?"

Some of the Scots laughed, though the notion of taunting ghosts and spirits did not sit comfortably with them. The moon was not yet up, and it was black as sin despite the crust of snow on the ground. The same sun that had warmed them through the day had melted the caps off the trees so that the forest crowding them on both sides looked like solid black walls—walls behind which things rustled and moved, where twigs snapped and the mist slithered from one branch to the next. The men leading the column carried hooded lanthorns, the glow restricted to a few feet on either side of the winding road; the men in the rear saw nothing but darkness, and had to trust that the men in front were not leading them straight off the edge of a cliff.

"We should be nearing the fork that takes us down toward Loch Moy," Blakeney said, his voice carrying over the heads of the soldiers. "I suggest we split into two columns and enter the glen on both sides, then converge on Moy Hall in force."

"Aye." MacLeod tilted his head, listening to the echo of the colonel's words ripple from one end of the column to the other. "Start the drummers beatin' while ye're at it; there might be some as haveny heard us comin' yet."

Blakeney ignored the taunt. "Check your powder, gentlemen. Be sure your charges are dry and full."

The command was an unnecessary waste of noise, for there was not one man among the fifteen hundred who had not checked and rechecked his weapon already. Their palms may have been damp and their tongues stuck from lack of spit, but a soldier's weapon was his life and if he came to battle unprepared, that life was forfeit.

Something—or someone—screamed up ahead. Any faint murmurs of conversation stopped and fifteen hundred pairs of eyes strained to see ahead in the darkness. The scream came again, this time identifiable as a voice.

"Rebels! Rebels up ahead! They be in the trees, in the bushes!" A forward scout from one of the Highland regiments came stumbling out of the darkness, his bonnet gone, his hair flying wild around his face. "They be everywhere, sar, an' they're formin' up tae attack. It's an ambush! It's an ambush!"

The news set the men buzzing and cringing tighter together, their muskets pointed into the black wall of trees.

"Hold your positions," Blakeney screamed. "How many, damn you! An advance guard? A company? A regiment? Speak up, Corporal, what did you see?"

"I dinna ken how many, sar. They were all around us, that much I could tell just by listenin'. They were swarmin' through the trees, thick as bluidy flies in June, but all quiet-like. Settin' up f'ae an ambush, I'd say. They already killed Jacobs—cut his t'roat like it were a gob o' lard—an' would hae done f'ae me, too, if I'd been a hair slower."

Two hundred yards ahead, Robbie Farquharson took his cue from the distraught "corporal," and discharged his pistol into the air. The smithy and his two apprentices did likewise, followed by the rest of the men scattered along the verge of bushes. They fired and reloaded as they ran, darting from bush to bush in the hopes of giving the impression of more men, all the while hollering and shouting the names of the clans, giving battle orders, screaming at invisible gunners to ready the artillery.

"Christ a'mighty!" screamed "Corporal" Jamie Farquharson, clutching the reins of Blakeney's horse. "That's Lochiel himsel'! They were waitin' on us! The bluidy bastards were waitin' on us!"

"They were waitin' on us!" MacLeod echoed the cry, his voice infected by Jamie's fear. He drew his broadsword and cursed in Gaelic. "Waitin' tae take us in our own trap!"

Blakeney's horse reared—no surprise, thanks to the point of the dirk Jamie jabbed in his withers. A musket ball whizzed by the colonel's leg and struck one of the infantrymen in the throat. The man staggered back, spraying his comrades with blood, his scream reduced to a liquid gurgle. The column started to split and men began to shrink back. More shots began to whistle into their midst and they turned like a school of scarlet fish and began running back along the road.

"Fall back!" Blakeney shouted. "Fire at will, and for God's sake, do not let them outflank us!"

"Fall back!" Jamie screamed. "Fall back! Run, ye bastards! Run all the way back tae Inverness!"

The barrage continued, an army of phantom clansmen created out of the frenzied screams of a dozen brazen men. Their efforts were spurred on by the lunatic Farquharson twins from Monaltrie, who chased after the stampeding Englishmen until they had expended all their shot, emptied all their weapons. It had been an insane idea concocted out of desperation, and they were under no illusions the ruse would work farther than the first bend in the road. There the colonel and his men would draw up, realize there was no army in pursuit, and turn back with a vengeance, but at the least it might have bought Anne the time she needed to spirit the prince away to safety.

Robbie stood in the middle of the road, swaying on his feet. Jamie was beside him, peeling off the scarlet tunic he had taken from the forward scout the smithy, Colin Fraser, had startled in the bushes. The unfortunate corporal and the soldier who had been throat-shot were the only two casualties until Jamie hauled back and punched his brother hard enough on the jaw to send him sprawling.

"That could ha' been me ye shot, ye bluidy daft beggar!"

Robbie didn't care. He stayed on his knees, where his twin joined him a moment later for an apologetic bear hug, both of them praying to whatever gods were left to watch over them when the English came back.

When Anne rode up the road fifteen minutes later, her cousins were still huddled on the road with the other men, only they were not praying. They were laughing.

"Gone? What do you mean gone?"

"I swear it, Annie," Jamie said, gasping for breath. "One o' the lads followed and said they didna stop runnin' until they were back on the main road. The stupid bastards just turned an' ran! We fired our guns, shouted a few names, an' they ran like the sin-eaters were after them."

Anne stared down the road. There was nothing to see, nothing to hear. The moon was just starting to crest over the distant mountain peaks, painting the topmost branches of the trees silver, giving texture and substance to the shadows below. The faintly acrid tang of exploded powder hung suspended in the mist—mist that thickened with her own disbelieving breaths.

"I cannot imagine they would have just *gone*," she said, and no sooner were the ominous words out of her mouth than the muted rumble of approaching hoofbeats sent her swinging sharply around in her saddle. They were not coming from the direction of the Inverness road, but from the moor!

"They have circled around," she gasped. "They have come up behind us!"

Robbie ordered the men to scatter into the bushes, fearing what was most probable: that Blakeney had split his force in half and these were the reinforcements.

"We've no more powder or shot," Jamie said. "If it's the English, we're done for. Come along, Annie. We'd best get intae the woods, out o' sight."

His prompt came a moment too late. Anne had barely kicked her foot out of the stirrup when the darkness exploded with horses and men. They came from all sides, the road, the trees, easily five score or more, all bristling with muskets, driving the small band of erstwhile defenders out of the bushes in front of them.

But Anne's men were not cringing in fear, they were dancing with joy, and it took a further jolt of astonishment for her to recognize the tarnished brass locks of John MacGillivray as he reined his beast to a rearing halt beside her.

"We heard shootin'," he said. "We saw the lobsterbacks runnin' down the road an' thought mayhap we'd missed the fight. Did Lord George make it back, then?"

She could barely do more than gape at him, at his men for seeming to have appeared out of nowhere. "No," she managed. "No, it's just us and now you."

"The prince?"

Anne's relief had barely begun to register when she remembered Douglas Forbes's warning about the young English soldier who had volunteered to escort Charles Stuart up into the hills. Conveying this new crisis to MacGillivray with a minimum of words, she turned The Bruce around and urged the gelding into a full gallop back to Moy Hall. No sooner had they streaked across the glen and organized armed parties to ride up into the mountains than Charles Stuart himself came riding into the torchlit clearing.

He was grayer than death, but unharmed. The same could not be said for Robert Hardy, whose tartan-wrapped body was draped over the saddle of his horse.

"What happened?" Anne asked, the tears building at the back of her throat as she watched the body of the beloved valet gently lowered to the ground.

"He threw himself in front of a lead ball intended for me," the prince said, sober and utterly humbled for the first time in many long weeks. "For his bravery and noble sacrifice, be assured that both he and you have the gratitude of an unworthy prince."

Anne did not know where to look, what to say, and when she glanced over the royal shoulder, her eyes widened at yet another shocking sight. The prince turned to follow her stare and nodded. "Yes, just so. The Lady Catherine was also injured in the exchange, but she lives. The wound is in the arm, and her brother—"

Damien Ashbrooke rode quickly past without deferring to the prince or anyone else in his haste to carry his sister to the house. Catherine rode before him, cradled against his chest, her face pale in the moonlight, her arm limp and bloody across her lap. For Anne, it was too much.

A wave of nausea swept through her and she had to grip The Bruce's reins tightly to keep from sagging to her knees in the snow. She was thankful for MacGillivray's solid presence by her side, and only dimly paid attention to the prince as he told John and the others how they had reached the safety of the caves up above, only to discover the treacherous spy in their midst. Corporal Peters had been prepared to kill him, and likely would have if Hardy had not intervened and if Damien Ashbrooke had not fought him to the death, sending his body over the edge of a steep, rocky promontory.

Anne felt as if she were on the edge of a precipice herself. The nausea and sense of standing on a tilt was getting worse, not better, and now there was a sticky rush of heat between her thighs.

"Are you all right, lass?"

She tried to focus on John's face, but he would not stand still long enough. He swayed side to side and split in two, then four. And just when she was about to shout at him to stop playing the fool, he reached out and punched her hard in the midsection. The blow took all the air out of her lungs and she doubled over with the pain. She heard someone screaming and felt hands reach out to grab her, but it was when she was falling, fighting the dancing spots in front of her eyes, that she saw the bright red stain of blood spreading down from the crotch of her trews.

Chapter Twenty-One

$\mathcal{M}$oy Hall quickly took on the aspect of an armed fortress, with lights blazing in every window, torches sputtering every ten feet outside. Patrols of MacGillivray's men crisscrossed the glen, the roads, the tree-lined slopes. Fires were lit to give the appearance of a fully occupied camp, and every man not dispatched elsewhere was placed in a position to give an alarm should a mouse stray within a mile of Loch Moy.

It was not mice but men who arrived with the dawn light: Lord George Murray rode in with the vanguard of his army. Hearing of the astonishing rout of fifteen hundred government troops by a handful of clansmen and servants, he brooked no arguments from the prince, who for once did not offer any, but whisked him away to the abandoned and more easily defendable Culloden House, there to be surrounded by three thousand of his own men.

When they took their leave of Moy Hall, there was no rider sitting tall in the saddle of her gray gelding to wave and cheer them on. There was only the hollow echo of the wind and the bleakness of a gray sky to mark the passing of the long day into night.

Anne heard whispers in the background. One of the voices belonged to her maid, Drena, and she was weeping. The other was not instantly recognizable, but a vaguely familiar Irish lilt brought a small frown to her brow.

"I think she's waking."

That voice she knew, and it inspired her to struggle against the pressure of the iron weights that were holding her eyelids shut.

"Aye, she's back with us," MacGillivray said, leaning forward in his chair. "Stop that caterwaulin', lassie, an' fetch the doctor."

Doctor? Who needed a doctor?

"J-John?"

"Aye, lass. Aye, it's me. I'm right here."

He looked dreadful. His hair was stuck straight up in yellow spikes, there was several days' worth of reddish blond stubble on his cheeks, and his eyes had more veins than a wall of ivy.

She tried to moisten her lips, but there wasn't enough spit to do it. A moment later there was a cool, wet cloth pressed over her mouth and she gratefully let the liquid trickle down her tongue and throat.

"Dinna try to speak yet, lass. Drena has gone to fetch the doctor."

Anne glared as best she could with her head spinning and her temples pounding. "Why," she rasped, "did you hit me?"

"Hit ye? I didna hit ye, lass. Ye let out a cry like someone cleaved ye in half, then the next I knew ye were bent over double an' not a wit left to tell us what was wrong. Then when I saw all the blood . . ." He offered up the kind of helpless shrug with which most men excused themselves when delicate subjects were broached. "I carried ye inside an' ye've been here ever since, not movin' so much as an eyelash."

"Ever since?"

"Four days." He frowned and thought about it a moment. "Aye. Four days."

"During which time Mr. MacGillivray has not moved from the side of your bed," said Deirdre MacKail. She was standing behind John, all but blocked out by his massive shoulders, and Anne realized it had been her voice she'd heard trying to comfort the weeping Drena.

"A-am I dying?"

"Not so long as I have aught to say about it, ye're not," MacGillivray growled. "So put that thought right out o' yer mind."

"Wh-what happened?"

He hesitated, and Anne saw him exchange a glance with the Irish girl. "Perhaps ye should wait for the doctor. He is just along the way in Lady Catherine's room—"

"Please, John. Tell me what happened."

He took one of her hands into his and rubbed his thumb gently across the palm. "Ye lost yer babe, lass," he said quietly. "Ye miscarried."

"Miscarried? But I wasn't even . . ."

"Aye, ye were. About two months gone, near as the doctor could figure it."

Anne felt the blood rush out of her head. Two months pregnant? She had been two months pregnant?

Two months ago she had been riding about the countryside gaining signatures for the petition to give her command of the clan. She had ridden to Aberdeen in dreadful damp weather, then to Falkirk . . .

Falkirk, dear God. She had ridden out onto the battlefield like an avenging Valkyrie, never knowing, never guessing. And afterward, the frigid ride back across the mountains . . .

How, indeed, could a tiny babe be expected to survive all that?

She turned her head to the side and stared unseeing into the shadows beside the bed. She was in Angus's bed, in Angus's room, and the smell of sandalwood was suddenly, inescapably cloying. She gasped and tried to choke back the tears, the shame, the guilt, for a combination of all three was rising in her throat, swelling her chest, causing her to clench her fists so tightly John clamped his teeth together as her nails cut into his flesh.

"I will see what's keeping the doctor," Deirdre murmured, touching his shoulder. "When he comes, you should leave for a little while and let him tend to her."

"No," Anne cried. "No, please don't leave me, John. Please don't go."

Stricken, tear-filled eyes sought his, and she tried, weakly, to reach out her arms. MacGillivray took the burden willingly upon himself, bending over and gathering her gently against his chest. He whispered her name and buried his lips in her throat, in her hair, in the sweet drenching scent of her; he held on so tightly his heart was pounding in his ears. "I willna go anywhere lass, I swear it. I'll stay right here by yer side as long as ye need me."

"Angus," she cried, her voice broken by sobs. "Oh, Angus, I'm so sorry."

MacGillivray opened his eyes . . . then slowly closed them again, squeezing hard enough to stop all but the smallest hint of a watery shine from escaping between his lashes. He held her and stroked his hand down the red tangle of her hair, gently rocking and soothing her until her sobs trembled away to heartbreaking whimpers. By then the doctor was standing by the bed, and John relinquished her grudgingly into his care.

"It's all right, lass," he whispered, pressing his lips over her ear. "Everything will be all right, I'll make sure of it. Here's the doctor now. Let him help ye with the pain. He'll give ye something to help ye sleep again, an' when ye waken, it will be that much better. I swear it will, on ma name an' on ma honor."

"You won't leave me?"

"I'll never be more than a heartbeat away, lass. Never more, never less."

Angus rubbed his eyes, feeling the grit beneath the lids. He was not sure of the time, but he guessed it was well past three in the morning. He was working by the light of a single candle, copying out numbers, names of regiments, commanders, supplies, equipment. It was more of an exercise to keep himself from going mad, since he had no idea to whom he should pass the information now that there were several hundred miles between himself and Adrienne de Boule. She had been his contact in Edinburgh, smuggling out packets of documents he had either copied or stolen from Cumberland's headquarters.

His billet had been in the same house he had occupied before the ill-fated foray to Falkirk. Roger Worsham was still down the hall, and Adrienne de Boule was once again a regular visitor. She had been taking larger and larger risks, carrying the documents under her corset, passing them on to whoever her contact was in Edinburgh. Twice in the week before he had shipped out, she'd had to find new conduits after the old ones were arrested. The city had turned into one huge garrison, with more soldiers on the streets than citizens, all of them impatient with the weather, the inactivity, the humiliating repercussions of the army's loss at Falkirk.

There were hangings every day, lashings nearly every hour. The city was placed under a military curfew that began at dusk; anyone found out on the street, citizen or soldier, was subject to arrest and punishment.

Angus's return had gone relatively unchallenged; he had simply reported to headquarters with the rest of the released prisoners. He had endured perhaps an hour of intense questioning as to his stay in the enemy camp at Falkirk, most of it conducted by the brooding, ill-tempered Duke of Cumberland and a select number of his senior officers. Garner had been among them, as had Worsham and the ill-fated Blakeney before he was sent north to Inverness. Hawley had been present, but for the most part had sat silent and ignored in a corner.

Round and swelling with fat, Cumberland was a month away from his twenty-fifth birthday. He had spent the last five years fighting wars in Europe, earning himself a well-deserved reputation for success. He had a precise military mind and appreciated order, discipline, and logic—the three things that seemed, to his analytical mind at any rate, to be most lacking in the Jacobite camp.

"I confess I am at a loss, gentlemen," he had said, fixing his cold stare on each of his officers in turn, "to explain the contradictions I encounter from one day to the next. I am assured by my advisors at every turn that this rabble is unseasoned and untrained, and comes to a battlefield armed with pikes and pitchforks. How then have they managed to humiliate two of my most brilliant"—his voice dripped sarcasm as he crucified Hawley with his eyes—"generals? How do they manage to escape us time and time again? I am told by people who should know these hills the best that there are no passable routes through the mountains at this time of year, yet my cousin has vanished into the high snowy reaches, apparently unaffected by the same weather that leaves our men gasping and strengthless in the drifts. I am told there are no possible encampments between Atholl and Inverness where more than five hundred men could subsist in a body. Yet Lord George has disappeared into the wilds somewhere with upward of three thousand men and horses, both of whom must have fodder to survive."

"Lord George knows the lay of the land, Sire; his family seat is Atholl."

"And my family seat is all of England, Scotland, and Wales, gentlemen. I will prevail over these skirted rebels. If it takes another ten years, I will prevail."

Angus had felt the bulging toadlike eyes fasten on him down the length of the table. "You, sir. You are related to Lord George Murray, are you not?"

"He is a cousin, yes, by marriage."

"Your lovely wife and he must have had a fond reunion at Bannockburn."

Angus had trod carefully there. A bundle of beribboned letters may have worked once to cast doubt on the reports of Anne's whereabouts in Inverness and Aberdeen, but too many captured soldiers had seen her at Falkirk.

"I doubt they met but once or twice before, Sire, and then only at official clan functions."

"And you, sir? You appear to have been given free rein of the Jacobite camp."

Angus had smiled as slyly as he dared. "The prince himself took my parole, and that once given, aye, I was allowed to keep company with my wife. I was able to move about with relative freedom, and was often invited to dine with the other lairds, some of whom, either through carelessness or misguided assumption, discussed matters with an unguarded tongue."

"Unguarded enough," Major Garner had said at that point, "to have let slip some vital information I intend to act upon within the hour. If it is true the Jacobites have stockpiled a vast quantity of weapons and ammunition at Corgarff Castle, its capture could seriously impair the Pretender's ability to re-supply his army. I plan to lead the assault myself, Your Grace, and you can be sure I will not return without a solid victory to report."

Garner had then raised his glass in a toast to credit Angus's cleverness. As Cameron had predicted, after Angus mentioned he had been in the company of the *Camshroinaich Dubh*, Major Hamilton Garner had turned from skeptic to guarantor almost in the blink of an eye.

"Indeed, a victory is much needed," Cumberland agreed. "Another humiliation would make us more of a laughing-stock than we already are. All the same, if I were a suspicious man, Lord MacKintosh, I might question such blind faith in your information, not to mention your motives for leaving your beautiful wife and returning here to us."

Angus did not have twenty-two generations of noble blood in his veins for naught. He had returned the duke's stare with an icy detachment and an eyebrow arched with just enough arrogance to mock the very notion of collaborating with such obviously inferior outcasts.

"I came back because I am a realist, Your Grace. I know it is only a matter of time before you catch up with the Pre-tender, and for the final denouement, I would prefer to be on the winning side."

"And your wife? What does she prefer?"

"It would seem she prefers to play games and raise havoc, but in the end, she will simply return home to her tapestries and embroideries and remember this as nothing more than a grand adventure."

"We are told she actually took part in the battle."

"Yes, I have heard the tales about the red-haired Amazon who took to the field in full battle dress"—Angus had paused to offer a disdainful smirk—"and if your men believe them, then the Jacobite dissemblers have done their work exceed-ingly well, have they not? I was with her less than an hour af-ter the first shots were fired and I can assure you, Sire, she was comfortably ensconced with the other wives of the offi-cers, drinking chocolate and laughing over the little gold braiding on her bodice that denotes her so-called *rank*. Better, I think, to put one's faith in the reports that may be proven true than in those designed to defy all logic and credibility."

Cumberland's eyes had narrowed and Angus had held his breath, for it all came down to whether or not they would believe his accounting of the events, or the vague reports of a handful of released prisoners, most of whom gave such varying descriptions of Anne he would have been hard-pressed to recognize her himself. In his favor, Alexander Cameron had given him the information about the cache of Spanish arms and ammunition the Jacobites were storing in Corgarff Castle. The fact that most of the guns were rusted and the ammunition was of so many different calibers it was more bother to haul than store would not be immediately apparent. With the news sheets in London depicting Hawley running from Falkirk with his napkin still tucked into his collar, the duke was almost desperate to put his faith in someone other than the incompetents who had failed him thus far.

And in the end, he had. Major Garner led an attack against Corgarff Castle and returned to Edinburgh with a dozen wagons full of muskets and barrels of lead shot. Within the week, the *London Gazette* was depicting the triumphant Duke of Cumberland poised atop a mountain of weaponry that could have supplied the continental armies for a dozen years. Assured of his loyalty, Angus had found himself onboard the *Thames Rose* within the week, bound for Fort George with orders to aid Lord Loudoun in his defense of Inverness.

Angus rubbed his gritty eyes again. The ship had been struck by a hellish storm and they had arrived in port battered, bruised, and a mere hour before Lord Loudoun declared he was abandoning the city. It had been decided to ferry the entire garrison across the Moray Firth to Easter Ross, which was under The MacLeod's control and relatively friendly to the Hanover government. Lord George took Inverness without firing a single shot, and although Loudoun watched hopefully from the opposite shore of the firth, Fort George capitulated shortly thereafter without the anticipated explosion of the powder magazines or storerooms.

Railing once again at the Jacobites' uncanny ability to root out a trap, Loudoun had moved his forces to Easter Ross, and that was where Angus found himself now, in a draft-ridden stone building that shook with every gust of wind, his fingers cramped and his back aching, less than twenty miles from Moy Hall but unable to do anything about it. Following Cumberland's example, Loudoun had imposed a curfew over the town, with standing orders to arrest civilians and soldiers alike if they were found out of doors after dusk. Anyone suspected of deserting was shot out of hand by armed patrols that roved the streets searching for violators.

He heard the clock chime the half hour and set his quill aside. His handwriting was verging on illegible anyway. He would have liked to write another letter to Anne, but he was not even sure she had received the last one he had sent.

There was so much he wanted to tell her, so much he felt he could set down with greater ease on paper than he could as a stammering, spluttering neophyte in love. He even caught himself quoting Shakespeare when he thought of her, for even his own words failed to touch on the depth of his emotion.

"Shakespeare," he muttered, cursing at the irony. " 'To sleep, perchance to dream.' "

" 'For in that sleep o' death, what dreams may come.' "

Angus felt the tiny hairs across the nape of his neck come to attention. The voice had been low and husky, as thick as the shadows that smothered everything outside the small circle of light thrown off by the candle. He'd heard no sound to warn him of another presence in the room. The flame on the candle had not flickered inside its glass bell.

He turned slowly, but his eyes had been impeded by the light and the shadows yielded nothing at first. After a moment he saw a slight movement in the far corner, and Angus wondered if perhaps he was dreaming after all. Like the eyes of a big cat, MacGillivray's glowed with an eerie luminescence out of the darkness, the only part of him not rendered invisible in the gloom.

"How did you get in here?"

"I've gotten in an' out o' harder places."

"So I should not ask how long you've been standing there?"

"Long enough."

Angus had always envied John MacGillivray his cavalier audacity, and this was no exception. The man had to be part ghost, part demon, part fool to make his way unscathed into a city locked up as tight as a keg of powder.

Or he had to have a damned good reason.

Angus felt a second chill bristle over the surface of his skin. "Is this about Anne? Where is she? Has something happened to her?"

The shadow moved, detached itself from the wall, and came forward just enough for the light to touch on a few threads of gold hair. "Yer wife's at Moy Hall, safe enough."

Angus heard the word "safe" and was able to breathe again. "Christ Jesus, you frightened me half to death. How the devil did you get in here? The door is still locked, is it not?"

MacGillivray's lip curled to express his opinion of locked doors. His gaze flicked to the decanter on Angus's desk. "If that is *uisque*, I'll not refuse a dram. 'Tis cold as a witch's teat out there an' I've been four hours or more in the damp. Long enough to realize I'm gettin' too bluidy old for climbin' walls an' slitherin' over rooftops on ma belly. Eneas wanted to come in ma stead; I should have let him."

"Why didn't you?"

John shrugged and accepted the glass of whisky Angus had poured. "He made ye a promise the day o' yer weddin'; he might have been tempted to keep it."

Angus watched the Highlander drain his glass and hold it out for a refill.

Something had brought MacGillivray here tonight. Something worth risking his life.

He fetched another cup and poured a measure of whisky for himself. "Are you planning to tell me why you are here, or am I expected to guess?"

"There's a fine, thick mist on the firth, an' Lord George has sent the Duke o' Perth to take advantage. They've a fleet o' fishin' boats ready to bring a thousand men across."

Angus paused with the rim of the glass touching his lip. "They're going to attack Easter Ross?"

"Aye. An' I didna want ye gettin' in the way of a stray bullet from some misguided clansman who would think yer head on a stake would make for a handsome trophy."

"I see. So I am to be taken 'prisoner' again?"

"I've a boat waitin' down by the shore, an' two horses saddled on the other side."

"And if we are caught between here and there? I am not entirely free of suspicion from the last time, and if I miss roll call, or I am not there to sign the Order Book—"

"I've no qualms about shootin' ye, if that's what ye'd like to make it look more convincin'. Make no mistake. I've come to take ye back an' take ye back I will."

With the threat soft and low in his voice, MacGillivray came fully into the candlelight, enough at least to show his face, heavily stubbled, and eyes that had not lost their eerie intensity though they were darker, wilder, than Angus remembered seeing them. A very clear image came to him of MacGillivray in the clearing in St. Ninians, his *clai' mór* drawn, his teeth bared. At the time Angus had been fool enough to tear open his shirt and offer up his chest for slaughter, not realizing that a man as dangerous as John would have no use for empty gestures.

"Has this something to do with Anne?" he asked quietly. "Did she ask you to come?"

The black eyes narrowed. "Annie disna ken I'm here. In truth, she disna ken too much at the moment. She's been abed this past week refusin' to eat; she says nae more than a few words at a time, an' then none that make much sense. She stays abed all day but she disna sleep. She just lies there starin' at the walls because she's dead afraid ye willna forgive her."

Angus blinked quickly several times. "Forgive her? Forgive her for what?"

MacGillivray's jaw tensed; the muscles worked for a moment. "For losin' yer bairn."

The hollow chill Angus had felt earlier was nothing compared to the plummeting sensation he experienced now. It was as if someone reached into his chest and shoved everything from his neck down to his groin, replacing it with ice.

"Anne was—?"

"Aye, she was. An' she needs ye more than any man's army right the now. She needs to hear ye say ye dinna blame her for the loss. And *I* need to hear ye say that ye understand if ye ever so much as breathe an accusation her way, ye'll find me crawlin' down yer bluidy throat with ma boots on."

Angus reached out his hand to grip the edge of the table for support, most of MacGillivray's threat lost behind the loud drumming in his ears. He and Anne had made a child together and now it was gone. She was alone, frightened, in pain, and he was worried about roll calls and Order Books.

He met MacGillivray's eyes and knew what it had cost the Highlander to come here tonight, knew why he would not have trusted Eneas Farquharson with the task.

"She just needs to see ye," John said quietly. "A day, two at the outside, an' there will be enough confusion, ye'll be back afore Loudoun even knows ye're gone."

"Then we're wasting time," Angus said, snatching his cloak off the wall peg. "I trust your boat has two sets of oars?"

"It has three. I couldna spare enough men to keep Gillies from followin'."

Anne stirred, waking slowly. Her face was pressed into a crush of her own red hair, and when she opened her eyes, the first thing she thought of was blood—lying in a pool of blood. She closed her eyes again but the image did not go away, nor did the hollow ache in the pit of her belly. All she wanted to do was sleep and forget, but the former came in restless patches, and the latter was simply not possible. The doctor had left a small bottle of laudanum, and she had resorted to it a couple of times when she thought her brain might explode from the sheer pressure of wanting to scream, but it only left her feeling more lethargic and dispirited than before.

The house was dark and quiet. Even MacGillivray, who had remained by her side for nearly a full week, had begged off earlier to tend to some clan business. She had not realized until now how much she had come to depend on his quiet presence. It had been comforting to know that day or night she could open her eyes and he would be beside her in the chair, his chin propped on his hand, his face gentled by the candlelight.

She heard a faint rustling sound behind her and lay perfectly still. She knew the sound of Deirdre MacKail's light footstep, and she knew the quick rabbit steps of her maid. She waited an extra minute until she was sure, by the scent of mist and woodsmoke and damp plaid, that it was a man attempting to slide quietly into the chair before she smiled and half turned.

"You were more than one heartbeat away, John MacGillivray."

But the eyes that met hers were soft pewter gray, not black. The face was lean and handsome, not bold and awkwardly apologetic.

"Angus?"

"If you would rather have MacGillivray for company—?"

She reached out, reached up, and before the gasp could leave her lips, he was on the bed beside her, his arms around her, his body cradling her close.

Behind them, clinging to the shadows that were his only shield against the naked emotion on his face, John MacGillivray watched the reunion between husband and wife. He watched Anne's hands twist desperately around his neck even as Angus's buried themselves in the spill of red hair and held her while he tried to silence her frantic whispers beneath his lips. He watched until it was senseless to watch any longer, then turned and quietly slipped out into the hallway, closing the door behind him.

That was where his legs failed him, and he stood with his hand around the doorknob, his forehead pressed against the wood.

"It's a fine thing you've done, Mr. MacGillivray, fetching the laird home. She needs him very much right now."

John looked up, startled to see Deirdre MacKail standing there, a witness to his sin of covetousness. He did not trust himself to answer decently, but he nodded and gave the door a final brush with his hand before he turned away.

"If anyone asks after me, will ye tell them I've gone to Clunas?"

"I will, yes. How long shall I say you will be gone?"

"As long as it takes, lass," he said quietly. "As long as it takes."

Chapter Twenty-Two

Alexander Cameron reneged on his promise to be back at Moy Hall within the week; he was gone more than a fortnight. Fort Augustus had surrendered, after a two-day siege, when one of Count Fanducci's well-aimed cannon shells had struck the powder magazine. Fort William proved to be more stubborn, however, and the talents of the gunners less daunting than those of the excitable Italian. They remained locked in a stalemate at Fort William for two full weeks, returning frustrated and short of temper, having squandered a deal of shot and patience trying to outgun the fort's determined commander.

Conversely, the Duke of Perth had completely routed Lord Loudoun's forces, chasing them out of Easter Ross and up into the hills of Skye. Another large contingent of prisoners was marched back to Inverness, and once again the prince, turning a blind eye and a deaf ear to the fact that most would break their parole—meaning they would only have to be caught and defeated again—released them.

In Cumberland's camp, the question of broken paroles was moot, for the option of laying down arms on a promise not to fight again was never offered. Nor were prisoners treated in accordance with any rules of honorable warfare. Most were beaten and starved, their wounds left to fester untreated.

Many were hanged without benefit of a trial; many more were simply loaded onto transport ships and never seen again.

Prince Frederick of Hesse, whose six thousand crack Hessian soldiers had come north with Cumberland, was appalled at the treatment the captured Jacobites received under the duke's command. The prince was Germanic. Nobility and honor were codes he held above all else, and he warned the English duke that his Hessians would not fight without those codes in place.

Cumberland's response was to immediately hang three prisoners who had been caught attempting to escape. True to his word, Prince Frederick ordered his men to Pitlochry and refused to acknowledge any further dispatches from Cumberland's headquarters.

March slipped into April with little more than skirmishes to mark activity in either camp. Charles, who had been ill since the night of his narrow escape at Moy, insisted his fevers were to be conquered if they could not be cured, and ordered days of hunting, fishing, and shooting. He appealed to the ladies of Inverness to organize balls, and for these special evenings he moved from Culloden House to Drummuir House, the guest of the Dowager Lady MacKintosh.

Angus was able to visit Moy Hall two more times; on each occasion, it was Anne who chided him for his recklessness even as she took full, shameless advantage.

"A month ago," he said, "when you were begging me to stay with you in Falkirk, I had a dozen good reasons why I should go. Here, tonight, with my hands on your breasts and my body held hostage between your thighs, I cannot think of a single one."

Anne sighed and rolled her hips slowly forward and back, feeling his response stretch deep inside her. She sat astride his naked, splayed body, her hair strewn about her shoulders, her hands braced on his chest. A cluster of candles were lit on the bedside tables so that not one flicker of reaction went unnoticed on either face.

"Whereas the dozen good reasons I had for you to stay all seem so selfish now. This one, for instance—" She arched her back and rose up on her knees, withdrawing her heat almost to the engorged tip of rigid flesh. "And this."

She settled back over him with a sinuous thrust of her hips, and Angus clamped his hands around her waist, the muscles in his arms bulging as he strove to retain some measure of control. He had been deathly afraid of touching her, of hurting her, of rushing into anything physical too soon after the miscarriage, and for the first two visits he had been content just to lie alongside her and watch her sleep in his arms. This time, however, he had not made it through the bedroom door before she was under his clothes with roving hands and an avid mouth that made short work of his noble intentions. He had, at the least, insisted on her assuming the superior role so that she could control their movements and stop at any time if it became too much. After the fourth time in as many hours, however, it was proving to be far more of a trial for him than for her. Judging by the deliberate slide of her hips, the flaring and tightening of all those wicked little muscles, she knew it, too.

"Each time you come here, I find it that much more difficult to let you go back," she said, withdrawing her heat again, hovering, sliding down his full length. "But I suppose the prince needs your help more than ever now."

"I was under the distinct impression," he said through clenched teeth, "your opinion of the royal progeny had dipped somewhat since Falkirk."

"But my opinion of Lord George has not changed. Nor that of Lochiel or Lord Drummond, or any of the men who are still willing to risk so much for the sake of honor."

" 'These deeds,' " he murmured through a shiver, " 'these plots, this ill-conceived folly born of midnight honor . . .' "

She slid to a halt, intrigued. "What did you say?"

"Oh, dear God," he rasped, "don't stop again; you'll kill me."

"No, before that."

"A quote. It was just a quote. Something that popped into my mind. I cannot even recall who said it."

She smoothed her hands over his breasts, ignoring his shivered urging to resume the sleek, rocking friction. She bowed her head and caught a nipple between her teeth, leaving it and the surrounding flesh well laved by her tongue. Her fingers combed through the dark swirls of hair on his chest, following the line down onto his belly. After a brief flirtation with the hard bands of muscle that made for such an inviting seat, she reached around and trailed her fingers up the insides of his thighs, teasing the little treasures she found nestled there until she heard him growl and felt him rise up beneath her like a volcano on the verge of erupting. She leaned farther back, inviting his torso to come up off the bed, and when he obliged, she shifted her feet forward, locking them firmly around his waist so that they each sat with their legs crossed behind one another's back.

Angus rested his head on her shoulder a moment, hoping to catch his breath, to steady his nerves before the next onslaught.

"You want something else, I know you do."

"I do," she agreed softly, "and I am getting it now."

She forced him to tip his mouth up so that she could ravage what remained of his sanity. The heat of her tongue lashed at him, while the moist silkiness of her body began to draw him in with bold, greedy strokes that were tight enough he could feel his foreskin sliding back and forth along his full length. The pressure soon had him groaning again, had him cupping his hands around her bottom and bringing her harder, faster against him.

Nothing shy of gunfire would have stopped either one of them that time, and Anne rode the heady waves of her release with her head flung back and the sound of wondrous joy quivering in her throat. Angus held her and poured himself inside her. His hands, his body, his entire being shook with the intensity of his climax; even so, he waited until the very last possible instant before grunting the air out of his lungs, knowing it would be several moments before he could suck in enough to replace it. Anne continued to shiver against him, around him, keeping herself pressed so close, the evidence of their pleasure ran warm and wet between them.

"The original terms of our agreement stand," he gasped at length. "No battlefields, no skulking about the countryside in the dead of night, no guns—although I am beginning to believe that not any manner of promise, oath, or pledge can keep you out of trouble, madam."

"The encounter with Blakeney's men was not my fault," she protested. "I was only attempting to defend my home."

"But sending fifteen men out to fight fifteen hundred?"

"It certainly was not by choice, I assure you. Just as it was not your choice to have to bow to Duncan Forbes's blackmail."

She said it so quietly it took a moment for Angus to raise his head and meet her eyes. When he did, he saw a world of mixed emotions reflected there: anger, confusion, pride, defiance, admiration, condemnation. There was not much left to choose from.

"MacGillivray talks too much."

"It wasn't John who told me; it was young Douglas Forbes. He thought it would cheer me to know how brave and honorable my husband truly was, sacrificing so much in order to guarantee the safety of his wife and clansmen. Frankly, it only made me want to hit you. And not just because you took it upon yourself to bear the burden of all this righteousness alone, but more because you did not tell me."

"And what would you have done if I had?"

She took his face between her hands, and Angus sucked in a breath as her hips wriggled against him again. "This is what I would have done," she whispered. "I would have loved you ten times more than I did already."

"*Then* you would have hit me?"

"Then I would have hit you," she agreed.

He continued to gaze deeply into her eyes, offering up a small, uncertain smile. "Perhaps I should bare my soul completely, then, and have done with all my confessions."

"There are more?"

"Only one, though it is somewhat related to the other." He swallowed to ease the dryness in his throat, but before he had a chance to elaborate, a low, distant rumble broke into the cocooned silence of the bedchamber. It was followed a few seconds later by a distinct rattling of the glass windowpanes and the trinkets on the mantel. Even the wine in the bedside decanter shivered in the glow of the candles.

Angus untangled their legs and left the bed to cross over to the window. He raised the curtain and peered outside, expecting to see gray skies and the roiling clouds of a thunderstorm. But the sun was shining, the blue of the sky almost painful after the subdued romance of the candlelight. Then he remembered.

"Eneas said they were going to commence blowing up Fort George today. I gather the English left more than enough powder in the magazine to do the job properly, and there will be no lack of volunteers for the job. Many of the men have been guests there at one time or another; many more have seen fathers, brothers, sons locked away for months on end without justification. I expect Fearchar would have been in the fore, lighting the first fuse, for was he not a guest of various administrations over the last century?"

When Anne did not answer, he dropped the curtain back in place and returned to the bed. She was fast asleep, snuggled into the nest of pillows, blankets, and tumbled sheets. He drew the covers gently up over her glorious nudity, then slipped back into bed beside her, listening as yet another distant rumble shook the windowpanes.

The explosions that eventually reduced Fort George to rubble stopped abruptly on April 14, when the shocking news reached Inverness that Cumberland's army had been on the move for a week. It had, in fact, already crossed the River Spey in three places, unchallenged by the brigades Lord George had set in place to guard against such a thing. The news could not have come at a worse time, for there were no more than a thousand of the prince's troops in Inverness; most were away either securing positions or foraging for supplies.

Food and fodder had become perilously low, and Murray of Broughton, a wily and inventive quartermaster throughout most of the campaign, had fallen ill and been replaced by John Hay, who knew even less about procuring field supplies than he did about guns—the one time he had discharged a pistol, he had shot off his big toe. When he sent men out foraging, he sent them to all the places that had already contributed more than they could spare, with the result that most wagons came back empty or not at all.

Several hundred men had, therefore, been dispatched to investigate a rumor of a Hanover supply train on the road to Nairn and returned instead to report they had seen the duke's army marching along the coast road, a rippling sea of red coats and glittering muskets propped at the shoulder. The royalists had marched eighty miles unmolested, in relative secrecy, and by nightfall of the 14th were camped less than half a day from Inverness.

It had happened so quickly, the escort removing the Cameron women to Achnacarry departed from Loch Moy at dawn and turned left along the Inverness road, while their men turned right and rode hard toward the city. Anne had been at the knoll to see them off, mounted on her gray gelding as usual, but this time there were few smiles. She had come to like and admire Catherine Cameron; moreover, she was not entirely sure she could have survived her own dreadful ordeal without the quiet, calm support of Deirdre MacKail.

"I feel so terribly sorry for them," she said to her cousin Eneas when they had ridden quickly back to the Hall. "It will take days, weeks for any news to reach Achnacarry."

"I suppose, then, it would no' be met with any enthusiasm if we were tae suggest ye take yersel' up intae the caves f'ae a few days?"

"The caves?" She pulled back so hard on the reins, Robert the Bruce reared up in surprise. "Why on earth would I do that?"

"Because Cumberland's whole bluidy army is half a day's ride away? Because Moy lies right in his path an' ye'll have no one here tae defend the place if he takes it in his heid tae circle round an' attack Inverness frae both sides?"

"I'll not be here at Moy," she said. "I will be wherever my clan is."

Eneas reached up and scratched his hand through his hair. "Och, Annie . . . ye ken The MacGillivray will have sparks shootin' out his arse if he sees ye near anither battlefield."

"John is not here to say me nay or yea," she said quietly.

"Weel, as a fact, he is. He an' his bride arrived back at Dunmaglass yesterday, an' he's up ayont waitin' on ye now."

Anne followed her cousin's reluctant gaze and tentatively pointed finger. A group of clansmen were gathered out front of Moy Hall, and since MacGillivray stood a head and half a shoulder above most of the others, he was easily recognizable.

They rode up the drive, where a hostler was waiting to take the reins when she dismounted. When he led The Bruce away, most of the men acknowledged a look from MacGillivray and followed suit, moving discreetly out of earshot.

Anne had not seen him since the night he brought Angus from Easter Ross. She heard he had left Dunmaglass that day and had been in Clunas helping his future father-in-law, Duncan Campbell, dislodge a small nest of government troops from the area. She had not heard he had married.

"I understand congratulations are in order," she said with genuine pleasure. "Eneas told me you and Elizabeth were wed."

"It was time. Besides, she liked the damned flowers so much she didna wait until we were alone an', well, her father found us on the brae an' thought it was past time I made an honest woman of her."

He looked different, somehow. More at ease. There was still a perilously dangerous air about him, but some of the tension seemed to be gone, and if Elizabeth had managed to do this for him, then Anne was doubly pleased. Lying abed, steeped in the tragedy of losing her baby, losing the steadfast Robert Hardy, she had come to realize how much John's friendship meant to both her and Angus; she was determined nothing would spoil that.

"You will make a fine husband, John," she said, smiling as she kissed his cheek. "The very finest there could be."

"I plan to do ma best."

"Will you take a drink with me? To toast the nuptials?"

"Another time, aye, I will do. For the now I've only come to collect yer cousins an' the rest o' ma men. We're needed in Inverness."

"Of course. Yes. I was not thinking. I'll just fetch my things."

She started past him, up the wide steps to the front door, but he reached out and caught her arm, halting her.

"Ye might be better off stayin' here, Annie. There is little ye can do in Inverness."

"There is a great deal I can do if there is a battle brewing. I can be with our men."

"*If* there is a battle brewing? Turn yer nose into the wind, lass, ye can smell the fear from here."

"We've beaten them twice before when all odds were against us doing so."

"Aye, an' both times Lord George was commandin' the army. He'll not be leadin' it now, however, because the prince has relieved him of his command."

"Relieved him of command! Has he gone mad?"

"He heard the general was invited to a parley with Prince Frederick. The German prince offered his services to negotiate a peace with Cumberland, an' naturally The Stuart took it to mean Lord George was settin' up to betray him. O'Sullivan were whisperin' in his ear all the time, o' course, helpin' convince him."

"Someone should have shot that damned Irishman a long time ago."

"Suggest it to any one o' the two thousand men freezin' their ballocks off on Drummossie Moor an' ye'll have no lack o' volunteers."

"Drummossie? What are they doing at Drummossie?"

"Waitin' on Cumberland," he said dryly. "An' have been since dawn, though ma men tell me the duke is in no hurry to roll his guns out o' Nairn."

"All the more reason for us to stop wasting time here," she said. "You can argue until you are blue, John MacGillivray, but I've not come this far just to run and hide now. You, of all people, should not even think to ask me such a thing."

He studied the firm set to her jaw and shrugged. "Gillies wagered good coin on the likelihood of ma ears gettin' boxed, but ye have to admit it was worth a try."

She glanced at the stocky Highlander and saw that MacBean was grinning, rubbing his thumb and fingers together to acknowledge his winnings.

"Give me five minutes," she said, and dashed up the steps.

"Ye've got one."

The roads leading out of Inverness were clogged with people, animals, and wagons. The latter, hastily packed with household possessions, were being trundled behind frightened townsfolk who had heard the battle for control of the Highlands was imminent.

Anne had changed into her trews and blue velvet

short coat. Sparkling white lace foamed at her throat and cuffs, an incongruous contrast to the two long-snouted brass pistols she wore strapped to her waist. MacGillivray rode at her side; MacBean and the Farquharson brothers flanked them, with about a hundred clansmen jogging along the road behind, muskets and targes slung over their shoulders, their faces grim, their strides determined. They were met on the crossroads outside the city by an open carriage bearing two occupants. One wore the black cassock of a priest, but Anne drew a deep breath, bracing herself for another verbal battle when she recognized the dour countenance of Lady Drummuir. Her fears were groundless, however. The old woman had tears in her eyes when Anne rode up to the carriage. From a huge basket on the seat beside her, she took a white cockade fashioned out of ribbon, decorated with a sprig of whortleberry, and pinned it to her daughter-in-law's breast just below the cameo locket that held Angus's portrait.

"Mind ye stay well back, Miss. I heard what happened at Falkirk, an' ye'll have me to deal with this time if ye dinna listen to The MacGillivray."

"Aye, you're a fair one to talk," Anne murmured. "He tells me you've refused to leave the city."

"Bah. I'm too old to lift ma skirts an' run. If it should come to that, I'm too old for anyone to think o' rape when they come bangin' on ma door. But you, ye old bastard—" She raised her voice and glared at Fearchar, who rode pillion behind Robbie Farquharson. "Where the de'il d'ye think ye're goin'?"

"I'm goin' where I'm goin', ye old dragon teat, an' never think a scowl frae you will stop me."

It only took a glare, however, for Robbie to nudge his horse to the side of the carriage. After the dowager fastened a cockade on each man's breast, she reached behind the younger man and grabbed the gnarled old face between her hands, kissing Fearchar squarely on the mouth.

"Try to at least stay awake," she chided. "An' keep yer plaid up around yer ears or ye'll catch yer death afore ye even reach the muir."

MacGillivray, MacBean, and nearly every other man was

called forward by name to have the sprig and cockade pinned to their plaids, then to bow their heads for a benediction from the priest. When the last of the clansmen had moved off down the road, Lady Drummuir remained standing in the open carriage, her lips moving silently in prayer.

Chapter Twenty-Three

Charles Stuart made his headquarters at Culloden House, a short mile from the moor. Having been apprised by his scouts that Cumberland's cook-fires were in full bloom at Nairn and the soldiers showed no signs of marching out that day, he gladly took the opportunity to ride up and down the field, a heroic figure in his scarlet-and-blue tunic. He brandished a jeweled sword overhead as if victory had already been declared, posturing for the men who stood freezing in their ranks, watching him.

It was late afternoon before the prince conceded and agreed that his cousin was not coming to answer his challenge that day. By then the men were too cold and tired to care. Some had cheered their prince until their throats were raw, others had simply stared and wondered if all royalty was a little mad. They were hungry; most of them had rushed onto the field without so much as a biscuit to break their fast. They wandered back to the parks around Culloden and huddled under what shelter their plaids could provide, or roamed farther into Inverness, where they begged scraps from angry townspeople who blamed them for the false alarm.

The few tents erected on the grounds of Culloden House quickly filled with chiefs and lairds who held heated debates over their prince's choice for a battlefield. Drummossie was flat and treeless, and would afford no protection against

Cumberland's artillery. Lord George had found a field a couple of miles to the east that was pitted with bogs and hills, far more adaptable to the Highlanders' way of fighting and far less friendly to heavy guns and disciplined rows of trained soldiers. But his efforts to persuade the prince to change his mind failed and on one of the few occasions since the campaign began, the dejected general was overheard to say: "We have lost, gentlemen. God save us all."

With nothing to be gained by spending a cold, hungry night out in the dampness, MacGillivray tried equally hard to persuade Anne to return to Moy Hall, but she would have none of it. Nor would she accept the invitation from the prince to dine with him or stay at Culloden House, making the excuse that it was her duty, in her capacity as colonel of the regiment, to remain with her men and keep their spirits high. It was only an urgent summons from Alexander Cameron that brought her away from the barn where a large body of MacKintosh men had taken shelter. Since she was still addressed as "Colonel Anne" by most of the lairds, she supposed another endless round of debates and arguments had begun. Naturally, for such mundane things as diplomacy, MacGillivray had made himself scarce.

Cursing her captain's selective nature—and secretly envying it—Anne tramped through the light drizzle that had begun to fall. The ground had been churned to mud and the wind was shaking the trees with a frosty hand, a harsh reminder that winter was not completely out of the air. The clouds were low and there were no stars, no moon; no pipes played and no singing echoed around the campfires. It was a quiet, forlorn contrast from the night before the battle at Falkirk and Anne shivered herself deeper into her plaid as she walked.

The twins, who had escorted her from the barn, melted away with the aplomb of their golden-haired captain after delivering her to the designated tent. Anne heard voices inside and refrained from sighing before she ducked beneath the canvas. Cameron was there along with his two brothers, Lochiel and Dr. Archibald. Aluinn MacKail was off to one side with Lord John Drummond and another tall Highlander. Leaning over a lamplit table, his hands braced to support his weight, was Lord George Murray.

A gust of wind came into the tent with Anne, causing him to look up from the maps he was studying. A corner of the topmost paper fluttered and curled back; the flame inside the glass candle shuddered and gave off a thin plume of black smoke.

"Anne. I see Monaltrie found you; I trust we have not taken you away from anything important."

His voice was completely devoid of any sarcasm, and she had no reason to suspect he was anything but tired and frustrated.

"I was just trying to stay warm and dry," she said with a faint smile. "If that would be considered important."

"I vow both sensations have become completely foreign to me, so yes. I would regard both as being crucial. Come in, my dear, come in." Lord George waved her closer to the small brazier that was glowing near the center of the tent. "Warm yourself. I'm afraid there isn't even a dry crust to offer, but lest we be accused of having forsaken our manners altogether," he addressed one of the other men, "have we something the Lady Anne might sit on?"

Since no one else was sitting and they were surely twice as tired as she, Anne shook her head. "I'm fine, really, I—" She lifted her hand in a staying gesture as the Highlander standing with MacKail turned and she saw his face.

"Ahh." Lord George followed her startled gaze. "Yes, I suppose that was cruel of us not to warn you beforehand, but even a whisper these days seems to spread like a roar. Angus . . . come and let your wife pinch you so she knows you are real."

Angus Moy hesitated as long as it took him to give his bonnet a twist in his hands, then came forward into the brighter light. Since Anne had seen him last, the circles around his eyes had deepened, his face was shadowed with stubble, and the rags he wore would have been better suited to a beggar.

"You look well, Colonel," he murmured.

"You look dreadful, Captain. Have they no barbers in the king's army?"

That caused an eyebrow or two to lift in surprise, since the last thing she was expected to notice was the unkempt shagginess of his hair. Another man's wife might have remarked first upon the long, ragged cut that ran from just below his left ear and disappeared beneath the collar of his shirt. The wound was no more than an hour or two old, still leaking fresh blood where it was chafed by the wool of his plaid.

"Perhaps you would like that seat now?" Lord George asked.

She still had her knees, but experience told her that her husband's presence in camp did not bode well. "Thank you. Yes."

"You have undoubtedly been apprised of the reason Cumberland kept his army at home today?"

"Someone mentioned it was the duke's birthday?"

"Indeed. He gifted his army with a day of warming their toes by their fires, toasting their valiant general's health with half a pint of brandy apiece. Would that I could even remember the taste of fine French brandy, never mind think to spill it down the throat of a common batman. Ah, well. Envy does not win us battles, does it? The way I see it, gentlemen—and Colonel—is that we should thank whatever God we pray to that the battle did not happen today. More men arrived late this afternoon, and Keppoch sends word he is but a few hours away. What is more, the duke may inadvertently have given us the opportunity we need to turn this fiasco into a victory. See here," he said, leaning over the map again. A long, slender finger touched on the black marking that denoted their present position, then followed a smudge of charcoaled lines to where a second mark identified Nairn.

"I have been told that this is in reality a long wynde that follows the river well to the south of Drummossie and comes out surprisingly close to Cumberland's camp."

He looked up for confirmation and Anne realized it was one of the maps she had drawn of the area. "Yes, my lord. But it is low ground, doubtless flooded with the spring thaw."

"But passable?"

"Not easily."

The general smiled. "Have we done one thing easy thus far? It is my intention to set a proposition before the prince. I

am going to press that we attempt a flanking move of our
own, leading the army out by two columns, dispatching one
here"—his finger tapped the area east of Nairn—"and one
here to the west, thereby taking the English camp between us
in a pincer that would allow Cumberland nowhere to retreat
but into the sea. If the action is conducted in stealth and surprise, we might just be able to catch them nursing their hang-
overs and yawning over their morning fires."

"A night march along a boggy riverbank?" Lochiel said,
frowning. "Christ, but, ma men have gone without sleep for
two days as it is."

Lord George straightened. "The choice, as I see it, is to
draw on our reserves or be prepared to line up on that damned
moor again in the morning. The only possible advantage we
can hope to gain at this point is surprise, and surprise will require a night march. It is roughly twelve miles from here to
there; we could cover it easily enough in, say, four hours.
Military etiquette aside, if we catch them abed or drunk as
beggars, it can only go in our favor. Angus, you say his artillery park is facing west, toward us?"

"They point the guns in the direction they intend to
march."

"Then it would behoove our vanguard to attack that position first and remove any possibility of their catching us in a
crossfire. Alex, I hate to ask . . . ?"

Alexander Cameron merely smiled. It had been solely due
to his rash heroics and those of his clansmen that the government artillery had been silenced at Prestonpans. A hundred
men had charged a battery of forty guns and captured them,
but at a terrible cost in brave lives.

"How many?" The question was directed at Angus.

"Ten three-pounder battalion guns, four signal-pieces."

Cameron pursed his lips and exchanged a glance with his
brother Lochiel. "We'll take Fanducci with us; he's brought
us luck before."

"Which leaves only one other satin-clad *prima donna* to
deal with," Lord George said wryly. "John?"

Lord Drummond sighed. "Aye. Ye're saddlin' me with the
prince?"

"Unless you would rather he come in my column, in

which case you would have to retrieve him after the battle, buried up to his neck in a bog and left by the side of the road."

"Och, he's no' that bad. If ye flatter him all the day long an' tell him ye like the cut of his tunic."

"Then the only question remaining is guides. We will need men who know the wynde like they know their own bodies. With the mist we have tonight, there are too many chances for error."

"MacGillivray and MacBean," Anne said at once. "They practically own the river. My cousins and me as well; we grew up"—she ventured a finger forth and touched the map— "here. Right where the wynde splits away from the bog. John can take the first column; we'll lead the second."

It was Angus this time, his objection halfway off his tongue, who forced himself to remain quiet. Just as Anne had refrained from crying out with wifely concern over the gash in his neck, he respected the sense of desperation in the group and held his fear in check . . . for the moment.

"That's it, then," said the general, rolling up his maps. "I'll take the final proposal to the prince, with the approval of those whose opinions matter, and put it to him in such a way as to leave him no options. I suggest you return to your clans and prepare them for an immediate departure. Angus, I thank you for the final count, and you may consider you have the grateful thanks of the entire army for the risks you have taken. I will have an escort waiting outside to take you back when you are ready. Unless, of course—?"

Angus shook his head, answering the unasked question. Lord George nodded to acknowledge his decision—and his courage—then signaled the rest of the chiefs to give Angus and Anne a few moments of privacy. Angus barely waited for the flap to drop over the door before he tossed his bonnet down on the table and gathered his wife into his arms.

When the first order of business was settled to a mutual, bruising satisfaction, he tackled the second. "I suppose it is my own fault. In the list of promises I extracted from you, I neglected to specify 'and do not volunteer to lead an army through a bog in the middle of the night.' "

"And you, sir." She touched the side of his neck, able to show her horror now at how close the cut lay along the jugular. "I suppose you earned this while you were copying out lists?"

"My visit tonight had not been prearranged, so I did not know the proper response to give the sentry. He held his knife to my throat with a little more enthusiasm than was warranted, though not as much as might have been displayed had I not been able to produce my brooch and prove I was who I claimed to be."

"I thought you were in Skye with Lord Loudoun."

"I was. Until three days ago, anyway. It seems Cumberland put in a 'special request' for myself and a dozen other prominent lairds. He wants all the Highland companies in the front line—and that is not the worst of it. He has deliberately chosen officers with no conscience, like Hawley, and given them command of battalions led by brutes and butchers. I have seen things of late that have left me sick at heart. Men hanged for simply stating their opinion. Women raped because they happened along the road and were wearing the plaid. Farms burned and livestock slaughtered for sport. They call the Scots barbarians, then turn around and disembowel a man for refusing to take a penny for his daughter's virtue. Just yesterday, a thirteen-year-old boy was accused—just accused, mind, not proven—of spying, and was hanged. He swung for over ten minutes before he died; all the while the duke's men took wagers. Another man was given eight hundred lashes in the morning and made to stand his post at night or receive eight hundred more. These are the men who want to bring the Highlands to heel, to make them bow to English discipline and order."

"Then what can you possibly hope to accomplish by going back? You are only one man, for pity's sake."

"Prince Frederick was only one man, yet he has refused to allow his Hessians to fight under such barbaric conditions. Perhaps there are more. Perhaps there are enough of us to stop the bloody sword of Damocles before it descends."

Anne was not entirely sure who Damocles was, but if Angus feared him, it did not bode well. "You sound as if you do not believe we can prevail."

"My belief, my faith has already been shown to be a poor

thing next to yours." He sighed and took her face between his hands. "I suppose the best I can hope for at this juncture is that you will trust MacGillivray and take your lead from him. If he says it is lost, believe him and run. Run for your sake and for mine. Will you promise me this?"

The tremor in his voice, in his hands frightened her, and she nodded. "I will trust MacGillivray. I will do as he says."

Even that much was a blessing and he closed his eyes, angling his mouth down to capture hers. The kiss was tender and poignant and conveyed a wealth of emotion in a simple gesture that had to end far too soon.

"I have to go. If Lord George prevails with the prince, I may be of some help at the other end." He hesitated a moment, then reached under his coat, withdrawing a silver brooch embedded with a large cairngorm, engraved with the MacKintosh motto: *Touch not the cat bot a glove*. "Take this. It is only fitting that the colonel of Clan Chattan wear the proper badge of office."

She said nothing as he pinned the badge solemnly to her plaid, but when he was finished, she slipped her arms up and around his shoulders, burying her face in his neck, breathing in the scent of his hair, his skin.

"Promise me," she pleaded softly, "that you will steer well clear of this General Damocles."

Angus drew a breath into lungs that were almost too tight to allow it, then claimed her lips one more time before easing her to arm's length.

"I shall avoid him like the plague, my love," he vowed, "and be back in your arms before you know it."

But she knew it already. She felt the loss before he had even left the tent.

Angus Moy returned to Nairn along the same route the Jacobite army would be taking, following the river east and circling up behind the encampment. A sentry saw him approaching along the road and stepped away from the guard tent to challenge him, but Angus knew the password and said it so sharply the lad lowered his musket and moved aside.

The wind had died down and the mist cloaked everything

in a murky haze. Lanthorns hanging on tent posts took on the look of yellow eyes as he passed the battalion streets. Like everything in the English army, those streets were laid out in neat, straight rows of peaked canvas, stretching off into the distant darkness. There were so many. Twelve battalions of Foot, three regiments of cavalry, and an artillery train all grouped in their orderly squares around the central headquarters of Balblair House, where Cumberland and his most senior generals were billeted. There were also eight companies of Scots militia, most of them sent by Argyle, men who would have no reservations about fighting their kilted kinsmen.

Bullocks had been slaughtered earlier in the day to provide meat in honor of the duke's birthday, and the mist still smelled of the sweet roastings. Angus had not eaten anything since early morning; having seen the condition of the Jacobite camp and knowing Anne would have stubbornly refused to take more than the same biscuit her men had been rationed, he had no appetite. Here and there sporadic bursts of laughter cut through the air, a sound that had been noticeably absent in the Stuart camp, and although he guessed it must be past midnight, a few of the campfires had solemn circles of men around them.

Balblair House was ablaze with lights. It sat atop a hill like a crown jewel, sparkling through the dark mist. Cumberland was likely playing at cards with a pretty woman by his side, a favorite pastime for someone who had banned gambling and women from the company tents. Angus had been told the duke had taken to smiling a great deal at Adrienne de Boule, which did not sit well with Major Worsham. William was the king's son, after all, portly and disagreeable though he might be, and royal scions were notorious for simply taking what they wanted if it pleased them.

Turning into his own row of tents, Angus dismounted and handed the reins off to a private. It had taken him nearly two hours to traverse the distance between the two camps, and his horse was muddied to the base of his neck for his troubles. The ground was so soft and spongy in places, he'd had to circle well out of his way, and he could only wonder how men on foot would manage. Surely they had departed Culloden by now. Even adding for the extra time it might take to circumvent the worst of the boggy terrain, Angus guessed they would not arrive before three or four o'clock in the morning. He had been cautioned that when the fighting erupted, he should stay in his tent if that was at all possible, or if not, to pin the white cockade prominently on his plaid to avoid being run through by another eager Highlander.

Smiling grimly to himself, he touched the cut on the side of his neck. His fingers came away dotted with blood, and he realized he would have to bandage it before the constant rubbing of his collar managed to do what the knife had not.

He lifted the flap on the tent and stepped inside, freezing just the other side of the pole. His cot was in disarray, his kit opened and the contents strewn about the blankets. A lamp was lit, but the wick was turned so low he had not noticed the glow against the canvas outside. It was barely bright enough to illuminate the figure seated in the corner, or the long, thin nose and pointed chin that identified Major Roger Worsham.

"Captain MacKintosh. I was beginning to think you were never coming back."

Angus glanced pointedly at his upturned kit. "So you thought you would ransack my personal possessions?"

"No. I merely did not trouble myself to replace them this time."

If he was expecting an indignant protest, he was disappointed. More than once Angus had opened his kit to find things slightly out of place, as if the contents of the trunk had been searched and carefully put back in order. He had been assigned a new subaltern, Ewen MacCardle, to act as his personal aide, but even though the man was no Robert Hardy, he was not so sloppy as to forget from one day to the next that Angus preferred his shirts laid top to bottom, not side to side.

In truth, he didn't give a hang how his shirts were packed, but after the first incident when he suspected his belongings had been thoroughly searched, he had expressed the preference to MacCardle, who had been obliging ever since.

Angus stripped off his gloves. "Find anything that interested you? Dirty laundry? Unpolished buttons? A commendation from Charles Stuart, perhaps, applauding me for my loyalty to his father?"

Worsham's eyes narrowed. "You make light of these things, MacKintosh, but I get the distinct feeling there is more truth behind your words than brevity. Where were you tonight, for instance?"

"My personal time is my own, sir. I do not have to answer to you."

"Would you prefer to answer to the duke?"

"I would prefer it if you removed yourself from my tent so I could get some sleep." He turned away from the major and shrugged his plaid off his shoulders. "It has been a long day and the muster is for four-thirty, if I'm not mistaken."

Worsham tipped his head to the side. "You seem to have cut yourself, Captain."

Angus instinctively touched a finger to his neck. "Yes. It . . . was an accident. My own carelessness."

"It looks painful. I'm surprised your wife did not dress it for you."

"She had other things on her mind and was a little preoccup—" He stopped. He clamped his lips together, barely refraining from cursing out loud.

Worsham, of course, was smiling. It had been too, too easy.

"It is a shame, really. You were doing rather well up until now. Even tonight, riding off in the direction of Kingsteps and waiting in the forest for an hour. My tracker, Hugh MacDugal, grew quite impatient and nearly showed himself."

"I wanted to see my wife. Is that a crime?"

"It is when she is a colonel in the rebel army, and when you spend nearly an hour in the company of Lord George Murray before your wife is even aware of your presence in the camp. It is when you've been passing documents and dispatches through Adrienne de Boule for the past several months, helping her play spy."

Angus felt a cool, ghostly shiver ripple down his spine.

"Oh, yes, I've known about her little games for some time too. I would have had her arrested long before now if she weren't so damned energetic in bed. I vow she can do more with a few little muscles than a man of twice her strength pumping with two fists. Believe me, I speak from experience."

He uncrossed his legs, then crossed them again as if the memory was a pleasant one.

"Where is Mademoiselle de Boule now?"

"Where she belongs. Flat on her back with her legs spread, entertaining the men of my company. An added fillip, you might say, in honor of the duke's birthday. Actually, I was informed about an hour ago that she bit one man so hard he had to strangle her before she would let go, but up until then she was a genuine little rebel hellcat, spitting and hissing, accommodating two men at a time, if you can imagine—"

"You godless son of a bitch." Angus started forward, but the sudden appearance of a pistol in Worsham's hand halted him two steps shy of reaching his goal. Worsham pushed to his feet, thrusting the nose of the cocked flintlock into the soft hollow above Angus's collarbone, pressing hard enough to almost crush the windpipe.

"Hands up, and back away, Captain. Your heroics do not impress me, and I would as soon pull the trigger as not."

"Then why don't you?"

"Believe me, it would be my pleasure, but I'm sure Cumberland will want to speak with you. And then there is the anticipation of seeing the look on that arrogant fool Garner's face when I reveal your duplicity, for you did indeed have him convinced you were the second coming of Christ. I have been savoring the moment far too long to let it end too quickly, but I promise you I could get over my disappointment if you press me. Now . . . hands up, if you please. And stand back."

Angus raised his hands slowly, palms out, fingers stiffly together.

"Very good. Now turn around and—"

Angus had seen it done once in Paris, at a demonstration of Oriental fighting skills, but he had never tried it, did not even know if it would accomplish more than causing Worsham's finger to squeeze the trigger. But he slanted both hands inward and brought them cutting sharply down in a V, chopping into the sides of the major's neck with as much force as he could bring to bear.

Surprise, more than skill of execution, startled Worsham into staggering back a step. The nose of the gun dipped down for a moment, which was all Angus needed to clench his fist and deliver a more conventional blow to Worsham's jaw.

The major's head snapped up and back and he staggered again, but he recovered enough of his senses to duck the next punch, even to swing his pistol up and strike Angus across the temple. The skin over MacKintosh's eye split, and in seconds the left side of his face was awash in blood, yet it did not slow him or hamper his aim in any way as he drew the dirk from the waist of his kilt and stabbed it forward. The tip of the blade skidded off a brass button and sliced through the scarlet wool of Worsham's tunic just below the breastbone. Angus barely thought about it as he drove the blade forward and jerked it up, slicing through skin and muscle and finally through the spongy mass of lung. He jerked the blade again, his rage lifting the major up onto his toes even as his body curled forward around the impact of the blow.

Worsham's hand sprang open, dropping the gun. His mouth gaped and his eyes bulged, and he stared in disbelief as Angus bared his teeth, jerking the blade a third time.

Worsham's hands clawed around Angus's shoulders for support. Blood surged up his throat and ran from between his lips; it bubbled through the scarlet wool and splattered the front of Angus's doublet.

"You're a goddamned snuff-taker," he gasped, his face twisting with the irony of his final few moments. "I've never even seen you draw your sword."

The strength went out of his arms, out of his legs, and Angus watched impassively as the major slumped to the floor. He reached over at the last and pulled his dirk out of the sodden red tunic, but Worsham's eyes were already glazing, losing their focus. The body continued to shudder a few moments more, but it was over.

Angus staggered back, the realization of what he had just done striking him like a blow to the chest. He backed up until he felt the edge of the cot against his knees, then sat down hard, the knife red and dripping in his hand.

He looked at it, looked at the major, and was grateful he had not had anything to eat all day. Even so, his stomach heaved upward and seemed to lodge at the base of his throat, remaining there until several deep gulps forced it down again.

Puking would accomplish nothing. He had just killed an officer in the king's army. Not just any officer, either, but the protégé of William, Duke of Cumberland.

"Aye," he whispered disgustedly. "I shall avoid Damocles like the plague, my love."

Jesus God, what was he to do now? If the body was discovered . . .

If the body was discovered, and if the Jacobite army succeeded in its surprise ambush of the camp, it would simply be assumed that Worsham had died in the clash! No one else knew what had happened tonight; their voices had not been raised; no one knew there had been a confrontation.

Except for Hugh MacDugal, the tracker who had followed him to the Stuart camp. But would he have said anything to anyone else? Or would Worsham have insisted on keeping it between the two of them until he had incontrovertible proof and could drag Angus in chains in front of his peers?

Proof.

Worsham was a meticulous note-taker despite his difficulty with the written word. His notes were marked in his own strange code, but if he had kept a record of Angus's movements tonight, and if someone was able to decipher his scratches, it could prove incriminating.

Angus pushed himself off the cot and forced himself to roll Worsham over onto his back. The eyes were fixed and staring, the centers dilated so that it looked as if two holes had been bored into his skull. Quickly, Angus opened the top three buttons on the bloody tunic and searched the inside pockets. He found nothing there, but when he lifted the flap of the leather belt pouch, he discovered several documents and a small notebook filled with scratched notations. Flicking briefly through the latter, he was able to read enough to know his suspicions were confirmed. Anne's name was there, as was his.

He opened one of the folded documents, dismayed to see his hands were shaking so badly he could scarcely hold it steady. It was an official copy of the company's battle orders, and he almost refolded it and returned it to the pouch, except that when he looked again, he saw it was dated that day, April 15, and signed by Lord George Murray.

It was a copy of the Jacobite battle orders, only there again, something was not quite right. He had seen this same document in the tent at Culloden just a few hours ago; it had been lying on the table with the maps. Angus had read it casually enough, for he had seen a dozen such battle orders over the past few months of military service. Most were worded almost identically—so identically the company commander rarely had to consult the page before reciting the contents aloud.

Angus read the document a second time, then a third before the hairs on his neck started standing on end.

It is His Royal Highness's positive orders that every person attach himself to some corps of the army, and remain with that corps night and day, until the battle and pursuit be finally over, and to give no quarter to the Elector's troops on any account whatsoever. This regards the Foot as well as the Horse. The order of battle is to be given to every general officer . . .

He did not have to read any further. These were not the orders he had seen on Lord George's table, nor did he believe, when he held the document up to the lamp and turned the wick higher, that it had been signed by his wife's cousin. It was a damned good forgery, but Lord George Murray was left-handed and wrote with a distinct slant—a slant that increased drastically for his signature.

There were several other folded papers in the pouch and Angus found what he was looking for in the third attempt. It was a copy of the original orders as he had seen them, noticeably absent the unconscionable phrase: *. . . and to give no quarter to the Elector's troops on any account whatsoever.*

The first sheet contained a forged order to take no prisoners, to slaughter without consequence even those who fell wounded on the field. To an English soldier, this would give rise to the vision of a screaming hoard of Highland savages falling on them, hacking them to bits whether they had surrendered or not. If copies of these false orders were given to every officer, and he in turn read them aloud to every man in his company, they would believe the prince had issued a command to show no mercy on the battlefield. It would inspire them to return the favor in kind, without reservation.

Angus withdrew his pocket watch. It was one-fifteen. He returned it to his sporran, along with the documents he had taken from Worsham's pouch, then rolled the body again, moving it to the far side of the tent against the canvas wall. Luckily Worsham had not been above average height and he fit beneath the camp cot with only a minor bending at the knees. When the blanket was draped over the side, it completely covered the fact there was a body beneath.

It was not brilliant, but it was the best he could think to do on the spur of the moment. Something dripped on the blanket while he was still bent over, and he remembered the cut over his temple. A quick glance in the shaving mirror was met by a reflection of charnel horror, for his scalp had bled profusely, adding to the stains that were already on his shirt and coat from the neck wound.

He stripped and cleaned himself as best he could, using the widest neckcloth he could find in the scattered contents of his kit, then winding it an extra turn around his throat to serve as both stock and bandage. The cut on his head was swelling by the minute, the skin was blue and ugly, but at least it was hidden by his hair. He fetched a clean shirt and donned his kilt and tunic. At the last, he remembered the white cockade Lord George had given him, and this, too, he tucked into his sporran after checking his timepiece again.

One-forty.

The Stuart army had to be close enough to smell the garbage burning behind the butcher's tents.

Chapter Twenty-Four

"What's that godawful stench?" Robbie Farquharson asked, his nose wrinkled up almost to his eyebrows.

"The shite o' the forty horses ahead o' us, mixed with the muck an' slime o' every fish what ever died in this bluidy river." Jamie, calf deep in the mire, struggled to free his left leg so he could sink it in front of the right. He'd lost his brogues a mile back, not clever enough or quick-thinking enough to have tied them on a string around his neck like most of the other men had done, and was barefoot. The wind that had blown earlier in the day was gone, its abrupt departure encouraging a heavy fog to creep up from the riverbank. The farther east they walked, the thicker the fog became, until it was difficult to see the man in front and impossible to know if there was better ground ten feet on either side.

Lord George Murray had led the first column of men out of camp at eight o'clock. With him were Lochiel's Camerons, his Athollmen, and the MacDonalds from Clanranald, numbering some nineteen hundred in all, guided by John MacGillivray and Gillies MacBean.

The prince and Lord John Drummond commanded the second column of two thousand, comprising mostly Lowlanders and French volunteers, and by the time they had struggled over the same trackless paths, marshes, and quagmires, the gap between the two columns had widened too much to ever hope to launch the simultaneous attack they had planned. By two o'clock in the morning they had covered only seven miles, and the conditions were worsening.

"Dear God!" Anne gasped as Robert the Bruce skidded in the mud for the fourth time in as many minutes. The valiant beast was doing his best to keep his footing, but she was afraid each time that the next slide would result in a broken ankle. Twice already she and her cousins had prevented the column from following the wrong branch of the river in the soupy fog. Thus far, she had managed to stay on her mount, but now she swung her leg over with a final curse and slid out of the saddle, instantly sinking calf deep in the churned mud. The Bruce must have sensed he had failed his mistress in some way, for he instantly began to tremble.

" 'Tis not your fault, my fine hero," she murmured, rubbing the velvety nose. " 'Tis the fault of all that snow melting down from the mountains and the ground still too frozen to suck it up."

"Weel, it's sucked me," said a man nearby. He threw himself down by the side of the tract, his arms splayed wide like a crucifix. "I canna go anither step. I canna catch ma breath. I canna hear f'ae the bluid poundin' in ma ears. I'd crawl the way if I could, but I canna. I simply canna."

An echo of his words rippled back through the ranks, some of the grumbles voicing sympathy, some anger. They were all exhausted and cold, and still as starving as they'd been that morning when they'd cursed over their ration of one small biscuit. The slowest clansmen, those who were lost well back in the fog and darkness, had simply stopped and turned around.

"It's no' possible, Annie," said Eneas, gasping for breath like an old man. "It's taken us five hours to cover seven miles, an' we've anither five to go."

She held her finger to her lips, for the prince's group was just ahead of them. "He'll hear you."

"I dinna care who hears me. The men are fallin' over on their feet. If they're expected tae go on, an' then tae fight, I can see disaster ahead even if he canny. What's mair, if he was hopin' tae surprise Thomas Lobster, he's lost that chance too, f'ae we've already found one o' Willy's scouts creepin' along the bank watchin' us. Lomach MacDugal. Do ye ken the name?"

It sounded as if it should be familiar, but Anne shook her head.

"He an' his brither Hugh have been trackers f'ae the *Sassenachs* since Loudoun took command o' Fort George. They're as close as oor Jamie an' Robbie, an' if Lomach were in the neighborhood, ye can bet yer kirtle Hugh is no' far ahind."

"Did you question him?"

Eneas frowned. "He would have had a mout o' difficulty answerin' through a slit throat."

Anne supposed she should react to the brutality, or at the very least ask if it had been justified, but she simply could not rouse either the effort or the sympathy. She could not find fault with Eneas's anger, or his sense of foreboding either. She was just as tired, hungry, and dejected as the men who struggled forward out of blind obedience. Her bonnet had fallen off somewhere back along the way and her hair hung over her shoulders in dark, tangled hanks. She had to speak through clenched teeth to keep them from chattering, and now she could swear she heard buzzing in her ears.

The buzzing grew louder; it was coming from up ahead. They walked without torches, but some of the guides carried hooded lanthorns and as she and Eneas strained to see through the mist, the dull glow cast by one of them appeared and swayed closer. The man carrying it was one of the guides who had been with Lord George's column and Anne recognized him as Colin Mor, the clansman whose bothy they had stayed at the night MacGillivray had oiled her legs to rid them of saddle cramps.

He saw The Bruce and veered across the sucking mud. "We've turned back, Colonel. The general an' the chiefs decided it were f'ae the best."

"Och, thank the good Lord above f'ae that," Eneas sighed. "It's over, then, is it?"

"All but the shoutin'," Colin said, hooking a thumb over his shoulder. Even before the words were out of his mouth they could hear the prince's voice rising in protest, screaming that he had been betrayed yet again.

"Where is Lord George?" Anne asked in a hushed voice.

"'Bout a mile ahind. He'll only go as fast as the slowest man, though now they've been told they can go back an' find their beds, they're movin' a fair speed."

"MacGillivray?"

"He an' The MacBean were no' very far ahind me. If ye stan' here, he'll see yer horse, like as I did, an' he'll find ye."

He saw another man coming past with a lanthorn, and gave his to Eneas before he set off back through the muck and trampled sod.

"Shall we go forward an' wait?" her cousin asked.

"No. No, we can hear the fuss well enough from here. I'd rather not enjoy it any closer."

"Aye. I'll leave the lamp wi' you, then, shall I?"

"Where are you going?"

"Just over ayont a bit where it's drier. I just need tae sit f'ae a wee minute. Catch ma wind. It were seven miles o' hell gettin' here, it'll be seven miles o' hell gettin' back."

Anne nodded, almost guilty she had ridden The Bruce as long as she had.

The feeling intensified a few minutes later when she saw MacGillivray and Gillies MacBean walking toward her. John didn't notice her at first; it took a tug on his arm from Gillies for him to lift his head and look in the direction his clansman pointed.

They both looked terrible, splashed head to toe in mud. Anne had never seen big John MacGillivray with his shoulders drooping, and she caught only a glimpse now before he pulled himself straight and walked toward her. "Ye've heard, then?"

"Aye. We spoke with Colin Mor."

"It was for the best. We got as far as Knockanbuie when they realized it was hopeless. As bad as this bit is, the river is flooded up ahead, an' the horses were sinkin' up to their bellirs. The men, too, for that matter. Gillies here thought he felt a snake crawlin' down his leg, but it were just the mud hangin' off his willie."

MacBean was too exhausted to even blush.

"Here." John handed Gillies his musket and cupped his hands. "Give us yer foot: We'll give ye a leg back up."

"No, I can walk. The Bruce is about done in anyway, and there might be someone needs the ride more than me."

MacGillivray did not even have the breath to argue; he simply took the reins and turned the gelding around.

When the sloping parkland around Culloden came into view, it was nearing six in the morning. Most of the men simply fell down in the grass and slept where they lay. Hundreds more never made it farther than the first point of the road where they could glimpse the roof of the Lord President's manor house. Anne stumbled as far as the same barn she had slept in the previous night; there, she and fifty other MacKintosh clansmen curled themselves into the hay. Most of them were asleep before their heads even touched the ground, but Anne found herself sitting with her back against the wooden slats, unable to close her eyes or even pretend to avert her gaze as MacGillivray stripped out of his coat and leaned over the water trough to scrub the mud and sweat away.

It seemed like months ago that she had stood in an upper window at Dunmaglass while he doused himself after a hard bout of practice with his men. Then his golden hair and muscled body had gleamed against the whiteness of the snow; there had been laughter and energetic camaraderie, and they had been preparing to set out on a great adventure to reclaim Scotland for their royal prince.

Now they squatted in dark, ugly places, most of the clansmen too tired to care about such mundane things as mud or how they might stink to the men lying next to them. She suspected that if she were not there, insisting unto the last on maintaining her role as colonel of the regiment, John might have flung himself down in all his glorious filth and been snoring as soundly as the others. Or he might even have been discouraged enough by the night's fiasco to keep going on to Dunmaglass, where his new bride would offer warmth and succor.

No, she thought, watching him as he flicked the water from his hands in a shower of bright droplets. John MacGillivray would never quit just because the odds were horrendously against any chance of succeeding. He had committed his men, his life, and his honor to fighting a battle he had been reluctant to join in the first place, but now that he was here, there would be no turning back. No compromising. No easy surrender.

Lord George had tried desperately to convince the prince to fall back beyond Inverness where they might rest, fill their bellies with hot food, and recoup the strength they needed to fight Cumberland's fresh, well-rested troops. The argument had overtaken Anne and MacGillivray where they trudged along the tract, and if not for her restraining grip on his arm, John would have taken out his gun and shot the Irishman O'Sullivan who, as soon as Lord George was out of earshot, began spouting more accusations of cowardice and betrayal.

But the prince refused to retreat again. He insisted his brave Highlanders would rally and fight, if only their leaders showed faith. "The Scots," O'Sullivan had said, "are always good troops until things come to a crisis, then the only word they know is retreat."

It was enough to send nearly every man's hand to his sword, and some to even want to turn around and march right back into Nairn.

"You should be trying to get some sleep," MacGillivray said, startling her away from her thoughts. He stood in front of the stall the men had set aside for her privacy, and fished a cigar out of his saddle pouch.

"I will. I'm just . . . trying to work the knots out of my legs," she said, rubbing the backs of her calves.

He watched the movement of her hands a moment, then leaned over and lit his cigar off the pale flame flickering inside a lanthorn. The smoke rose around his head in a cloud. When he had puffed a good enough glow at the end, he dropped the shield back into place and savored a long, deep draw.

"May I?"

He looked down at her and frowned. "May ye what?"

"May I try it," she said, pointing at his cigar.

"No, ye may not. It's bad enough ye dress like a man an' ride like a man; I'll not be the cause of ye horkin' an' spittin' like a man."

"Then will you at least come and sit beside me for a minute? I have grown quite fond of the smell of those things and it would be a vast improvement over whatever occupied this stall before us."

He smiled, but still hesitated. "Annie, I—"

"Yes, of course, how selfish of me. You need your sleep as well. Please, go ahead. I'll just close my eyes and think of heather after a summer rain."

"That was no' what I was about to say."

She glanced, as he did, at the rows of sleeping men on the barn floor. The area was dark save for a few cracks in the boards where daylight sliced through in dust-laden slivers, but no one else appeared to be awake, or if they were, they were thinking of their own blistered feet, not the impropriety of a whispered conversation in a hay-filled stall.

MacGillivray exhaled another stream of smoke and lowered himself gingerly past the cramps in his own legs to sit beside her.

They were both silent with their thoughts for a few moments, listening to the patter of the icy drizzle that had begun to fall.

"I never had the chance to thank you."

"Thank me for what, lass?"

"For bringing Angus home to me that night."

"Ah. That. An' here I thought ye were goin' to thank me for puttin' ma name on that petition so ye could be here with us, freezin' off yer . . . well, freezin'."

"You are an impossible man to flatter, John MacGillivray." And before she could think about what she was doing, she leaned over and laid her hand on his cheek, turning his head so that his lips were a mere inch away. A kiss, given thus, would not have been interpreted by anyone as being anything other than a friendly, playful gesture, but there was suddenly a wealth of caution in his dark eyes.

"You have been a good and dear friend to me, John," she said softly. "I don't ever want that to change."

"It never will, lass, ye have ma oath on that."

She smiled and reached down, plucking the cigar out of his unresisting fingers.

The end was damp and tasted slightly bitter when she put it to her mouth; it drew easily enough but she knew the instant the smoke was on her tongue that it was probably the least pleasant sensation she'd experienced since the twins dared her to lick a toad when she was small.

MacGillivray grinned. "Dinna swallow it, lass," he warned.

"Mmm?"

"Let it out. Blow it out afore it goes up yer nose."

She expelled the smoke on a "Bah" and handed the cigar back quickly enough to earn an amused chuckle. "I may no' take flattery well, but ye were always the one who had to hold her finger in the flame to believe it was hot. Are ye happy now that yer mouth tastes like the backside of a scorched log?"

She smiled "yes," but her eyes filled inexplicably with tears. They were hot, stinging two silvery paths down her cold cheeks; try as she might, she could not stop them.

MacGillivray swore and stubbed out the cigar. Then, heedless of who might or might not be taking notice, he opened his arms and drew her against his chest. Anne went willingly, even a little helplessly, and it was John, gently stroking the damp tangle of her hair, who went straight to the heart of the matter.

"He'll be all right, lass. He's no' half so soft as ye think he is."

She shook her head, keeping her face buried against his throat. "I just wish I knew where he was this very minute, what he must have thought when we failed to attack the camp."

"He probably thought the prince came to his senses. An' he's likely still warm in his bed, or havin' a good stretch an' tuckin' into a hot meal. Right the now, he'll be thinkin' what a bluidy fool he was for goin' back; that he should have stayed here with you instead of leavin' ye in the care of a rogue like me."

She made a strangled little sound that was half sob, half laugh, and he tried not to hold her too tightly, to give away too much of his own weakness as she curled herself gratefully against the warmth of his body.

"I'm sorry," she whispered. "I'm so sorry for being such a burden."

"Och, ye're no' a burden, lass," he said, pressing a kiss into the soft crush of her hair. "A trial, sometimes," he added with a crooked grin, "but no' a burden."

Anne did not know how long she had slept, or when the heat had left her side. It was the pipes that woke her. Pipes and the paradiddle of beating drums that called the Highlanders to arms, warning them that Cumberland's army was approaching Drummossie Moor.

Anne shook herself awake in time to see MacGillivray strapping his great broadsword across his back and fastening the wide studded leather belts that held his arsenal of smaller, lethal weapons, including a brace of claw-butted pistols. Gillies was beside him, kicking awake some of the men who had not yet stirred.

"Wh-what's happening? What time is it?"

"Gone eleven," John said, his voice as raw as his mood. "The first four brigades o' the duke's army are already on the field, with more comin' up behind. Half our men are still dead asleep; the others have wandered away in search o' food." He looked at the barn door and bellowed, "Is ma horse saddled yet? I'll only need him as far as the moor."

Someone shouted back and he acknowledged it with a grunt.

Anne scrambled to her feet, earning an instant, ominous glare from MacGillivray.

"Ye're stayin' right here, lass, make no mistake. Try so much as to breathe a quarrel with me an' I'll have Gillies tie ye to the post."

"He wouldn't dare."

Both men answered in unison, one saying "He would," the other saying "I would," and she knew they meant it.

When the last clansman was rousted, the last sword and musket retrieved from the hay, MacGillivray sent them out on the run. Unable to find his own bonnet, he snatched another from beside the trough and waved it at Gillies as a signal to go on ahead.

"If things go bad," he said, cramming the bonnet over his blond hair, "I want ye up on The Bruce an' riding hard for Moy Hall. 'Tis where Lord George has said the clans are to rendezvous if we have to take the prince up into the mountains."

"Promise me you will be careful."

"Ye could have five thousand men there by nightfall, so ye'd best make preparations. There will be wounded."

"Promise me you will not be one of them," she said, shivering.

His gaze held hers for a long moment before he turned away.

He managed two long strides before a curse brought him sharply back. With his hands taking a fierce hold on her shoulders, he dragged her up and kissed her hard and full on the mouth. It was not a friendly kiss, nor could it ever have been mistaken for one. It was a kiss full of passion, exploding with the pent-up hunger of a man who understood he might never have the chance to do so again—not because conscience or morality might stand in the way, but because he knew the odds were not in his favor to leave the battlefield alive that day. He had already accepted the inevitability of death, and he was not afraid of it. Moreover, he had lived his entire life expecting it to come at the end of a musket or sword and, as a fighting man, he would not want to cheat the devil any other way.

What he could not accept, what he could not have tolerated, was going through all eternity knowing he had been too cowardly to take one last, glorious taste of life.

"Try to forgive me, Annie," he gasped against her mouth. "But I do love ye. Know that I've loved ye all ma life, and know that I'll love ye long after ye've forgotten me."

He released her then, his eyes being the last to relinquish their hold before he turned and ran out of the barn. His horse was saddled, waiting, and he swung himself up on its back, kicking it into a gallop before Anne could even find the breath to gasp his name.

Chapter Twenty-Five

*A*ngus had paced in his tent until he heard the signal drums beating the General Call to Arms at four-thirty. He guessed something had gone terribly wrong with the planned attack; his fears were confirmed when he heard men talking calmly outside his tent on their way to muster.

Worsham's body had then become a major concern. It was still dark outside, but within minutes the streets would be filled with soldiers filing toward the central parade ground, there to fall in with their company and begin the march toward Culloden. There would be confusion, but not enough to distract from a man carrying a dead major over his back. Nor could he explain the death as an accident or even self-defense and leave the corpse where it was to be discovered after the battle.

The dilemma of what to do was temporarily taken out of his hands when he peered through the canvas flap of the tent and saw another eyeball peering in.

He jumped back, his heart lodged in his throat. A moment later his adjutant, Ewen MacCardle, ducked through the flap, bearing a small tray with some foodstuffs and a cup of steaming black tea.

"Mornin', sar. The general has ordered no fires lit an' no

meal f'ae the men. He thinks they'll fight better on an empty belly. I managed tae find ye some biscuit 'n' cheese, but."

Angus felt sweat gathering on his brow as he studied his aide. Had it been Robert Hardy attending him, he would have had no qualms bringing the man into his confidence. MacCardle was politely indifferent, however, and one never knew where one stood with him; if he approved, disapproved, resented, admired.

"I have a small problem," Angus said slowly. "I was hoping you could help me with it."

"Aye, sar, if I can."

Angus reached inside his tunic and withdrew the white ribbon cockade. If MacCardle recoiled or shouted an alarm, the game would be up then and there, and it would not matter if the body was discovered in his tent or not.

MacCardle's eyes fixed on the cockade and remained there for almost a full minute before rising slowly to Angus's face. Once there, he seemed to notice the purpling lump over his temple and the lame attempt to conceal it beneath a wave of brown hair. The hazel eyes, which MacKintosh had considered to be rather dull up to now, flicked back down to the cockade and considered it another long moment before he pursed his lips and nodded.

"You don't seem too surprised."

"That ye're a rebel playin' at bein' an officer o' His Majesty's Royal Scots?" He shrugged. "Half the men in the Highland brigades would be wearin' the Stuart colors if they didna have tae worry about their wives an' bairns bein' burned out o' their homes."

"What about you? Do you have a wife and bairns?"

MacCardle grinned, showing a mouthful of rotten teeth. "In truth, I've two wives, one in Glasgy, an' one in Perth. The Glasgy one has a face like a cooked boar, but her faither is rich an' said as how I had tae jine up wi' the Campbells tae protect his land. The lass in Perth is rounder an' sweeter, an' her brithers are with Lord John Drummond. So if ye're after askin' me where I'd rather be right the now, I might tell ye Perth, but if ye're askin' me tae help ye drive a blade intae the belly o' fat Willie, I'd have tae tell ye Glasgy."

"The blade, I'm afraid, has already been driven." Angus expelled a breath and crossed over to the cot. He lifted the edge of the blanket, watching the hazel eyes flick down and widen slightly when they saw the stiffened body.

"Aye, sar," MacCardle murmured. "Now that's what I would call a problem."

"I am due at the parade ground with my regiment. God only knows what will happen on the field today, but if Major Worsham's body is discovered here, I am a dead man regardless."

MacCardle's jaw twisted slightly as he weighed his choices. "Aye. Go on, then. Leave the bastard wi' me. I'll think on sum'mit tae do wi' him."

"You would be putting yourself at great risk to help me, Ewen."

"Then ye'd best get on about yer business afore I think on it too much an' change ma mind."

Angus tucked the white cockade back inside his tunic and snatched up his bonnet. After a parting glance at the cot, then at MacCardle, he ducked out into the freezing drizzle and joined the flow of men moving toward the parade ground. He found his own regiment and stood to attention in the miserable cold, guessing there were upward of nine thousand others standing and waiting for the order to march.

At a signal from the drummers, they came to the ready, moving out right foot first, toe to the opposite heel of the man in front, the firelocks of their muskets tucked beneath their arms to keep the pans and chambers dry. They marched in columns six abreast, heading west along the valley of the Nairn, saluted by two heavy guns mounted on the slopes of Balblair House as they passed.

His Grace, the Duke of Cumberland, sat on his horse watching the men strike past, admiring their precision and determination. He was not easy to mistake: His frock coat was scarlet, banded with thick gold braid. Wide, pointed lapels of royal blue framed a face that was as dark and ominous as the sky, for he had made the promise well known throughout the entire camp that he would hang every last one of them by his own hand if they even gave a thought to turning and running from the field this day. He had also heard that his cousin often inspired his troops by marching in their ranks, and so, when it came time for him to join his men, he dismounted and handed the reins to an aide, then fell into step beside a regiment of Foot that cheered loudly enough to drown out the timekeeping of the drums.

Twelve miles later he mounted his horse again and assumed the higher ground on the southeast bank of Drummossie Moor for a vantage point. It was cold and the weather was abominable, but at least the sleet was driving at their backs and not into their faces, as it was for the Jacobites.

Angus could not help but stare across the field at the howling wall of plaid and steel, wondering at the insanity of so few standing up against so many. Major Hamilton Garner rode past, distracting him momentarily by asking if he had seen Major Worsham that morning. Out of the corner of his eye, Angus saw Ewen MacCardle blow a puff of steam into the misty air, for he had caught up with his captain on the road and casually mentioned the "problem" had been disposed of in the huge pit where the cooks burned their garbage.

And then there was nothing to distract him as he heard the officers passing up and down the lines, ordering the men to prepare their weapons.

MacGillivray had ridden straight into a sodden gray curtain of driving rain and sleet that swept from one side of Drummossie Moor to the other and obscured what lay half a mile away on the other side of the field. When the squall passed, he was not the only one who drew back on the reins in shock.

There were thousands. Eight, nine, maybe ten thousand scarlet-clad soldiers lined up in squared divisions, marching onto the field in perfect precision, like blocks of Roman centurions. Each wore the red tunic and white crossbelts, the knee-high spatterdash gaiters and stiff leather neck stocks. To the right, the first division extended so far it straddled the moor road. Far, far to the left, on an angle that seemed to jut away from the Jacobite front line, divisions of cavalry were standing patient, the animals trained to wait until the artillery did its terrible damage before they thundered out onto the field.

The Jacobite army was half the size and spread half the length of the moor, even though the chiefs attempted to draw their companies out to give the impression of substance. Lord George was in command of the right wing, comprising Camerons, Stewarts, and his own Athollmen, the last with their collective shoulders butted up against a sod dike that had been extended over the years as the parklands of Culloden spread eastward. It had been another point of contention between the prince and his general that the edges of the field had too many dikes and low stone walls that could encumber the men. The prince argued they would afford some protection; Lord George worried they could become a trap.

Lord John Drummond had command of the center, and it was here that MacGillivray rode to meet the cheers of the men from Clan Chattan, five hundred strong and near enough to their own lands and homes that they took comfort knowing if they fell on this field of honor, they would not lie alone and forgotten in some faraway unmarked ground.

The Duke of Perth commanded the left, and had to deal with the thousand-strong MacDonalds of Keppoch, Glengarry, and Clanranald, some of whom had only arrived at Culloden that morning, and were angered over being so far from their traditional place on the right. It was the crusty old Keppoch, swallowing his ire a moment to study the field, who also noticed the left wing was aligned at a skewed angle, making the distance between the two armies as little as five hundred yards at the one end and as much as eight hundred yards at the other. He sent a runner to Lord George to see if this should be corrected, but before he could receive any answer, the first of the prince's mismatched artillery guns was mistakenly fired by a half-asleep gunner.

Anne had never liked storms; as a child she had thought the sky was cracking apart and would come crashing down over her head while she slept. When the cannonading began, it sounded and felt just like a cataclysmic thunderstorm, and fears she had not thought of for twenty years came back to haunt her. The ground shook and the planks of the barn trembled. Straw and dirt fell in gritty showers from the rafters. Ten minutes into the incessant pounding, a loose beam crashed to the floor, missing her by a few feet and hastening her decision to move out of doors.

The wind caught her plaid, tearing it off her head. Freezing rain pelted down at a sharp slant, cutting into her face, making her gelding more skittish than the sound of the guns. She pulled him under the protection of an awning of trees and craned her neck to see through the mist and sleet, unsettled by the sight of huge gray plumes of smoke rising over the vicinity of Drummossie Moor. From half a mile away she could hear the sound of pipers and men screaming their *cath-ghairms*. She had seen them at Falkirk and she could envision them now, the clans stretched across the field in a swirling, turbulent mass of red and green and blue tartans, waiting for the signal from their general to unleash hell on the English lines.

The prince would be on the high ground, cheering them on. His huge silk standard would be snapping in the wind, and he would be mounted on his white stallion, presenting a regal figure in royal blue and gold, his eyes possibly even streaming tears as they had at Falkirk to see his brave Highlanders charge into battle.

Anne tilted her head and listened, still hearing the distant cacophony of screams and skirling, but now there was something else familiar. Above the roar of the heavy artillery, she could hear the crackling pop of musketfire. That, too, brought a vision into her mind, of the clans breaking out of their ranks and running forward. The chiefs and lairds would lead the bloodcurdling rush, for the hierarchy of the feudal system dictated the order of honor. They would be followed by landowners and anyone of ranked nobility, then their tenants, then the lower classes of common workers, shepherds, and humblies. The second Jacobite line consisted of the Irish, French, and Royal Foot guard. Here, too, were Lord Elcho's Royal Horse, the cavalry of gentlemen. Their animals had been sorely decimated by the harsh winter and lack of forage, but there were still about a hundred smartly suited officers who would be eager to enter the fray on a signal from their commander.

Anne stroked The Bruce's neck, feeling the same impatience and excitement shiver through his muscles as she felt in her own. MacGillivray had said to stay away from the battlefield; he had not expressly forbidden her not to find a better vantage point. With that small qualification in mind, she swung herself up into the saddle and nudged the gray into a quick canter, heading for the higher ground beyond the moor road.

The clans were stunned by the swift and savage damage wrought by Cumberland's artillery. This was the first time they had encountered English gunners, for they had caught their enemy by surprise at Prestonpans, and at Falkirk the cannon had been mired in mud and abandoned when Hawley's troops fled the field.

At Culloden, they had been rolled onto the moor ahead of any men, and were manned by officers who knew their business. Round after round was loaded and fired with precision, first upon the cluster of mismatched Jacobite guns, unseating them and blowing them to hell within the first ten minutes. Next, the elevation was adjusted and the big black snouts were pointed into the Jacobite front line. The screaming Anne had heard was not so much from the taunts and war cries of the clansmen but from the men who were being torn apart where they stood. The prince, startled to find his own position under heavy bombardment, was forced to move back, but neglected to pass the order first for the chiefs to release their men. By the time he did so, the English gunners had changed to grapeshot—hundreds of tiny lethal balls packed into an exploding shell that sprayed the field like hail, against which there was no defense but the body of the man in front.

Lord George, furious at the prince's incompetence, unleashed his men without waiting for the royal order. He was followed by Lochiel and Lord Drummond, and so on down the line like a staggered wave. Last to realize the charge had begun were the MacDonalds, who also had the farthest distance to cross, every step of it under the repeated volleys of musketfire exploding from the unmoving and as yet unscathed wall of scarlet-clad soldiers.

The men of Clan Chattan charged headlong toward Cumberland's front ranks. With MacGillivray in the lead, they veered to avoid a sunken morass of mud near the center of the field, and found themselves running shoulder to shoulder with the Camerons. They were the first to reach the government line, scattering the terrified soldiers with the sheer impact of their fury. Lochiel went down, his ankles shattered by grapeshot, but his brothers Alexander and Archibald brought the full wrath of the clan forward, hacking and slashing their way through the infantry lines, carving such a deep and bloody swath through the government troops that they unwittingly opened their own flanks to fire from the divisions on either side. Caught in a deadly crossfire, they had no choice but to withdraw and wait for support from the other clans, but there were no other clans close enough to come to their aid.

Lord George Murray struck the line on the right, where the fighting had become so intense his men had to climb over their own dead to reach the soldiers. Cumberland's troops kept up a steady, precise drill of fire, reload, fire, not even needing to aim in the closely packed mass of kilted Highlanders. Those who survived the grapeshot and synchronized fusillades were met with fifteen inches of serrated steel thrust at them from an unmoving wall of well-disciplined infantrymen.

Frustrated by the redcoats' refusal to turn and run as they had before, appalled by the dead mounting before them, the Jacobites began to fall back. Cumberland observed this with a triumphant smile and gave the nod to the men of his second line, who moved forward, fresh and eager to relieve the battered front ranks.

Lord George, seeing this new barrier of infantrymen six deep step up into firing position, realized the action was hopeless and screamed the order to retreat. That was when he saw, to his further horror, that the stone walls he had pleaded to have taken down were now lined with Cumberland's men, sharpshooters who propped their muskets on the topmost stones and took deadly aim at the unprotected backs of the retreating Highlanders.

Blinded by the rain, the smoke, the confusion, the clansmen

fought their way back over a field littered with their own dead and dying. MacGillivray had lost sight of Jamie and Robbie Farquharson in the frantic charge, but he saw them now, lying together in a tangle of bloodied arms and legs, the one shot while trying to pull the other to safety. Eneas was beside MacGillivray. At the sight of his slain brothers, he turned and raised his sword, screaming obscenities at the English. Two, three, five shots smacked into his chest, his belly, his shoulder and still he charged back toward the government line, hacking the hands and sword off the first man who stepped up to meet him, cleaving the skull of the next, and going down, finally, under the bayonets of a dozen infantrymen.

Just when it seemed some of the clans might make a safe retreat, Cumberland unleashed his cavalry, five hundred strong. These were the dragoons who had run at Prestonpans and again at Falkirk, and now that they could see the Highlanders were crippled and helpless, they took special glee in running them down, killing even those who threw aside their weapons and raised their arms in surrender.

The beating rain gave the smoke nowhere to rise, and the air was choked with sulfur. Lord George, wounded in half a dozen places, his face awash with blood, saw there was only one escape open to them and shouted for the clans to stay together and retreat along the moor road. The prince's standard had already been taken down. There was no sight of the royal figure or his white charger, and for that they could be grateful, for within minutes of the cavalry being unleashed, the high ground was overrun.

It fell to the Camerons and the MacKintoshs, both of whom had lost half their men in the slaughter, to protect the retreat. Alexander Cameron took the right, and on a waved acknowledgment from John MacGillivray, the MacKintoshes positioned themselves to protect the left flank. Throughout the charge and the terrible aftermath, MacBean and MacGillivray had managed to stay together, and they fought side by side now, rallying their men to hold off the assault of the soldiers who pressed toward them in an unrelenting sea of scarlet and white.

"Moy Hall is it, then?" Gillies snarled, fixing his gaze on a pocket of soldiers who were advancing across the field and smirking along the lengths of their bayonets.

"Aye, we'll meet there, brither," John said, his attention drawn to a cluster of Foot converging on three wounded Athollmen.

"Ye think we'll get some meat? An' a real bed tae lie on?"

"I'm sure of it, lad. That an' a crock o' sweet ale to quench our thirst."

"Aye, well." Gillies looked over his shoulder and grinned. "It might be worth the trouble, then."

John reached out and the two men, who had been friends since their reckless youth, exchanged a fierce handclasp, then parted. Gillies ran screaming toward the startled infantrymen, slashing his broadsword with such ferocious power that two of their number lost their heads and a third saw his entrails spilling onto the ground before the rest could form up and bring him down.

John, unaware of Gillies's fate, went to the aid of the three wounded Athollmen, dispatching the first of the king's Royal Foot before the *Sassenach* was even aware there was a rampant lion behind him. A second and third redcoat were sent writhing on the ground with hideous wounds, while a fourth actually dared to turn and raise his bayonet. One swipe from MacGillivray's broadsword broke the musket in half and left the soldier gaping down at the bloody stump where his arm used to be. The injured Highlanders fell on another man and, because they were without weapons, wrested his own musket from him and clubbed him unconscious with the stock.

The last of the royalists, a lieutenant, flashed his saber in MacGillivray's direction and actually managed to cut the sleeve of his shirt off at the shoulder. John looked at the tear, cursed at the officer, then drove five feet of honed steel through his chest and punched it out the back of his spine.

"MacGillivray!"

He spun around in a half crouch and saw the blood-spattered face of Hugh MacDugal looming out of the mist. They had a long history of bad blood between them, and John knew by the snarl on the ugly face that it had worsened over the past twenty-four hours.

"Yer bluidy kinsmen killed ma brither Lomach last night.

Slit 'is throat they did, an' left him in the bog. I found him this mornin', drowned in his own bluid."

"Must have been a sweet change," John said, "from the shite you breathe all day with yer nose stuck up Thomas Lobster's arse."

"Aye, an' you would know all about arses, would ye not? I hear tell The MacKintosh's wife bends over f'ae ye on a regular basis. Mayhap I'll try her a time or two maself after I'm done wi' you an' her rebel husband. Oh, aye, I know all about that one, too, an' I'll be the first tae raise a cheer when they string him on the gibbet."

John wiped at a persistent trickle of blood over his eye. Coming up behind MacDugal were ten or twelve more infantrymen, and when they saw the golden-haired Highlander standing firm on the road, they started to spread out into a half-circle.

"Hold!" MacDugal roared. "This bastard is mine! I've waited too long f'ae this no' tae have the pleasure o' tearin' his heart out wi' ma own hands."

He raised his broadsword and charged forward with an unholy scream of fury. John waited for the ugly Highlander to come to him; when MacDugal was half a dozen paces away, he gripped the hilt of his *clai' mór* in both clenched fists and swung it hard enough for the exposed muscles in his arm to bulge like polished granite. He caught the tracker low, hacking through a knee, slicing upward to sever through the artery and lodge the edge of his blade deep in the opposite thigh bone.

MacDugal was still screaming when he went down in a fount of blood, taking MacGillivray's blade with him. The circle of soldiers melted back in awe for a moment, staring in horror at the limbless and bleeding tracker, then, as one, looked up at The MacGillivray.

"If ye're going to kill a man," he said quietly, "just kill him. Dinna boast about it beforehand."

One of the soldiers swore and raised his weapon. John's hand moved to his waist and in the blink of an eye, the man went down clutching at the hilt of the dirk protruding from the split in his forehead. Another saw a flash of steel coming toward him a half-second before the blade struck his shoulder with enough momentum to send him back off his feet.

Having determined MacGillivray was now weaponless, the eight survivors spread out to close the circle and, confident of a kill, started to edge forward. John stood completely still, his black eyes defying each of them in turn, and when the first man lunged forward with his bayonet, MacGillivray bent over and snatched up a broken wagon axle that was lying at his feet. The swing caught the *Sassenach* full in the face, splitting it like a bladder. A second scything sweep tore the throat out of a second man and knocked a third senseless. He pressed forward, roaring his rage, downing seven of the eight foot soldiers before the last one was able to fit his trembling fingers around his musket and pull the trigger.

The shot caught MacGillivray high in the chest and spun him around. By then, another pack of soldiers had seen the encounter and rushed to give aid; several of them raised their bayonets and stabbed the unmoving Highlander repeatedly before running off in search of more challenging prey.

What they saw instead was a huge gray gelding bearing down on them. The screaming red-haired woman on its back raised two flintlocks and fired, blasting one man off his feet, sending another scrambling over a low stone wall. The wall proved to be the lip of a deep well, and while his scream was reverberating off the stones, The Bruce's hooves trampled another of his companions. Anne's sword made short work of the last.

She had witnessed the horror of the charge, the futility of the attack, the slaughter during the retreat, and at one point had been nearly swept away by the horsemen forcing the prince off the field and leading him to safety. Charles Stuart had indeed been weeping, but not out of pride this time. He had been weeping with shame and fear, screaming at the Highlanders to keep heart, that they would rally to fight another day.

The road had begun to clog with Jacobites retreating toward Inverness, but Anne had turned The Bruce toward the moor and fought her way to the verge, where she saw what was happening to the Camerons and the valiant men of Clan Chattan. She saw Gillies MacBean, bloodied head to toe but still fighting like a dervish. There was no sign of her cousins, but she saw MacGillivray . . . and she saw what lay beyond him: a field of horror littered with the bravest hearts of Scotland.

By the time she recovered her shock enough to spur The Bruce forward again, both Gillies and John were down, the brutality of MacBean's wounds leaving no doubt that he was dead.

She thought MacGillivray was dead also, but when she slid out of the saddle and slumped onto her knees beside him, she saw a faint movement in his throat. When she touched his face, his eyes fluttered open and she cried out, rolling him gently onto his side, taking his golden head onto her knees.

"John! John, can you hear me?"

His eyes stayed open, but they could not seem to focus. There was blood everywhere, in his hair, spattered on his cheeks and lips. She wiped what she could with the corner of her plaid, and for the smallest instant he was able to look up and meet her gaze.

"John—?"

A sigh brought the copper-colored lashes down and the effort it had cost him to see her one last time was expended. His head lolled gently to the side. He was gone.

Anne clutched the folds of his doublet and hugged him close to her body, too stunned, too shocked, too numbed by the horror to even be aware of the danger coming up behind her.

The English soldiers were crossing the moor in pursuit of the straggling Highlanders, but victory was theirs and they were not in any great hurry. They moved across the field in packs, like ravening dogs, searching the fallen bodies for gold or valuables, killing and mutilating anyone they found wounded or helpless. Some were red to the tops of their thighs from moving through the dead; others looked like butchers as they hacked and slashed.

Anne looked wildly around for help, but the road was clear save for a few limping stragglers. She tried to haul MacGillivray's body up by the shoulders, but she knew she would never be able to lift him onto The Bruce alone. The thought of just leaving him there, however, was never a consideration.

She heard a shout and saw two of the king's soldiers running toward her. Snarling, scrambling to her feet, she snatched up her sword and braced herself to avenge her brave MacGillivray's death.

She was nearly blinded by the heat of her tears, but she saw enough to know both men were wearing scarlet-and-white tunics over the cursed dark plaid of the King's Royal Scots. One was an officer, and this was where she focused her rage first. She clutched her sword with both fists in the same manner as MacGillivray, and with the clan cry on her lips, she lunged forward. At the last possible moment she thought there was something vaguely familiar about the ashen face and dark chestnut hair, but it was too late to stop the momentum of her sword and she felt it punch through the hated scarlet wool and slice into flesh and bone.

Instinct more than anything else made Angus stagger back when he saw the blade coming. He threw up his hand and managed to deflect the blade from piercing his heart. Even so, he felt the raw edge of steel scrape between his ribs, and it was all he could do to shout at MacCardle to lower his musket and hold his fire!

"Anne!" He gritted his teeth and braced himself as she withdrew the sword and set herself to thrust again. *"Anne, it's me! It's Angus!"*

He brought his saber up this time to block the second strike, but already he could see some of the confusion in her eyes clearing. On the third parry he was able to drive the point of her sword into the ground, after which she stopped cold and stared at him, her eyes as wide and haunted as those of a wounded, cornered animal.

"Anne . . . it's me, love. It's Angus."

Her gaze slid to MacCardle and, seeing only the loathsome scarlet-and-white uniform, her lips drew back in another cry.

"Ewen, get behind me!"

"Aye, sar. That I'll gladly do."

The subaltern stepped quickly out of Anne's line of vision, forcing her to focus all her attention on Angus.

"Annie," he said as gently but as urgently as possible.

"Annie, listen to me, darling. We have to get you out of here. You have to leave here and you have to leave *now*. Let me help you up on The Bruce."

"I'm not leaving John behind," she rasped.

"What? John? Where—" Angus looked at the bodies scattered around the shallow scoop of frozen ground, shocked by the welter of gore. He saw one big body sprawled on its side, a hand still clutched around the broken axle of a wagon, and he almost did not recognize the tangled, bloodied ruin that was John MacGillivray.

"Oh, good God," he whispered. "Good sweet God."

"God was not on this field today," Anne declared savagely. "Look around you. Is this the work of a compassionate, loving Creator?"

A commotion near the moor road drew Angus's attention. He heard two gunshots and saw a woman with long blond hair running away from a band of pursuing dragoons. One of the dragoons was Hamilton Garner, and he used the heel of his boot to knock the woman to the ground.

"Anne, we have no more time. We have to get you out of here."

She bared her teeth and raised her sword again. "I am not leaving this field without John MacGillivray."

Angus cursed, but he nodded. "Hold The Bruce steady, then. Ewen—"

MacCardle stepped warily forward, one eye on Anne, the other on the big gelding as he and Angus heaved the body up between them, then draped it over the seat of the saddle. They were starting to attract attention and some of the soldiers were shouting at them to hold up, but Angus ignored them. He grasped Anne around the waist and hoisted her up behind MacGillivray, and handed her the reins.

"Get out of here. Get back to Moy Hall—and for pity's sake, stay there until I come for you. Now, get going. *Go!*"

He slapped the gelding's rump with the flat of his sword and stood his ground until he was sure Anne had cleared the field and was on the moor road. Only then did he let his legs give way. Only then did the agony send him slumping down onto his knees.

"Cap'n?"

MacCardle dropped down beside him, noticing for the first time the huge wet bloodstain that ran from just under Angus's armpit to the lower hem of his kilt.

Chapter Twenty-Six

*A*nne knew she would not make it as far as Moy Hall with John MacGillivray's body draped over the saddle. Dunmaglass was closer, but there were open fields to cross. Twice since leaving the moor, she had been forced off the road and into the trees as groups of howling dragoons rode past, chasing after the fleeing Highlanders. Bodies lay on both sides of the road, some having lain down to die there of injuries gained on the battlefield, some freshly slain by the dragoons. At one bend in the road, Lord George had positioned men to discourage a blood-crazed company of Kingston Horse from following too closely. Once Anne passed through, they closed ranks behind her and a few minutes later, she heard gunfire and screams when the government troops were ambushed.

After that, the Elector's troops were more cautious, for the Camerons and Athollmen were still a threat as a fighting force. But the progress of the dragoons was persistent and lethal. Even hapless civilians who had ventured onto the high ground to watch the battle were summarily cut down and hacked to death along with the fleeing Jacobites.

Only a handful of the prince's cavalry were still on horses. Either the animals had been shot out from under their riders, or their riders had been shot out of the saddles and the beasts left behind, trembling on the field of carnage. The Bruce's

forelegs and withers were streaked with the blood dripping
down from the saddle; he and Anne made a gory sight crossing over the bridge into Inverness, but at that point she truly
did not care. She stared back at the faces that peered out from
behind parted curtains as she passed. She ignored the only
other horse and rider she saw—a well-dressed gentleman apparently going about his business as if half of hell were not
erupting five miles down the road. He, in turn, veered to the
opposite side of the road and gaped at her aghast. Her arms
and the front of her tunic were soaked with John's blood from
holding him on the battlefield. She expected her face was
streaked as red as her hair—a suspicion that bore fruit when
the front doors of Drummuir House opened and the dowager
covered her mouth in horror as Anne drew close.

"God an' all the saints above, it is you," she cried.

Anne dragged the cuff of a torn sleeve over her cheek but
she only smeared the stains more. "I didn't know where else
to take him where he would be safe."

If not for the leonine mane of tarnished gold hair, it was
not likely the dowager would have known whose body was
draped across the saddle. She crossed herself, her expression
a mixture of pain and sadness, and touched the hem of Anne's
coat.

"Are *you* all right, child?"

Anne was not even sure, but she nodded dumbly. "I didn't
know where else to take him. The soldiers—" She turned her
head slightly as if she could see through the hills and trees to
the battlefield. "They were doing such terrible things to the
bodies . . ."

The dowager clouted one of the servants on the ear.
"Dinna just stand there, ye clarty fools! Help get that brave
man down." She waved two of the house servants over. "Be
gentle with him! Take him inside where we can clean him
proper. Annie, child, come out o' the saddle."

"I have to go to Moy Hall," she said, her voice a ragged
whisper. "Angus told me to go there."

The dowager clasped a hand to her throat. "He's alive,
then? My Angus is alive? Ye saw him?"

Anne frowned. She was fairly certain it had been Angus she
had seen at the last, but there were too many images crowding

into her mind. Too much blood. Too much pain. Not ten minutes ago she'd seen a child no more than four years old lying by the road, him and his mother both bayonetted.

"I have to go to Moy Hall," she repeated. "Angus told me to go there."

Lady Drummuir felt a chill as she looked up at her daughter-in-law. Her eyes were huge, the blue completely swallowed by the black centers. She was trembling as if in the grip of a terrible fever, her cheeks so pale the spatters of blood looked like splashes of crimson paint.

"Aye," the dowager said gently. "An' ye will go back to Moy, just as soon as ye're able, but for the now, come down off that great beast an' let me help ye. Ye'll take some hot broth an' a bath, an' when ye're a fit sight for yer men to see, then aye, ye can go to Moy Hall. Please come down, Anne."

Anne's eyes filled with tears again as she watched the servants carry MacGillivray's body into the house. She felt Lady Drummuir's hand on her wrist, and she looked down through another blinding rush of tears and nodded. She was colder than she had ever been in her life, shaking so hard she could not dismount on her own but had to wait for the servants to lift her down out of the saddle. The dowager did not even give her the option of walking. She ordered the stoutest of the men to carry her into the house and up the stairs, where she threatened to bring down the wrath of all the MacKintosh ancestors if a tub was not filled with steaming water upon the instant.

Once upstairs, Anne sat numb and unresponsive at the edge of the bed while a maid stripped her of her bloodied clothing. She stared at some cuts on her hands, but could not remember how she came by them. One whole side of a hip was marked with purple-and-black splotches, but there, too, she could not recall being bruised.

The maid helped her up and guided her into the huge copper tub that had been hauled in front of the fire. The shock of the hot water startled Anne into looking around and slowly coming to realize she was safe. At least she was away from the death and the blood, and she was not alone any longer.

The steam and the heat and the smell of soap being rubbed into her hair restored her a little more, and by the time she had been rinsed and left to soak, she was able to hold a cup of hot broth to her lips without dribbling half of it down her chin.

Lady Drummuir left for brief moments at a time, but always came back to sit by the hearth. It was obvious she was aching with questions, but she did not ask anything of Anne other than to inquire if she wanted more broth.

After three bolstering cups Anne felt well enough—and warm enough—to climb out of the tub and sit by the fire. Wrapped in a thick woolen dressing gown, she sat dutifully still while the maid brushed her hair dry and twined it into a thick braid.

"Thank you," she said. She glanced up from the hot flames and looked at the dowager. "I don't know what happened back there. I don't even remember how I got here."

"Ye were in shock, lass. I'm no' surprised. There have been men coming to the door, bringing the news before they flee."

Anne just looked at her, and waited.

"The soldiers are on their way to Inverness. They're no more than a mile down the road."

"I have to get to Moy Hall," Anne said, setting her cup aside. "The men will need help. Have you had any news of the prince?"

"He's away safe. They're taking him to Ruthven. Are ye sure ye want to ride out in this, lass? It might be better ye stay here. There are rooms below the stairs that the soldiers would never find in a hundred years—ye could hide there until it was safer to go out."

Anne shook her head. "I feel much better now. I can almost think clearly. The men will go to Moy Hall, and I must know how they fared. With John and Gillies gone . . . they will not know what to do."

Her voice trailed away and the dowager clutched the crucifix she wore around her throat. "Gillies is gone too?"

Anne nodded and had to press her lips very tightly together for a moment. "I did not see Eneas or the twins, so perhaps they escaped. Lord George was commanding the rear guard, protecting the retreat, but there were so many who scattered into the woods and across the fields; it will take several days to know who survived and who did not."

Lady Drummuir rose slowly and walked to the window.

"Did ye see Fearchar?"

"Not for but a moment this morning. I told him to stay away from the moor, but—"

"Aye, he takes to orders as well as you do," the dowager said on a soft sigh. "If ye're that set on ridin' to Moy today, ye'd best go now, then, while the way is still clear. Follow the river road out to the east bridge and make a wide turn south. I'll send a couple of the lads with ye, well armed, just in case."

"What about you? What will you do?"

"Me? Och, dinna worry about me, lass. I've had one prince under ma roof an' I survived it. I'll likely have another strutting through the rooms before the day is out, an' I'll survive that as well. In truth, it should be the wee toady himself who should worry about me. I'm no' above poisoning his soup if he galls me."

"You'll look after MacGillivray?" Anne asked quietly.

"They willna find him. He'll have a proper Christian burial ere I draw ma last breath."

"I would like to see him before I leave."

The dowager touched her cheek. "Get yerself dressed, lass. I'll wait below. An' no trews an' plaids for you either," she warned. "Wear yer best ridin' suit. The more lace at yer throat, the less likely the soldiers are to think ye've just come from a battlefield."

Anne descended the stairs ten minutes later, an elegantly clad young woman in a blue velvet riding habit with founts of lace at the throat and cuffs.

The dowager nodded her approval and led the way down into the wine cellar. There, after manipulating a hidden catch behind one of the tall wooden racks, the entire section of shelving swung open and, holding a glass lamp over her head, she took Anne through, cautioning her to watch her step as they went down a flight of shallow stone stairs.

Anne had heard rumors of smuggling ventures in the dowager's family history, but she had never been in the "vault" below the house on Church Street before. It proved to be a huge, cavernous room excavated beneath the house and,

and despite the shortages brought on by the blockade, was surprisingly well stocked with black-market goods. The walls were stone block, the ceilings supported with massive beams. The smell of earth and worms was tinged with the faint hint of distillation from the row upon row of casks and barrels that lined the walls.

"Some of these bottles," the dowager said, pointing to a dusty wine rack, "date back to Angus's great-great-grandfather, and some of these casks of *uisque* are older still. Knowing him, Big John would have appreciated his surroundings."

A trestle table had been propped between two barrels, lighted by a halo of candles stuck into bottles, the wax dripping down the sides in yellowish globs. The dowager tipped her head at the two women who had been working over MacGillivray, and they moved discreetly back into the shadows.

His face and hair had been cleaned; the latter was still wet and fell back from his temples in dark brassy streaks. A linen sheet covered the hideous wounds on his body, and he almost looked as though he were just sleeping; Anne half expected him to open his eyes and give her one of his big, careless grins, telling her it had all been a mistake.

She reached out and combed her fingers lightly through the damp locks of his hair, then leaned over and pressed her lips to his brow. "I haven't much time, John," she whispered, "but I wanted to thank you for always being there when I needed you. I wanted to thank you for being my friend. For loving me. And I wanted to tell you," she added, faltering as her lips brushed one last time over his, "that part of me will always love you, John MacGillivray, and that my life will be that much richer for having known you. And no, there is nothing to forgive, nor will I ever forget you."

She straightened with an effort and looked over at the dowager. "If you could send word to Dunmaglass. Elizabeth is there. They were wed in Clunas not long ago, and she will be frantic."

"Aye. I'll let her know he is here."

Anne nodded. "That's it, then. I'll be on my way."

"You be damned careful, lass. If ye dinna think it safe, keep riding right past Moy Hall and take yerself up into the hills. A velvet suit might fool a common soldier, but never think that Cumberland will not know exactly who ye are. Off ye go, now. I think I'll sit here a wee while with Big John."

Anne exchanged a quick hug with her mother-in-law before hastening back through the vault and up the stairs to the rear door of Drummuir House. The Bruce was there, his gray coat restored and dry, though he was not saddled. Two armed groomsmen waited for her to run her hands over The Bruce's flanks and withers to make sure the gelding was not injured in any way. When she was satisfied, the three of them mounted and rode down the crushed-stone drive, leading The Bruce behind. At the wrought-iron gates, they heard the popping of distant gunfire and looked toward St. John's Chapel. A dead Highlander lay sprawled on the steps, and even as they turned west and headed toward the bridge, they could hear hoofbeats and shouting behind them as a company of dragoons galloped onto the main street of Inverness.

The dowager's warning proved to be unnecessary. It was evident at once that the soldiers had not yet come as far as Moy Hall, for the slopes around the loch were littered with weary, wounded clansmen. The road had been clogged with Highlanders as well. Upward of a thousand men limped, staggered, and fell to their knees beside the cold, sweet waters of the loch, there to cleanse their wounds and quench their thirst, and try to understand what had happened on the field that day. When Anne arrived, she ordered cattle slaughtered for meat. Every vessel that could hold water was set to boil over enormous fires, with chickens barely wrung and plucked before they were tossed in whole to make broth. The cupboards were emptied of linens, which were torn into strips for bandages. The grand dining hall was turned into a surgery where Dr. Archibald Cameron worked furiously to save shattered limbs and stitch impossible wounds. His own brother, Lochiel, had been carried from Culloden on a tartan sling and lay unmoving on the floor, ghastly pale, both ankles shredded by grapeshot. Alexander Cameron had been dragged from the field unconscious, his arm slashed to the bone from wrist to elbow. There was no sign of Aluinn MacKail or the giant Struan MacSorley, and though Anne asked everyone who might know, no one had seen her cousins or her grandfather.

Lord George Murray sat with his head between his bandaged hands, obviously fighting and refighting the battle in his mind. There had been so many errors, so many grievous errors that day, most of them wrought by the man they had forsaken everything to follow.

The prince had stopped at Moy but was gone before Anne arrived, so she did not hear his impassioned speech to the clansmen vowing they would rally to fight another day. The only rallying she witnessed was when wagons arrived from some of the neighboring farms bearing baskets of bread, extra blankets, and sheets for making bandages.

She had not troubled herself to change out of her velvets, though she had torn away the various tiers of lace to make bandages along the way. Thus, when another two-wheeled cart rolled to a halt outside the front of the Hall, she stood like a splash of azure blue in the doorway and watched as the Highlanders crowded around to help carry the goods away and distribute them. The sky was darkening, it being past five o'clock, and a runner had just come from Inverness with the news that Cumberland had entered the city like a grand conqueror, the citizens greeting him with ringing bells. His first stop had been the Tolbooth, the combined courthouse and gaol at the bottom of Bridge Street, where he immediately released all the prisoners the Jacobites had under lock and key. Word had also arrived that the duke, who had a fondness for sleeping in the same beds his cousin had slept in, had made his way to Drummuir House and demanded the dowager's hospitality.

All these things were spinning through Anne's mind, so she did not realize at first that the burden the Highlanders were unloading from the wagon was a man. An old, frail, broken shell of a man.

"Granda'," she whispered.

Fearchar Farquharson shrugged off the assistance of the two Highlanders who lifted him out of the cart. He took one stiff step after another, shuffling his way slowly to the bottom step before he stopped and looked up at her with tear-filled eyes. "I can say now that I've lived tae see mair than I ever wanted tae see. All those brave lads," he whispered. "All those brave lads."

Anne did not think her heart could break any more, but she was wrong.

"The bairns are gone," he said. "All three o' them. I looked f'ae Big John an' Gillies, but I couldna find them." His eyes held a hopeful gleam for the moment it took for Anne to shake her head. "Ahh, weel, better they died in battle, rather than see . . . what I saw."

"Come inside, Granda'. There's hot broth and blankets—"

"What need dae I have o' hot broth an' blankets when there are a thousan' men lyin' on Culloden field, stripped naked, left in the cold, beggin' f'ae even a small sip o' water. What's wrong wi' the rest o' these men," he said loudly, turning and waving his walking stick in the direction of the park. "Why are they no' goin' back tae help their kin! Why are they sittin' here wrapped in blankets an' drinkin' hot broth when their faithers an' brithers lie dyin' f'ae lack o' a sip o' water!"

"Do you think we just left without trying?" Lord George asked, coming quietly up behind them. "Each time I sent men back, they were slaughtered for their efforts. I could have kept sending men until we were all dead, I suppose, but what would that have gained? Believe me, I would gladly give my life if I thought we had the smallest chance of bringing even one man out alive. Cumberland has refused an appeal to parley. He demands nothing less than the prince's formal surrender in exchange for the right to treat our wounded and bury our dead. Loathe me if you will, blame me if you will, but do not disparage the honor of these brave men. Know that they would return to Culloden on the instant if I asked it of them, but that, in all good conscience, I will not do. Lady Anne, may I have a word in private?"

She nodded and entrusted her grandfather into the care of two clansmen. When she and the general were alone, she inquired if she might change his bloody bandages while they spoke, but he shook her concerns away.

"You know, of course, the army will come to Loch Moy."

"I would be surprised if they did not."

"It is to be hoped that when the heat of blood lust passes, as it surely must, logic and reason will prevail. I strongly doubt the Duke of Cumberland will want to be seen as a conqueror who makes war against women and children; even so, it might be prudent to remove yourself from Moy Hall."

Anne shook her head. "Angus told me to wait for him here, and so I shall until I hear otherwise."

"You saw your husband?"

"Briefly. He helped me move John MacGillivray's body."

Lord George pursed his lips, and she could tell he was searching for some delicate way to say what needed to be said. "That may not have been the wisest thing for him to do. If he was seen, or if his efforts on our behalf have been exposed . . ."

"If he has been arrested, or if he needs my help, how would I know this if I were in Ruthven or hiding in a cave up in the hills? No, my lord, I know you are only thinking of my welfare, but I have done so many things to disappoint him throughout our marriage, been so stubborn, behaved so foolishly at times." She spread her hands in a gesture of helplessness. "He would not even be facing a possible threat of hanging if not for me, if not for my challenging him, after Falkirk, to take more risks. At the very least I owe him my loyalty now."

Lord George bowed his head a moment, then looked up. "You give yourself too much credit for the risks he has taken, my dear. Angus was taking risks for us long before Falkirk."

"What do you mean?"

"I mean . . . there were other occasions on which your husband helped us when he could have as easily, and far more safely, helped himself. We had spoken, you see, just after Loudoun and Forbes began calling upon the lairds and blackmailing them with threats of arrests and forfeiture if they joined the rebellion. I can tell you that Angus, for one, was quite incensed by the Lord President's arrogance. Moreover, the veiled threats levied against Lady Drummuir, yourself, and the other clan lairds had the exact opposite of the desired effect, and might have put him in the front ranks at Glenfinnan had I not suggested he might be helpful to us in other ways."

Anne stared at him, wondering if perhaps he had taken a blow to the head. "You asked him to spy for you?"

"He was in the perfect position, after all. He had been away on the Continent long enough for his lack of political zeal to be convincing. He was an important enough man to win a position of favor and trust with both Forbes and the Earl of Loudoun. Despite giving me a very firm and clear no at the time—I believe he made reference to leaping out of the pot and dancing in the fire—I began to receive intriguing and interestingly worded letters. They pertained to mutual business interests, for the most part, but the odd one contained a phrase or two that made no sense at first, not until one began to realize the 'shipment of grain' he was alluding to coincided with the arrival of troop ships. Or that the 'meat shortage' they were experiencing in Perth and Stirling meant that there were far fewer troops garrisoned in either city than the government boasted. I doubt we would even have attempted to go up against General Cope at Prestonpans had we not known beforehand that the 'apples in the orchards were still very green and quite inedible.' By this method he told us General Cope had little more than raw recruits to send to the field that day. On at least two other crucial occasions, he was able to warn us away from potential traps."

"Angus did all of that? But why did he not tell me—especially after Falkirk, when he openly agreed to go back to Edinburgh to spy?"

"Perhaps he wasn't entirely sure how you would receive the news. I expect it came as a shock to him that you were able to raise the clan without his approval, and perhaps he regarded his own contributions as being too little, coming too late."

"Midnight honor," she whispered.

"I beg your pardon?"

"That was what he called it. Eleventh-hour heroics."

She looked down at her hands. They had begun to tremble so badly she had to clasp them tightly together. All those months she had railed at him with her contempt! All those times she had fallen less than a hair's breadth short of calling him a coward, questioning his loyalty, his honor! He had said, on his last visit to Moy Hall, that he had one more confession to make to her. Was that what he had been about to tell her: that all the months she had thought him a Judas, he had been secretly working for the prince's cause?

There had been hints, even outright contradictions in his behavior that she should have noticed, if not for her own arrogance and self-righteous pride. The night she had stolen the treaty agreement out of the Lord President's study, for one. He could have simply stepped out from behind the curtain and stopped her, but she had been too wrapped up in her own cockiness at the time to even ask why he had not. Was it because he had gone back to the library intending to steal the dispatches himself? Was it because he knew if she took them, they would eventually find their way into the right hands anyway?

"Oh, what a dreadful, posturing fool he must think me," she whispered.

Lord George smiled. "On the contrary. He believes you are the bravest woman he knows, and that both your courage and your loyalty come without compromise—a rarity even in most men."

"Well," she said, returning a faint imitation of his smile, "if he thinks so highly of me, how indeed could I disappoint him now by quailing before a few thousand of Cumberland's soldiers?"

"I am sure he would not want you to deliberately place yourself in danger, Anne."

She thought about it a moment, but shook her head. "No. I cannot run away, either. I must be here when Angus comes home. And he will come home. I know it."

Lord George sighed and took one of her hands in his, raising it to his lips. "It has been an honor to have you in my army, Colonel. I pray you are right and Angus is soon back by your side, where he belongs."

Chapter Twenty=Seven

*T*he soldiers came to Moy Hall three days later. There were upward of two hundred, half of whom had split away to circle the loch to the north, the other half to the south. Their scouts must have waited to hear Lord George had moved the clans out the previous afternoon, for although their approach was cautious—especially along the tree-lined route Colonel Blakeney's brave men had taken six weeks earlier—they strutted into the glen as if they owned it.

Word had preceded them from Inverness that Lady Drummuir's blatant condescension toward her houseguests had earned her a gaol cell at the Tolbooth. Because of Angus's service in the king's regiments, there had been some debate over what must be done about his Jacobite wife, and it was Hawley who suggested that if they were balking at the thought of hanging a woman, he would instruct his executioners to use silk cords.

Cumberland was only slightly more pragmatic. He issued an order for the arrest of "Colonel Anne" and dispatched a company to fetch her to Inverness. Since Anne had been forewarned of this, she dressed with extra special care. Her hair was plied with hot tongs and swept back in a crown of glossy curls. The gown she wore to greet her visitors was rose-colored watered silk, cut low enough to display more flesh

than the flimsy gauze tucking piece could modestly shield
from view. The small army of servants had cleared every trace
of her recent guests out of the house, and Lord George had ordered that every cart, blanket, and scrap of refuse be taken
away when the clansmen departed. Thus, at a casual glance,
the parks looked relatively unused, and the officer in charge
of the detail wondered if perhaps the reports had been exaggerated or wrong altogether. It would not be the first time they
had been misinformed of a rebel's whereabouts, or indeed of
a rebel's very participation, and he was particularly reminded
of an incident less than a month ago when the laird of a
manor was hanged from his own gates for being a spy, only to
be cleared later of all charges.

The officer had been sent to arrest a "red-haired Amazon"
of such manly proportions as to have been mistaken on the
battlefield for a Highlander. The lovely young woman who
greeted him at the door of Moy Hall was perhaps taller than
the average female, but there the description faltered.

"Lady MacKintosh? Lady Anne MacKintosh?"

"One and the same, sir," she replied, smiling. "Whom do I
have the favor of addressing?"

"Lieutenant-Colonel Thomas Cockayne, Pulteney's Royal
Foot, at your service." He started to salute, but saw her be-
mused expression and bowed instead. When he straightened
and saw that she was still frowning with polite bewilderment,
he added, "Is your husband at home, by any chance?"

"Forgive me, no. I believe he is in Inverness with his regiment. Perhaps I might be of some help? But first, please,
where are my manners; will you not step inside and take
some tea or a cool drink? I am expecting some ladies from the
Inverness Orphan Society at any moment, but I am certain
your company, as well as your input as to what aid we might
hope to expect from the king's representatives, would be most
welcome."

Thomas Cockayne wavered. He frowned and chewed his
lip, and if not for the second officer who stepped up beside
him at the head of a party of armed troops, he might have
considered getting back on his horse and riding away.

"The search party is ready, sir," the captain said. He was
an older man, uglier, with one eye covered in a milky white

film. The scarred eye triggered a memory, and although it had been several months since Anne had seen Captain Fergus Blite at the Forbes birthday party, she knew he would not be so easily distracted from his duty as Lieutenant Cockayne. Already his one good eye was flicking past her shoulder, anticipating rooms full of valuable booty, all of which had been proclaimed legal plunder—as much as a man could carry on his back—for soldiers engaged in the dangerous task of searching the homes belonging to known rebels.

Angus Moy's affiliation with the Scots regiments notwithstanding, there were two hundred men who had volunteered to make the march to Moy Hall knowing they would be returning with their haversacks several pounds heavier. A pink dress and a winsome reference to orphans were no deterrent.

"I have a copy of the arrest warrant here," Blite said, producing the document with a flourish. "And if the *lady* will just step aside, we can be about our business."

Cockayne was a gentleman and had the grace to flush. "If it please your ladyship, we do have our orders. Hopefully it will all be set aside as a dreadful misunderstanding, but in the meantime—"

"In the meantime you intend to invade my home, violate my privacy, and steal my possessions?"

"Aye," Blite said. "That and take you back to Inverness, where they've a nice cozy gaol cell waiting on you."

Anne's blue eyes sparked with fury despite her vow not to lose her temper.

"Shall I have my horse saddled?" she asked tautly. "Or am I to be dragged along the road in chains?"

"Nothing quite so drastic, my lady," Cockayne said hastily. "I am certain it is a formality, nothing more." He signaled one of his men. "Have Lady Anne's horse brought around. Captain Blite, you have one hour to conduct your search."

The captain grinned and waved his eager men forward. They were not fully inside the gloom of the doorway when Anne heard the first cupboard shatter under the butt of a musket stock. They would likely damage a good deal more in the hour they were given, for they would be frustrated to find little of any value inside. Heirlooms, sentimental or otherwise, had already been loaded into boats and rowed out to the tiny island in the middle of the loch. They had been buried and the sod carefully replaced so that no sign of a disturbance could be seen from any point on the shore.

"Do you have a wife, Lieutenant? A family?"

"Why yes, I do. A lovely wife and three daughters. They are at home in London."

"They would be very proud of you this day," she said, speaking softly over the crash of glass and porcelain. "Even prouder had they seen you on the moor three days ago, I'm sure."

Cockayne's grin faded. They spent the next long minutes in an uncomfortable silence, and when Robert the Bruce was led around from the stables, the lieutenant suffered another pang of indecision, for the gelding was well groomed, unmarked, and would have won praise walking a promenade in London's Hyde Park.

It was not until Anne was bundled into a warm cloak and mounted on the sidesaddle that he had cause to question his own doubts, for when he gave the signal to the drummer to start the escort moving back toward the road, the magnificent beast raised his head and took up the march as if he were back at the head of an army.

Anne was taken directly to the Tolbooth, an old stone building with one large main room in which the town magistrates normally held their meetings. The walls were rough, without plaster or paint; the furnishings consisted of a long trestle table and a dozen plain straight-backed chairs. A door at the rear led down a narrow corridor to a cramped labyrinth of cells, few bigger than three paces by two, even fewer boasting a window slit wide enough to let in a meager breath of fresh air.

Situated directly across the street from the Tolbooth was the largest inn in Inverness. It had been turned into the officers' mess, with the rooms on the second floor being assigned to senior officers and their staff. Since there were only four main streets in Inverness, all of them converging in the vicinity of the courthouse, the immediate area in front of both buildings was crowded with soldiers, all of whom stopped what they were doing to stare at the elegantly caped and hooded woman who was helped down off her horse and led into the Tolbooth.

Before she went inside, Anne turned and glared back at the curious redcoats. She made it easier for them by lowering her hood; when she turned her face briefly up to the warm sunlight, she heard the low rush of whispers identifying her as "*la belle rebelle*," and the equally vehement hissings that said it could not possibly be so.

"If you please, my lady." Lieutenant Cockayne stretched a hand toward the open door. He removed his lace-trimmed cocked hat and waited for her to pass through before instructing that no one else should be admitted.

It took a moment for Anne's eyes to adjust to the dimmer light inside the courthouse. There were only two windows, and they were shuttered from the inside to discourage noses from being pressed against the glass. There were tall, multi-tined candelabra set at intervals along the walls instead, lending the room the gloomy atmosphere of an inquisition chamber. A single chair had been placed about five feet in front of the trestle table, behind which sat ten bewigged, uniformed officers, all of whom had been conversing, sitting in various stages of lazy repose until Anne came into the room.

Their conversations ceased at once. One false bark of laughter lingered the longest and drew Anne's attention to the cruel, hawklike features of General Henry Hawley, seated at the far right end.

There was no mistaking Hawley from the descriptions she had overheard, but the rest, save one, were unfamiliar. The Earl of Loudoun's rounded, split-veined jowls quivered as he straightened and busied himself arranging a few documents that were before him, and although she stared at him for several long moments, he did not look up again.

The one face she had hoped—and dreaded—to see was that of her husband, but Angus was not there. She had not heard any word from him but she had managed to convince herself that no news was good news. He was an officer, a laird, a chief; his death would have been reported. Moreover, she suspected her arrest would have been much less civil had there been no fear of repercussions from the local government officials, the most important of whom was the Lord President, Duncan Forbes—the man who supposedly had given her his personal warrant of immunity.

"And so she comes before us," said a quiet voice from the back of the room. "The red-haired rebel hellion."

Anne kept her eyes forward. Solid, decisively placed bootsteps brought the speaker slowly forward out of the shadows where he had been concealed, the sound echoing in the empty room, shivering off the walls as it was likely orchestrated to do.

"Your reputation precedes you, Lady Anne," the voice said. "Or would you prefer to be addressed by this tribunal as 'Colonel Anne'?"

Now Anne turned, but she did so keeping her gaze deliberately level. The fact that the Duke of Cumberland was a full head shorter than she required an immediate—and obvious—adjustment, one that was supplemented with a slight arching of her brows.

"Since I wear neither the uniform nor the rank for which you credit me, sir, you may address me as Lady MacKintosh."

"And you may bend your knee and address me as Your Grace," he replied evenly.

"Ahh. Please do forgive my ignorance, Your Grace," she countered, dipping down in a perfectly elegant, graceful curtsy. "The light is so poor, and with no formal introduction, I was not aware to whom I was speaking."

He continued to walk around her, cutting a wide, deliberate circle that took him in and out of shadow, seemingly content to observe and prolong the tension—something Hawley apparently could not abide.

"You have been brought before us today, madam, to answer charges of sedition and treason," he said, "and to account for your actions of the past five months."

"Would that accounting be by the day, sir, or by the week?"

"By the deed, madam. Do you deny, for instance, that you took up a sword and raised your clan in support of the Pretender's treasonous efforts to usurp the throne of England from King George? Do you deny you led those men to join ranks with the Jacobite rebel Lord Lewis Gordon at Aberdeen, and from there proceeded to engage in an act of war against the king's army on the field at Falkirk? And do you deny you were present on the moor at Drummossie not three days hence?"

"Do you intend to credit me with starting the entire rebellion, sir? For if you do, I think it only fair to warn you I have not that much influence."

"You had influence enough to lure"—he looked down, consulting a sheet of paper—"at least five hundred clansmen to your cause."

"It was not my cause, sir. It was Scotland's. And in actual fact, the number was closer to eight hundred."

Hawley's face was sharp as a blade in the candlelight. "So you do *not* deny your affiliation with the Pretender?"

"My loyalties to Scotland's rightful king and heir have never been a well-kept secret, as I am certain Lord Loudoun may attest. Yet while I may have applauded the prince's victories and supported the decision of some of my husband's clansmen to follow the course their honor dictated, I would not say I had any more or less influence over their actions than scores of other wives, mothers, and sisters."

"Most of whom did not take up a sword and join their men in battle." Hawley half rose out of his chair. "You were *seen* on the field at Falkirk!"

"Was I, indeed?" she remarked wryly. "And would this have been by the same brave men who swore they saw three thousand Camerons and MacDonalds lurking in the trees the night Lord Loudoun dispatched soldiers to Moy Hall to capture the prince?"

Loudoun looked up at that, reddening as each of his fellow officers leaned forward to glance his way. The beginnings of a spluttered defense were silenced when Cumberland raised his hand.

"So," the duke said. "You deny being at Falkirk?"

"No. I do not deny it at all, Your Grace. I was there, just as dozens of other wives were there, for it was, above all else, a grand and glorious adventure the likes of which cannot be found hereabout in the pastures and moors of Inverness."

"You are claiming it was a diversion, nothing more?"

"An *exciting* diversion, Your Grace."

"And you ask us to believe you took no part in the recruiting of men? Or that the reports we were given that place you on the battlefield at Falkirk were mistaken?"

She sighed. "I would put the question to this panel of august military men instead, asking if they would sanction the presence of women on a battlefield, much less allow them a position of command? Would you, Lord Loudoun, encourage your wife to take to the field? And if you did, would you expect your officers and men to follow her blindly over hill and dale?"

A few of the officers lowered their heads to conceal their smirks, for Lord Loudoun's wife was as big as a bullock, and the thought of her hiking her petticoats to heave over a mud wall did nothing to maintain their sense of decorum.

The duke resumed his slow pacing again, but only as far as the table. His gaze strayed downward from her smile to the deep V of her cleavage. Her cloak had become loose and sat precariously balanced on the rounds of her shoulders. Somewhere along the way she had lost the gauze tucking piece as well; her skin took on an almost luminous quality in the candlelight, emphasizing the low scallop in the bodice and the deep shadow between her breasts. Strands of her hair had flown loose, the wisps catching the light and glowing like a fiery halo around her head.

"I confess you are not in the least what I expected, Lady MacKintosh," Cumberland murmured. "Reports have invariably put you a foot taller, several stone heavier, with a full moustache that would do a brigadier proud. I will also confess I find it difficult to envision you running out onto a battlefield in full armor."

"Thank you, Your Grace. It was a charge against which I did not know quite how to defend."

"Oh, I think you have done admirably well. The gown, the hair—" He waved a fat hand to include the entire presentation. "Not one man on this tribunal failed to give pause when you came through that door. And these are hard-hearted brutes, my dear. Hard-hearted brutes. Would there were indeed a few score women like yourself who did take to the field of honor, we might have been harder pressed to win a victory. But win we did. And since you have rather cleverly avoided answering any of our questions directly, nor have you denied your politics or your involvement in this uprising, you leave us no choice but to find there is more than sufficient evidence to warrant arresting you on charges of sedition and rebellion. I expect we could hold a trial right now and find you guilty, but, as I have said, this is a delicate situation and we must preserve the appearance of civility and fairness, must we not?"

From the moment Anne had walked into the courthouse she had known what the outcome would be. She had also bitten her tongue enough times to taste blood, but this was too much and she could not prevent the two blooms of color that rose to stain her cheeks.

"*Civility* and *fairness*? Is that what I saw on the road coming into Inverness today? I counted fourteen bodies stripped naked and mutilated, left lying on the grass to be kicked and spat upon by every soldier who walked past. I am told there are still men alive on the field at Culloden who have been left out in the bitter cold, their wounds unattended, guards placed around the moor to prevent their families from taking them so much as a sip of water so that they might die easy. Yet you offer me *civility* and *fairness*? Why, because I am a woman and you would be called far worse names than 'Butcher Billy' if you were to hang me"—she glared directly at Henry Hawley—"whether you used silken cords or not?"

The duke's eyes bulged a little wider. "Your mockery does you no credit, madam."

"Nor does your gullibility, *sir*," she countered. "If you are willing to give credence to a report that there were women on the field at Falkirk, what must that do to further enhance the fine reputation of the brave men under your general's command who turned and ran that day?"

Hawley made a choking sound in his throat and might have leaped across the table if not for another officer, who introduced himself as Colonel Cholmondeley, taking up the challenge.

"If, as you say, you were only keeping company with the wives of the other officers, we would remind you your husband wore the regimental colors of the Royal Scots brigades!"

"He had his preferences for company, sir; I had mine."

"You are the niece of Fearchar Farquharson, are you not?"

"I am his granddaughter."

Cholmondeley took up a quill, dipped it in ink, and scratched a notation down on paper. "Was it he who persuaded you to disobey your husband and call out your clan for the Pretender?"

"Since I was a child, sir, I have not been persuaded to do anything I did not want to do."

"We notice you have not yet inquired as to your husband's health," Cumberland pointed out. "Are you not curious to know how he fared in the recent dispute?"

"If Lord MacKintosh were dead," she said, attending upon a loose thread on her cuff, "I expect I should have heard by now."

"You have not had any contact with him over the past three days?"

Anne dismissed the notion along with the pulled thread. "I have neither seen nor spoken to my husband in several weeks, nor, to my knowledge, has *he* made any inquiries as to the state of *my* comfort or health. I expect, in fact, you will hear from him long before I do, when he discovers his prize herd of cattle has been appropriated and his home left in shambles by your soldiers. These would be far more likely to draw his attention than the peccadilloes of an errant wife."

Cumberland smiled. It was an evil, sly kind of smile that began with a thoughtful pursing of the too-red lips and spread across his porcine face like a bloody slash.

"As it happens, my dear, your husband is quite close by. Within a hundred paces, I should think." He turned to consult one of the officers. "The hospital is a hundred paces away, would you not say?"

Anne stiffened. "Hospital?"

"Well, not in actual fact a hospital," Cumberland said, swiveling on his heel to look back at her. "But we could not very well put our wounded officers in with the common rabble."

It took two attempts for the rasp in Anne's throat to form audible words. "Angus was wounded?"

"He was struck down on the battlefield—he took a saber

in the belly, I believe. The doctors will, of course, do all they can, but . . ." He shrugged as if the devil cared more than he. "Belly wounds, in my experience, are usually quick to turn morbid."

Anne felt the floorboards shift beneath her feet. The room took a sickening turn as well, and the faces of the officers behind the trestle table blurred and became nothing more than flesh-colored blobs over splashes of crimson.

A saber wound in the belly . . . ?

For the last three days, each time she closed her eyes, she relived nightmarish reenactments of the battle. In most of them, MacGillivray was lying in her arms, dying, and a soldier came running up behind her. She would leap to her feet and engage his sword, and at some point, she felt the blade strike and punch through living flesh. In her dreams the face had been distorted, but now, even as the faces of the tribunal faded away into the shadows, the face of the soldier came clearly into focus. It was Angus.

"Dear God," she whispered.

"Indeed, it is in God's hands," Cumberland said. "Or so the surgeons tell me."

"May I see him?"

"Of course you may, my dear." The smile spread insidiously across his face again. "Just as soon as you tell us what we want to know."

She frowned, her thoughts tumbling too fast to follow his words. "Tell you—?"

"Names, my dear. We want the names of all the chiefs and lairds who wore the white cockade. You say you went on this grand adventure to Falkirk merely to keep company with good men . . . we want to know who those good men were. Lord Lovat, for instance. We suspect he was an active participant, but we have no proof. We need sworn, signed statements, for it is not so easy to win a guilty verdict against members of the peerage as it is against common cotters. They must be taken to London and tried before the House. . . ." He spread his hands as if soliciting her acknowledgment that it was, indeed, a great hardship.

"And you expect me to give you these names? To bear witness against these brave men?" Her voice had turned soft and low. It trembled around the edge of each word and anyone who knew her would have instinctively stepped back a pace or two. "In exchange you will permit me to visit my husband, who may or may not be dying of a morbid wound?"

"You have the gist of it, my dear. Cooperate, and all charges against yourself will be set aside as well. We will even release your esteemed mother-in-law, the Lady Drummuir, much to the relief of the guards who have been forced to listen to her incessant pontificating day in and day out."

Anne squeezed her fists tighter—tight enough she could feel the tips of her nails cutting into the flesh of her palms. The room, thankfully, had stopped slipping and sliding. The faces of the gallant gentlemen officers were beginning to clear as well, and she looked down the line, impaling each with her contempt, resting at the last on John Campbell, earl of Loudoun.

"You claimed friendship with my husband, sir. Have you nothing to say against this travesty?"

Loudoun harrumphed into his hand. "You have the conditions before you, Lady Anne. I suggest you accept them."

Anne hardened her stare. He bore the full brunt of her loathing for nearly a full minute before his hand crept up to his collar. He thrust a finger between his skin and the linen neckcloth to ease the pressure, and when that failed, his jowls began to quiver, his chin to sag, and he began to wheeze like an overweight bulldog. In the end, his choking became so severe, the officers on either side helped him to his feet and led him, stumbling, out the rear door, where he could be heard coughing, spluttering, and wailing about "cursed devil eyes" for some time after.

"Shall we assume you require some time to think about your answer?" Cumberland asked, lazily scraping a speck of dirt out from under a fingernail.

You cannot show him you care. You cannot show him you care too much, or both you and Angus are lost.

"You may assume, sir, that there is not enough time left for either you or me on this earth wherein I would bow to such *uncivil* demands."

"Bravely said, my dear, but perhaps a few days in a gaol cell with rats as big as sheepdogs will temper your imprudence somewhat."

He nodded to Colonel Cockayne, who came forward with the greatest reluctance. "Escort Colonel Anne to her new quarters, if you please. I would also caution you to search her well before you turn the key; if the dowager could smuggle in a knife large enough to put out the eye of one of the guards, I'm sure this one could do the same. One last chance to reconsider, madam?"

Anne gave him her answer, having collected just enough spittle under her tongue for it to reach the duke's highly polished boot.

Chapter Twenty-Eight

Inverness, May 1746

The fear was like a blanket, smothering her. The slimy stone walls of her cell seemed to be shrinking around her, closer each day; the air was so thin and sour she had to pant to ease the pressure in her lungs. The sounds from the other cells were as bone-chilling and piercing as the screams that haunted her dreams day and night.

Cumberland had come to the prison three times over the past six weeks, offering to free her in exchange for giving evidence against the Jacobite leaders. All three times she had sent him away spluttering German oaths under his breath.

Her hair was dull, matted with filth. Her skin was gray. Deep purple smudges ringed her eyes. Her hands were stained black, her nails cracked and torn from repeatedly pulling herself up to the narrow window cut high on the cell wall.

She did not know what she hoped to see, other than a glimpse of the fading light to indicate another day had drifted into night. Both were endless, the one filled with the nightmares of the living, the other with nightmares of the dead. There were times she almost thought it would be a blessing if she simply did not waken one morning. Cumberland said Angus was still alive, but she had no reason to believe it. If he had lived through the fever and putrefaction of a belly wound, if he were still alive, surely he would have found some way to get word to her. Not all of the guards had been chosen for their cruelty. There were some who didn't leer and rub themselves when they walked by her cell, some who smuggled in an extra cup of water or, once, a half-gnawed chicken leg in exchange for a rosette button off her bodice.

The buttons were gone, the silk of her bodice was more gray than pink, and the only thing of value she had left—the one thing she would never part with unless it was removed from her dead body—was the silver-and-cairngorm brooch Angus had given her the night before Culloden. She kept it against her breast, tucked beneath her corset, and when she felt herself growing weak, when the despair threatened to overwhelm her and the sounds of the dying men nearly deafened her, she pressed against the metal until it cut into her skin.

She would not give Cumberland the easy way out. If he wanted her dead, he would have to give the order to hang her, and because she was the wife of a prominent chief, that could not be done without taking her first to London to stand trial.

Common soldiers and deserters were not so lucky. Thirty men who had been found amongst the ranks of the Jacobite prisoners but who were recognized as having once signed on to serve the king were summarily tried and hanged, the courts-martial taking place on the stroke of one hour while their bodies hung naked and dead the next. One such man was led past Anne's cell, called out to the courtyard by the drums, and when he paused a moment outside her door, she nearly did not recognize young Douglas Forbes through the blood and filth. He managed a parting smile, however, and she was told later that he walked to the gallows with his head high and refused the blindfold, preferring to stare at the vastness of the sky overhead before the trap was sprung beneath him.

More prisoners were brought in every day, and when the Tolbooth filled beyond its capacity, they were taken to the churches, then onto ships that were subsequently converted to prison hulks.

In the latter days of April, Cumberland posted orders that all known and suspected Jacobites were to be reported to the

Crown officers. Ministers were told to make lists of those in their kirks who had been absent during the months of the rebellion; warrants were issued for all chiefs and noblemen, with rewards offered for their capture and arrest. A price of thirty thousand pounds was put on the head of Charles Stuart, with lesser, but still substantial, sums allocated for those names that had sounded most often on the battlefield: Murray, Cameron, Glengarry, Clanranald, Ardshiel. Regiments of infantry and dragoons were sent out to hunt down the fleeing Jacobite contingents. Lochiel's stronghold at Achnacarry was demolished, the castle reduced to rubble, while the chief and his kinsmen were forced to hide in caves in the hills. Gray clouds of smoke hung over the glens as clachans were burned, the sheep and cattle driven back to Inverness. Cumberland had been given the authority to do whatever he deemed necessary to suppress the rebellious nature of the Highlands, and in his determination to be thorough, he gave little thought to the innocence or guilt of the general population. With so many prisoners to deal with, a lottery was organized wherein every twentieth man was marked to stand trial. The rest, if they could afford to buy their freedom, were released on the condition they leave Scotland and never return; those who had no money were loaded on transport ships and sent to the colonies as indentured servants.

Four members of the peerage were arrested and slated for execution by the ax. One of them was the Earl of Kilmarnock, whose wife had entertained General Hawley the evening before Falkirk. It was rumored, in the whispers that circulated around the Tolbooth at night, that it was Murray of Broughton, the prince's former quartermaster, who turned king's evidence on the earl in exchange for a pardon. It was also whispered that Lady Kilmarnock escaped the patrol that had been sent to bring her to Inverness by infusing their wine with enough opium to render them senseless.

Anne would have liked a little of that wine now. She was hungry and cold; she knew Cumberland would come again soon, offering her food, a clean bed, a hot bath. She was not sure how much longer she would be able to refuse, or how much longer he would tolerate her insolence, but there were indications the stalemate had to end soon. The king had given him a free hand to deal with the rebels in any way he saw fit, but after six weeks of unchecked slaughter and bloodshed, the atrocities were beginning to have the opposite effect, turning fear to anger, creating fierce zealots out of men who might have gone quietly home and nursed their wounds. Stories in the London papers had began to openly refer to the duke as "Butcher Billy," and there were protests in Parliament from lords demanding a more civilized means of resolving the Scottish problem.

Cumberland's free hand would soon be reined in. Lady Drummuir had already been released to more comfortable quarters, though she was still under house arrest. Sixteen other ladies—wives of suspected Jacobites—who were held for a time in churches or inns had been sent back to their families after the wives of several parliamentarians had interceded on their behalf. Anne knew she had not been forgotten in her fetid little cell; she had only to survive another day, she told herself, and perhaps one more after that. . . .

They came when she was asleep. The rusted hinges on her cell door screamed in protest despite the stealth with which the door was opened, giving entry to two shadowy figures who hauled Anne to her feet before she came fully awake. It took several moments for the fuzz to clear from her mind. By then, her hands had been jerked forward and bound with a leather thong, a filthy length of canvas stuffed in her mouth, and a burlap sack pulled over her head.

She made a sound in her throat and tried to kick out at her assailants, but something hard, blunt, and decisive struck her across the temple, causing her to lose all but the frailest thread of consciousness.

She was dimly aware of being picked up and tossed over a broad shoulder, then of being carried out into the hallway and through a door cut so low her assailant had to duck to clear the lintel. She felt cold air on her legs and heard the snuffling sound of several horses. A cloak or blanket of some sort was wrapped around her shoulders, then she was manhandled up onto a saddle and her hands bound to the pommel.

"Hold on." Dazed, she felt the sharp bite of leather slap across her fingers. "I said hold on to the saddle, bitch, or we'll tie you across it like a sack of offal."

"Smells like offal already," said another voice, sniffing loudly. "How far do we have to take her? It's a bloody cold night an' the fog's already drippin' down my neck."

"We have our orders. We follow them. Grab hold of that lead and look smart. We'd all look like ruddy fools if she managed to get away now."

"I say we just take her to the river. Can't see, other than the time it will save us, that it matters whether we kill her down by the bridge or out in the woods."

Anne blinked and tried to focus her eyes, but aside from the odd twinkle of lamplight that managed to pass through the weave of the sacking, she was as good as blind.

So. It was happening. The stalemate was ending. Cumberland had finally run out of patience—or time—and instead of a trial had issued the order to take her out and have her quietly murdered, buried in a bog or a forest where no one would ever find her or know what happened. She remembered finding a skeleton once when she was younger. Jamie and Robbie had been digging a hole for a new well and the skull had flipped up on a turn of the spade. The jaw had been open, the eyes great gaping holes, and part of the bone had been crushed inward, suggesting that whoever it was had been killed by a hard blow with a rock or cudgel. Ten years or a hundred and ten years from now, someone might be digging in the woods and turn up another skull. It would be hers, but no one would know it; no one would have mourned her passing, either.

She choked back the taste of panic that rose up her throat and tightened her hands on the pommel as the horses moved forward. The bindings on her wrist were cutting off the flow of blood, and her fingers were half numb. She had traded her shoes away weeks ago and her feet were bare, hanging inches below any protection the hem of her tattered skirt might have afforded. The saddle was cracked, and the uneven edges gouged her thigh with every jostling motion, but at least the pain helped clear her senses. She knew when they turned off Kirk Street and rode down Bridge Street and, when they crossed over timber planking, that they were across the river and heading out of Inverness. She also guessed, by the sound of saddles creaking and hooves beating, that there were at

least a dozen riders in the group—far too many to try to break
away from, tied and hooded as she was. On the other hand, if
they were taking her into the woods to kill her, what did she
have to lose?

"Don't even think about it, dearie," came a low growl
from beside her. "Half these men were at Falkirk and would
just love an excuse to fire their muskets into the back of your
pretty rump. Me? I've a mind to put something else up your
backside, and might do it yet if you give us any grief."

Anne turned her head slightly. Her hearing was distorted
by the woolen hood, but the voice had sounded familiar
enough to freeze her marrow and bring forth an instant image
of a scarred, milky eye.

They rode in silence for a mile or more, though it was difficult to judge distance or time. By sound, once again, she
knew when they left the firmness of the road for the swishing
thickness of long deer grass. She could smell spring in the
dampness of the mist. The sweetness of saplings and green
growth was mixed with the rich compost of rotted leaves and
pine needles. There were no sounds of rushing water, so they
had not followed the river. Just south of Inverness proper,
however, was a dense band of forest about five miles wide
that could absolutely suit their purpose this night, and she
wondered if they would at least remove her hood in the final
moments so she could take one last look at the sky and the
trees overhead.

One of the men swore as a branch snagged his tunic.
"How much farther, dammit?"

"The clearing should be just up ahead."

Branches brushed across the top of Anne's head for another hundred paces or so, then her horse was led off to one
side and halted. More protesting leather indicated her escort
was dismounting and again there were hands reaching for her,
untying her from the pommel, dragging her down out of the
saddle. The grass was wet and cold beneath her feet, the earth
spongy between her toes; despite her resolve, she began to
tremble.

A tug at the back of her neck brought the hood off her head,
and she blinked again. They were in a clearing surrounded by
heavy-limbed fir trees. The mist was waist deep, lit from above

by a crescent-shaped moon and from the two pitch-soaked torches that had been stuck into the ground nearby. Flanking her were eight redcoated soldiers with muskets cradled in their arms; across the clearing, six more looked as though they had been waiting impatiently for their arrival.

The six were escorts for another familiar figure, short and squat, dressed in a dark coat with frogged gold braid down the front, his face shadowed by the brim of a tricorne.

The Duke of Cumberland stared at Anne for a long moment before signaling one of her guards to remove the filthy gag from her mouth. When it was gone, she used her tongue to scrape bits of thread and dirt from her lips, but there was no spittle to call upon this time. She tasted blood from a tear in the corner of her mouth, and she took quick, shallow breaths to glean what moisture she could from the mist.

The duke came forward slowly, his hands clasped behind his back. The look in his eyes, as he inspected her bedraggled appearance, was clearly contemptuous, his smirk triumphant.

"A lovely evening for a final chat, do you not agree?"

Anne clamped her lips together and simply stared back.

"Determined to defy me to the end, I see," he murmured. "In truth I will confess you have made an admirable adversary. I would have thought to break you weeks ago. There is still time to reconsider, however; we have a few moments before the stroke of midnight."

"I have nothing to say to you," she said, her voice little more than a dry rasp.

"I did not think you would, and yet we do have one other small piece of business to attend to before we can proceed." He smiled, and brought one of his adjutants forward with a wave of a hand. The soldier carried a leather-bound ledger, which he opened and presented to the duke. He then produced a small bottle of ink and a feather quill from a satchel he wore slung over his shoulder.

"I have a document here," the duke said, turning the ledger around so that she might see it contained two sheets of paper, "which requires your signature."

Anne tore her gaze away from his long enough to glance down, but the light was too poor and the script was illegible. "What is it?"

"Nothing that should give you any cause for concern. Nothing that will compromise your principles or your politics or, God forbid, your heroic stature within your clan. It is merely a statement of fact, that you are a Jacobite, that you willingly disobeyed your husband by calling out your clan, and that you enthusiastically participated in acts of war against the Crown."

"A confession? Is this to ease your conscience before you have me murdered?"

"My dear Lady Anne, if I had merely wanted you murdered, I would not have gone to all this trouble, I assure you. As for my conscience, I would warn you not to test its limits much further, nor my patience for that matter. Both are perilously close to the end of their tether. Now sign. We are running out of time and these games grow tiresome."

"It is all right, Anne. You can sign it."

Startled, she looked up, looked around, searching for the source of the voice. She was not the only one who scanned the ring of trees; the soldiers turned their heads, brought their muskets up, and braced themselves as the woods came suddenly alive with sounds and shadows. From behind each tree, each thicket and bramble, emerging like ghosts out of the fog, came a score or more of MacKintosh clansmen, most armed with swords, pistols, and muskets. Detaching himself from the rest and walking fully into the blaze of torchlight was Angus Moy, his shoulders clad in forest green tartan banded with leather crossbelts. Gone was the image of the perfect gentleman. Gone was the polished elegance in his stance, the casual insouciance in the set of his jaw. His hair fell long and loose to his shoulders, his chin was dark with stubble; the gunmetal gray of his eyes blazed as hot as the torchlight and called forth all the blood and history of his warlike ancestors.

"It is all right, Anne. You can sign his little scrap of paper; it was part of our agreement. There should be a second document there for His Grace to affix his signature to in front of these witnesses, granting you a full pardon."

Anne felt weak, breathless. Her lips parted around the soundless escape of air that was her husband's name.

"You have something for me as well?" Cumberland demanded, turning to face the laird of Clan Chattan.

Angus turned his head slightly, and another figure wearing the black frock coat and plain white neckcloth of a clerk stepped forward from the edge of the wood. He looked plainly ill at ease in the presence of so many bristling soldiers and armed Highlanders, and he hastened across the clearing, sending little pinwheels of mist spinning off in his wake.

"I have the d-document in question, Your Grace," he spluttered, barely loud enough for the duke to hear without tilting his head. "I also have a letter from His Royal Highness's First Minister, Lord Newcastle, suggesting that you comply with the terms of the agreement as laid out by Lord MacKintosh and his London solicitors. He states that should the House or the infernal news sheets get wind of any suggestion that the battle orders were forged, or in any way, ah, tampered with that day, the repercussions could be perilous and far-reaching. Moreover—"

"Yes, yes." The duke cut him off, aware of Anne's proximity and of the heavily armed clansmen who, although they might not be able to hear or understand what was being said, were a viable threat nonetheless.

"You are a grave disappointment to me, MacKintosh," the duke said. "I had high hopes for your future here in the Highlands. I could have made you a rich man, a powerful man; you could have had a seat in Parliament, become a Minister even, and replaced that milksop Forbes."

"I have all the wealth I need right here," Angus said, his eyes locked on Anne. "And if I have disappointed you, Your Grace, then *I* can die with a clear conscience."

The duke smirked and murmured under his breath, "Sooner, perhaps, than you think."

But Angus heard him and grinned as he raised his arm again, bringing another circle of armed Highlanders forward out of the woods. These men were on horseback, the beasts clearly outfitted with the military saddles and trappings that identified them as mounts of the King's Royal Dragoons.

"Did you meet with any difficulties?" Angus asked.

"No, sar," said Ewen MacCardle. "Found 'em right where ye said they'd likely be, lying in wait for an ambuscade. Left the lot of 'em trussed up like hogs in a bog."

Angus's smile was as ominous as the assortment of knives

and pistols that glittered in his crossbelts. He came forward, and the duke, it was noted by all, took an instinctive step back. The soldiers who had escorted him suddenly found themselves disarmed, as did the guards who had brought Anne from the Tolbooth. Fearing the worst, the officious clerk from London took out a large white square of linen and began to mop his brow.

"Oh dear, oh dear," he muttered. "This was supposed to end peacefully."

"And it will," Angus said, snatching the quill and ink out of the frozen hands of Cumberland's adjutant. "Just as soon as His Grace signs the pardon."

"You would dare threaten violence against my person?" Cumberland hissed, his eyes bulging.

"I would not only threaten it, I would happily slit your throat and the throat of every man in your guard. Moreover I would bury you so deep in these woods the hellhounds would never find the bodies, much less learn what had become of you—a similar fate, I expect, to the one you were planning for my wife and me?"

The duke pursed his lips for a moment, then took the quill, stabbed the tip in ink, and scratched out his signature on the designated page. Angus removed it from the ledger and blew gently on the angry scrawl before folding it and handing it to the clerk. "If anything happens to this, I will personally come looking for you. If I do not hear from my London solicitor within the week telling me that he has received it, I will come for your family as well. Do I make myself clear?"

The clerk swooned backward, swabbing his temples and throat. "Oh . . . inestimably clear, my lord."

"Good. Now go with my men. They will stay with you until your ship sails."

"Wait," Cumberland demanded. He shoved the ledger at Anne and tapped the confession. "I insist on having her signature as well, if you please."

Angus looked disdainfully at the pudgy finger. "I hardly think you are in a position at the moment to insist on anything."

"No," Anne said, "I would be happy to sign it."

She reached out for the quill. Her hands were still bound

together, which made the movement awkward and brought a savage curse to Angus's lips. Torchlight flared off the blade he drew from his crossbelt; with a single stroke, she was free.

Anne waited until her fingers steadied, then signed her name with an elegant flourish: *Anne Farquharson Moy Mhic an Tosaich, Colonel, HRH Charles Stuart Royal Scots Brigade.*

Epilogue

Anne traced her fingers gently over the ugly welt of scar tissue that marred the smooth skin below her husband's ribs. He was lying on his side, asleep, but at the touch of her fingers, then her lips, he stirred and rolled slowly onto his back. He saw the threat of tears in her eyes and he sighed, enfolding her in his arms and holding her close against his chest.

"It wasn't your fault," he murmured, burying his lips in her hair. "You didn't know what you were doing."

"I knew enough to nearly kill you."

"You were enraged, and I did not move out of your way fast enough, an error I will not make again, you can be sure."

"I thought you were dead," she whispered. "All that time, when I did not hear from you, I thought I had killed you."

"The first two weeks, I thought you had, too. MacCardle tells me I was out of my mind with the fever. Then, when I recovered"—he paused and kissed her again, tightening his arms around her so that she was encouraged to slide over and lie directly on top of him—"I was told you were in prison, and there was little that could be done to set you free. I damn near lost my mind again."

Anne folded her arms across his chest and propped her chin on her hands, content just to look at him, content to feel his hands stroking up and down her back. They had spent the better part of the last ten days in bed, most of it sleeping, eating, *bathing,* sleeping. Angus slipped away now and then to oversee the repairs to Moy Hall, for the English had come back several times during Anne's incarceration and there was hardly a chair without its stuffing ripped open or a cupboard not smashed to kindling. Most of the servants had returned when they heard the laird had somehow miraculously won his lady's freedom. There were also two hundred clansmen camped around the loch, with more appearing every day, many of them MacGillivray and MacBean men who had no homes left to go to and no one to lead them. Of the twenty-one lairds of Clan Chattan who had stood in the front line alongside MacGillivray, only three had survived the charge, and two of those had died later of their wounds.

The clansmen who found their way to Moy were still some of the fiercest fighters who had taken to the field that day, and with Anne standing proud by his side, Angus declared that he would have need of every one of them in the weeks and months to come. There were a thousand fugitives hiding in the hills who would need food and clothing and transportation out of Scotland, and MacGillivray's men were the best smugglers in Caledonia. The English were systematically stripping the Highlands of cattle, sheep, and livestock, hoping to starve the people into submission, but to an exceptional band of reivers and rustlers, what was stolen once could easily be stolen twice.

Angus had received word the previous afternoon from his solicitor that Anne's pardon had arrived safely in his office, along with affidavits from the three royal ministers to whom Angus had shown the forged battle orders. Cumberland had immediately destroyed the copy Angus had taken from Major Worsham's pouch, but the gesture had been theatrical at best, petulant at worst. On its own, there was nothing to prove the order false. But there had indeed been other papers in Worsham's possession, including copious notes taken during the meeting with Cumberland, when it was explained how easy it had been to forge Lord George's signature and add the clause that had led to such unjustified, unconscionable slaughter. Angus had gone to London himself to present the evidence to the First Minister, and to name the only terms on

which he would not send copies of all the documentation to
the *London Gazette*.

In the days following the battle at Culloden, Cumberland
had been regarded as a valiant hero; he had triumphed over
the savagery of a Highland army twenty thousand strong! He
had saved England! He had saved his father's crown!

But then, as the stories of the hangings and brutalities began to seep south, the papers were less enthusiastic in their
praise. Prince Frederick of Hesse had returned home with an
entire army that had refused to fight under such a "butcher,"
and the people were appalled to learn the reason why. They
were also becoming curious to know why, out of the thirty-
five hundred rebels currently imprisoned in the Highlands, so
few had actually been taken on the field that day.

Angus was in a position to give further eyewitness ac-
counts of the total lack of compassion and honor and the
needless cruelty to the dying and wounded; that, plus evidence of the duke's complicity in forging false battle orders,
would turn the hero into a beast overnight. The triumph
would become a shameful disgrace, and in the backlash of
sympathy, both in England and abroad, the Scots might well
emerge in a stronger position to challenge the throne than before.

In return for his silence on the matter, Angus demanded
Anne's immediate release from prison and a full pardon. Further, since he had served in the king's regiment right up to the
moment he had taken a near-fatal wound from a "Jacobite"
sword, he expected the original terms of his immunity agreement to be upheld, and to include the surviving lairds and
families of Clan Chattan.

It had taken three weeks for couriers to go back and forth
from London to Inverness, but in the end Angus had won. He
had appeared before the minister wearing the scarlet tunic
and gold braid of an officer in the King's Royal Scots, but he
had returned to Scotland wearing the tartan and crossbelts of
a man fully in command of his own destiny. Cumberland had
made the exchange that same night. Now, ten days later, Anne
was warm and safe in his arms; she was still terribly thin and
her nights were not entirely peaceful, but at least she was
sleeping, and eating well enough, and she only wept when

she was left alone too long to think about all the dreadful losses.

"I have arranged to have John's body moved to Petty, to a small green hill overlooking the firth."

"He would like that," she said softly, "being able to look out over the water with the mountains at his back."

"And MacBean by his side, as always. We found Gillies's body and asked Elizabeth if she minded them sharing the brae together. She said I should be asking the priest instead, for with the two of them in the churchyard, they'll be sure to raise the devil."

The shine was back in her eyes, but it came with a smile this time. "Granda' told me yesterday that Elizabeth is with child, so he's not completely gone. There will still be a MacGillivray at Dunmaglass."

"If it's a son, I suppose I will have to give him back his father's bucklers."

Anne's eyes narrowed beneath a wry frown. "I wondered where you had come by all that impressive armor in the clearing. I almost did not recognize you as the fastidious gentleman scholar I married."

"It suited my mood. And besides, I thought I needed a little of MacGillivray's roguish courage to bolster me."

"You have more courage than it would seem wise or safe to have these days, my lord. Or do you think Cumberland will forget that you blackmailed him?"

"He will not forget. But he has already taken his army to Fort Augustus. In a month, when he becomes bored with the lack of opera and swans' liver, he will go home to London, and we will not seem quite so significant. Besides—" He rolled carefully onto his side, taking Anne with him; another deft shift and she was beneath him, her eyes round and wide and blue as sapphires as he settled himself between her thighs. "I have more important things to worry about at the moment than the wounded vanities of a fat little tyrant."

"You do?"

He moved his hips forward and savored the heat of her welcome a moment before curling his hands in the fiery silk of her hair and holding her through a long, molten kiss.

"Unless, of course, you would rather talk," he said against

her lips. "Which is what a fastidious gentleman scholar might well do under the circumstances."

"In that case"—her hands smoothed down his waist and grasped his hips—"I think I prefer to keep my roguish warrior awhile longer."